For Angela
"Twenty-eight and counting . . ."

EMMANUEL PAIGE

DEATH RIDES DARKLY

A NOVEL

Stark Raven Press

www.StarkRavenPress.com

Library of Congress Control Number: 2020932208

ISBN 978-0-9824312-4-5

CONTENTS

PROLOGUE

1

In the Autumn, during Halloween, also known as All Hallows Eve, the holiday first observed by western civilization and Christians on October 31 of the liturgical year, it is a time of feasting, festivities, and commemoration of the dead. This is a time to remember deceased saints, martyrs, and other departed faithful servants. In other parts of the world there are similar celebrations to pay tribute to the dead, deceased, and dearly departed. A related pagan holiday observed by Celtics during the harvest season, particularly the Gaelic tribe, known as Samhain, is widely believed to be the origin of Halloween. As with many primitive traditions and rituals, Christianity incorporated this pagan celebration long ago, westernizing the customs and beliefs, in effect bringing it to the rest of the world. Another similar holiday that was absorbed by Christianity was All Souls' Day, a commemoration of all the faithful departed. In Mexico *Dia de los Muertos*—the Day of the Dead—was a festive Mexican holiday celebrated in remembrance of the dead, a predominantly Catholic and Latin American influence. Around the world and throughout history there has always been a celebration to show respect and reverence for the dead with all tribes, races, civilizations, and peoples of the Earth. They all share one common theme: death. Halloween is now a world-famous holiday and a long-standing tradition and has reached worldly influence.

Trick-or-treating is the tradition of dressing in costumes modeled after supernatural beasts and monsters, skeletons, ghosts, witches, devils, and vampires, and more, are all worn by children who go door to door asking for treats, and in the exchange, the bogeyman will be appeased and kept at bay. If there are no treats to be had, there will be tricks, shenanigans, and pranks played on the unwary property holder. The trick-or-treaters go door to door singing songs in exchange for treats.

The costumes are from mixed traditions across the world, Europe, Canada, the United States, Mexico, where children and groups of people disguise themselves to blend in with the creeping dead and bogeys walking amongst the living. The costumes served a primary purpose: to protect against spirits of the dead that return from the grave; to ward off demons and bogies that rise from the depths of the underworld and walk abroad around the world on Halloween. It is believed that adorning a disguise will fool the roaming souls of the dead and keep them from taking hapless victims back to the underworld or the grave. The candy, toys, and treats are supposed to appease the wandering supernatural creatures and make them go away, moving on to other haunts. This is a widespread belief and custom shared by various cultures around the world throughout history and prevalent today.

Christians consider Halloween a wicked holiday and Jehovah's Witnesses are strongly opposed against the celebration of the pagan tradition. They hold a bitter and antagonistic view of the rituals of the holiday and considered it to be the source of evil streaming directly from Satanism. The Church of Satan, Wiccans, cults, pagans, and heathens worldwide are happy and proud to celebrate and partake of the festivities. It has become a favorite tradition in the Western Hemisphere, and the world, at large, commercialized and exploited, influencing the rest of the world that anxiously idolizes and adopts, watching and waiting with baited breath, the antics and exploits of Western culture.

For many people worldwide, Halloween is a time to congregate, celebrate, indulge, dress up in costumes, and let loose in festivities and activities that result in consuming massive quantities of devilishly delicious treats and sweets. Many adults attend parties, dressed in lavish and outlandish costumes, that have music, contests, prizes, intoxicating beverages and sinful and wicked activities that may lead to wanton excess or wild expressions of sexuality, liberating inner repressed frustrations, and releasing repressed inhibitions that lead to acts of romance and sex of extreme proportions. Halloween is celebrated by adults, as well as children, and often it is a season and a reason for grownups to indulge in decadence and riotous self-expression, all while disguised in costumes that bring secrecy and anonymity.

People love to play dress up and scare each other with death, attending costume parties and festivals, and that is why Halloween is so popular. Additionally, people love to have wild and uninhibited sex, sometimes in groups, at clubs, in private, in public, on film and the Internet for all to see. People have an inclination to be exhibitionists and voyeurs and it is in our nature to feel lust, desire sexual gratification, and seek out release. People like to party and have sex. Vampires embody the spirit of this desire and we act out our fantasies frequently, sometimes making it into a reality. There are drinkers of blood amongst us; this is a fact, and they like to party, too.

2

A brief history of the vampire . . .

The superstition is of Eastern origin, originating with Arabians, then when Christianity became prevalent it spread to the Greeks. It was at that time that the present myth and superstition took its form, the Latin churches believed that a body entered in their territory could not be corrupt and stories of the dead rising from the grave sucking on the blood of the innocent and youthful and beautiful increased. In Western countries, there were variations, such as Hungary, Poland, Austria, Romania, where vampires rose from their tombs and went in search of victims to exsanguinate, and the prey would become emaciated, losing strength, and quickly die from consumption. The "human" or "undead" bloodsuckers would become engorged and their blood vessels would distend and expand to a point that the capillaries became plump and swollen so that the blood would flow vigorously through their veins and arteries and would permeate the epidermal membrane and bead and glisten on the surface, exuding from their porous skin.

In Hungary, during the 18th century, there were tales of vampirism, which occurred throughout Europe, and it was said that certain dukes and noblemen were confronted on the Turkish Servia by a vampire, and after using methods to rid themselves of the hideous and foul creature that involved eating dirt and rubbing themselves with the blood of the beast, they had staved off attacks for a short time. Unfortunately, some of them succumbed to the curse—for that is what they believed it to be, a curse of evil—and were themselves converted into the living undead. To prevent further attacks the local villagers took up the bodies, which were noted to have not been corrupted by the grave and had mouths full of blood, and also were emitting blood from the eyes, nose, and ears. They were quickly dispatched in the customary tradition with a stake through the heart. Arnold Paole, was a Serbian hajduk, believed to have been converted into a vampire during this time, and when he was killed with a stake to the heart, after being removed from the grave, he was said to have screamed like a living man dying from such a wound. Afterward, they beheaded the corpse, burned the body, and placed the ashes back into the grave. This news and evidence rapidly spread to Western Europe and influenced the dissemination of the reality of vampires and the belief by educated Europeans. The rest of the corpses that had been suspected of being vampires were disinterred and disposed of in a similar fashion.

This initiated an epidemic and horror that resulted in vampire hunting locally that killed sixteen villagers in Maduegna, by West Morava river in Trstenik, Serbia. This is a well-known and documented example from history where vampirism was taken literally and believed to be true by the Austrian authorities, physicians, and officers who testified to the truth of the existence of vampires.

In literature, cinema, comic books, and video games the vampire is a staple archetype that reigns supreme within the horror genre. "Dissertations on the Apparitions of Angels, of Demons and of Spirits, and on Revenants or Vampires of Hungary, of Bohemia, of Moravia and of Silesia" written in 1746 by Antoine Augustin Calmet, a French Benedictine monk, who discusses vampires at length proves an academic interest in the legend and folklore of vampires. "Thalaba the Destroyer" is an epic poem composed in 1801 by Robert Southey that mentions vampires. "The Vampyre," written in 1819 by John William Polidori, was the first and most definitive fictional tale of vampires. "Carmilla," a Gothic novella written in 1872 by Joseph Sheridan LeFanu, was the next major fictional story about vampires that also involved undertones of lesbianism. Then came *Dracula,* the definitive and classic Gothic horror novel of vampires, written by Bram Stoker in 1897 and is, arguably, the single most influential work involving the subject. The movie *Nosferatu* was a silent German film from 1922 inspired by *Dracula* and believed to be an unofficial adaptation of the classic novel. Many more novels, stories, movies, and video games followed afterward, and a few are worth mentioning: *Salem's Lot* by Stephen King (1975). *Interview with a Vampire* by Anne Rice (1976). *Buffy the Vampire Slayer* was a film released in 1992 and spawned a popular TV series adaptation (1997) and a video game (2000) which were all popular. A comic hook, *30 Days of Night* (2002) was a success and was also made into a film (2007) that breathed new life into the trope. The final smash on the vampire scene to date was the novel *Twilight* (2005), from the series of the same name, by Stephanie Meyer that went on to be adapted into a series of films beginning in 2008 which inspired a slew of fan fiction and caused a sensation in the small logging town of Forks, Washington, the setting for the story.

The belief in vampires is ancient and longstanding and can be summed up as a fear of mythical blood thirsty creatures who sleep during the day and lurk at night to prey on the innocent; anyone who gets bitten and sucked by a vampire will in turn become a vampire themselves, and as a result they will go out and return the favor in kind to other unsuspecting victims. This is a persistent and visceral fear that is primitive and poignant, almost as potent as fear of the dark, itself.

Empirical evidence for vampirism is readily available. All one needs do is consider the mosquito, the arachnid species of ticks, the common leech, or the vampire bat to realize that vampirism truly occurs in nature. It is not a far stretch to imagine that humans may be intertwined with a lineage of humanoid beings who feast on the blood of the living and are themselves the undead, having existed since the beginning of the Universe and perhaps thriving in the shadows for eternity, waiting for the perfect moment to strike, eager to bite the neck and suck the blood.

3

In 1732, a blonde haired and blue-eyed girl, ten years of age, named Stephanie Dascălu, lived in the countryside of Hungary. She lived in farmhouse with her mother Mioara and stepfather, Nicolae, on the outskirts of a small village where the sloping hills were covered with deciduous forest of oak and beech, and in other areas varied forests with beech and fir, and in the alpine regions, in the distance, there grew larch and pine trees on the mountain sides. The woods, teaming with deer, stag, rabbit, pheasant, fox, badger, marten and partridge, chamois, groundhog, eagle and mountain jackdaw, were often foggy, eerie, and mysterious, in a land filled with beasts and mythical legends. The woods were said to harbor ghosts, demons, vampires, and witches. All children knew of these legends and stayed away from the spooky places they were warned about.

When Stephanie was only thirteen years old, still an innocent young girl, she had a terrible encounter while she was feeding the rabbits out in the pens on the farm. It was a pivotal moment that would forever change her life. A lecherous old

"Whatever you do . . . you better not tell anyone about this. You hear? I will come back and kill your entire family. Understand?"

Stephanie lay on the ground with her dress still raised exposing her nakedness, and she sobbed uncontrollably. She sobbed, wiped her runny nose, and nodded in agreement.

"Good," Grendel said. "Now go about your business. This never happened. I bid you good day . . ."

He turned and hurried away through the bushes and was gone like a shooting star.

Stephanie sat up, pulled down her dress to cover herself, and then slowly got up and stood looking out where the fiend had disappeared. She was scared, unsure, but decided she should hurry home to be safe inside, wary that the man might come back and do it again.

She ran through the woods, the branches in the trees grabbing her hair and scratching her face, and it was like she was running against the wind because she could not get across the open ground fast enough and she was scared and worried that the bad man would be waiting for her by the rabbit pens and would jump out and grab her and molest her again. The thought of what he had done to her made her cry again and tears rolled from the corners of her eyes, hot on her cheeks, salty on her tongue.

After what seemed like an eternity, she made it safely to her home and burst through the door with a bang. She ran into her mother's arms, still crying. She buried her face in her mother's bosom and cried.

"What's the matter, dear?" her mother, Mioara, asked.

Stephanie just shook her head and cried. She was not going to speak of the incident or the details, ever, and she had come to that conclusion already. She would never tell what happened. She did not want the bad man to come back and harm her family.

Mioara patted her daughter's head and tried to get the story out of her, but it was useless.

After Stephanie calmed down, her mother gave her a bowl of warm soup and a sandwich, but the little girl had no appetite.

She went to bed and lay deathly still, in shock, and was never the same after being molested by the lecherous pervert named Grendel. She would always remember this terrible event . . . always, forever, and it changed her life profoundly, creating a strong and driving force to seek justice against men like Grendel. She became an independent woman who would strive to make assholes and pedophiles suffer dearly for their atrocities in the future. She would make good on this promise, for sure, and she swore a solemn oath before God and all the angels in Heaven.

Unfortunately, due to this act of molestation, she was inhibited and uncomfortable around men, and as a result she stayed at home with her parents long into her adulthood until she was a grown woman. When she was eventually courted by a man from the village, Oswald Spencer, who came from a well-to-do family that owned a farm across the valley, she did not want to have anything to do with him. Her parents had agreed to a dowry and promised her to Oswald and his family in return for money and livestock. Stephanie would be a bride to Oswald in return, her hand offered in marriage, her life reduced to a wedding gift of human flesh, her life given as a possession, an acquisition to a wealthy family, to a man she could never love.

She refused to obey her parent's command, and swore to never love the strange man, ever, never, whatsoever. Oswald's honor was now at stake. He was furious. He wanted his prize.

When she refused to oblige Oswald, his parents were highly upset. They said she was an old maid and possibly a witch, since they had recently harvested spoiled milk from their cows and animals were dying for mysterious reasons. They said she had placed a curse on them, and she was guilty of witchcraft.

The community heard of the incident, a witness accusing her of witchcraft; they were certain that she was a witch. When they consulted with the preacher at the church it was decided that she was indeed a witch, and she should not be allowed to live, because the Bible said "though shalt not suffer a witch to live."

One night, with their suspicions aroused, they went to the farm, intent on killing Stephanie—and her parents, if it became necessary—for witchcraft was punishable by death. They gathered in a mob with torches and pitchforks outside the farmhouse. They called to the occupants inside the house.

"Bring out the witch," the leader of the mob, a balding man with crooked yellow teeth, cried out loudly. "We will make her suffering come to a quick end. We will spare everyone else if you cooperate."

Stephanie was secreted by her parents and ushered out through the back door.

"Run into the woods and hide," her father said. "Run as far away as you can and never look back."

"I'm scared," Stephanie said. Here eyes were wide and her complexion frightened.

"Just go, dear," her mother said. "We will always love you. Just remember that."

"Now go!" her father said. "Before it is too late."

"I love you," she said, turning away.

Stephanie slipped out the back door and ran into the woods, following the familiar trails that led deep into the forest. She did not look back, at first, until she was at a safe distance on a slope, behind the ferns and bushes that grew there in abundance.

The vigilante mob of witch killers surrounded the house

and set it on fire. When her parents came running out through the door, they grabbed them and tied their arms with rope.

"Where is the girl—the witch?" the yellow-toothed man asked, his breath reeking of garlic.

"She is gone," her father said. "She is no longer here."

"You have betrayed us," Yellow-Teeth said. "Hang them for sympathizing with the witch."

Quickly they took ropes, fashioned nooses at the end, then put them over the heads of the parents and took them to a nearby tree with a large enough limb to support their weight. They hanged them by pulling the ropes with horses and lifting the bodies, kicking and jerking, into the air, tongues protruding, eyeballs bulging, faces turning blue from asphyxiation.

Stephanie observed the entire event. She was frightened and angered and vowed to seek revenge for the murder of her parents. She turned and ran away as the house burned to the ground in the wake of the horrendous scene behind her.

4

As she walked down the road alone, a horse-drawn coach approached from behind on the dirt road. The driver sat up in the seat, bundled in blankets and clothed in a thick coat and gloves to protect him from the cold. The coach stopped and the door opened. A dark, handsome, and mysterious stranger opened the door and peered out at her. He took off his hat and greeted her warmly.

"Hello, my dear," the man said. "What is such a lovely young lady as yourself doing out on the road all alone at night? It is dangerous out here. You never know who might pick you up. What is your name?"

When she looked upon the man, she was instantly enamored; however, her distrust of men, particularly strange men, caused her alarm. She was not sure she trusted this stranger.

"My name is Stephanie," she said. She was choking on the urge to sob that was welling in her throat. "My parents have just been hanged, and my house was burned down. I am alone, now. I have nowhere to go."

"My fairest young lady," he said. "It appears that I am here to rescue you, then. My name is Vincent Lazar. You may refer to me as Count Lazar. I am arriving back from travels abroad and currently am on my way back to my castle here in Hungary. May I offer you a ride?"

There was an unknown cargo strapped to the top of the coach. Stephanie was suspicious of this man and his strange cargo.

"What—rescue me?"

"You are a damsel in distress," he said, smiling. "Are you not? You need help?"

"I am terrified," she said. "They have accused me of being a witch."

"You are accused of being a witch?" He breathed deeply, taking in her scent, his nostrils flaring. "I know your smell. I can sense your essence. You are no witch; of that I am certain."

"That is right. I am not a witch."

"It makes no difference—witch, or not. You are welcome with me. Come up her, dear," Count Lazar said, extending his hand to help her climb inside. "I won't bite you . . . not yet, anyway."

She hesitated, then reached out and took his hand, noticing it was deathly cold to the touch. As she was climbing up into the coach, he cleared a spot for her on the seat, and allowed her to sit down. He signaled through the window to the driver. The horses began pull and the coach moved as the driver lashed the horses and said *yah, yah, yah,* the whip cracking sharply. The horses neighed and whinnied as their hoofs clopped on the ground.

"I have nowhere to go. What will I do?" she asked.

"Well, do you know what that means?"

"I have no idea."

"You belong with me."

"I do?"

"Yes. You can come and live with me in my castle."

"I don't even know you."

"That matters little, dear. I see no reason you should not come and live with me. I will take loving care of you. What other choice do you have?"

"You have a point."

"Fine. It's settled then."

"Okay, I'll go with you." She looked at the handsome Count Lazar and became lost in his soporific eyes.

"I will protect you and keep you from harm. You have much to learn. If you want to survive in this cruel world, I must teach you the ways to prosper."

"I want to learn. Please teach me."

"It is settled then."

"Yes."

"There is much you need to know," he said. "But there is plenty of time . . . patience is a virtue."

"What do I need to know?"

"Just watch and learn."

"Absolutely," she said, mesmerized by his presence. "I will do anything you ask of me."

"Anything?"

"Yes. Anything."

"Wonderful, my dear. We have much to do and discuss and learn. I will teach you. I have a place just for you in my castle."

This sounded like a wonderful idea and she decided she would go with him to his castle.

The driver steered the carriage through the night and just before dawn they managed to make it back to the gates of the magnificent castle on the outskirts of the village of Markaz. The Count could afford this opulence, he said, since he was a wealthy businessman and entrepreneur wise beyond his years. He told Stephanie he loved living in the massive stone walls of the castle he called "Castelul Muntelui" which was interpreted as "The Mountain Castle."

5

After several years of living with the Count in his castle, Stephanie learned that he was a vampire. She was curious about this, and she wanted to become one herself. She begged Count Lazar to turn her into a vampire, but he refused to do so, telling her that she was better off waiting until she was older as she would be stuck as a young woman, a naïf, perpetually, and this would cause her problems later on in life if she was a young woman that never grew to maturity. So, he made her wait until her thirty-fifth birthday, when he felt she was mature enough to be a responsible vampire.

"Tonight you will become something special . . . a vampire," Count Lazar told her, pushing her back on the bed and gently opening her garment and exposing the pulsing vein on her neck. He kissed her gently, licking the pale skin, sucking on the spot where he intended to enter her. He bit her on the neck, drawing her blood and drinking deeply. He did not let her die, however, and rolled up his sleeve and ran a fingernail along the veins beneath his wrist. He drew blood from his own wrist and made her drink it, transforming her into a vampire.

She was wracked with exquisite pain, convulsing and thrown into spasms with cramps worse than anything she had ever experienced during the worst menstrual cycles, and she doubled over in pain, but there was an underlying pleasure as the Count's blood coursed through her veins, mixing with her own blood. The transformation had begun. Her eyeteeth began to elongate and grow into points, fangs extending, protruding out from her moist lips, still fresh with blood. She was intoxicated and ecstatic. It was complete. She was now a vampire and her senses were acute and sharp. She could feel the essence of life and death coursing through the air all around her.

"Thank you," she said, looking at the Count. "I have waited so long for this moment."

"It is an honor," he replied.

After that, She had an insatiable appetite for meat, her menstrual cycle was always heavy and she suffered from iron-deficiency anemia and although feeding on rabbits, chickens, rats, and other small animals could satiate her desire to feed on humans, she still wanted to bite everything in sight and suck the blood. Her desire to feed on human prey grew stronger and stronger, and eventually she killed a neighbor child, a young boy, sucking his blood and leaving him for dead behind the barn. "What have you done?" Count Lazar said, scornfully. "You've killed a young child."

"I could not help myself," Stephanie said, staring down at the floor in shame, unable to meet his eyes.

"You've attracted the attention of the locals. I should banish you from the castle at once."

"I have nowhere to go, my Lord."

"You should have thought of that before this."

"I'm sorry."

"Sorry is not good enough, I'm afraid. You must leave at once."

"I cannot. Don't make me," she said, pleading. "I will never survive on my own."

"That is not my concern," he said, turning away. "Be gone from my sight, now! Leave at once. I never wish to see you again."

She knew he was serious and that arguing was useless. She went and gathered her belongings into a bag and left out through the door from the castle and wandered into the night. This was the second time in her life that she was alone and left with nowhere to go, and she was saddened. She could only hope that her new vampire abilities would guide her. She hoped she would become a capable creature of the night and be able to make it out on her own.

The castle faded into the night behind her and she traveled quickly away down the road until she found a nice place in the woods to hide in a cave during the coming morning. She was aware that light would harm her, intuitively, and she hid away from the daylight.

6

Back at the castle, Count Lazar could hear noises outside in the night. It was a familiar sound and he knew right away what was taking place.

"They have come for me," he said, peering out through the window.

There was the sound of a battering ram against the castle gates.

The sun was rising over the horizon and there was no chance

23

of escape for Count Lazar. He would be required to retreat to the cellar and hide away from the coming of the vigilantes. He did not want to die as a coward and decided it was best to lie down in his coffin and take it like a man. He would die on his terms. He would die in his place.

The vampire hunters, a traveling band of Christian warriors hellbent on destroying creatures of the undead, crashed through the gate with the battering ram and rushed inside, bound and determined to capture and kill any vampires inside.

They went down into the cellar and found Count Lazar lying with his arms crossed in his coffin and they killed him quickly by driving a stake through his heart.

7

Stephanie was able to escape the following night, leaving the safety of the cave, and traveling by night to Budapest where she had to fend for herself, working as a servant of the night, posing as a prostitute and tempting men into the darkness, killing and drinking their blood, and taking any valuables they may have in their possession. Eventually, she was able to work her way into a high standing position and moved into a mansion where she lived the good life of luxury and wealth.

After that, Stephanie spent many years as a wealthy vampire, preying on victims at will, but eventually as she grew older, she was forced to move on to greener pastures. Having lived for centuries she became wealthy, which typically happens to all vampires who are seasoned because they have lived so long that gathering fortune just comes naturally.

After living for hundreds of years as a countess in Budapest, she eventually attracted the attention of the vampire hunters of old, and they came for her during a craze that swept the country where the locals believed that vampires were real and they were going to get rid of them all, one by one, and purify their wretched corpses with fire—after beheading them, of course.

In 1778, Stephanie took all her savings and liquidated it into fine gemstones and gold, and she crossed Europe and boarded a ship in England, heading for the United States of America. It was the promised land and she thought she could go there and start anew, hoping that the vampire hunters would lose track of her in the New World.

She took a room on the ship and remained hidden within, leaving only when necessary, during the arduous trip that took nearly a month to cross the Atlantic from Liverpool and the English Channel to the port of New York.

When she arrived, she waited on the ship until it was dark and then she deboarded and went into the city of New York to seek out her new life. She was forced to find shelter quickly, and she opened a brothel and again made magnificent sums of money.

The vampire hunters found her again, after living in the city for a century, and she was forced to flee, once more. This time she chose to move to Canada and picked the furthest point on the map she could find, Vancouver, British Columbia.

8

When she arrived in Canada, she was pleased with the city of Vancouver, British Columbia, and she knew that she would make this her new home. She had amassed enough of a fortune of the years that she could live in high style, and she immediately went about buying property on the hillside in the country and hired masons and builders to construct her new home, a castle, which she aptly named Château de Dascălu in the tradition of the castles she had grown so fond of in Europe. It was a major undertaking, and it took several years to complete the construction, and it was finally finished in 1895, nearing the turn of another century. When it was finished it had all the appearance of a Gothic castle from the old country in Hungary.

Over the years it became equated with ghosts and Satanic rituals and terrifying events that caused the locals to create legends about the history . . . murders have taken place there, and strange things have been observed, like creatures lurking in the shadows and ghosts . . . and today it is a spooky sight at night during a full moon as it looms on the hillside, overlooking the city of Vancouver.

9

George Vivaldi, the groundskeeper at the Château de Dascălu, was up early that morning, he had his shovel and wheelbarrow, there was a tractor with a trailer and other landscaping tools. He was planting new rhododendrons in one of the many flower gardens in the landscape on the estate. He took off his baseball cap and wiped his sweaty brow. The sun was only now coming up over the horizon and he had made and early start that morning.

He was thirsty and parched after digging the deep holes in the earth, his work gloves dirty and grimy as he gripped the bottled water and took a long drink. He guzzled the water hastily, droplets leaking from his dry and chapped lips, rolling out of the corners of his mouth and falling onto his boots, washing away the sand and dusty film covering the worn and tattered brown leather, trickling off in streams and leaving trails of dark, clean, lines like the trail of a snail. Those boots had walked many a mile on this property. His eyes had seen many a thing, too. He was familiar with the legends and rumors surrounding the mansion. He knew things. He kept quiet. The job was regular, and the pay was good, and it was in his better interest to just ignore things that did not concern him.

He had been the caretaker of the property and mansion for twenty years, working with the previous caretaker, Jim Stow, who had been there twice as long and had eventually died of old age and retired from the job. George had learned many things from Jim, and together they had seen many things during their days spent maintaining the landscape, the structures, the plumbing, and seeing that the overall functioning of the mansion stayed in working order. It was a hard job as the property was vast, covering many acres as it sprawled along the wooded hillside of the mountains, a massive wall and fence bordering the property line with wrought iron and spikes and designed to keep intruders out, and perhaps to keep things in, too, and that was a frightening prospect that George tried not to concern himself with. He was allowed free access and could come and go as he pleased and that was all that mattered to him.

The rumors were extraordinary . . . and the funny part was that just that morning there had been an article about haunted castles and mansions around the British Columbia, and lo and behold, there was a piece about the Château de Dascălu. He had been eating his breakfast and drinking a cup of coffee when he saw the article just in front of the obituary column. He nearly choked, his mouth full of bacon and eggs. He had to take a second look to make sure he was not seeing things or that his imagination was not getting the best of him.

He read the article and was not surprised by the content.

10

HAUNTED CASTLES AND MANSIONS IN VANCOUVER?

By Brent Treadwell

The Vancouver Courier

Did you know that there are haunted castles and mansions in Vancouver? Probably not. Since Halloween is here, we thought it would be fun to talk about the legends of some of the oldest structures in existence in our community.

Yes. Vancouver has castles, and other antiquated mansions, and they are of historical significance. Although they are not as old as ancient castles of Europe, they are still officially known historical sites that have all the trappings of their medieval counterparts.

The most notorious of these being Château de Dascălu. Although it is officially called a mansion, it is, in fact, a quasi-castle castle complete with motes, turrets, spires, and a large wall surrounding the entire estate. The history of the castle is shrouded in mystery, as the original builders were secretive and kept outsiders away, and it was not until the mid-20th century that visitors were openly welcomed into the mansion. The government and historical society do not recognize the structure as a true castle because it does not come from royalty or have significant historical value to be listed in the registry. For all practical purposes, it is a castle, and we would argue that it should be recognized as such, however, it remains a tourist attraction, nonetheless.

Currently, the property is owned by Stephanie Dascălu, a wealthy heiress who has ties to the old country in Hungary through a long family lineage of wealthy land barrens who came to the new world in Canada and the United States and found riches in the railroad and timber industries, as well as architecture and real estate. They are amongst the wealthiest citizens of Canada, and Stephanie is known to be a flamboyant jetsetter and celebrity on the club scene where she makes regular appearances and indulges in the decadent lifestyle of the nightlife downtown. She is beloved by many and her lifestyle is notorious, and she is known to throw lavish parties at the mansion.

This is where the rumors and legends come from. Visitors have told stories of strange things going on behind the gates of the quasi-castle.

Legends and rumors surround the Gothic styled structure. On a full moon it is claimed that wolves howl into the night, endlessly until the sunrise. There are rumored to be ghosts that haunt the cemetery on the premises. It is like something right out of a horror novel. There have been claims of people vanishing into thin air when they have ventured too close to the mansion, and paranormal investigators have gone into the woods nearby to conduct experiments and tests and see if they can conjure up any spirits of the lost souls who have vanished, but nothing significant has ever been found.

This Halloween should prove to be an exciting time at the mansion as locals pass by to take pictures and see if the dead really do rise at walk down the lonely road that leads to town. There have been stories of a ghostly hitchhiker, and it reads like a scary story of fiction, but many motorists passing along that stretch of road have claimed to see a young woman in a white dress flagging them down to ask for a ride. There have even been incidents where drivers have given the girl a ride only to find she vanishes into thin air right before their very eyes.

This all seems quite fantastic, and as everybody knows, ghosts do not exist. We find it interesting and entertaining and think that this Halloween is a perfect time to spotlight one of our local haunts around town and speculate on the question, what if ghosts really did exist? Who knows? Maybe there are haunted castles here in Vancouver.

Be warned, if you should attempt to go out to the castle and spy on the inhabitants you will find a pack of trained dogs that run loose on the property and will attack any intruders. Not only that, it is also illegal to trespass, so we suggest that you pay respect and be courteous if you should decide to visit the mansion this Halloween or during the next full moon.

11

George pulled a rhododendron from the trailer, scooted it into the wheelbarrow, and grabbed the wooden handles and pushed it over to where he had dug the large hole. This was a transplant and it was going to look magnificent in its new home. He had other plants to work with today, Japanese maples, apple trees, and junipers were on the list of chores to be tackled before he stopped for the day. He planned to work until sunset, and then he would go home to his wife and family.

He looked and saw the black limousine as it pulled up in front of the mansion, parked, and the driver got out, dressed in a tuxedo, and wearing a black hat. He went inside through the heavy and solid wood doors. The mansion was built like a fortress, and George was not sure it that was to keep intruders out, or keep prisoners in, because he knew things, had seen things, had *heard* things.

There he goes to pick up someone privileged and well off, he thought. *Must be nice, having everything handed to you on a silver platter.* It was not for him. He had never been in a limo and doubted that he ever would. He was dirt poor and that was how he had always experienced life, from the eyes of a laborer. He made the best of it. He made a living. He supported his family, a wife, and three lovely children who were his pride and joy.

The lady of the house, Stephanie, had always treated him well, and gave him large bonus stipends at the end of the year, so he had no complaints.

Although, he wondered what went on inside the mansion. He thought about the article, and the stories passed down from elders in town that knew some of the dark secrets about the place. It was rumored to have been built by Chinese immigrants who slaved away, pushing the large stones and beams into position with their bare hands. It was back breaking work, or so it goes, and some of them died in the process, what with all the digging and labor involved with laying the foundation, and some of them died from exhaustion and were buried right on the property. Nobody would miss them, and back then it was a different time, and the contractors were on a time schedule and wanted to save money, so they did what they had to do, and nobody was going to cry over a couple of dead Chinamen.

Also, after the mansion was complete, there was a dark period where no one was allowed to enter the premises, and it was rumored that the landowner was a wealthy count from Hungary who arrived by stage coach late at night, and witnesses claim to have seen large black boxes being unloaded and hastily carried inside the castle. The curious onlookers wanted to know what secret cargo was being transferred in at such an hour and why did they have to do it under the cover of darkness and with such secrecy?

Nobody knew for sure, and it led to many strange theories and speculation. There were even tales of Satanic rituals and cannibalism that supposedly took place within the walls after the place had been established for a while. Robed figures had been observed gathering in the courtyard with torches and strange sounds of screaming and chanting were heard coming from within, a large bonfire lighting up the night, and the locals feared for their safety, going inside and hiding so the demons and beasts being conjured would not fly through the night and carry them off to Hell. After that, the locals stayed away from the area and genuflected with the sign of the cross when passing by the evil estate. It was shunned for some time and even the local authorities, including the police and RCMP would not go out there for fear of being possessed by demons.

George knew all of this, and more, as he had seen things, strange things, ghostly things that crept around in the darkness, with glowing eyes and ghastly voices that sounded like creatures from another world, a place deep in another dimension, and he had felt his skin crawl at the sight of shadows creeping along the walls, sinister and looming, then disappearing and leaving him alone in silence with only the sound of chirping frogs in the bogs and crickets in the tall grass outside the fence.

He would continue to come to work and ignore those things that did not concern him. It paid his bills and he had lived this long, so he did not feel that he was in any danger. He made sure to eat a diet rich in garlic because that kept the dark ones at bay. He knew that much. They would not bother him if he just kept to himself and continued to do his thing. Planting trees and tending to the garden. That was all he would do. Never mind the stories. He did not put much faith or belief into it.

He knew one thing . . . he was going to go home before dark set in. He did not like being around the mansion after sunset. There were strange things that lurked about and creatures that flew through the night and swooped down low and came close enough to lift the hair on your head. He had experienced this on more than one occasion, and he would not stay late unless it was absolutely necessary. The lady of the house was generous, and she paid double time when work required him to stay late, but that did not make it any better or less . . . frightening. That was the word for it. It was eerie and unsettling, and although he was not one to go for ghost stories and spooky myths, he did know that something was strange and weird about the Château de Dascălu and the less time he had to be there after dark, the better.

Tonight, was no exception. As he watched the sunset with colors of pink, orange, and blue, he hurried and finished for the day, putting his tools away and parking the tractor in the shed. He dusted himself off and shut the door, making sure it was locked, although he had a suspicion that no thief would ever bother to attempt to break into the shed, or even venture onto the property, because it had never happened in the history of the mansion, or at least no one had ever lived to tell about trespassing on the property. If there had ever been an attempting theft or intrusion it had gone unreported and the perpetrators were never heard from again. Anyone in their right mind would not want to sneak onto the property, and that was a fact.

George took his lunchbox and ambled over to his old Ford F-150 truck. He opened the door, threw his work gloves on the passenger seat, and put down his lunchbox. He looked at the ribbon of colorful light looming on the horizon as the sun sunk down over the landscape. He felt gooseflesh on his arms and the hair on the back of his neck stood on end. Something was astir and he did not care to stay around and find out what it was. The spirits walked on these grounds after dark and he had every intention of getting the hell out while there was still light and time.

He got into his truck, shut and locked the door, and put the key in the ignition. He turned the key and started the engine with a backfire and belching blast of black smoke.

"Come on, Betsy," he said, patting the dashboard, speaking to his truck as if it were a sentient being. "Don't fail me now. Let's get out of here while the getting is good."

The engine fell into a regular idle, and he put it in gear and stepped on the accelerator, rolling down the driveway and stopping at the gate. He stepped on the brake, hesitated, then roll down the window and reached out to the keypad and punched in his code. He was afraid he might not get his arm back inside in time, and he was anxious and uneasy as the heavy iron gate slowly opened and let him pass through, unscathed.

He did not feel safe until he was better than a mile down the road and cruising just above the posted speed limit of 80 km/h. He looked in the review mirror and sighed. He would have to go back tomorrow, and it was a job that paid well, but he always had reservations . . . at least it would be morning and the sun would be out and he felt safe in the daylight.

He had survived for another day . . .

PART ONE

THE WICKED CITY

The prince had provided all the appliances of pleasure. There were buffoons, there were improvisatori, there were ballet-dancers, there were musicians, there was Beauty, there was wine. All these and security were within. Without was the "Red Death."

—Edgar Allan Poe,
"The Masque of the Red Death"

CHAPTER ONE

1

The party scene downtown on Main Street in Vancouver, British Columbia was exciting and intense, and there was never a dull moment on weekends and special occasions. During the night of Halloween, however, the spirit of celebration was heightened, and the party goers kicked it up a notch, consuming massive quantities of alcohol and intoxicating substances and dressing up in outlandish costumes. They took to the streets to let loose in a raucous and decadent celebration that would last well in to the next day, littering the streets with party favors and refuse that blew away in the wind, left to be swept up by city maintenance crews.

At a club known as The Royal, found at 666 Main Street, there was a six thousand square foot private event facility located in the urban core of the city that hosts large events and parties. This is where the annual fetish Halloween party known as Wicked City Fetish Halloween party was thrown, which was the wildest party in the city It is a state-of-the art party presented with world-class entertainment offering an exciting and unparalleled event experience with a flexible floorplan and high-tech audio and lighting displays for hosting concerts, dinner events, corporate meetings and presentations, fundraisers, private parties, or anything else that may need an event host with a place to transpire and flourish in the heart of the city.

This was the site of a costume party that involved dressing in outlandish attire with themes of fetish, bondage, burlesque, and drag. There were staged scenes with actors and attendees performing various acts of bondage and indulging in fetish acts, spanking, licking, kissing, all sorts of depraved and wretchedly lewd acts were acceptable here in the assigned play areas with dedicated furniture and props. There were DJs, dancing, and socializing, and, of course, drugs and alcohol and sex. There were two levels with four rooms with an attendance of over six-hundred kinky and perverted Halloween partygoers.

Main Street in Vancouver B.C. had an extensive history as a fashionable and trendy scene for hipsters, party seekers, and all walks of nightlife in general. It was usually a casual and relaxed atmosphere, with a focus on music and a not so demanding attitude about style and decorum; however, it did have a reputation for getting wild during certain times of the year, during certain holidays, weekends, and on a full moon, and Halloween was no exception.

Wicked City Fetish Halloween was a specialty event produced and presented at The Royal, a trendy nightclub found in the city core, downtown, and had a strict dress code for fetish, bondage, and kinkiness. They did not tolerate "normal" people , or kink-less outfits—none would be admitted to the club in plain clothes or non-kinky attire—and the more outlandishness and grandstanding one could be and the more attention seeking self-indulgence one could achieve with a costume, the better, because it was required fetish and bondage apparel at the club. They did not tolerate lower genital nudity, although partial upper nudity was acceptable. One could use the power of suggestion, or slight exposure of genitals or nudity was acceptable, however no direct displaying of sexual body parts. Attire that included PVC, vinyl, rubber, leather, tuxedo, themed and full outfit costumes, period, fantasy, cross-dressing, body-paint, bondage, lingerie, skirts and kilts, and just about any other sensational or risqué and sexy costume were preferred. The more perverted the imagination was . . . the better. Whatever the case, no one wanted to simply show up in nothing but tighty-whities or plain underwear. That would be unacceptable, a parody, but a social gaffe, nonetheless.

This Wicked City Fetish Halloween party was going to be legendary and wild at The Royal; the attendees were giddy with excitement and anticipation, dressed to the T and already well on their way to being intoxicated. They were already gathering outside the club, The Royal, lined up down the street, grouped, and congregating all the way down the block and around the corner out of sight.

The party goers were dressed in spectacular and striking costumes of fetish and Halloween themes, with traditional skeletons, ghouls, zombies, and vampires, as well as more garish and gay attire that leaned toward extreme fetish and extreme dominance of leather, lace, and lingerie, often the lack of a costume and exposure of flesh and genitals were the main attraction. Here was a queen dressed in a burlesque outfit and there was a bear dressed in a stud leather outfit showing a hairy chest beneath the vest, and there was an angel with wings, and here was a drag queen dressed in fishnet stockings and platform high heel boots all the way up to the groin. Some costumes were lacking and left little to the imagination, breasts, asses, and crotches nearly exposed beneath G-strings and thongs, leather, plastic, and PVC underwear, and chains and frilly lace panties. It was more about what was missing than the costume itself. The party goers were covered in makeup and wore wigs and masks.

The air smelled of excitement and sex; assorted flavors of alcoholic smoking cigarettes, cloves, and marijuana beverages lingered on the breeze. The crowd was full of party goers popping Ecstasy and Molly, LSD, and amphetamines, getting primed and ready for the show. They were getting charged up and anxious to get it on. They were already hanging on one another, kissing and making out, swapping partners, and anticipating a good night of sex and pleasure amongst friends or strangers.

Party goers were magically drawn together at The Royal to attend the Wicked City Halloween Fetish party and they would become acquainted there, exchanging phone numbers and social media pages. It was going to be an exciting and sin filled night with sex and promiscuity to rival the legendary escapades of Sodom and Gomorrah. Their lives would be forever changed.

Men and women would meet there, sample the wares, swap tongues and other more delicate personal body parts, choosing mates, and going home with one another to extend the party after hours. Some would go home in twos and threes and others would go in groups and packs, hands in each other's pockets, arms slung over shoulders, staggering drunkenly and out of step, feeling what bulged and sweated beneath the fabric, anxious to get to know them better.

There would be smeared lipstick, mascara, and eyeshadow, an overpowering mix of cologne and perfume, and saliva and other bodily fluids exchanged and drained. The condom machines in the bathrooms were sold out and emptied, and thank goodness for that, at least they were thinking about being safe; they did not want to exchange or contract any nastiness that might be lurking just below the surface, and catching an STD was not on the itinerary for any of the party goers.

2

The doorman, Max Chase, dressed in a tailored blue Armani suit, was checking identification, ripping tickets, and letting guests in slowly, methodically, opening the red velvet stanchion rope for couples and groups, careful and watchful for anyone unwelcome or troublesome. This was a legit show, and no one was going to blow it for the rest of the exuberant and enthusiastic crowd that came to have fun. Sometimes there were those who wanted to get in and spoil the fun, but Max, had seen it all, and he had been a security and bouncer for the event for years. He had a good eye for miscreants and troublemakers, and he would instantly send them packing, kicking them in the ass with a Gucci leather shoe if they were stubborn or defiant. He did not mess around. This was a night for fun and sex, not trouble or violence, and he would see to it that the assholes did not make it inside.

3

Rudge Goodburn was a bartender at The Royal and he was ready for the party on Halloween scheduled for Saturday, October 26, 2019. He had worked at the annual Halloween fetish party since its inception twenty years ago when it began in a small and seedy bar, The Voyeur, across town and back then it only attracted a few souls and they were packed in like a tin of smoked oysters. The party had grown over the years and eventually it moved from place to place, until it found a home in the new facility at 666 Main street downtown Vancouver at The Royal. This facility was large enough to manage the hundreds of guests that would be in attendance. It was an extreme and sexually charged event and there was never a dull moment in his experience.

4

Manson Stokes, lived in the South Main "SoMa", just south of the city's urban center around 6th Avenue and extends south as far as Riley Park, and all the way to 33rd Avenue, in a studio apartment. It is an area that is experiencing a resurgence in upswing in popularity, inhabited by young urban professionals and humanitarians, hipsters and millennials, with converted studio and loft apartments, artists, actors, and performers called it home. The area was at one time the industrial center; however, it had become a source of shops with retro, vintage, and eco-friendly apparel, galleries with sawdust floors and contemporary taste, craft beer and microbrew pubs, art and acting studios. The entire scene was set with the backdrop of an Art Deco flare, with a resolute blue-collar etiquette, taste and culture surrounding each new upstart venture and food trend. Residents in SoMa knew that they were at the forefront of a stylish movement and that their easygoing lifestyle was on the rise. People who lived there were happy and content.

Main street was packed with cafes, restaurants, bars, and pubs, and an emerging beer connoisseur scene with local craft and micro-breweries, complete with beer tasting rooms. In Mount Pleasant there were parks, playgrounds, jogging and bicycling trails, and a beautiful view of the North Shore mountains.

5

Zoey Lavay was an energetic and sprightly young woman, a devastating beauty, dark and tall with a frame like a fashion model. In a word, she was terminally pretty. She had long raven hair and big sapphire blue eyes. She consistently wore black corsets with ruched sleeves and bows and ribbon lacing at the back, a black Gothic leather dovetail robe jacket with eyelets cap, black knee length laced up platform boots with a 4-inch heel and black lace knee stockings. She was beautiful and men were instantly drawn to her dark charisma, and she had no problem attracting a potential mate.

She and her family lived on the upscale West End side of Vancouver, in a quaint four-bedroom home with her mother and father, two older brothers, and one younger sister.

When she heard about the Halloween party at The Royal, she was did not need to think about it, and she decided she would be there with bells on, dressed to kill, and ready to rock and roll.

6

Shortly after sunset, right around 7:30 p.m., twilight had set in and the sky was growing darker by degrees, and Stephanie Dascălu, a socialite and a cougar who lived in the mansion called Château de Dascălu, an old mansion that was literally a castle on the outskirts of Vancouver, nestled in the hillside on a sprawling estate that she owned and maintained, wealthy and a woman of means, she lived to party and life was good. Tonight, she was anxious to go out on the town . . . because it was Halloween and there was a great party to attend: The Wicked City Fetish Halloween at the club The Royal, and she would be there dressed to impress.

Stephanie was in a hurry to get ready since it started at 8 o'clock sharp and she did not want to miss a single thing. She hurried and climbed inside the limousine and told her driver to step on it, she did not want to be late, as the party would start without her. She had a table reserved, but that did not matter, she would be fashionably late, of course, but she wanted to arrive and look marvelous as she walked down the carpeted entrance in front of the cameras and onlookers.

She lit a cigarette and cracked the window in the limousine. She was drinking a gin and tonic from a tall glass with ice and it had a wedge of lemon floating at the top. Her lips were brilliant red, her makeup done immaculately, and she was wearing dark sunglasses to cover her eyes. She would take them off in the club, but for now she enjoyed the incognito anonymity that they afforded.

The party started in less than an hour, so she wanted to get their early and get seated in her special allocated table at the VIP section where she would be provided with a wide view of the festivities. The stage would be right in front of her and she had one of the only tables with seating in the entire event. Everyone else was forced to stand, or sit on the stools along the bar, and it did not matter to them because they were all dancing, grasping and groping each other, or watching the activities on the stage with so much sex and promiscuity in the air that you were guaranteed to get horny at the event.

The black stretched limousine crept down the driveway, pulled through the gate, and turned onto the main drive toward the city. The gates closed. The sun was setting. It was going to be night soon.

It was one of many limousines that pulled up in front of the club at 666 Main Street downtown carried Stephanie Dascălu, and the driver got out and opened a rear passenger door. She put her drink down and climbed out, a crowd had already gathered out front and she was greeted by cheers and applause as she walked down the red carpet and entered in through the front door.

She was dressed in her finest costume, a Wicked Queen, and she intended to steal the show. She had attended many of the parties before and it was always fun and exciting, and she usually found someone to bring home to her mansion and have an after-hour party. They rarely made it through the night alive, as she would wind up sucking their blood after the festivities were over and she would discard of their corpses in the deep basement beneath the castle. There were piles of bones and rats in the cellar.

The patrons of the party at The Royal would not know that she was a vampire and they would just see her as a beautiful socialite who attended the party scene, a cougar who tempted the young men and women with her domineering personality and enchanting beauty. They could not resist her, and she was always on the VIP list when the parties were thrown around town. She attended all the parties during the year, but the Wicked City Fetish Halloween party was her personal favorite, because the freaks came out in force and she fit right in with them.

The lust and sexual antics were exactly what she was looking for and it made her giddy to watch the queens and boy toys dance around and spank each other and perform lewd and visual motions with each other.

Tonight, she planned to bring some fresh meat home to fuck and consume whole. She had a ravenous appetite and she was in the mood for some serious flesh and fantasy.

This was going to be a great night. She knew it for sure.

She could already taste the blood . . .

Inside the party was just getting started and the smell of sex and sin was thick in the air mixed with cloying perfume, cologne, and sweat.

CHAPTER TWO

1

Manson Stokes was late for band practice, so he stepped down hard on the accelerator in the black 1975 Monte Carlo and raced down the street, engine rumbling, steering the heavy metal vessel like a locomotive barreling over the asphalt. Built of steal and rubber in Flint, Michigan, the car had raw horse-power cranking from a customized high-performance engine, guzzling down gas like a thirsty beast. He loved his car and he had worked hard to turn it into the classic hotrod that was now worth a mint. It was old and massive and built like a tank, but it was his pride and joy, and because it was shiny and black and covered with glistening chrome it turned heads wherever he went. Tonight, since he was running late, he broke the speed limit and did not care if he got a ticket. He was willing to take that chance.

He played guitar in a punk metal band, Sinister Fiends, with his best friend, Skeeter Dinglewood, a bass player, in a garage across town. His friend, Skeeter, had a funny name, and every-body knew it and made fun of him, singing a song about having a skeeter on his peter, whack it off, whack it off. Peter often took exception to this song, but he knew the joke was not on him, so he let it ride. Despite the funny name, Skeeter's parents were the owners of the Dinglewood Pharmacy, and it was a favorite store for the locals and a family tradition. How they ever got a last name like Dinglewood was beyond Manson, and he thought the name Skeeter fit his bass playing friend quite well.

The garage was their lair and they spent many days and nights there, writing their masterpiece and practicing for the gigs they took part in around the clubs in Vancouver.

Skeeter's father, Monty, thought the garage was a pigsty, and he was always telling him to "clean it up . . . and turn it down. It's too firkin loud. We can't even hear the TV in here."

"Alright, already," Skeeter would reply, still holding his bass, the volume knob turned down to zero and mute. "I heard you the first time. We're trying to practice out here. Quit interrupting."

His father would shake his head, handwave the noisy kids away, and turn and go back inside through the interior door.

The music would instantly resume, and the drums and base would shake the windowpanes in the garage and the house. It was a reoccurring incident without remedy, and as old has electricity, at least, maybe holder, as Wolfgang Amadeus Mozart was known to annoy his parents many centuries past, or so Skeeter liked to argue—not knowing if it was a true or false fact. The truth is that Mozart had parents that encouraged his musical talents, only upset when he was out of tune or missed practice, and the same went for Monty and his wife, Gertrude; they encouraged their son to express his passion for music and create art, despite how loud and obnoxious it could be at times.

There had been noise complaints in the past and the police had even come to visit on weekends when the festivities got too loud and out of control. They shut the party down and sent the crowd packing, much to the parents' relief—they were too lax and easy going to shut it down themselves, and they always let Skeeter have his way. The police warned them that they could be held responsible for underage drinking and illegal drug use, and the parents complained to Skeeter, but it fell on deaf ears, literally because his ears were always ringing from the loud music he loved to play. It was a constant headache, but a common scene for many families in the world. Music attracts the youth like honey attracts bears, and the end result is sometimes a world famous superstar, but more often than not, just a bunch of adults who go on to work remedial jobs and earn minimum wage, still cleaning to a decrepit dream into their forties and fifties.

It was a double wide construction with two doors and he always parked his old Chevy pickup in one of the bays where it sat like a sleeping dinosaur, perpetually waiting for an oil change and tune-up. It was his work truck, so he was not afraid of it getting damaged when Skeeter had guests over, to play music or just hang out on the ratty old sofa against the far wall by the drum set; he was not worried about scratches or dents accrued when the boys in the band got too drunk or out of hand and threw things—bottles, drumsticks, bricks, tools, microphones, you name it—in a random volley instigated by angst and intoxication. It happened in the past, and he supposed it could happen again, in the present, or the future, so he did no park his nice Chrysler sedan anywhere near the garage (he kept it parked out on the street where it was better to risk the passage of public vehicles getting in a collision). He did not enjoy the music, or the constant flow of kids coming and going, nor the drinking and smoking pot—the cannabis smoke made his allergies act up for some odd reason and his eyes itched but he was tolerant because he loved his son. One day he knew that Skeeter would grow up and move out and the whole thing would come to a sudden end—he hoped it would be sudden, anyway.

Manson and Skeeter were out in the garage early one morning, practicing some new material, reworking the riffs to a difficult section of complicated chords and rhythm changes, when the gang came over to visit and help with the song writing tasks.

Kramer stepped into the open garage retracted doorway. "What's up, hosers?" he asked, picking up a spare set of drumsticks from the window seal.

Peter and Stuart joined him. They stepped inside and sat down on the couch. Peter took out a pack of cigarettes and lit one. Stuart scratched his ass intently, then sniffed his fingers.

"Oh, man," Skeeter said, cringing. "That's disgusting."

"I know," Stuart said. "My ass itches. What can I say?"

They laughed and shook their heads. Stuart was the guy bringing the gross-out factor to the group, always doing something disgusting or cutting up with crude jokes. He just could not help himself. "Smell my finger," he would say, or rub it under someone's nose and call it a "buttstache." It never got old, at least not to him.

They all said hello and slapped high fives, except none of them wanted to touch Stuarts shit scented fingers. Although, Manson realized too late, gripping Stuart's hand, and feeling his sweaty palm, pulled his hand back, grimaced, and then wiped it on his pantleg.

"Yuk," Manson said, scowling. "You've got shit stains on your fingers."

They cracked up over the imitation of John Lennon riffing about having blisters on his fingers.

"Hey, yo," Kramer said, patting Manson on the back. "What's happening?" He flipped a drumstick in the air, then said, "I heard you were looking for a drummer?"

"We were," Manson said, scratching his head. "Is Neil Pert coming over, because I gotta tell ya . . . we need a real drummer in a bad way."

"Yeah, whatever," Kramer said, sitting down behind the drum set. "I taught him everything he knows." He did a drum roll and then accentuated the punch line with the snare and crash cymbal. "How you like me now?"

"We love you, Kramer," Skeeter said, taking a swig of warm beer from a bottle that had been sitting on the amplifier for too long. He grimaced and smacked his lips.

"How about you two?" Skeeter asked, looking at Peter and Stuart. "You guys ready to rock and roll?"

"Hell fucking yeah," Peters said. "We got out gear out in the car."

"Well, don't just stand there," Skeeter said. "Go get your shit and let's kick this pig. Me and Manson been working hard on this new set and you guys gotta catch up."

It was a typical day in an average neighborhood in the outskirts of the city. They were living the dream. A big gig at The Royal, a dream, was looming in the future. They had to practice and get ready. It was paramount that they be at their best and kick ass during the show.

"I think we are going to completely blow the fucking The Royal up, man," Manson said, tuning up his electric guitar. "This new music we are working on is going to bring down the roof."

"Let's run through the set," Skeeter said. "Enough jib jabbing. It's time to get to work."

Peter and Stuart went out to the car and brought back their

guitars. Sinister Fiends was a three-guitar band, and Peter sang lead vocals. They had a loud and full sound that most four-piece bands could not compete with, reminiscent of Blue Oyster Cult with a heavier and more sinister tone and mood. Their music was more in the nü-metal genre, with a slight bent on themes of death, carnage, and mayhem. It was like a wall of sound that shook the ground and split the ear drums with screaming guitars, booming bass, and machinegun rhythms on the drums. Kramer's double bass footwork was phenomenal, and it sounded like a runaway locomotive when he stood on the pedals and hovered off the stool, seaming to float like a genie on magic carpet ride. They were good and people knew it. They might be getting a record deal soon, and things were looking up for the dark metal Goth punk band.

They got everything plugged in and tuned up and began working on their new set of songs. It was magnificent. The music filled the garage and spilled out into the surrounding neighborhood and rocked the house. Children passed by on skateboards and bicycles and looked at the band in the garage, amazed and awestruck, wondering *what was all the commotion and who were these strange looking rock and roll rebels? They might be famous someday.* They wanted to meet them and get an autograph. It was a big deal for a kid to see such a sight in the neighborhood. Skeeter was always accommodating and gave the kids signed CDs and flyers and group photos with the band logo, Sinister Fiends, in a jagged and toothy metal font, emblazoned on all the promotional material.

The band played for the rest of the day, a full three hour tour de force, and they were exhausted when they were finished, especially Kramer, as playing the drums was, in his opinion, the hardest part of the job. They called it a night, and everybody went home.

"That was a good day's work," Skeeter said to Manson after the others had gone.

"I think so," Manson said. "We're getting it down pretty good. I think we'll rock this new material at our next gig."

"I think you're right," Skeeter said, putting his bass away in the hard-shell case.

"Hey, you want to go out and grab a beer and a bite to eat?" Manson asked, following suit and putting his guitar away. "It's my treat."

"Nah, I'm good," Stewart said. "I'm going to wind it down early tonight."

"Suit yourself," Manson said. "There are some hot chicks that have been hanging out at the Rockhouse. I've been working on them for a few nights. I think they are about to give in to my dark and sinister charm." He waggled his eyebrows. "Know what I mean?"

"Yeah. No. I'm good," Stewart said. "Maybe next time. I'm bushed. Go ahead without me."

"Alrighty, then," Manson said. "The bush master rides alone tonight. I got this. You take care, bro."

"You, too," Skeeter said.

They slapped a high-five to each other and then hugged in a heartfelt embrace.

Manson went home and took a shower. He was looking to find a date tonight, and planned on hitting the clubs and seeing what, or whom, he could dredge up from the scene. There were usually a dozen girls, regulars, hanging out at the Rockhouse Pub, where he could get some good food and drinks and possibly a date.

Manson drove in his 1975 black Monte Carlo, the hotrod standing out in the street and turning heads, as the engine rumbled and chugged along through the night. He was proud of his car as it was a classic that was the envy of many a car aficionado. Anyone could buy a brand-new car off the lot, but it took time, patience, and devotion to restore such a fine automobile. He pulled up at the pub and parked in the back lot, getting out and locking the doors.

He went inside and sat down in his usual spot. It was an eventless night. The girls were not interested, the beer went down smooth and the rare T-bone steak was delicious, but it was a slow night and after watching the news on the TV over the bar, he decided it was a wash and was going to go home. He left and went out to get into his car.

When he got out there, he noticed a flyer on his windshield.

"What have we here?" he said, aloud. "Who put this shit on my car?"

He pulled the paper from beneath the windshield wiper and looked at the images and text, reading the message:

> The Royal is hosting the annual fetish Wicked City Fetish Halloween party on Saturday, October 26, 2019 at 8 p.m. through midnight. This is the wildest party in the city, hands down, and paddles up. We are going to spank that ass if you don't show up. You don't want to miss the most wickedly delicious party of the year. We'll see you here to trick or treat the night away. Don't forget to wear an awesome costume. No bores, only crossdressers, queens, boytoys, and Gothic whores will be let through the door, so dazzle us with unique attire, and bring your lust for flesh and desire. Be there or be square.

The club was The Royal, and Manson was familiar with the place because he was going to be playing a gig there soon. He noted the address was 666 Main street downtown, in the heart of Vancouver. It tickled him to no end that the address was the exact number as the mark of the beast, right out of the New Testament in the Bible, and he found this delightfully wicked. Whoever thought of that was a genius. This party sounded too good to be true. Fetish and bondage sounded fun, and there would be some hot Goth chicks there to flirt with. He was going, no doubt about it, and he would invite his mates from the band, too. Sinister Fiend would be there with bells on, representing the neighborhood of SoMa in full, living color, make-up with black eyeliner, teased up raven hair, and musty leather.

He folded up the flyer and stuck it in his pocket. This was a serendipitous score, and he was glad that someone had placed the flyer on his windshield. This was going to be fun. He got into his car, started up the engine, and drove home, thinking about what costume he would wear to the Wicked City Fetish Halloween party at The Royal.

2

Manson was dark, tall at six feet high, and handsome. He was a young man, with blue eyes and a dimple, who was in his late twenties. He had medium length black hair he kept combed back neatly in a ducktail. He wore a hip length black leather jacket, long sleeve button up silk shirts with lace and large lapels, a special gold necklace with a Devil's eye ruby amulet that was sentimental, and Calving Klein jeans, and Gothic style New Rock leather boots with buckles, zippers, and steel tacon heel.

He was a rebel and had a feisty demeanor. He grew up in a small three bedroom house with his parents in the city of Vancouver, on the rough side of town, the Eastside on East 17th Avenue just a hop, skip, and a jump away from skid row downtown where the drug use and heroine junkies were rampant on the corners with needles and diseases, where prostitutes sold their goods, and the mentally ill walked around aimlessly, talking to themselves, whacked out on methamphetamines and whatever else they could get their grubby hands on, panhandlers begging change, homelessness run rampant, crime, thugs, thieves, and community service workers and VPD police officers in the middle trying to keep the peace. The long-term residents in his neighborhood had a strong sense of community, and they believed in the power of change, and morals, and values, and that humans were resilient, that there was power in social activism and a can-do spirit.

Although it was a rough neighborhood, Manson was tough and he was a survivor, and he could take care of himself. He had been in more than one fist fight, defending himself against bullies, thugs, and robbers trying to take whatever they could from him, including his ass, if that were the only thing he had to offer. They would rape you in a second, if you let them, and Manson was not about to let that happen—although, he did believe that you cannot rape the willing, and he was fond of going both ways, if the conditions were right. He like men and women and did not care much for one over the other. Sex was just sex, after all, and it all felt good, if you just went with it and let yourself go; he liked women, and he liked men, but he had penchant for dark cuties with Goth makeup and lifestyle. He considered himself to be a dark soul, and he had a taste for black cloths, black hair, black eyeshadow, and black lipstick.

3

When he turned eighteen, he graduated high school, and his parents offered him a hand-me-down car for his graduation present. It was a black 1975 Monte Carlo his father had owned for years and kept in the garage under a tarp. For some reason, the car spoke to Manson. It was big and gaudy and brash, looking like a Gothic funeral taxi. He could imagine himself behind the wheel, racing down the road, picking up dates and fucking them in the backseat. It was his dream car.

He did not like imported cars, the little rice burning Hondas and Toyotas of the fast and furious crowd; he preferred a muscle car that was big, loud, and powerful.

The Monte Carlo matched his character and he had to have it. He told his dad and they went down and paid cash, four thousand dollars total, for the beast of a car. It had brand new Michelin tires and a dual exhaust with chrome pipes. Man, it was remarkable sight, and Manson was forever grateful to his parents for giving him such a nice ride. He knew his father had been saving the car for him, to treat him for being a good kid, with good grades, and sticking in there to see school through to the end.

He spent many hours reviving the old car, turning it into a customized hotrod that was of show quality with a massive beefed up 454 engine overhauled with high performance parts, a nitrous oxide kit, a four-barrel carburetor, header pipes, Turbo Hydra-Matic transmission, and dual Flowmaster exhaust system and mufflers, sitting on monster racing tires and centerline wheels The interior was black all-vinyl and upholstery, carpet and instrument panels, swivel bucket seats, plus center console floor shifter. It had four vertically stacked rectangular taillights with horizontal louvers as red as blood. The steering wheel was black with faux wood strip outlined in chrome and Chevrolet stamped in the center. It is adorned with a red and chrome knight's crest emblem decked with a Corinthian helmet with chrome filigree. This emblem was on the grille and sail panel quarter glass—he liked it because he thought it looked Gothic.

When the car was running at idle it sounded like a rumbling menace, a lion growling preparing to attack, and when the throttle was hammered down to the floor it would roar like a monstrous king of the jungle, deafeningly loud and fine-tuned to precision. It cost a lot of money and time, and blood, sweat, and tears, but it was well worth it in the end. When Manson passed by in the Monte Carlo, he turned a lot of heads, a showstopper, and even the kids with the fast-and-furious rice burners had to stop and take notice. Manson was a force to be reckoned with in his mean street machine. It was a beautiful car and in immaculate condition after the complete restoration and he was proud to drive it everywhere he went.

4

Downtown on Main street, Manson passed by a building with the sign saying it was The Royal, and it as found at 666 Main Street. He thought the address was delightful and charming. He looked in the windows to see what he could see. He wanted to go inside, because this was a new venue, and he had yet to go check this place out. Recently, he had been booked to play a gig there with his band, Sinister Fiend, and he wanted to see what it looked like inside to check out the interior for the stage layout, aesthetics, sound quality, and amenities. He saw a flyer taped in the window for the Wicked City Fetish Halloween party and it was coming soon. He had attended this party before at a different location, and he knew it was an annual fetish Halloween party that was a tradition downtown, but now it had found a new home at The Royal.

"Looks delightful," he said, aloud. "I would not miss it for the world."

Next to that, there was a flyer for the current band playing at night called The Candy Pistols, and it was formed of two girls and three guys, and Manson had heard of them before. They were posing for their promo picture, holding their instruments, and huddled together, a combination of punk and synth-pop musicians in garish and outlandish costumes, which had a good reputation around town. Manson had never attended any of their shows, but he had heard of them before, and he had even met the lead singer, Katy Saxon, a pink and blue haired nymph who wore a nose ring and had numerous facial piercings, she was an icon to her fans, and she dressed like a warped and twisted Salvador Dali painting in strips and swaths of plastic, leather, spikes, and lace, with custom made outfits that were always a crowd pleaser. They were acquainted, on a first name basis, even, but that is as far as it ever went, and he had made a mental note to get to one of their shows, but had yet to make good on the thought.

His curiosity was piqued since this was a new club and he wanted to see what it looked like inside, so he decided to go in and have a peek. He tried the door, and it was unlocked. He pulled the door open and went inside, greeted by the cool interior and the smell of absinthe, a mix of wormwood, anise, and fennel, a mélange of cologne and perfume, gourmet coffee, and candle wax—there were candles lit and burning at some of the tables in the large hall where there were floral arrangements and potted plants with streamers of ivy trailing over and down the tables. There was a hint of something else, an electric scent like hot wires and lights and energy that crackled and vibrated, tickling the olfactory. It was a delicious aroma, spicy and alluring, and for some strange reason it reminded him of entering a cathedral.

The stage was fabulous, a high ceiling with track lights and spotlights, below were wash fixtures and spot fixtures, the lighting bright, vibrant, and colorful, casting an ambient glow of purple and green across the stage. There were drums, a keyboard, large PA system with speakers and monitors, amps, and mixers, along with microphone stands and mics. There were long, lacy curtains hanging down in strips, alternating in colors of white and dark russet like massive ridged ribbons, and the stage itself was up high, at least four feet above ground, and it was constructed of solid hardwood. It looked slippery, so he took note that he might be careful to avoid falling during his performance. It was amazing and he was feeling excited to get up on the stage and perform.

As he stepped further inside, it was quiet, as the hall was virtually empty, except for a stagehand attending to the microphones and wires and mixing boards, and a bartender washing and towel drying glasses behind the bar. He walked past round tables with mauve tablecloths that sparkled as if they were made of sequins with small centerpieces holding large white roses and sprigs of evergreen, and there were small, square black stools nearby. There was a seating area with stylish white upholstered loveseats and chairs in a Victorian style, complete with throw pillows, surrounded by trellises and ivy and a faux weeping willow tree. There were lights streaming overhead on runners, and in the nooks, up high, there were Chinese imperial guard statues, and the high ceiling was covered with immaculate acoustic tiles. In the middle of the room there was a divider with rails and trellises, where the floor dropped down a level and the main floor of the dancehall was spread out before the stage.

He watched the bartender as he was busy straightening and tidying up, the chandeliers overhead and candelabras casting a bright glow across the bar. He had obviously arrived at a slow moment, between events, at an off hour. The bottles of liquor and beer made Manon thirsty, and he considered ordering a drink, despite that it was still early in the day—only alcoholics drink before noon, or so they say—and he knew that they were probably not open for business right now, anyway.

"May I help you," the bartender said, looking at Manson as he dried a glass with a towel.

"Ah, yeah," Manson said, putting his hands in his pockets and raising up on his toes, doing a little jig. "I just came in to check the place out. I was just curious . . . this is where the big Halloween party is going to take place?"

"That's right," the bartender said. "Should be quite a party."

"Excellent. I am looking forward to it. By the way, I'm booked to play a gig here next month," Manson said. "I kind of wanted to check the place out."

"Well, were not technically open right now," the bartender said, "but I guess it wouldn't hurt for you to take a look. Help yourself."

"Thank you."

Manson walked past the chairs and the willow tree, down the step onto the level of the dance floor and stood looking at the stage. Manson looked longingly to where his devoted fans would be slam dancing and moshing around in a pit while he and his band performed. It was going to be a great show. He knew it would be impressive; he could feel it in his bones; he had a sense for such things. Of course, they were going to have to change the decorations because this place was too quaint and cheery; they were going to install some dark and gloomy stage props that would bring more of a sinister mood to inspire all of the fiends in attendance. His shows usually attracted a wild bunch and they liked it dark, hard, and rough.

They would all be dressed in jeans and leather with teased

up hair and piercings and tattoos, a riotous throng, and they were truly loyal to the dark themes and music. He knew he could count on them, usually numbering in the hundreds, but in some instances, he had pulled in thousands of fans in a show. He was going to advertise the show on the radio, Internet, and with fliers, and he knew he could count on the regulars showing up, too, and it was guaranteed to be a good show.

Manson watched the stagehand setting up the equipment for the current entertainers, The Candy Pistols, and he was curious how well their shows were being received at this new club. He nodded at the stagehand and decided it was time to get going, as his band mates would be looking for him to have band practice this afternoon. They would give him all sorts of hell if he was late. He turned and walked back across the large club, his books clomping on the hardwood floor, the lights dazzling and brilliant. He was pleased with this new club, The Royal, and he could not wait to break it in; he hurried outside and back to his car to go tell his bandmates about the place.

CHAPTER THREE

1

Zoey Lavay worked as a barista at the Golden Bean Coffee Shop downtown, but also, she was an aspiring tattoo artist that worked at the Naughty and Nice Ink & Piercings tattoo parlor just down the street. She could leave one job and walk to the other and make a night of it. She did not like working at the coffee shop, but slinging tattoo ink was her passion. She could not wait for her shifts to end at the Golden Bean and hurry over to meet up with her mates at the tattoo and piercing parlor.

The coffee shop catered to an upscale clientele and the boss, Terry Kent, was always warning her about her piercings and tattoos and that she should remove the facial jewelry and wear long sleeve shirts to keep the ink illustrations covered. She had argued with him that it was a new century and people were used to seeing tattoos and piercings now, but he was from puritanical descendants and did not believe in any of it. That kind of nonsense was for trollops and hoodlums, and he did not want his business establishment portraying those types of values. Ultimately, Zoey was convinced to oblige and in an obsequious manner she would cover everything up, remove the facial piercings, and dress appropriately in long sleeved shirts and her raven black hair done up nicely in a tight bun behind her head.

She was a beauty, Terry had observed, and he told her that she should not ruin her looks with all of that dark and Gothic self-mutilation; it was such a waste of a perfectly fine young woman. She blew him off, and she could care less what he thought about it, but she acted the part when she was at work at the coffee shop. When her shift was over and she left the restrictive environment where she served coffee and scones to uppity patrons with hipster outfits, yuppies, and businesspeople dressed in suits and ties, she would let her hair down and change into a t-shirt with a band logo, or some other image she felt like sporting for the night, and she would put on her leather jacket and walk the few short blocks down the street to do her work as a tattoo artist and professional body piercers. That was where she really felt at home.

Her fellow artists at Naughty and Nice were always happy when she showed up and put on her apron. She would come in, usually with a travel carrier full of large coffee for everyone: Stewart, Lindsey, Casey, and Paul, were the regular artists and body piercers in attendance at the booths and when she came in they had grown accustomed to the coffee.

"Finally, you show up," Lindsey said, blowing a tuft of dark bangs out of her eyes. "Did you bring coffee?"

"Don't I always?" Zoey said, passing the carrier to Stewart, who took it gladly and looked for his favorite, white chocolate mocha latte.

"I gotta have it," Stewart said, passing the coffee around.

"Thank you," Casey said, smiling. "I love it when you come

to work, Zoey."

"I love you, too," she said, patting him on the shoulder. Zoey looked for Paul, but he was absent. "Where is Paul?"

"He called in sick," Lindsey said. "He said he was throwing up this morning . . . so I told him to just stay home."

"Aw, well I hope he gets to feeling better," Zoey said.

Lindsey had a client in the chair, a device that looked like a dentist chair, black and sterile, and the man was a heavy dude getting a smiling devil with a pitch fork and wings drawn on his arm. The skin was red and raw, and the ink was fresh and dark, making clean lines. It was professional work and Lindsey was a professional. Many tattoo enthusiasts and aficionados sought out her work, often from afar, traveling to downtown from hundreds of miles away, even from the United States, to come and have her work drawn permanently on their skin. The client looked at Zoey and smiled, he looked like he was ready to be done, but the artwork on his arm was not finished.

Zoey looked at the man in the chair and said, "Do you want a coffee? Paul is not here . . . so you can have his."

"Sure," the man's said.

"Don't move," Lindsey said, scolding him as he reached for the coffee. "Let me finish this line . . . then you can have the coffee."

"Fine," the man said, his expression that of a reprimanded child.

Lindsey ran the tattoo gun around in a circle, with a flick of the wrist, making a flourish, then sat back and admired her work. "Now you can drink the coffee," she said.

The man took the coffee and sipped at it, looking at his nearly finished, new tattoo.

"What do you think?" Lindsey asked.

"I think it looks badass," the man said.

"Has it been busy today?" Zoey asked, taking off her coat and hanging it on the rack.

"Not really," Stewart said.

"I wish," Casey said.

"There is a client coming in for some body piercings in a minute," Lindsey said. "You know her. She is a regular . . . Mandy Cline. Do you remember her?"

"Yes," Zoey said, rolling her eyes. "How could I forget."

"She thinks your cute," Lindsey said, grinning. "I think you should give her the piercings. She asked for you by name. Are you up for that?"

"I suppose," Zoey said. "Why not?"

"Okay, go get set up," Lindsey said. "She'll be here any minute. Make sure you give her the royal treatment. We want her to be happy. She an important customer."

"Got it," Zoey said, going to her station and getting her equipment ready.

"Are you going to the Halloween party downtown?" Stewart asked, coming up behind her.

"I'm sorry," Zoey said. "Which one? There are going to be bunch of parties."

"The wild one at that new club," Stewart said. "It's called The Royal. It's the new club where they are going to have the Wicked City Fetish Halloween party."

"Oh, that one," Zoey said, raising her eyebrows. "I know about that place. It sounds like fun."

"You should come with us," Stewart said. "We're all going. You can ride with us."

"Are you wearing costumes?"

"Yes. Of course," he said. "It has to be wild and dark, too. They give out prizes for the best costume."

"Sounds fun and kinky," she said.

"It is."

"Count me in," she said.

"Be here at seven o'clock on Halloween," Stewart said. "We are going to close early and all head over there to participate in the festivities. It starts at eight, so we don't want to be late."

"I will," Zoey said, excitedly. "I know what I'm going to wear already, too."

"Oh, yeah. What's that?"

"I've got a Dark Angel costume with wings and everything."

"Ooh, sounds sinfully wicked."

"Where is this client?" Zoey said. "I'm ready to get to work."

"She's coming," Stewart said. "You should ask her if she is going to the party, too. She might like to meet up with you there."

"I'll do that," Zoey said.

As if speaking of the devil, the client walked in through the door. Mandy was wearing her finest outfit, a tight black plastic jacket with zippers, and tight yoga pants with high platform shoes, her face was adorned with hoops, barbells, and her ears were dangling with studs and rings. She was a masterpiece of pierced perfection.

"Are you my next client?" Zoey asked, looking at Mandy.

"Yes. I'm here to get some new piercings in my . . . you know . . . clitoris."

"Oh, I see," Zoey said. "Well, come over here and get in the chair. We can take care of that for you. No problem."

Mandy went to Zoey's booth and undressed, climbed onto the chair, and spread her legs, exposing her vagina.

"Right, then," Zoey said. "Let's get to work."

The job was slightly painful, but Zoey was experienced, and Mandy was a devoted piercing and tattoo fashionista, so it went well. When it was over, Zoey gave Many a mirror to admire the new studs in her clitoris.

"I love it," Mandy said. "And I love you."

"I'm glad I could be of service," Zoey said, admiring her work.

"Can I give you my number?" Mandy asked. "We could hook up sometime and go out for drinks."

"Sure," Zoey said. "I'm up for that."

They exchanged phone numbers via text messages.

"I'll hit you up sometime," Mandy said. "I think you are just adorable. I would like to get to know you better."

"Speaking of going out," Zoey said. "What are you doing for Halloween?"

"I'm not sure yet."

"Well, there is an awesome sexy fetish party at The Royal," Zoey said. "We are all going. Maybe you would want to attend that with me?"

"I've heard about that place," Mandy said. "It sounds like fun. It's kinky and fetish. I've heard they like to get right down to business there . . . I'm up for that."

"Good," Zoey said, putting away her instruments and cleaning her equipment. "I'll look forward to seeing you there."

They parted ways and Zoey was certain that she was going to have more intimate intercourse with Mandy at some point, because she did find her attractive, and she was single. Those were two winning combinations, and, although she enjoyed her freedom, she would not mind having a regular partner, maybe even a serious relationship could develop.

The closed the shop, everybody hugging one another, and saying goodbye as they left through the front door, turned out the lights, secured the locks, and went home for the night.

Life was good, and Zoey was happy as she went home and crawled into bed. She would get up in six hours and do it all over again, rinse, repeat, and love every minute of it.

2

She was a happy child with pigtails and ribbons in her hair. She was good in school and got good grades. People loved her and found her to be adorable. Her mother, Nancy, dressed her in cute little outfits of dresses and stockings and patent leather shoes. She could have been in a beauty pageant; however, her parents did not believe in such nonsense. They thought that vanity was the cause of most of the problems in the world today, and they would not expose their child to the likes of a little miss junior beauty pageant for weirdos and freaks to ogle her with lewd intentions.

Zoey had a happy childhood with her siblings. They played together and got along well. Although, her older brothers did tend to treat her like a boy, at times. She was a tomboy, for sure, there could be no doubt, and she did not mind being thought of that way. She liked to wear bib overalls and run around barefoot, the bottoms of her feet black as coal. She liked to catch frogs, snakes, snails, and slugs. Often, she would end up playing football with her brothers when they needed an extra player, and they were rough with her, and it toughened her up, making her have a scrappy and testy attitude. She was not afraid to fight, and many times she had been in tussles with neighborhood kids. The results were always predictable: fat lips, bloody noses, and black eyes. It was a tough life, but she was making it through, one day at a time.

One day she got into a fight with a nasty girl named Tawny Miles, who was her nemesis. It was after school and the bully was waiting for her out on the playground.

"What are you doing, you bitch?" Tawny asked, looking cruelly at Zoey.

"I'm going home," Zoey said, matter-of-factly, clutching her schoolbooks in her arms.

"I think I'm going to kick your ass," Tawny said, scowling.

"Why are you picking on me?"

"Because your ugly."

The other girls standing around snickered at this, agreeing wholeheartedly.

"Whatever," Zoey said, knowing that it was not true. She knew that she was attractive because some of the cutest boys in school had paid attention to her this year. Maybe that was the problem, she thought, that the cutest boy in school, Bradly Newcomb, had asked her to the dance. She was considering telling him that she would go, but she was not sure her parents would let her go, and that was the deciding factor. Her stepfather was strict and did not like for her to talk to boys, let alone go to that dance; her mother, on the other hand, would allow her to go, and she might be able to make it happen. "I don't care what you think." Zoey shifted her books, as they were getting heavy, and she was in hurry so she would not miss the bus.

"You better stop talking to Bradly," Tawny said, pointing her finger. "He's going to the dance with me. Do you hear?"

"Why are you worried about it?"

"Because you are not good enough for him."

Another girl, Rachel, a tagalong and stuck-up to Tawny, chimed in, saying, "You're a slut. That's why. Bradly doesn't go out with girls like you."

"Really? Is that so?" Zoey asked. "Because he asked me to the dance. I think you already know that."

"You better tell him you can't go," Tawny said, stepping forward. "Because if you don't . . ." she raised her arm and brought it down forcefully, knocking the books out of Zoey's arms. The books clattered to the ground and landed in a cluttered pile, papers and bookmarks falling out and landing askew on the pavement at her feet. ". . . I'm going to kick your ass. And I'm going to tell everyone that you have herpes."

"Hey! What the hell?" Zoey said, enraged. "You're a liar, for one thing." She wanted to reach down and pick up her books but she did not trust Tawny, and thought that she might try to kick her in the face. "I don't have an STD . . . so nobody is going to believe that."

"Are you still a virgin?" Rachel asked, tauntingly. "I heard you are a slut and give a good blowjob. You suck dicks at the park in the bathroom. That is what I heard. I saw your name written on the wall. It had your phone number and everything."

"That's a lie, too," Zoey said.

"It doesn't matter, "Tawny said, making a fist. "I promise I will punch you in the face if you don't tell Bradly you can't go. Do you hear me?"

"I don't care," Zoey said. "I can't go anyway. My parents won't let me. So . . . don't worry about it."

"Good. Momma's little baby," Tawny said. "Pickup your books and get the hell out of here before I decide to give you a fat lip."

"Go home to your stepdaddy," Rachel said. "I bet he's the one that gave you herpes, isn't he?"

This hit close to home, as Zoey was fearful of her stepfather and thought that he might tend to be a sexual deviant, and she was uncomfortable with the topic. She blushed, picking up her books and tucking the papers inside. All she wanted at that point was to just get away from these mean girls. The would go smoke cigarettes and focus their attention on other things if she could just hurry and get away from them, get out of their sight, and give them a moment to forget about her.

There would be more incidents like this in the future, and eventually, Zoey had to stand up for herself and fight Tawny. It was a one hit fight. Zoey punched her in the eye and gave her a shiner and that was the end of it. The bully never bothered her again after that.

The best part was that she got to go to the promenade dance with Bradly that year and it was magnificent. He brought her a corsage and dressed in the finest black tuxedo and she wore a lovely, long, blue dress. The were a lovely couple and, no surprise, crowned the king and queen.

Tawny sat at the far side of the gymnasium and pouted.

It was a victory for Zoey, and she was happy.

3

When she became a teenager, everything changed. That is when her father died from cancer and soon, she was introduced to her stepfather, Robert Dillard. He was nice at first, but after he moved in with his mother, he showed his true colors: he was an asshole and a drunk.

Her mother loved the man, and Zoey could never really understand why because he was mean and spiteful. He would complain about the bills, his job, money, food, and rent, and running out of bear was fodder for a potential tirade of rage and aggression. There was always beer in the refrigerator and whiskey in the cabinet because no one wanted to see Robert go without his alcohol.

If he were in a passive mood—which was almost never—he would sit down in the living room and put his feet up. If he were watching his favorite shows like COPS and Live PD, or WWE wrestling or Ultimate Fighting Championships matches, he would leave everyone alone, until it was over. Zoey and her mother knew that if he was focusing attention on the TV that he would not be paying attention to them, and that was a blessing.

CHAPTER FOUR

1

Stephanie Dascălu sat at the wet bar in her mansion and drank alone. This was out of the norm for her because she was a socialite and loved to be out on the town and enjoying the party life. Tonight, she felt like being alone. It was one of those nights. She sometimes grew depressed when she thought about her past, about her dead husband, and sometimes it was a major buzzkill. This was one of those nights.

She wore her blonde hair tied neatly back into a tight-fisted bun, and gold and diamond earrings and necklace that shimmered and sparked from the floodlights overhead. She was a remarkably beautiful woman, an enchantress, attractive, a popular socialite and jetsetter, charming and eccentric in a mysterious yet amiable way. Although she was well over two hundred and fifty years old—very few souls were privy to this fact—she was perpetually thirty-five, immortal, and gorgeous for a middle-aged woman. She was often referred to as a "cougar" and—it did not bother her to be looked at and doted upon by lustful men, or women—she drove the boys and girls crazy with her charm and terminally pretty visage. She was a bisexual and liked men and women equally, fond of both, and able to please all comers.

Tonight, she was staying home alone and resting up for the big party coming up in a few nights. The fetish Halloween party downtown was always a blast and she never missed one, ever. She lit a cigarette and let it hang from the corner of her lips. She poured a drink, Maker's Mark bourbon whiskey, neat, and sat down, crossing her legs, and looking out the window at the cityscape, the lights twinkling against the nights sky, the water reflecting with shimmering and lapping waves. She looked like an actress, Sharon Stone. She still had an accent from her youth growing up in Hungary. She did not like to think about her past too much, as it caused her to get angered, and typically she would want to take out her angst on some lecherous men who deserved to be castrated for child molestation or rape. She delighted in seeing perverts get their comeuppance, and she was not above seeking them out for a night of pleasure and revenge.

2

Stephanie was a countess who lived in her mansion Chateau Dascălu and she loved the party life. She lived in the castle with her servants, but had no mate, no husband to speak of (since the death of Count Lazar many years past back in Hungary, she remained unmarried), and she did not want on either. She was a headstrong woman who did not need a man to lord over her.

She knew that the locals viewed her as strange, and that her castle had become associated with ghostly legends, rumors and speculation, and even stories about how she worshiped Satan and was the leader of a cult. The rumors, she knew, spoke about ceremonies and horrifying events that triggered the natives to generate myths about the castle and her history (and with good reason, she thought, because, she was a vampire, after all). There were speculations about murders and blood-letting and torture, amongst other strange things, which were seen on her estate. There were purported to be boogiemen skulking in the dark recesses of the land and phantoms and apparitions . . . and it did not bother her at all, because the rumors had a tendency to keep the snoops and nosey curiosity seekers away.

Living in British Columbia, Canada was amazing. She loved the city of Vancouver. She was proud to call the city home. It was eclectic and anything but ordinary. Her fortune was built from years of demanding work, fortitude, and shrewd business investments and a strong portfolio full of high-end stocks, bonds, real estate, petroleum, and precious metals and gemstones. She was highbrow, high-minded, and lived in high style, treating herself to only the best things in life that the world could supply and that her wealth could afford. Her real estate investments were far reaching around the globe, and she owned properties in every continent. In Vancouver alone, she owned several buildings in the city and massive sprawling estates on the hillside, apartment complexes downtown, and rental houses in the suburbs.

She had contractors and construction workers lined up to help her build on her properties, and they often came to her parties to indulge in drugs and sex. They helped her to build the Château de Dascălu. It was traditional castle like something right out of medieval Europe. It was hard work and took several years to complete, and in 1895, it was finished, and looked much like a Gothic castle similar to those she had been familiar with as a child back in Hungary.

3

She was typically a night owl and loved to stay up till early in the morning. Usually, she would entertain guests and friends and they would party until just before dawn. Tonight, was without incident and she had a few drinks, watched some TV, surfed the web, and then just before sunset, during the small hours of the morning, she sauntered upstairs to her room. She was dressed in slinky Guia La Bruna lingerie and a silky nightgown, soft fur slippers on her feet, as she traipsed up the stairs toward her sleeping chamber. It was a lavish room at the end of a hall past a knight in shining armor, a statue, which stood guard, a sentry forever still and lonely in the hall. She ran her fingers over the marble bust of Pallas, Athena, Pericles, and walked beneath her family crest hanging on the wall.

"Goodnight, my lovelies," she said. The marble was cold under her fingers. She touched her nipples with the tips of her icy fingers and they instantly became erect, tightening up into two points of plump flesh. She felt a tingling sensation run through her body, and she was making herself horny just thinking about sex, so she decided to go to her room and please herself.

She went through the door and entered her room. Moving past the writing desk made of walnut and the golden lampstand, on the wall were oil paintings, above her handcrafted chiffonier and wardrobe composed of exotic hardwood. The wood, the cloth, the old paintings, the flowers in the vase, all mingled together in an earthy, pleasant, alluring, and weird scent that delightful to her senses. It was a familiar and comforting smell of an ancient castle, the wafting fragrance of dried flowers and frankincense and myrrh commingled in a lovely potpourri. It reminded her of roses, hyacinth, and honeysuckle. For some reason, it always made her think about the musky aroma of her long-lost love, Count Lazar. He smelled manly and musky and masculine. She could still remember how he smelled after all these years. It was the smell of home; it was the smell of her true love, forever lost to the ages. She missed him dearly, even after all these years.

She went to the dresser and pulled open the drawer, exposing a plethora of assorted sex toys, dildos, Ben Wa balls, anal beads, butt plugs, and assorted vibrators. There were tubes of KY jelly, Astroglide, Anal Ease, and edible underwear, and mint flavored condoms, and just about anything a sexually promiscuous nymphomaniac could dream of or desire. She took out her favorite ebony dildo, "The Stallion," a twelve-inch rubber schlong with four double AA batteries concealed inside and sat down in the chair in front of the desk. She spread her legs, slide the lacy panties aside forcefully, and rubbed her moist vagina with her fingers. She was getting more exited and hornier and had the urge to have something thrust inside of her. She turned on the vibrator and rubbed the tip along her pink slit, back and forth, the sensation deliciously arousing. She teased herself, waiting, rubbing, waiting, withdrawing, then she plunged the tip in deep, pushing, shoving, out, then in, deeper, deeper, deeper, until it was all the way to the hilt. The vibration was buzzing and stinging like a bee and she let out a soft moan and a whimper as she felt herself rising to a climax.

After she came to a high point of masturbation, she relaxed and let the tension release from her tense body, slumping in the chair and basking in the glow of orgasm. She then lit a cigarette and sat back and enjoyed the smoke. She poured a shot of Grand Marnier from bottle she kept on the desk and sat back and sipped the sweet liqueur. It was delightful.

"So good," she said aloud, looking into the mirror. "So good. But not as good as the real thing. I need to get Crandall up here to finish this." She stared blankly at the looking glass, her reflection empty and vacant, unsatisfied and wanting.

Crandall was her live-in houseguest, she called him her "boy toy" and he was blessed with a large manliness and young enough to endure the fucking that she desired. Unfortunately, he was out of the house at the moment as the moon was full and he liked to go out on the prowl and lurk beneath the lunar light, frolicking in the darkness. Something about the full moon brought out his wild side and he never missed an opportunity to indulge himself.

She made a mental note to grab him as soon as he came home and fuck his brains out.

Winding down and seeing that the night was coming to an end and a new day was dawning, she decided it was time to call it a night and lay down and go to sleep. She finished the cigarette and liqueur and hit the sack, tired now and ready to get some sleep.

She would look into fucking Crandall later. For now, she would sleep, the sleep of the dead, because now she was exhausted from the massive dildo.

4

When she awoke from her slumber, she was refreshed and rejuvenated. She got up and stretched. There was much to do tonight. She had to go downtown and see some old friends and conduct some business. She took a shower, dressed in a tight red sequin dress and matching high heels, put in her diamond earrings, and put on her red lipstick to make the outfit complete. Her blonde hair was pulled back and she wound it up, rolled it into a bun, and pierced it with a pin.

She was breathtaking, a knock-down drag-out gorgeous

woman, and she knew it. She walked with confidence, her heels clicking on the stone floor, and her ass and thighs moved in sequence, her gate that of a thoroughbred show horse. She had runway swagger and exquisite tastes, so wealthy that she could afford to have a limousine take her anywhere she wanted to go; however, tonight, she was going to drive her Jaguar into town and take care of business.

She went outside, got into her car, and revved up the engine. She took off down the driveway, opened the gate with the remote, and raced away down the street toward the heart of the city where she had placed to go and people to see.

CHAPTER FIVE

1

Crandall Hanson, a handsome rogue, was born in South Carolina, but relocated to Bangor, Main with his parents when they moved early in his childhood. When he was eighteen, he decided to leave home, and hitchhiked across the country running from his past, the moon changing him into a beast along the way, and her did not enjoy his lycanthropic condition. He did not know how he had become a werewolf, other than he had been bitten by a wolf-like creature in the woods of rural Main while on a camping trip with his parents. The wound took some time to heal, and after he turned twenty-one, the wound finally healed, and he was left with a permanent scar on his leg from the bite.

He returned to his hometown in Bangor, returning to live with his parents. He began to have nightmares in which he was transformed into a wolf, and he had sexually explicit dreams where he was involved in lewd and graphic acts of sodomy, and oral sex, where he has being fucked and raped by men and women with foreign objects inserted into his rectum, and eventually even dreams of bestiality invaded his thought, with images of him having sex with wolves, dogs, cats, monkeys, and goats. He was sure he had become a deviant pervert and attempted to lock himself away in his room at his parent's home, upstairs, never coming out unless it was absolutely necessary—to eat, to use the restroom, to shower and shave. He found that he was somnambulistic and would sneak out of the house, unaware the next day, with dirt on his shoes and footprints leading upstairs on the rug, his cloths covered with blood.

When the moon was full, he would make a horrific and terrifying transformation into a werewolf and he had no way of stopping it.

There were murders in the neighborhood, and he seemed to be the cause. No one could prove it, but he knew he was guilty. What was he to do? Turn himself in to the police? That was not an option.

He needed to relieve his parents of the burden he was imposing on them, so he packed his backpack, made a bedroll, and kissed them goodbye. They did not want to see him go, but he insisted that he had to leave, or there would be trouble.

He set out on the road, traveling north to Main, at first, and wandering along backroads, into the wilderness. The new of murders occurring during the full moon seemed to be following his path, and he knew that he was the culprit. He had to live with himself, however, and he did not know what to do; he kept on moving, running away, trying to find a place where he could fit in and live in peace. This was probably asking too much of his current situation, he realized.

He traveled south the Florida but found the heat and the city life in Miami too hot and vacuous. He wanted more out of life than beach babes, sand, booze, and cocaine. He decided to head west, moving through the southwest to Louisiana, then Texas, then Arizona, and finally arriving in California. He was an aspiring scriptwriter and had been working on a movie he hoped to pitch to a big producer someday, although it was not quite finished, and he needed a little more time to polish the writing and finish the script.

He found the lifestyle in Hollywood to be wanting, and he could not get anywhere with the big executives at any of the movie producers or studios, and found only other aspiring writers and wayward ruffians that would cling to him and try to use him for what he was worth. Eventually, he grew tired of the vagrant lifestyle and with the beaches and silicone implant-ed bimbos playing in the surf, sand, and sun. Los Angeles was full of crime and drugs and superficial people, and although he was able to fit in—he had resorted to killing victims during the full moon, running away into the night, and narrowly avoiding being capture by the police—the did not like the California sun and heat and the police were constantly harassing him for his vagrant lifestyle.

Ultimately, he headed north through Oregon, then to Wash-ington, traveling along Highway 101 to the legendary city of Forks, looking for werewolves there, but he found nothing. Just locals and tourists in recreational vehicles and in trucks with boats on fishing trips at La Push. He moved along to Port Angeles, then caught the ferry across the Puget Sound and stopped in Seattle for a while. The Space Needle was marvel-ous and spectacular, much more impressive in person. The city offered everything he required, and he could crash anywhere he wanted without being harassed too much by the authorities. Homelessness was common here, and he fit right in; although he did not feel like he was homeless for he was a vagabond for different reasons. He liked alcohol and drugs, but he was willing to work and be a productive member of society. After an incident during a full moon when he killed two people in the park, he decided it was time to move on again, and realized that he wanted to see what Canada was all about. He had never been that far north before, and he even considered going all the way to Alaska and visiting the North Pole. Maybe he could find a pack of wolves to live with there.

2

When Crandall was a boy his parents were poor, father worked at a factory and mother was a teacher, and they struggled to keep afloat. There were always bills due and having expendable money for lavish things was not a priority. They had to tighten their belts and pull themselves up by the bootstraps, be frugal, and learn how to survive on meager rations. This meant that he went without certain things that other kids had regularly. He did not have the newest toys, bicycles, or clothing that the other kids in the neighborhood always seemed to have in abundance. At Christmas time he always got one big gift that he could choose and that was the high point, and he was a grateful child and appreciated everything that was under the tree and wrapped with care and love.

Like many children his age, he collected Tonka trucks, Hot Wheels, GI Joe action figures, marbles, and road a Huffy bicycle, and spent many hours building dirt cities and forts where he played with the other kids in the neighborhood for days on end. They would gather down at the swamps and catch frogs, snakes, and butterflies. It was a wonderful and joyous childhood.

He was not the cleanest kid in the neighborhood, a boy who liked to play in the dirt, his mother was constantly after him to bath, telling him to wash behind his ears and between his toes. He would wear the same socks and boots for days on end, at the end of it all his feet would have to be peeled like a banana, and when he was placed into the bathwater it would turn brown from all the dirt he had accumulated during his romps through the forest, playground, riverbank, and gravel pit.

One day, he went to class and the teacher had decided to have the students do a project that involved tracing the outline of one of their feet on a sheet of paper. It was a great idea, in theory, and they would post their finished papers up along the walls in the classroom so everyone could observe the different shapes and styles of feet. They were to put their names on their papers when they had finished. Crandall was happy to do it, at first, until he realized that his feet were stained with dirt and grime, and when he peeled his foot out of his boot and sock, he was embarrassed and worked his way into a corner of the room so he could hide his dirty foot, ashamed, as he put his filthy little foot down on the white paper and traced the outline.

He struggled to keep his dirty foot a secret, not wanting anyone to see, and the teacher was walking around observing the students to see how they were progressing, and he maneuvered himself around, hunkered over, keeping his hind end between himself and the teacher to keep her prying eye off of his dirty foot. When he was done, he had to peel the paper from the bottom of his foot because it had adhered like tacky paper to his sticky, dirty foot. When he looked at his work, he saw that the dirt had created a perfect footprint on the page, and he did not even need to trace the outline with a pencil. His face turned red out of embarrassment and he quickly put his sock and boot back on, feeling the tops of his ears burning with shame.

The projects were hung on the wall and for the next week Crandall got to relive the incident throughout the day as he looked at his dirty footprint on the wall. The other students snickered and sniggered, the girls whispering and pointing at him, and he would sit at his desk and tap his pencil and want badly to be out of the room and away from school. He could not wait for the last bell to ring so he could go out and play in the dirt once more.

When he met Tiffany, a sprightly blonde with pigtails and bows, she was new to class and she had not yet spoken to Crandall, only sneaking glances as she was introduced on her first day, and they were both bashful and shy. When the art-work of outlined feet was placed on the wall, she stood looking at Crandall's drawing and smile, while all the other kids were making fun of the dirty footprint, she looked at it thoughtfully and pondered long.

Crandall pretended to not notice that she as looking, and when she came over and slipped him a note, he was surprised and abashed. She went back to her desk and sat down, sneaking a glance at him, and then turning to her books and school-work. He did not open the note in class because Mrs. Pinchley would take it and embarrass him in front of the other students, so he stuck it in his pocket and saved it for later.

When he found a secret place on the playground to read the note—he opened it with trepidation in anticipation of what it might say—and unfolded the sheet of paper and read the neatly scrawled girly penmanship.

Hi Crandall,

I would like to be your friend. I think you are cute, and I want to play with you sometime. Do you want to be my friend? Answer Yes or No and send it back. And I also love your footprint drawing. I think it is cute. I don't care what the other kids think. Have a nice day.

Best Friends Forever,

Tiffany.

Crandall read the note twice, his heart beaming with joy, as he did not have a special girlfriend yet and this was exciting news. The "Yes" or "No" section of the note had checkboxes drawn for him to select and then return the not to her. He knew the answer right away: "Yes." The part about his footprint was uncomfortable, but he thought it was wonderful that she did not care that he had dirty feet inside his boots. That meant he could easily get along with her and not have any reservations or inhibitions, although he would anyway, regardless, and he was excited and ecstatic that a girl was showing interest in him—the new girl, a pretty girl, a wonderfully delightful intriguing girl who wanted to get to know him better. This was most excellent.

They became best friends and had a long-lasting relationship that lasted all the way through graduation from high school. They laughed together, played together, cried together, went to the prom together, and pretty much did everything together, virtually inseparable, until college ripped Tiffany away from him. She was accepted to Yale and her parents were paying for everything. This meant she had to go, and, unfortunately, she would be leaving town, and Crandall would be alone, without her. They promised to write to each other and keep in touch, and they did, but it was a painful separation, and eventually they had to say goodbye, with a promise to reunite someday.

It was one of the most painful moments Crandall had ever experienced in life, and when she found a boyfriend at college and told him that she was engaged it was even worse, because he had intended to be with her for the rest of his life. It just was not meant to be however, especially since they were from different social and economic classes, and their relationship would never have been approved by the patriarchs.

Crandall knew at that moment that he was not meant to eat from a silver spoon and that the two classes, upper and middle, were not destined to intermingle, and if you wanted to be happy for the rest of your life you should not make a wealthy girl your wife. It was a painful lesson, but true. The worst part was that Tiffany never acted like money was an issue. She did not seam to care about that when they were kids, and just playing out in the sun and having fun after school, or going down and swimming in the river on summer vacation was enough, it did not have a price, and childhood was a nostalgic place that everyone always longed to go back to, never could in the end. It was nothing but memories after a while, and then old age would set in, and the places and people that have passed through our lives were permanently etched in our memory, and then we were left with whatever road we had chosen and the mates and people we had surrounded ourselves with. Money was a decisive factor, and as Crandall learned, it was better to stay on the same side of the railroad tracks when considering a life mate.

He lost contact with Tiffany after a while and then she was gone from his life forever, nothing more than a memory, and although he found her on Facebook and added her to his friends list, it never was the same and they did not communicate anymore.

That was his first experience with love and heartbreak, and after that he was much more cautious with whom he gave his loyalty and love.

3

Crandall wanted to write screenplays. That was his passion, his love, his art. He dreamed of creating a screenplay that would be the source of an award winning movie along the lines of something written and directed by the likes of Stephen Spielberg, William Goldman, or James Cameron, although he had many favorites, and picking just one was nearly impossible. Spielberg was the best, in his opinion, and that was where he would put his money.

He had been working on a script for several years, and this one was a winner, he could feel it. When he was younger, he took an online course that taught him the fundamentals of scriptwriting, and he had attacked the craft with ardor. It was titled, Beyond the Fierce Planet, and it was a science fiction piece about the colonization of Mars in the future after Earth has been wasted by the ruination of mankind.

He wanted to take a trip to California and visit Universal Studios and stalk down any directors and producers he finds and pitch his script to them. He knew that if he could get his foot in the door down there in Hollywood that they would love it and he would become famous after they bought his script and made a blockbuster movie out of it. He hoped it would star Ryan Gosling as the lead character, a masculine and no-nonsense hero, who would save the Universe from imploding when a secret weapon was detonated in a black hole located at the center of the Milky Way galaxy. For the villainous force he would like to see, Marylin Manson, as he would make the best evil genius ever. He had a complete list of actors picked out for the parts, but he also knew that casting was entirely up to the director and producer and screenwriter rarely had any say in the matter.

He kept the screenplay between two blue cover pages with three holes punched along the edge and two brass brads binding it together. It was his pride and joy and he treasured it as if it were the holy grail and made of pure gold; he did not want to go anywhere and present a poorly constructed script and cast his pearls before swine. When he finally gave it to anyone important, he wanted it to look perfect.

4

When Crandall met Stephanie, he was instantly attracted to her, and he just had to know more about her. He was sitting at a quaint and cozy bar, The Ritz, downtown Vancouver and enjoying a craft microbrew when she walked in through the door. She was wearing a tight-fitting black sequin dress and high heels, blonde hair pulled back into a tight bun, and diamond earrings and necklace glittering brilliantly. She was stunning. He took one look and knew that she was an older woman known as a "cougar" and he wanted to introduce himself.

She sat down at the bar and lit a cigarette, ordered a drink, and sat primly on the barstool watching the TV overhead. She paid no attention to her surroundings, completely engrossed in her drink and cigarette, and she was not aware of Crandall admiring her from afar.

He got up and walked over to her and sat down, clearing his throat and telling himself not to blow. *Steady, easy, don't blow this,* he told himself. *Just act natural, and be yourself, but don't say anything stupid or naive. She obviously has taste and sophistication, so be good, and don't act like a fool.*

"I could not help noticing such a lovely lady walk in through the door," Crandall said. "May I buy you a drink?"

She turned and looked at him with brilliant and stunning amber eyes that pierced him to the core. She looked like a movie star he knew that he was probably outclassed by her social stature, however, he was always up to the challenge, and after his experience with love and loss when he was young, he still did not head the lesson of staying within one's own social class, and he was willing to take a chance and see if he could impress this MILF with his swagger.

She took a drag off her cigarette and exhaled, not speaking, just looking at him and smiling.

He was losing her, he could tell, and he needed to act fast, say something witty, make her smile, charm her with his brilliance and style.

"Are you from around here?" he asked, tapping nervously on the bar.

"Yes," she said.

"Yes, I can buy you a drink," Crandall asked, "or, yes, you are from around here."

"Both," she said, smiling, tapping the cigarette ash out in the ashtray.

"I see," Crandall said, looking at the bartender and waving to get his attention. "What are you drinking?"

"Crown and Coke," she said, finishing her drink. She slid the empty glass down the bar.

"Bartender," Crandall said, "two Crown and Cokes, please."

"Right away," the bartender said.

The next thing they knew they were involved in a deep conversation about everything under the sun, and soon they were talking about love and lust and carnal knowledge. She said she had a mansion on the hillside and invited him back to join her for a little private party. He said he would love to oblige, and they hopped in her private limo and headed for the hills.

CHAPTER SIX

1

Adrian Burgendorv, a paranormal investigator (ABCPI Inc.) and self-proclaimed "vampire hunter," was 49 and middle-aged, and growing older by the minute. He did not feel old, but he was beginning to show signs of aging on his physique with belly fat, wrinkles, and graying at the temples of his thinning hairline. When he looked in the mirror, he could not believe he was already almost fifty years old. His Chevy van was a reflection of how he lived his life: old, dilapidated, and in need of a tune-up—traded in for a new model, actually. The van was on its last leg, bald tires, backfiring from a standstill, and suffering from all sorts of ailments. He would pat on the dash, coaxing it into action, hoping it would last for just another day. It worked; so, why fix it? He planned on buying a newer model, but he was strapped for cash, his credit taking a hit from maxed out credit cards and defaulted loans, and he just had not gotten around to shopping for a new van, yet . . . *damn it all to hell, he thought . . . if it ain't broke, don't fix it. It still rolls and drives . . . and that's all that matters.*

Growing old caused him to ruminate, thinking back to a time long ago, when he first learned of his true calling, like his dad used to say "back when he was still knee-high to a grasshopper and not as old as dirt," back when he was still "young, squat, and full of snot," another of his father's favorite aphorisms.

One weekend, on a Friday night, he stayed up late and watched *Salem's Lot* on the *Monster Mash Movie Marathon*. He got so scared he could not sleep alone for a week, and took to sleeping with his older sister, Sarah, in her bed; she did not like the arrangement, but she had little choice and she loved her brother, Adrian, so she humored him—although she enjoyed playing on his fears and telling him scary stories before they went to sleep. His favorite was "The Tale of The Hook," a story about a deranged lunatic murderer who escaped from the insane asylum and had only a sharp hook for a hand; the murder liked to hide out at places where young lovers would go to kiss and make out and rip them open with the hook; eventually, the hook gets ripped off as a young boy who has been denied a kiss races away, rushing the girl home, and goes to open her door to find a shiny hook hanging in the door handle of his car. The ending was always satisfying. Adrian would plead with her to stop, but it was delightfully terrifying, and he enjoyed it despite the fear that it invoked in him, because he knew he was safe with here in bed.

Soon he got over being scared by the movie and went back to his own bed. He did not learn his lesson, however, and continued to watch scary movies with an addiction and morbid curiosity that bordered on obsession. He became a consummate connoisseur of horror movies and stories and read novels and short stories frequently; he was a died in the wool horror buff.

As the years passed by, he learned about the supernatural

forces at play that created monsters, ghosts, and bogies, but was especially intrigued by vampires after reading the novel titled *Dracula* by Bram Stoker. He watched the movie version of Francis Ford Copula's *Dracula* and then *Van Helsing* and even went as far as watching the TV series *Buffy the Vampire Slayer* one too many times. At some point he decided that he would pursue a career as a vampire slayer just like Buffy. He decided that he wanted to be a vampire hunter, like Van Helsing, and he was convinced beyond a shadow of a doubt that was what he wanted to be when he grew up.

When he was old enough, he ordered a "Vampire Slayer Kit" off eBay and was fascinated when it arrived. He looked at the wooden stakes and mallet, the crucifix, a sharp knife, a mirror, candles, powders, potions, and elixirs, a large syringe, an authentic Bible, and handled it all with care. This was to be his occupation, his passion, his calling, because someone had to do it, after all.

2

Adrian was a much younger man back then, still in his early twenties, and still living at home with his parents. He had graduated from Georgetown University in Washington D.C. and his mother had urged him to become a Catholic priest. His father wanted him to become a police officer. He did not want to become either of those; he wanted to explore his options. In his opinion, playing rock and roll in a band sounded like much more fun.

He and some friends took over the basement and filled it with miscellaneous musical equipment: guitars, bass, amplifiers, drums, microphones, PA and monitors, the usual stuff. It was a decked-out cave for a handful of miscreants to waste away the days playing power chords and screaming songs out of key and intonation.

One day, they got to messing around with a Ouija board and summoned up a spirit named Zoso. The guys thought it was because Adrian was infatuated with Led Zeppelin and that he was joking around, but it was an eerie event, nonetheless.

They had summoned a demon and Adrian was forced to deal with it for quite some time afterward.

He had to perform an impromptu exorcism to get rid of the entity known as Zoso.

That changed everything. He still did not fancy becoming a priest, but he was into fighting off evil.

3

After his incident with the Ouija board he joined a paranormal ghost hunting group and set out to look for ghosts. They filmed their excursions and even had some of their footage optioned for the popular series *Paranormal Discoveries*.

They visited a supposed haunted mental hospital in Indianapolis, Indiana, Central State Hospital. It had been closed in 1994 when the goal of community-based care became more predominant. It was rumored to be haunted by many ghostly entities since it was the scene of terrible treatment and deaths of patients during the course of its activities for a century and a half.

Central State Hospital was founded in 1848 with an initial group of five patients, and back then it was called the Indiana Hospital for the Insane, and the first patients were admitted to be treated for mental illness and other disorders, such as addiction and substance abuse. Farming and colony style work, along with recreation and physical activity, were used as therapy. It was renamed to Central State Hospital in 1927, a nicer and kinder name, eventually growing in scope and size until it housed 3,000 mentally ill patients over a period of 146 years, before it was closed down and many of the buildings were demolished and destroyed.

Adrian and his team, "Big Dog" Billy Mathers, Terry Pendergrass, and Roy Levitz, including several assistance (not worth mentioning right now), gathered their tickets and itineraries, all courtesy of the producers of Paranormal Discoveries, and the team paranormal investigators, or ghost hunters, if you like, flew to Indiana and brought their equipment. It was going to be a great show and they expected to find some clues as to the paranormal and getting good ratings with this adventure.

The Central State Hospital was on the west side of Indianapolis on Washington Street, spanning several blocks, and the dilapidated buildings stood like crumbling Gothic castles from distant past. The red brick walls stood eerily against the cityscape and had all the appearance of a sinister institution from yesteryear. It was now a museum, but back then it was just an abandoned building, and it stood spooky and foreboding on the horizon. The locals were afraid of the place and there were rumors of things being seen there creeping around at night. The truth was that it was just vagrants and vandals, but rumors and tall tales and urban legends began to grow around the abandoned institution and eventually it was picked up on the radar of the ghost hunters. They knew this was a goldmine of spooky settings and haunted buildings that would film well and scare the shit out of everybody. They were able to get permits from the city of Indianapolis and stay for the night in the haunted buildings. What happened next changed their lives forever.

It turned out that some of the underground tunnels and

buildings were still intact and there were even old furniture and documents that could be found in some of the offices and building and other structures.

The strangest story was about a ghost that haunted the tunnels. It was the ghost of a woman who disappeared while in the care of the institution. She was believed to have been molested by some of the orderlies back near the turn of the 19th century and she became pregnant. The orderlies wanted to hide their evil deed and fed her poison. They then placed her dead body in the incinerator in the basement and claimed that she had run away and never came back. During those days mentally ill women were not prized possessions, in fact many husbands had their wives institutionalized when they wanted to be rid of them, and the authorities would accommodate, without much convincing, and take in the women and brand them as mentally deficient, or insane.

Adrian and his crew looked at the spooky building when they first arrived, there was the brick walls, Bedford limestone, and white wooden trim, and smoke stacks of the power plant, and there was the Pathology Building that was in surprisingly good condition as it had weathered the years well. It was a two story, peaked roof, brick building with arched and circular windows in the front, and cement stairways leading up to the main entrances. It had brick chimneys on the shingled rooftop and was surrounded by small ornamental Canadian Red Chokeberry trees. Next to that was a utility building that functions as a maintenance shed for the groundskeeper.

Adrian and his team pulled up in a F-150 Econoline van they had rented from Enterprise rentals. The got out and opened up the rear cargo doors. They started pulling out their gear. It was getting late and the sun would be setting soon, so they were in a hurry to get inside and setup for a long night of filming and attempting to catch ghosts. They had all the usual equipment EVP recorders, EMF meters, full spectrum night vision cameras, IR sensors and lights, SB7 Spirit Boxes, flashlights, laptops, and other assorted equipment used to track, locate, and communicate with ghosts. They had found interesting paranormal activity in earlier investigations, and they were counting on this one to be a jackpot.

"Let's go inside and get setup," Adrian said.

"This place looks spooky as hell," Bill said, hefting his heavy backpack on his shoulder.

"I think it's a wonderful," Terry said. "This is going to make some good footage." He was the lead cameraman and he knew his stuff about filming ghost and haunted buildings. "We need to get some good footage of this place. I guarantee this is going to look good on film."

"It gives me the creeps," Roy said.

"That's a good thing," Adrian said. "If you are uneasy now . . . then imagine the possibilities once we get inside and it gets dark."

"Yeah," Roy said, spitting on the ground. "That's what I'm afraid of."

"If we meet ghosts, we are successful," Bill said, heading toward the main entrance to the Pathology Building. "That's our job, after all . . . to interact with ghosts."

"I guess so," Ray said, picking up the hard-shell cases that contained some cameras, and tripods. "Let's go before I lose my nerve."

"Excellent," Adrian said, excitedly. "I'm loving this place. It's got history and charm. Imagine all the crazy people that lived her for a hundred and fifty years. They are still around, in spirit. I can feel their presence."

4

That night while they were setup in the basement of the building, they picked up on the spirit of a ghost that spoke to them first, plainly.

"Get out of my house," the voice said on the EVM equipment. They had it captured on digital media and recorded it directly to their laptops.

"Did you hear that?" Adrian asked, thrilled.

And then another voice said, "We will kill you if you don't go . . . leave now."

This last one freaked them out and set raised the hair on their arms.

There was a final voice that said, "They killed my baby."

Bill was ecstatic. He said, "This is too good to be true."

"That must be the ghost of the woman that got raped and burned in the furnace," Ray said.

"I recon so," Adrian said.

The next thing they saw was a shadow figure pass before their infrared cameras, accompanied by a falling object somewhere off in the distance, sounding like a pipe or metal hitting concrete.

"Holy shit," Terry said. "What was that?"

"I don't know," Adrian said. "Rewind that footage and see if we can make out what moved in front of the camera."

They examined the footage and sure enough there was a ghostly figure passing before the camera, lit up in vibrant colors of orange, yellow, red, and blue, a human shape, passing down the hallway and out of sight.

"That's a real ghost," Bill said. "I think we've made contact."

Adrian decided to try to communicate with the ghost, saying, "Who are you and why are you here?"

There was only silence, and then one of their meters lit up and change colors.

"I just got a cold flash," Ray said. "I can feel the temperature dropping . . . but it's only in this one spot, right here." He held out his hands and touched the pocket of frigid air that was lingering next to him. "Do you feel that?"

"I do," Billy said.

"Me too," Adrian said.

Terry agreed, too. He could feel it with his hands. It was spooky.

When they played back the EVP recorder there was another voice that said, "Help. Murder. They killed us."

"That's freaky," Bill said.

"It was rumored that a lot of people died here," Adrian said. "The conditions were terrible at one point and there was not control . . . some of the patients killed other patients. It was a true madhouse."

The night passed by and they visited many different areas in the institution, and they were amazed at all the contacts they made with spirits. They caught it all on film and they recorded enough footage to fill in a complete episode. The producers were going to be pleased with this adventure and they would be rewarded handsomely. They stayed awake all night hunting down the ghosts in the abandoned mental hospital until in the morning when the sun came up and the birds began to sing outside.

They packed up their gear and went outside. The sun was just rising above the horizon, bright and glaring, and the sky was a beautiful, clear blue.

CHAPTER SEVEN

1

The night was young and the festivities at the Wicked City Fetish Halloween party at The Royal were bizarre and sexually charged. The costume party was alive with thrill seeking guests dressed in weird and outlandish outfits that had themes of fetish, bondage, burlesque, and drag. Tonight, the joint was jumping, and the crowd was charged and primed, bellies full of gin, absinthe, whiskey, wine, and beer and libidos at full throttle. The air was electric with sexual excitement and the freaks had come out to play.

There were DJs, dancing, and socializing, and, of course, drugs and alcohol and sex. The loudspeakers blasted out hits from diverse and eclectic selections of music from different genres, and currently the room was pulsing and bouncing to a song "Weit Weg" by Ramstein. A spotlight spiraled and cut across the crowd, the air hazy with a mist composed of sweat, hormones, perfume, cologne, and lust, stage lights flashing brightly, red, purple, green, strobes and pots pulsing to the music and beat. It was loud and captivating, and the vitality and enthusiasm was contagious. The song ended and the crowd stopped momentarily got gather a quick breath before the next song started.

The MC grabbed the mic and shouted out to the crowd: "Hey! Good evening guys and ghouls. How is everybody? I'm Rick Strickland from KFIX one oh one, the rock radio of Vancouver, and we are here to give you're your fix of music, sex, and fun . . . let's make this a night to remember."

The crowd screamed back in tumultuous agreement and applauded vehemently.

"Alright! Happy Halloween. And welcome to the annual Halloween Fetish party presented by The Royal," Rick continued.

There were whoops and hollers and cries of joy and excitement from the crowd.

"Let's have some fucking fun tonight," Rick continued. "Is everybody ready to have some sinfully delicious fun?"

Yes. The crowd agreed. Yes. Indeed.

"Grab a guy or girl and give them a kiss," Rick said. "Make sure to visit any of our stages and take part in the activities. Don't forget to stop by the bar for refreshments. We will be announcing the winners of the raffle contest later tonight at nine o'clock sharp. Be here or be square. Don't forget to tip your bartender or waitress. And most of all get your balls or boobs out and spank that ass. We are here to get it on. Yeah? No? I think so. Now let's get back to the festivities."

The crowd went wild, jumping and jouncing, and bouncing and frolicking, and frothing in a frenzied sexual anticipation.

"Welcome to our guest DJ . . ." Rick said, pointing at the ghoulish figure propped up behind the turntables and soundstage, the spotlight lighting him up like a Grim Reaper beneath the full moon. "Let's give it up for The Mortician. He is here to rock the house tonight."

The crowd was happy to have the DJ and his wonderful performance. The Mortician waved back at the anxious crowd, spun up a record, and the music began to blast through the speakers, a Marylin Manson hit flooding the crowd and filling them with beats from the song "The Dope Show."

The dance floor was once again throbbing and bouncing, and the liquor flowed like Niagara Falls. Drinks were spilled, theatrical blood was flowing from lips, fangs were biting lips and necks, and illicit chemicals were consumed by the fistful. They were getting high and ready to ravish one another. It was a true mosh pit and there were pulsing sexual organs everywhere, hands groping and grabbing, and tongues sucking and waggling, and pleasure and pain in store for all. It was going to be night to remember.

Across the venue, guests were indulging in everything under the sun, sucking faces and probing and leaving nothing to imagination. The crowd was full of sweaty and stoned guests all dressed in fabulous and dark costumes, dressed to the T and many of them were clad in slinky, kinky, trendy costumes that conjured up visions of exquisite pleasure and excruciating and painful sex. The air was charged with excitement, and energy that urged everyone to get naked and fuck one another, no questions asked.

The stage was set and there were drag queens prancing along a runway, showing of their wares, and there were kinky nude models in nothing but G-strings suspended from ropes hanging down over the crowd, doing acrobatics maneuvers and showing of their hot bodies. There was a burlesque show taking place on a stage to the left, and dancers in cages to the left and to the right, and laser lights flashed and sliced across a sea of dancers grooving to the beats coming from the center stage where a high-profile DJ known as The Mortician, dressed in black trench coat and hood with a skull face mask, was performing a remix.

There were two levels with four rooms with an attendance of over six-hundred kinky and perverted Halloween party-goers. Here there was a vintage Victorian ornate chair with crushed red velvet and party goers and queens were posing together for pictures to keep as mementos of this wild night. A scantily dressed man in a costume made entirely of leather pranced suggestively in a thong, studded straps across his chest, police hat on his head, and engineer boots, while he held a short, braided whip. He was spanking another man, wearing leather fringed chaps, buttocks exposed and red with welts and striations, grinding his hips and rising to meet the strokes of the whip, his face and expression of exquisite pleasure and pain. Photographers and videographers captured every moment.

There were staged scenes with actors and attendees performing various acts of bondage and indulging in fetish acts, spanking, licking, kissing, all sorts of depraved and wretchedly lewd acts were acceptable here in the assigned play areas with dedicated furniture and props.

There were vampires, ghouls, Goths, and Vikings, muscle bound boy toys in G-strings, and bears and queens flaunting their flamboyant goods, as well as dapper gals and gents dressed in tuxedos with faces painted white in Dia de los Muertos makeup, and frilly fringe colors and cuffs, with shiny leather shoes and stiletto heels. There were dark and brooding vamps with massive breasts bulging beneath tight shirts and rainbow-colored hair, and anime tarts dressed in Pippi Long-stocking pirate outfits and girls who looked like Wednesday from the Adam's Family. There were plastic fangs between sultry lips and gallons of stage blood splashed liberally.

On the dance floor, guests bounced and hopped, in full costume, completely entranced by the thunderous music blasting from the speakers mounted on every wall. It was invigorating and cathartic, and they joined, gyrating and grinding, intoxicated and enthralled. The smell of sex and sin and lust permeated the air. Everybody knew they were going to get what they desired tonight, and only the meek and mild would be left out, and hopefully they stayed home and did not attend the raucous party.

At the doors, the crowd had congregated and there were paparazzi and famous guests walking along the red carpet between the braided gold ropes that portioned off the mob. Flashbulbs and spotlights flickered and shone across the arriving guests and limousines that pulled up at the curb. The street was congested with partygoers spilling out onto the street, the sidewalks cluttered with scantily clad beauties dressed to kill and young, hung, gigolo studs that walked with swagger, dressed like gay leather studs, pants bulging with large, sweaty packages, ready for action. The party in the streets rivaled the party inside The Royal, and tonight promised something for everyone.

There were partygoers on couches getting spanked with leather belts and straps, large red handprint welts on their buttocks, grinding to the music. There were tongues and kisses, wet and sloppy, hands groping everywhere, first breasts, then hips, then sweaty crotch with panties exposing sexual organs. It smelled of perfume and cologne, angst, sweat, alcohol, anxiety, and tension. The mood was sexual, sensual, and invigorating. It was one big prelude to a fuck fest.

2

Manson arrived in a costume dressed as the lead character from the movie *The Crow* staring Brandon Lee. He was with the members of his band, Sinister Fiend, comprised of a group of his friends from the neighborhood, and they had all dressed in dark and disturbing costumes to attend the Wicked City Fetish Halloween party. They would not have missed it for the world. This was a chance to see some of the hottest and most flamboyant freaks in town as they got loose, strutted their stuff, and spanked one another's asses on the dedicated furniture around the arena. Manson and his friends were seated at a table near the far wall, and this afforded them a magnificent view of the festivities.

Manson and his friends, Stuart, Kramer, Grover, and Peter were hot to trot and ready to get laid.

"Hey, check that out," Grover said, pointing at a couple who were spanking each other over a leather sofa with a whip, taking turns, exposed asses as red and rosy as a freshly slapped cheek.

"Ooh," Manson said. "That's gotta hurt."

"I think I want to try it out," Kramer said.

"Do you want to pitch or catch?" Peter asked.

"Both," Kramer said.

"It's Halloween," Manson said, shrugging his shoulders. "What better time than now to get your freak on?"

"You're a freak," Stuart said. "Why don't you go over there and ask them if you can join in?"

"I might do that," Kramer said.

"Why don't you order another round of drinks while you're at it?" Peter said. "And do hurry back."

Manson happened to glance toward the entryway, and he

noticed when a girl in a Gothic fallen angel costume complete with feather wings, a Victorian black lace choker collar necklace with teardrop beads and a silver crucifix, and a silky dress and knee length laced, leather boots with heels.

He wanted to get to know her. He did not have the nerve to approach her. She as leaving the building toward the exit, and he wanted to catch her before she got away. He followed her outside. Manson was pleased to see the beautiful lady in a Goth fallen angel costume, looking much like a devilish sprite sitting outside the building, smoking a cigarette. She was beautiful, and Manson was astounded by her ravishing good looks. He must meet this girl, he thought. She was a stunning beauty, and he knew he must introduce himself at one.

He walked up to her and cleared his throat.

"Hello," he said.

"Hello, yourself," she said, blowing out smoke through her painted black lips. She looked away, disinterested.

"What is a lady such as yourself doing out in the evening unattended?"

"I'm sorry," she replied. "Do I know you? Who says I am unattended?"

"Forgive me for being curt," Manson said. "I am assuming you are alone. I don't see a gentleman anywhere. Surely a woman as beautiful as yourself would not be without a . . . date."

"You assume too much," she said.

She smashed out the cigarette under her leather boot.

"Easy, buddy," she said. "I'm not into random guys with bad pickup lines. Do you always start up a conversation without properly introducing yourself first? Don't you have any manners?"

"I do apologize," he said, bowing. "If you will forgive me. My name is Manson Stokes."

"What a wonderful name," she said. She giggled.

"What's so funny?"

"Oh, nothing," she said. "I was taken aback for a moment. Never mind. It's very nice to meet you, Manson.""Either works for me," he said. "Just don't call me late for dinner."

"Funny," she said. "I see what you did there."

"You can call me Luke."

"I love your costume, Luke," she said. "You are 'The Crow,' right? Eric Draven. I am a big fan. Brandon Lee was so hot in that movie. Too bad . . . what happened to him, you know?"

"It was a tragedy—thank you for the compliment," Manson said. "I am a fan of The Crow, too, obviously." He looked away for a moment.

There was a beat of silence; an uneasy awkwardness.

"I love your costume," he said, breaking the silence. "A dark angel. You wear it well."

"Thank you," she said.

"And may I ask my lady for her name?" Manson asked. "If I may be so bold."

"Yes. You may," she said. "That doesn't mean I'm going to tell you."

"Hard to get, aren't you?"

"Absolutely."

(Another awkward beat).

Manson did not show his embarrassment because of his painted face and darkened eyes with makeup, however his awkwardness was obvious by his body language. He sighed, putting his hands in his pockets, shifting from foot to foot nervously.

"You are quite cute, you know? I wouldn't just tell any stranger my name. But, for you I will make an exception. My name is Zoey. And you have no chance with me. I just want to get that out right now. I'm honest and I will tell you what I think. Some men don't like that in a woman."

"I'm not trying to be pushy, or anything like that," Manson

said. "I only stepped outside to get some air. I saw you. You're beautiful. I just wanted to say hello. I am not looking for a date . . . necessarily."

"A date?" Zoey said, smiling. "Then why are you here at this meat market? This is the most sexist party in the world. It's literally all about fucking and getting stoned. I'm not buying it. You came here to find someone to fuck . . . didn't you?"

"Oh, uh, I'm here with some friends," Manson said. "We came here to party and have fun, yes. But I am not a typical asshole. I have manners. Don't get the wrong impression. I mean you no harm. I just thought you might like to talk. That's all."

"Now, now," Zoey said. "Do not insult me. I am no common slut. I have class and style. What makes you think I would even consider talking to you, in the first place? In this day and age, a girl has to look out for herself."

"Are you going back into the show?"

"Yes."

"Are you alone?"

"What kind of question is that? I am here with friends."

"I see."

"If you are asking if I am engaged . . . the answer is no. I am single, and available. But . . . I am not easy."

"Okay," Manson said. "That changes everything."

"Would you like to go back inside and have a drink with me, Luke?"

"Of course."

"Can I get your number—I mean, can we talk more later?"

Manson looked around, nervously, he knew he was blowing it. This girl was too pretty to let get away so easily. He must get her number, at least, to continue a friendship with her in the future.

"You are trying too hard," Zoey said. "But, yes. I will give you my number . . . in a moment."

3

Manson and Zoey went back inside the club, the bass music and laser lights setting the tone and mood of the atmosphere. It was loud and brash, and the club scene was one of lechery and debauchery.

Stephanie Dascălu, was dressed as the Wicked Queen in an extravagant Elizabethan dress with feather collar and ruff, elegant and posh, clearly a showstopper at the party.

Manson and Zoey were invited to sit down at her table, and they were much obliged, taking a seat next to the eye-catching queen, who was stunning in her Elizabethan dress, the obvious focal point of the party. She stood out above the rest, and she was charming and beautiful, in a dark and delightful way. She ordered more drinks for everyone surrounding her and they started to party, hard. It was a sexually charged atmosphere.

After doing more booze and drugs—lines of cocaine were spread out on the glass table and snorted with a hundred dollar bill; Molly capsules were handed around and swallowed; magic mushrooms were choked down and washed back with absinthe; various other drugs were consumed as well, and it was a volatile cocktail of illicit chemicals that put them in an aroused and euphoric state—they begin to flirt with each other. They wound up drinking more, heavily, doing shot after shot of different types of distilled spirits, and doing more drugs: whiskey, gin, vodka, tequila, and more absinthe glowing fluorescent and chartreuse like radioactive spill out, and more cocaine, another big dose of molly, and some marijuana. They were as high as fucking kite and loving every minute of it.

Stephanie put her hand on Manson's crotch, grabbing what bulged in his jeans, squeezing, and massaging gently. He looked at her and smiled. He looked at Zoey, and she smiled back. Sex was inevitable; they would share each other; it would be a wonderful pile of bodies and sexual organs. It would be beautiful, young, vibrant people exchanging fluids and organs, tasting each other's sweat and cum and pheromones. It would be decadently delightful, and they were horny as fuck and ready to get out of there and have sexual bliss.

"Bang the gong, honey," she said, "because it's time to get it on. We should fuck like animals."

"Oh, my," Manson said, surprised but delighted. "Very nice to meet you."

"And your darling Dark Angel can join us, too," Stephanie said, glancing at Zoey and smiling. She leaned forward, put her hand behind Zoey's head, and pulled her close and gave her a wet kiss full of tongue, her breath minty and intoxicating.

Zoey was happy to oblige, and she met the kiss with her own tongue. After the enthusiastic kiss ended, she agreed, saying, "I would love to have some fun tonight."

The music was invigorating with the light show and the atmosphere was intense. It was a feel-good vibe, and everybody was there to be pleasured and get high.

"Would you like to come back to my place?" Stephanie asked, looking at both.

"Yes," Manson said.

"Most definitely," Zoey said, wiping her lips.

4

Stephanie invited Manson and Zoey back to her mansion, a castle, and they went outside of the club as a black limousine pulled up in front and the party goers climbed inside the coach. Inside the limousine they were given long glasses filled with fizzing champagne and a mirror with lines of cocaine and a rolled up 100-dollar bill was passed around.

"You are going to love my castle," Stephanie said, raising her glass of champagne. "Here is to a lovely night of wild sex and pleasure unlike anything you have ever experienced."

She raised her glass. They made a toast, drank deeply of the bubbly effervescent alcoholic beverage. It went to their heads. It was intoxicating.

After a short drive across the city and toward the outskirts where buildings gave way to rural landscapes. When they left the city and made their way toward the countryside and mountains, they arrived at a sprawling property with fences and gates at an antiquated castle built in the Gothic Revival style nestled in the North Shore Mountains that overlooked Vancouver and the Burrard inlet. The view was magnificent, and it was a beautiful sight to behold at night with a grand vista of the cityscape as it glittered and glimmered with polychromatic lights, causing an aura to linger in the clouds overhead in a visible halo like a glowing mist.

The limousine approached the gate to the castle; they were amazed.

"You really do live in a castle," Manson said.

"I told you," Stephanie said.

"It's beautiful," Zoey said.

At the entrance was a massive granite stone gate with wrought iron bars and a sign that read: **Château de Dascălu**. It was magnificent and exciting to be going to a real castle. The gate opened when the driver entered a code on the keypad. They passed through the gate and traveled slowly up the driveway toward the mansion.

At the door, a butler greeted them. He was dressed in a bow-tie and tuxedo. He was wearing a traditional attire of a butler, dressed nicely in a black tuxedo tailcoat, double breasted vest, white dress shirt with wing collar and a black tie, and white gloves. He looked regal and sophisticated and held his head high in a regal pose. A pocket watch chain hung from inside his coat.

"Good evening," the butler said, bowing slightly, "and welcome. Please come in."

The butler stepped aside and allowed them entry, and they stepped through the threshold and went into the mansion. Inside the decor was lavish and ornate with chandeliers, wood and marble, plush carpets, taxidermy animals mounted, paintings of portraits of aristocrats and landscapes done in dark themes.

"This is incredible," Zoey said, eyes wide in amazement.

"You live in a real castle?" Manson said. "I thought you were joking."

"No joke," Stephanie said. "But, beware . . . it is rumored to be haunted."

"What?" Manson asked. "By ghosts?"

"That is what the locals say," Stephanie replied.

"Nice," Zoey said. "I just love a creepy ghost story."

Stephanie removed her fur coat and the butler took it and draped it over his arm.

"Please take our guests coats, William," Stephanie said.

"Yes, ma'am," William said.

"You have a butler, too?" Manson said. "This is unreal."

"It's like a dream," Zoey said.

"It's not a dream, my dear," Stephanie said. "Come into the great room and we shall have party favors while we get comfortable."

William led them to the great room and opened the large wooden doors, allowing them access to a room full of lush plants, lighting, furniture, a massive widescreen TV, lavishly decorated. The furniture was immaculate, a mix of modern and vintage, with sofas, easy chairs, rocking chairs, and a chair that resembled a throne.

"Make yourselves comfortable," Stephanie said.

5

The doors opened and a handsome young man with golden locks of shoulder length curly hair and amber eyes came into the room unannounced. He had a straight nose, full lips, and a trimmed mustache and goatee. He joined the party, grabbing a glass of Champaign.

"Allow me to introduce my boytoy, Crandall," Stephanie said.

"Please," Crandall said. "You're embarrassing me."

"You know it's true."

Manson and Zoey looked at each other surprised.

"It's nice to meet you," Crandall said, extending his supple hand.

They shook his hand and greeted him warmly.

"He is my live-in love slave," Stephanie said, smiling.

"Why didn't you go to the Halloween party?" Manson asked, looking intently at Crandall.

"I did not feel like going out tonight," he replied.

"I tried to get him to go," Stephanie said. "He was a wet blanket tonight. Said he was tired."

"Who feels like getting high?" Crandall said, pulling out a bag of dope from his pocket. "I got some good molly . . . if anyone is interested."

"Me please," Manson said.

"Sure," Zoey said.

"Let's do it," Stephanie said.

They took capsules of the MDMA and began to be overwhelmed with sensations of euphoria and sensuality.

After a few more drinks and some cocaine, the four of them moved to a bedroom and proceeded to engage in an orgy of magnificent proportions, tongues, protruding members, pink parts, anal crevices, and breasts, oiled and lubed, all culminating in a happy ending and sweat dripping . . .

Exhausted and spent, they passed out in one another's arms and closed their eyes, gratified and satisfied and content . . . sleep overcoming them like a warm blanket on a cold day, and the sandman stood above them pouring sand in their eyes, causing the lids to grow heavy and droop as they dozed off, blissfully unaware of the terrible danger and horrors that lurked around them, oblivious to the reality of what was in store and, for now, they would rest like newborn babies just brought into the world. It was the sleep of the intoxicated, caused by too much alcohol, drugs, and overindulgence, and tomorrow they would have the most excruciating hangovers imaginable, but for now sleep was of the essence.

"Goodnight, my children," Stephanie said, standing in the doorway with her hands on the door, looking at them huddled on the bed together, innocent and cuddling, snuggling contentedly together. They were a beautiful couple. She knew that she loved them. She knew that she wanted them to stay with her forever. She would have her way, and they would adore her always. "Goodnight, my pretty ones. Tomorrow will be a new day, and we will have much to do . . . but for now . . . sleep tight.

Stephanie closed the door and left them alone, moving down the hall, going to her chamber, and lying down in her place of rest. It was her lifestyle to stay up all night and sleep all say. She lived to party, and she needed her beauty rest to look her best tomorrow night.

It would be morning soon.

A new day was dawning.

A rebirth was coming.

The winds of change were blowing.

6

Spiraling down the vortex, floating upside down, in a perpetual skydive, like stuntmen falling to the Earth in a black void . . . now spinning, head over heels, round and round, in a perpetual state of vertigo . . .

Down . . . down . . . down . . .

The wind rushing past their hair, clothing rustling in the rushing wind, limbs outward, flapping like birds, floundering like fledglings trying to right themselves . . .

Landing lightly on the ground and standing upright, it was still pitch black all around them, and suddenly they noticed that they were in a long tunnel, dark and mysterious, and there was a light looming up ahead where there was an opening in the shape of an arch, they could see it, so they moved toward it, pushing against the air that seemed as thick as molasses, like they were swimming in a vat of Jell-O, not making much progress. It felt like a dream, worse, a nightmare, and something bad was about to happen. There was an uneasy feeling, like being chased by a big hairy monster, and a pack of rabid wolves howling and growling, and other sinister creatures staying just out of sight, but following their progress, tailing them and stalking them, beasts so foul they would tear you limb from limb, that you could not see but you knew they was there and you wanted to scream but could not, only a click in your throat coming out, panic setting in and terror rising to the surface like a bubble in the dark lake of consciousness.

Then they were standing on a vast plane, a void, an expanse stretching out in all directions for as far as the eye could see, immersed in a thick fog, but at least there was some light now and it was getting brighter. Daylight was coming as the sun began to rise over this surreal landscape, and they were happy for that, because monsters must hide from the light, everyone knew that, however there was something sinister and foreboding about the light . . . it was painful, bright, and menacing. It was beginning to cause a burning sensation on their skin and boils and blisters were forming there, the flesh beginning to smolder and smoke, and the pain was excruciating, so they ran, and ran, and ran, getting nowhere on the empty vastness of nothingness.

Up ahead, there was a withered tree looming in the fog, a large gnarled oak tree with a tremendous barrel of a trunk that had burrs and knotholes that resembled a face with holes and sockets and valleys and rifts for eyes, nose, and mouth, worse it resembled a skull. The tree was huge as they approached it, and they could hide in the shady side, but it was stripped of leaves and had only crooked and scraggly branches that afforded little protection from the quickly rising sun. They must find shade, that was all they knew, and they must find it fast because now they realized that the sun was poisonous, and the harmful ultraviolet rays would cause sickness and death. What they needed now was a big tube of SPF 150 sunscreen to keep them from being exposed to the cancer-causing rays of the sun.

There was a castle on the hill appearing suddenly out of the fog, gray walls and towers and spires reaching toward the sky, a refuge in the wasteland, and they knew they must go there to find safety.

Where were they? That was the question. What was happening to them?

Upon awakening, they looked around at the room and orientated themselves with their situation and reacquainted themselves with what had happened the night before. The sat up and looked at each other, slightly embarrassed and feeling the sting of guilt, they realize where they were now, at the mansion where they had partied like it was 1999 all over again. It occurred to them that there may have been some kind of drugs involved in their deep sleep, it felt like they had been roofied because they got fucked up and whacked out and there was some kinky and painful sex involved, and then after that it was blank . . . there was nothing . . . they could not completely remember everything.

Manson and Zoey had blacked out during the festivities and now there was a gap of missing time. Now it was early in the morning and they were hungover and confused, sitting in an awkward silence, and looking at each other in awkwardness and humiliation. The buzz and intoxication that alleviated inhibitions was gone and now they were sober and solemn and full of regret.

The looked for their host, Stephanie, and her guest, Crandall, but they were both gone without a trace. Manson and Zoey were alone in the bedroom in a strange mansion of which they knew nothing about, and worse, there were blood stains on the sheets. Their eyes were wide at the blood stains . . .

They looked at each other with confused expressions, knowing what each other were thinking: *What have we done?*

7

After the wild sex was over and Crandall had left the room, Stephanie sat alone with Manson and Zoey, who were passed out and incapacitated on the bed.

The process involved with turning someone into a vampire is shrouded in mystery, a painful creation and sinister transformation. Stephanie had drugged them and attended to them while they were passed out in the bed. She opened a vein on her wrist and put it to the innocent victims' lips. The florid blood dripped into their mouths and onto their tongues.

"You will become creatures of the night," Stephanie said, rubbing their cheeks lovingly as they lay passed out on her bed. "I have waited for a couple like you to come along. Now I will make you my own. We can be like a family."

Bianco quivered and twitched, moaning in her sleep, she was on the verge of a silent scream. She was having a nightmare. Manson was deathly still as the blood trickled into his mouth and down his throat. As the fresh vampire blood began to take effect the two sleeping victims began to suckle at the bloody wrist, wanting more, feeding vigorously, biting and snipping the skin.

"Easy, my sweets," she said. "Don't take too much too fast. This is a delicate procedure and you must take your time. My precious little ones. Drink my blood . . . it will make you immortal."

8

When Manson and Zoey woke up again, they were lying in a bed with white satin sheets stained red with blood. They looked at each other, at the stained sheets, around at the interior of the apartment. They felt hungover from too much alcohol and drugs, their heads pounding.

There was an awkward moment of embarrassment as they realized what had transpired the night before.

What have we done? What are we going here? They wondered, and why were their necks throbbing with a dull beating sensation, where they discovered deep bite marks in the flesh. They had holes pierced in their throats and it was painful.

"What has happened?" Zoey asked, feeling the holes in her neck. "I've been injured, somehow." She looked at Manson and noticed he had marks on his neck, too. "And so have you . . . look, you have some kind of wounds on your neck, like . . ." She trailed off, thinking of the implications.

"Huh?" Manson said, reaching for his throat. "What is that? I feel it. There are scratches there. We must have had some really kinky sex, and biting and licking and such, but . . . I can't remember everything."

"I remember being bitten," Zoey said. "It was all part of it, but . . . this is weird."

"That was some night, eh?" Manson said. "I've never had so much fun and not be able to remember it."

"Yes. It was great," Zoey said, her eyes darting away ashamedly. "I'm not sure about this. Have we done something wrong?"

"Not at all. It was a night of decadent indulgence. Don't worry about it," Manson said. "I would do it all over again . . . without question. How about you?"

"Absolutely," Zoey lied. She was having some feelings of remorse. "No sweat. It was a ravishing party."

The looked at the bite marks on each other's throats and wondered what had really happened. This was leading up to something mysterious, leading up to a conclusion that they did not want to contemplate, leading them to believe that they had been involved in something sinister, but unable to recall all the details. Their minds and memories were still in a drugged haze and separating reality from fantasy was still out of their grasp.

"Where is our host?" Manson asked, looking around the

room.

"I don't know," Zoey said. "Maybe we should look for her."

Suddenly, the door to the room opened on creaky hinges and the butler, William, popped in through the door, sharply dressed in tuxedo jacket, hands in white gloves. He had brought them breakfast in bed.

"Madam Dascălu sends her apologies, as she has stepped out on an errand," he said, in a French-Canadian accent, wheeling the cart to the side of the bed, "but she has instructed me to tell you that you are welcome to stay as long as you want, or need. Please do make yourselves at home. And I have brought you breakfast in bed. Would you like for me to serve you?" He lifted the sliver lid off the serving tray and place it beneath the cart and presented an extravagant breakfast of scrambled egg, bacon and sausage, potatoes, fresh fruit, croissant, and juice, with a bottle of Champaign.

"Here is your breakfast," he said, waved the palm of his hand over the steaming food as a presentation. "Enjoy. I have brought some Tylenol and Advil in case you are in need of relief for whatever ails you. I know a hangover can be quite painful. By the way, I will have the housekeepers make that bed for you shortly. You are welcome to relocate to the grand room, if you please. This room is such a mess and needs a good cleaning."

"Excellent, my good man, William," Manson said, looking at the cart. "I see you have thought of everything. But, no . . . that's quite alright. We'll take it from here. You can just leave the cart right there. You are too kind. Thank you."

"It's a pleasure," William said, stooping in a slight bow. "Will you be requiring a bath? I can draw the water for you . . . or perhaps you would prefer a shower? We have ample facilities for your convenience. A swimming pool, jacuzzi, sauna is at your disposal. We have all the amenities. There is an exercise room with fitness equipment, a tennis court, and, if you like, you can take a walk along the gardens and paths along the property. It is a lovely morning—but, on second thought, you may not enjoy the bright light . . . that is if you are suffering from a hangover or headache."

"I would love a hot shower," Zoey said. "But first I am starving. Can I eat first?"

"Of course," William said. "Just ring me if you require assistance."

"Ring you?" Manson quizzed.

"Yes. That button on the intercom by the door," William said, pointing a gloved finger. "Just press the call button and I will be at your service."

"Excellent, my good man," Manson said.

William then left them to eat in peace. He bid them good tidings. He left the room while they were still in bed, allowing them privacy so they could make themselves presentable and enjoy their breakfast in peace.

"What have we done?" Manson asked.

"Where are we?" Zoey asked. "I don't remember anything. Did we all fuck each other last night?"

They were both embarrassed at their actions from the previous night. They did not feel normal. Something was wrong. Although the shades were drawn, they could not stand the daylight creeping in through the cracks in the curtains at the large windows. The sun was up high in the sky, blaring and beating on the glass.

They sat at a table next to the wall with a fabulous painting by Picasso and ate their breakfast in silence.

There was a knock on the door. Manson answered it. It was the housekeepers, two Latino women dressed in French maid outfits, and they came in and quickly made the bed, replacing the linens, tossing down a new bedspread, and turning down the pillows and sheets. The bed was inviting and new. They dusted the room, emptied the trash, cleaned out the attached bathroom, and then quickly exited, never saying a word.

"Well that was nice," Zoey said. "Now we have clean sheets."

"Yes. About that," Manson said. "I wonder . . ."

"Don't ask," Zoey said. "It may be better if we just ignore it and pretend that we never saw it."

"You may be right."

They finished breakfast and turned on the flat screen TV hanging on the wall. They watched the news for a while and moved back over to the bed.

"I am getting back in bed," Manson said. "My head is pounding. I think I could use some more sleep."

"I am going to join you," Zoey said. "I don't feel so well either. I've never had a hangover like this."

"We did some incredible things last night," Manson said. "No wonder we are suffering for it this morning."

Zoey climbed back into the bed, pulled the covers over her body, and covered her face with a pillow.

"That sunlight from the window is making it worse," Manson said.

He got up and went to the window. Behind the curtains were electric louver blinds. He found the switch on the wall and pressed it; the curtains turned and closed tight, blocking out the light.

"Problem solved," Manson said.

"Thank you."

He climbed back bed, still mostly naked except for their under garments, and started kissing passionately. It led to more sex. After they reached climax and orgasm, they both eventually nodded off to sleep, resting comfortably in each other's arms.

9

When they awoke in the bed again, they did not know if it was morning or night, or how long they had been sleeping. Stephanie standing in the doorway, looking at them, smoking a cigarette. She looked different from how they remembered her at the party with her costume and makeup. She was dressed in a black robe, dark sunglasses covering her eyes. When she spoke, her voice was hypnotic and soporific.

"Regretfully, I have to admit that I have done something terribly selfish. . . ." she took a long drag on the cigarette, the ash long and curving away on the end, the smoke swirling over her head. "You will both want to come out and join me in the great room. I have something important to tell you." she said, turning and heading toward the door. "Please follow me. We will bet more comfortable out on the nice sofa and chairs. I want you to be ready for the news I am about to share with you."

"What happened here? What was there blood on the sheets when we woke up?" Zoey asked. "Did you bite us last night? I mean, I know the sex was kinky and all, but why did you have to break the skin? That might be a bit extreme, don't you think?"

"Don't worry your pretty little head," Stephanie said, rolling her eyes. "You will understand after I explain everything."

Manson sat up, covered his nakedness with the sheets, reached for his jeans on the floor. Zoey wrapped herself in the bed spread, got up and found her cloths on the chair. Manson slipped on his tight jeans, donned his shirt, and shoes. Zoey put her skirt and blouse back on and found her choker collar and put it around her neck with the intention of hiding the hickeys and bite marks, slightly embarrassed by the remaining signs of last night's sexual encounter. The collar was uncomfortable and made her neck itch, she instantly fussed with it and scratched around the edges, irritated by the strange sensation.

They dressed quickly while Stephanie looked on and finished smoking her cigarette.

The got up and went through the door.

Out in the great room, they sat down on the plush white sofas.

"Do you want a drink?" Stephanie asked. "I have a pitcher of Bloody Marries mixed up just for the occasion."

"Yes. Please," Manson said. "Anything to help with this splitting headache."

The servant, William, was standing quietly in the corner. He produced glasses and poured Bloody Marry mix for each of them with a sprig of celery. He handed the drinks to the wide-awake young lovers.

"Now, prepare to hear what I must tell you," Stephanie said. "Please understand I meant you no harm. What I have done for you was out of love and affection."

"Did we have an orgy last night?" Zoey asked. "I can't remember a thing."

"I think we did more than that," Manson said, sipping from his drink.

"My dearest Manson and Zoey," Stephanie said. "I don't know how else to say this but, welcome to your new lives as vampires. You will no longer be mortal. You have been reborn. I have created you in my own image, man and woman, as creatures of the night. You will now know what it means to serve the darkness and live forever."

"What are you talking about?" Manson said. "Vampires? Are you serious? This is crazy."

"I don't believe it," Zoey said, sitting up on the sofa. "And, don't you think drugging us was a bit extreme?"

"It was the only way. The drugs were just a means to an end."

"You could have asked us first," Zoey said.

"You would not have agreed to this," Stephanie said, shaking her head. "I know it was wrong. But I had to have you . . . you are so precious to me. Please understand. I have been lonely and I long to have you two by my side."

"Really?" Manson said. "That makes it alright?"

"No, probably not," she said. "Please forgive me. I could not help myself."

"What happens to us now?" Zoey asked.

"You will no longer know life as you have before," Stephanie continued. "You will long for blood and lust for flesh, craving the taste of the blood of the innocent. You will feed in the darkness, consuming the vitality of souls to invigorate your own. I know you probably wonder why I have done this, but I must confess it was out of loneliness. I have longed to have companions for so long now, that I just had to have you when I saw you. This is a most beautiful gift I have given to you and I hope you don't hold me accountable for turning you in to vampires."

"This is nonsense," Zoey said. "I don't believe in such things as vampires."

"I think she's telling the truth," Manson said. "I believe her."

"Forgive me for my selfish ways," Stephanie said. "I just knew I had to have you two for my own. You are my familiars now."

"No. I refuse to believe it," Zoey said. "This is not true. There is no such thing as vampires."

"Who are you, really, Stephanie? Where do you come from?" Manson asked. "What is this you speak of, about vampires and such? Surely you jest."

"I am a descendant of a long lineage of vampires from a bloodline that comes from Hungary, in a small village. I have lived here in Vancouver, for about a hundred and fifty years. I moved here to get away from my past. I no longer desire to retrace my footsteps to a long life in the old country."

"Why would you do this to us?" Zoey said. "We have done nothing to deserve this."

"You have been blessed with a new way of life, Zoey," Stephanie said. "You will come to thank me one day. I promise you that."

"We must leave here at once," Manson said. "I don't believe a word of what you are saying."

"We will show ourselves out," Zoey said.

"I think you will find that going out into the daylight is not going to be a pleasant experience," Stephanie said. "You will no longer be able to walk in the daylight. You are now creatures of the night."

"Bullshit," Manson said. "Come on Zoey. Let's leave this place at once."

They stood up quickly, moving toward the door.

"Wait," Stephanie said. "Do you think it is any coincidence that all of the blinds are shut in this castle during the day? I have gone to great lengths to block out the daylight. Watch this." She went over to the window and opened the blinds. Bright sunlight spilled into the room.

Manson and Zoey cringed away from the piercing light. It was excruciatingly painful. They had to block their eyes with their hands. Stephanie was wearing sunglasses and still she squinted away from the piercing bright sunrays.

"Stop. Please," Zoey said "Close the curtains this instant. It's giving me a migraine headache."

Stephanie closed the curtains quickly, blocking out the deadly sunlight.

"As you can see," she said, "the daylight is dangerous to you now. You can only go out at night."

"What ever shall we do?" Zoey said, looking at Manson. "What has become of us?"

"You evil whore," Manson said. "You have killed us."

"On the contrary," Stephanie said. "I have brought you a new life, Manson, silly boy. One day you will thank me."

Realizing that they were now relegated to the confines of the castle for the expanse of the day, Manson and Zoey sat back down on the sofa and sipped on their Bloody Marries.

"We can keep each other company for a while," Stephanie said. "Please do make yourselves comfortable now. We have so much to discuss."

They talked for hours, getting acquainted, coming to terms with this new life as a vampire and what it meant for them now.

The crucifix on Zoey's choker was causing an irritating burning sensation in her throat. Zoey reached up to her neck and fidgeted with the choker, moving it back and forth to alleviate the burning sensation.

"I don't know why, but this thing is irritating my throat," she said. "I can't stand it. I must take it off. And my teeth hurt. Why do my teeth hurt so bad?"

"The transformation is beginning," Stephanie said. "You will experience some strange sensations and physical changes now. Prepare yourselves. It can be painful."

"Vampires? Are you insane?" Manson said. "There is no such thing."

"I'm afraid that's not true," Stephanie said. "We do exist. And now you are one, too."

"I don't believe you," Manson said.

"Is this some kind of sick joke?" Zoey asked, standing up from the couch. She reached behind her neck and loosened the choker with the crucifix as it was burning excruciatingly into her neck, leaving a red mark. She threw it down on the ground. She put her fingers to her mouth and felt her canine teeth. They were throbbing painfully, like he worst toothache she had ever experienced. She could feel the pointed teeth, her eyeteeth, were growing longer tapering to a wicked point.

"What is this all about?" she asked. "What is happening to me?"

"I told you," Stephanie said. "You are going through the change."

Manson was taking the pain better, but he too was beginning to experience the symptoms of transforming into a vampire. His canine teeth were becoming elongated, and his eyes were turning dark with red undertones. He had no pupil, only a solid, dark iris that completely obscured the whites of his eyes. His skin was turning pale and his blue veins showed through the thin epidermis. He could feel all his senses were heightened, his touch was tingling with a static charge, his taste was like copper, his smell was filled with the scent of blood, his sight was painfully bright, his hearing so finely tuned and he could hear the dim heartbeats of servants and pets in the castle. He could smell humans and their blood. He was struck with the urge to tear someone apart and eat their heart.

"You are crazy," Manson said. "Why should we believe you?"

Manson stood up and went to the mirror on the wall. He looked into the mirror, expecting to see himself, but saw no reflection. The mirror only showed the room to be empty; neither Zoey nor Stephanie were visible in the mirror, either.

"That's just some kind of trick or illusion," Manson said. "Any funhouse mirror will do that. I don't believe it."

"I would not lie to you, my children," Stephanie said. "I've created you in my image and now you share my power . . . and curse. Look in the mirror for yourselves. You will see that you are morphing into another life force. You will be so much more of a perfect creature now. You will be the undead that live forevermore."

"So, this is like in the movies?" Zoey said. "You've changed us into vampires? Like in the movie Dracula? Salem's Lot? Twilight?"

"All of those, and more," Stephanie said. "My personal favorite is Nosferatu. I like all the stories, too. They are based on truth. We do exist, but the world has tried to keep us hidden for so long. We live right next to mortals, unnoticed and unfeasible. They pretend we don't exist, so they won't be frightened by their meager existence. They've invented myths to explain us away."

"Why would you do such a thing?" Manson said, touching the mirror. "I have no reflection. Your telling me I'm a vampire now? Why should I believe you? Does this mean I have no soul? Am I the undead, now?"

"Yes," Stephanie said. "And no. Believe me because I have no reason to lie about this. As for being the undead, yes, it is true. But, you are alive, and well. You have no soul, but there was never a soul to begin with—religion has concocted such fallacies to mislead the populace—so you have lost nothing, except for mortality. You should be thanking me. You can live forever now, never growing old, forever young . . . forever beautiful."

"We have to drink blood?" Zoey asked, cringing at the thought. "That doesn't sound to appetizing."

"Yes. You will need to feed," she said, putting her hand on Zoey's shoulder. "You will acquire the appetite soon enough.

Human blood is the most exquisite thing you will ever taste. I can assure you of that."

"We have to bite people on the neck and drink their blood. Do they die?" Manson asked. "Do they become like us? I've never killed anyone in my life."

"What if I don't want to suck on someone's neck? I'm not sure that I can do that," Zoey said.

"What in God's name do you expect us to do now?" Manson asked, bemused. "We can't just run around biting innocent people and sucking their blood. I still don't believe this is true. It's all make-believe, right? You are one of those crazy people who claim to be a vampire, but it is really all in your head. You drink blood, to be sure, but you are only a human, and not supernatural at all."

"Don't mention God," Stephanie said. "He has nothing to do with it. You are a god, I am a god, and Zoey is a god. We have transcended beyond what is human and achieved the sublime state of immortality. You can now be part of something that is so much more than ordinary."

"So, you do believe in God?" Zoey asked. "How can there be a god and vampires at the same time?"

"Even the devils know His name," Stephanie said. "And they tremble and shake when they hear it. Vampires are part of the natural world. You don't question the existence of the vampire bat, do you?"

"Well, of course not," Zoey said, shrugging. "But that's different. They are just animals and not monsters. Are we devils? Demons? Evil?"

"You are . . . what you are," Stephanie said, with a long sigh. "You are darkness and wickedness. You will always walk in the shadows and by the light of the moon at night. You will never be able to go inside a church or touch a Bible or crucifix again.

You are lost souls that belong to the darkness now.

"I don't understand that part," Zoey said. "But how do we know we are really vampires? We were just normal people last night. Now you are saying that we are devils. Do we worship Satan now?"

"Satan is the dark Lord, and you will do well to give him reverence," Stephanie said, sternly. "There is so much more to vampires than you know, or what you have seen in literature and movies. We are on an order of beings that exist next to angels. We are superior to mortals. We have our place in the universe, and someday you will understand."

"Why did you do this to us?" Zoey asked. "If this is true, then we are cursed forever?"

"You are a witch, a sorceress," Manson said, growing angry, his brow creased and his teeth showing. "I should kill you, now. If this is true, what you speak of, then you have destroyed us."

"Relax. It isn't so bad," Stephanie said. "You will come to enjoy your new life. Believe me. I felt the same way when I was changed so many years ago, but over the centuries, I have learned to love my life."

"Have you ever turned anyone else into . . . a vampire?" Zoey asked, raising her eyebrows like an innocent child asking if Santa Claus really exists.

"Yes. A few times," she said, lighting another cigarette. "I try not to do it too often. But, with you two, it was perfect. I could not resist. You were so innocent and misled in life. Your inner darkness is strong, and I knew you would be perfect. You will stalk the night forever and keep the legend alive. You are my legacy."

"We can't go outside in the sunlight anymore?" Manson asked. "Will the sun hurt us?"

"You must stay inside in the daytime," she said, exhaling

smoke. "Remember that. The sun will cause you great discomfort and can lead to death if you stay out too long."

"But I thought you said we are immortal," Zoey said. "How can we die, then?"

"You are immortal," she replied. "You can live forever, but you are not immune to death. That means that you can die, too. So, you must be careful. You will learn with time how to avoid those things that threaten your existence. Just take your time and embrace the transformation."

"Can we stay here today, just to relax and absorb all of this?" Manson asked. "I mean, since we can't go out in the daylight."

"What will we tell our families?" Zoey asked. "How will we live a normal life?"

"You will have to leave your families," Stephanie said. "They will find out and put you to death. Even loved ones cannot accept vampires in their clan. Once you have become a creature of the night, branded as the undead, you will always be at odds with mortals. Especially those who are religious. They have persecuted us since the beginning of time. They are jealous, you see?"

"I don't know," Manson said. "This is too much for me to handle right now. I need a drink. Can we still drink?"

"Absolutely," Stephanie said. "Please. What would you like? I have a fully stocked bar. Drink whatever you like."

"What about cigarettes?" Zoey asked. "Can I still smoke. Because I'm dying for a cigarette right now. I see that you are smoking. Can I have one?"

"You can smoke," Stephanie said. "It's a bad habit, but you can do it if you want. Feel free to light up anytime you like."

"What about getting high?" Manson said. "You were getting high with us last night. We all took drugs. Does that mean we can still indulge in the forbidden fruits?"

"You can do anything you want," Stephanie said, stamping her cigarette out in an ashtray. "You will discover what is right, and what you should, and shouldn't do, in time. There is nothing that goes into you that defiles you. It is what comes from within that defiles you."

The transformation was well underway, and they could feel the vampire blood coursing through their veins, infecting them like a virus. They were not aware of the implications yet, but they would be soon, once the transformation was complete.

It was still too much to believe this vampire business all at once, and they both had their doubts, unconvinced.

"I am going to step out for a moment," Stephanie said. "Please feel free to make yourselves at home here. You are my children now. I will take care of you. Stay as long as you want. I hope we can have a long-lasting relationship and share everything . . . and I mean everything." She grinned a devilish grin, licked her lips, and rubbed her breasts in a sensuous manner. "How I do adore the both of you . . . and I look forward to more fun like last night."

"Okay," Zoey said, taken aback. "I think I like it, too. It will take me some time to get used to this new thing . . . whatever this is."

"Me three," Manson said. "You can't rape he willing, darling. I am always up for a second round."

Stephanie smiled flirtatiously, and sashayed to the doorway, glaring at them both with bedroom eyes that promise more fun in the near future.

"I will see you two very soon," she said, opening the door. "Don't leave me . . . I long for you to be my companions."

Manson and Zoey looked at each other, then at her, knowing what everyone in the room was thinking, and it was erotic and intoxicating, the energy buzzing audible. It was hot, hot,

hot and they were tempted to start fucking right on the spot.

"I'm going to go before I'm tempted to stay," Stephanie said. "I have some important business to address, or otherwise we would take care of this right here and now."

"Right, then," Manson said, "We'll see you when you get back."

"Goodbye," Stephanie said, going through the door and shutting it behind her.

They looked at each other with expressions of confusion and perplexity.

Could this really be happening? Was it true? Do vampires really exist?

Perhaps . . .

10

They decided to explore the mansion . . . the room they were presently in was modern and stylish and had all the appearance of hotel room with clean and simple decor, however as soon as they stepped out through the doorway and into the hallway they were transported back into a previous century with antiquated furniture, chandeliers, oil paintings of aristocrats, stately gentleman and noble women hung in ornate frames, hearkening back to a time in the past when electricity was yet to be discovered and horse drawn carriages were the primary mode of transportation; indoor plumbing was not common, there were no jets or automobiles, and men often settled their differences with pistols in a duel out in the courtyard.

The hallways were enchanting, like something out of an old novel, like *The Castle of Otranto* by Horace Walpole. With hardwood floors and stone walls and large doors leading to unknown rooms. It also could have been right out of Bram

Stoker's novel *Dracula*, they suddenly realized, with a shiver of dread. The figures in the oil portraits were dressed in Victorian era styles of high collar coats and suits, and the women wore long and billowing dresses with cages beneath to make them flair out like a bell, their waistline cinched tightly in a corset to give them a classic hour glass figure. They looked back at Manson and Zoey with eyes that followed them down the hallway as they walked into the grand hall where the ceilings arched high into the air and crystal chandeliers hung down like tinkling diamonds and ornate glass wisteria flowers suspended from chains.

"This is incredible," Manson said, rubbing his neck where the bite marks still throbbed and tingled. "I can't believe we are in a real castle."

"A vampire's castle, no less," Zoey said. "Do you believe any of this? I mean the vampire nonsense."

"I'm not sure," Manson said. "Let's look around and see if we can find out more about Stephanie. She should have something that will expose her if she really is a vampire."

"This is kind of scary," Zoey said, "but fascinating at the same time. I've always loved the dark side . . . but now that I am being pulled in, I'm not so sure I still like it."

"The dark side?"

"You know . . . the whole angsty Goth thing."

"Oh, yes, of course," Manson said, turning and looking at her. "What was I thinking?"

"This may be a wish I never wanted to come true."

"It may not be so bad," he said, rubbing his neck again. "It might turn out to be a blessing in disguise. Imagine the advantages to being a vampire . . . you can suck the blood from the innocent and live like an aristocrat. Look at this mansion. Obviously, she has great wealth . . . but the question is, really

. . . who is she, exactly."

"Let's find out."

"I intend to do just that," Manson said, taking her by the hand. "Let's explore this castle and see what secrets we can uncover."

"Where is William, the butler?"

"I don't know. He said to call for him if we needed him."

"What if he catches us being nosy," Zoey said. "I'm sure they don't want us snooping around."

"If they were worried about that . . . would they have let us alone in here?"

Zoey shrugged.

"I don't think so," Manson said. "Quickly. I am curious, now."

They went into the great room and looked that the furnishings, amazed, flashbacks of the previous night of drinking and sex and debauchery filled their thoughts. They were not ashamed for one moment, and they had thoroughly enjoyed all of it.

There was a stairway that led up to a balcony with marble banisters and balustrades, and more oil painting portraits of noble aristocrats watching down on them from afar. The carpet on the stairs was blood red and the scene looked like something out of a setting for Shakespeare's *Hamlet*.

"What's up there?" Zoey asked. "Can we go up there?"

"We can go anywhere we want," Manson said, leading her up the stairs.

When they got to the top it seemed like they were at such a height that to fall would be lethal, hitting the marble floors below would break bones, and there was a pleasant aroma in the air of incense, and old books, like a library, and musty old leather. There were statues and figurines placed in strategic nooks and crannies, a bust of Pallas and Athena and Pericles, a family crest hanging prominently at the center of the ceiling above the stairs, and a real armored knight standing at attention, complete with helmet, a shield, and long ax. The knight stood fast, looking ahead, paying no attention to the explorers.

"It's a knight in shining armor," Zoey said, wanting to reach out and touch it. "I never thought in my life that I would be in a castle like this. It's amazing . . . and spooky."

Manson led her down the hallway and they found a double door at the end. Their curiosity was getting the better of them now.

"I wonder what is behind those doors?" Manson asked, pulling her along behind him.

"I'm not sure I want to find out."

"Where is your sense of adventure?"

They stopped in front of the doors and Manson tried the doorknob. It was unlocked. He looked at Zoey and she shook her head.

"No. I don't want to go in there."

"It's too late now," Manson said, twisting the knob and pushing the door open. "We've come this far . . . why turn back now."

"I think I need a drink."

"There is a bar downstairs," Manson said. "We can stop there on the way out."

"Sounds good to me."

Inside the room they were greeted by the smell of ancient catacombs and funeral flowers and incense. It was the smell of primeval graveyards and wildflowers growing in a swamp. It was earthy, sweet, enticing, and strange. It was a chamber, there was a hardwood writing desk and lamp, more paintings on the walls, a chiffonier and a wardrobe both constructed of antique hardwood, and there were dressers and mirrors, but no bed. In the middle of the room, beneath a large chandelier, was a stand with stout wooden legs, ornately carved from ebony and inlayed with alabaster, and on top was the most unexpected sight.

"What is that?" Zoey asked, pointing to the stand.

"I think it's a . . ." Manson was stunned, ". . . I'm not sure I believe what I am seeing."

"It looks like a coffin," Zoey said.

"It sure does."

On the top of the stand was an ornately decorated coffin with hardwood and gold trim. The lid was raised and on the inside was plush, purple satin lining and a pillow. On the pillow they could see a few stray hairs of golden color that were obviously from Stephanie, an indentation in the pillow where she had lain her head.

"She has a coffin?" Zoey asked, raising her eyebrows.

"It looks that way," Manson said. "It all makes sense. Why wouldn't she have a coffin?"

They thought about this for a moment and it became crystal clear that they were dealing with a vampire.

"It's true, then," Manson said, rubbing his neck and feeling the holes where he had been bitten. It was strangely arousing to think about it. "I don't know . . ."

"I do," Zoey said. "We are cursed now."

Behind them, without warning, William, the butler, appeared and cleared his throat, startling them.

"I say," William said, eyeing them sternly. "I see you have found the quarters of the Countess Dascălu . . ."

"What does this mean?" Manson asked, turning, and looking at William. "She sleeps in a coffin?"

"I imagine this is shocking for you," William said. "You have much to learn. You should not be in here."

"We want answers," Zoey said. "We've been bitten and told that we were turned into vampires and now we want to know the truth."

"The truth is a twisted tail," William said, sighing. "Suffice it to say that . . . yes, you are now vampires. Your lives will change forever, after this. You must stay here and let the Countess teach you the ways you must know."

"What if we don't want to?" Zoey said. "I did not ask for this."

"It's going to be alright," William said. "You will come to know a new life that will be so much more than you are used to."

"Are you . . . are you one of them?" Manson asked.

"Truthfully, I am not," William said. "I must keep the estate functioning and do things that require mortal blood. I have considered the transformation . . . but for now it is in my better interest to remain normal."

"Normal?" Zoey quizzed. "Is that what you call it? We are abnormal now?"

"Relax, young lady," William said. "You will appreciate this . . . I promise you. The Countess has longed for a family for quite some time . . . and the fact that she has chosen you two is an honor. You should be grateful."

"It was against our will," Zoey said.

"I'm don't mind, really," Manson said, at last. "I think I'm going to like it. I've always been considered a dark and gloomy freak, anyway. I might as well go all the way . . . being a vampire seems kind of like my destiny."

"Speak for yourself," Zoey said. "I'm into the whole Goth thing . . . but a vampire? Are serious."

"As serious as a heart attack," William said. "The Countess is from a long lineage of vampires in the old country of Hungary. She lived there in a small town when she was a child, and the stories you have heard about the vampires of old are all true. Don't fight it. Just go with it. It's too late to turn back now."

"I need that drink now," Zoey said.

"Follow me down to the bar and I will make you anything you desire," William said.

"Consider it done," Manson said.

They turned to leave, casting one last glance at the coffin on the stand in the room. It was eerie and unbelievable, but now they were convinced of the truth. They had been converted into vampires bay an elder vampire known as the Countess Dascălu who had immigrated from Hungary in a previous century, and now they were her proteges.

They left the chamber and the coffin behind and went down the stairs to the bar. William fixed them both double shots of Chivas Regal in crystal glasses and they drank deeply, requiring more liquor to deaden the pain in their throbbing necks from the vampire bites and the harsh reality of what had become of them, seemingly overnight.

11

It was midnight before Manson and Zoey left the mansion. Unsure, they were afraid to go out in the daylight, so they waited until after dark. They left the mansion in one of Stephanie's personal limousine, trembling in fear and loathing at what they had been told.

This is not be happening for real, was it? They both wondered the same thing. This was all too confusing and overwhelming. Did they even believe in vampires, really? Could it be true, the myth, the legend, the curse?

"Do you really believe all that vampire nonsense?" Zoey asked, looking at Manson intently. "She made it all sound so . . . real. I don't know if I believe her, or not."

"I don't know," he said, looking back and meeting her gaze. "I love the legend and myth of vampires. Wouldn't it be cool if it was true? I mean, Dracula is one of my all-time favorite horror novels. Vampires could be real, I guess. Who knows for sure? Anything is possible."

"No. I'm serious," she said. "Do you believe that Stephanie has turned *us* into vampires?"

"I think *she* believes it is true," he said, turning the steering wheel sharply and heading out on the highway. "Do I believe it's true? Maybe. I know I've got bite marks on my neck that look suspiciously like a vampire's bite. That much is true. I feel different, somehow . . . alive, revigorated, excited."

They both felt it: a tingling sensation, a longing and lustfulness that emanated from their inner being, and a sexual arousal that was invigorating. They were extremely aroused, even more so than normal, and it was growing stronger by degrees. They would have to fuck soon, because it was becoming unbearable.

"Yes. But, shouldn't we be upset by all of this?" Zoey asked. "I mean, she drugged us and abused us while we were unconscious. Are we supposed to forgive her for that?"

"I'm not too worried about that," Manson said, shrugging. "After all, if you want to play you have to pay. We asked for it, in a manner of speaking. We are no angels, you know?"

"That doesn't mean we deserved to be taken advantage of," she said, crossing her arms.

"I'm not too butt hurt by all of this," he said. "I kind of liked the whole experience . . . although I could have gone without the roofy. I've got a splitting headache from that stuff."

"It's a date rape drug," she said. "That's illegal. Shouldn't we report her to the authorities?"

"No. Absolutely not," Manson said, resolutely. "I don't agree with it. But, I like her, for some reason. I want to stay with her . . . and with you. We can have so much fun. She's a cougar, and wealthy, too. That doesn't appeal to you?"

"You are a gigolo," she said, hitting him on the shoulder. "Just an incorrigible swinging dick."

He looked at her and grinned, waggling his eyebrows, a favorite facial expression and tick for him, and showed his teeth, which were now taking on the appearance of sharp fangs. "I do resemble that remark."

"Your teeth," she said, noticing his fangs. "They are sharp . . . like fangs."

"What?" he asked, snatching a quick glance in the mirror and grinning, examining his teeth. They were indeed sharp and pointy. "Holy shit. They are . . . like fangs. Damn it. That's new."

"Are mine like that, too?" she asked, showing her teeth to him.

"They are looking very sharp," he said, surprised. "Maybe there is something to this vampire thing, after all."

"That explains the painful bright light this morning," Zoey said. "I thought it was just a hangover . . . but the light was excruciating."

"I noticed that too," he said. "And our reflections in the mirror . . ."

"Come to my apartment," Manson said. "I will get my car and drive you to wherever you need to go."

"Okay," Zoey said, softly. "I trust you."

Manson and Zoey returned to his apartment and he quickly gathered some clothing and essential items in a duffel bag and placed it in the black Monte Carlo. He took Zoey home, although she did not want to go there because she despised her stepfather, and she managed to gather some belongings and make a hasty escape. She never wanted to return there ever again in her life.

They got into the black Monte Carlo and raced away with the engine rumbling and roaring into the night like a beast.

12

Manson and Zoey went back to the castle and stayed with Stephanie for quite some time after the transformation. She was like a mother to them. They did not know much about this mysterious woman of wealth and means, but she was accommodating and her lavish lifestyle full of drugs, booze, and sex was alluring enough to make them stick around. They loved Crandall to death, and they loved the sex with one another. It was a match made in heaven.

"Will we be able to stay here forever?" Manson asked, looking at Zoey.

"I don't know," she said. "What do you mean."

"Do you think she will grow tired of us?"

"Maybe," she said, "but how should I know. She seems to love us right now."

"I know. But what happens when she gets bored with us?"

"I guess we'll have to deal with that when the time comes."

"What about Crandall? What will he do if she kicks him out?"

"He can come ride with us."

"Ride?"

"Yes. Ride. We are riders on the storm. We basically live in my car, so he can have the backseat. We will be death riding darkly, the three of us, terrorizing the innocent and drinking their blood for sport."

"You are taking to this vampire thing naturally, aren't you?"

"I think so," Manson said, rubbing his lips with his fingertips.

"We should just roll with it," Zoey said, patting him on the shoulder. "Que sera sera. Whatever will be will be. You know . . . we can't predict the future."

"Or can we?"

"What do you mean?"

"Don't we have Tarot cards? Are we not supernatural beings now? I mean, if we are vampires—and I'm pretty sure we are—then we should have all kinds of special powers. At least from what I know of them . . . they can do many powerful things."

"Don't get carried away, man," she said, "because you might get a big head and float away into the clouds."

As they were talking, Stephanie pulled up in front of the castle in her Jaguar. They could see her through the picture window, illuminated by the porchlight, as she got out of the car and gathered up some shopping bags from a trip of evening shopping down on Robson Street. William, the butler, opened the door.

"Good evening, Madam," he said. He took the bags out of her hands.

She came in through the front door and took off her coat, handing it to him, and then straightening her clothing and hair as she went into the living room where Manson and Zoey were sitting and watching TV on the curved screen.

"Hello, my most beloved house guests," she said.

"Hi," Zoey said.

"Hello to you, too," Manson said. "How was the shopping

trip?"

"Fabulous, and invigorating," she said, plopping down on the loveseat. "I do love spending money."

"Me too," Zoey said. "But I don't have much to spend, unfortunately."

"I can give you money," Stephanie said. "I have plenty to go around."

"I wouldn't feel right taking—"

"Perish the thought, dear," Stephanie said, waving her hand. "I would be insulted otherwise. Just take one of my credit cards and you kids can go out on the town and treat yourselves to something nice."

"I'm down," Manson said. He sat up, grinning. "You don't have to tell me twice."

William stood by with his nose raised high, ignoring the conversation, looking off into the distance at something that interested only him.

"That is a lovely gesture," Zoey said. "Maybe we will take you up on it."

Manson agreed.

"Okay, well then," Stephanie said, standing up. "It is time for drinks and a chance to powder up our noses, don't you think?"

"Indeed," Manson said, standing up as well.

Zoey stood up and followed them into the dining area and they all sat down at the bar and got drunk. The snorted a few lines of cocaine. The smoked some marijuana.

Crandall must have smelled the skunky ganja because he appeared like a phantom out of nowhere and strolled up to the bar.

"Mind if I join you?" he asked.

"No. Please. Be my guest," Stephanie said. "I was thinking

about you last night, but you were gone. I missed you so. I was in need of your strong hands and hard dick to keep me occupied."

Crandall blushed and grinned, looking away embarrassed. "Sorry. I was preoccupied."

"No worries," she said. "We can make up for lost time to-night."

"Certainly," he said. He sat down and had a drink, snorted a line, and took a toke off of a joint.

The next thing you know . . . the four of them were naked and fucking on the sofa, tangled in arms, legs, smothered in tits and vaginas, and deeply penetrated by dicks and balls.

What a wonderful way to end the night, they all agreed.

13

It became a regular habit for them to go out at night and go to clubs and drink and live the high life of sex, drugs, and music, in high fashion and glamor. They were known by the regulars and were trendsetters on the club scene. It got to be a habit. They loved the nightlife. The loved to boogie. They loved to go back to the castle and fuck one another's brains out. This was going to be a great and wonderful life, if it never came to an end, but as with all things good, eventually it does come to an end, just like the wildwood flower in the song by Jim Staf-ford, as their lives were merely the equivalent of the Wildwood Weed . . . soon it would come to an inevitable end, and they all knew it was a fact, but pretended not to notice.

CHAPTER EIGHT

1

Manson, Zoey, and Crandall discovered that they shared a common history of being used and abused by sick and twisted adults with mental disorders that led them to be abusive; however, there was no excuse for a grown man taking advantage of a child in such a fashion, and they all would fight to the finish should they be confronted by such an individual again. They had overcome tragedy from the past and they made a perfect match. They accepted their histories and looked past the sexual abuse bestowed by figures of authority and control. It would not define them. They would be their own glorious entities and aspire to greatness, regardless of what the world had done to them. Sex had become power, and power begets abuse, and corruption follows suit. Although they had experienced sexual abuse early in life, it had the effect of making them into sexual creatures, allowing them to utilize their looks and bodies to control others, for right or wrong, it is just how they learned to navigate through the world of corruption and vice. Sex was a powerful method of control, and Manson and Zoey knew how to work it well.

2

When Manson was a little boy, his neighbor, a black man named Sambo Reems who was a pimp and a player, attempted to molested him and he had tricked Manson into coming over to his house for some candy. Despite all the warnings his parents had given him about accepting candy from a stranger, he did not think of Sambo as a stranger. He trusted the man, and that is how he ended up getting sodomized and molested completely one sunny afternoon in June. Sambo said he had some gumdrops and bubblegum and licorice whips and Manson could come over and have as much as he wanted. He was excited and looking forward to having some candy. When he got inside the house next door, Sambo locked the doors, and stood looking at Manson. Sambo said they were going to play a little game, and it required them to strip down to their underwear. Manson was not sure about this game, but he did not see how it could hurt anything. He just wanted some candy. The next thing Manson knew, Sambo was holding his big black dick and waggling it back and forth. It looked like a summer sausage.

He gripped his penis in his hand and said, "Why don't you come over here and suck it?"

Manson as dumbstruck and confused; he was not sure what to do. Should he run, scream, stay and play the game? He had no idea, other than it was just weird and scary.

"What . . . er . . . are you doing?"

"I'll give you some quarters from my change jar, too," Sambo said, making a promise. He pointed to the jar he kept over the stove on a shelf. He let go of his protruding member and walked, wang wagging, across the kitchen and took it down and showed it to Manson; there must have been twenty dollars in change in there.

What do you think?"

Manson did not think he would play the game again, ever; there was no amount of candy worth this; he wanted to leave and get away from this weird old black man immediately. It was not until he was much older that he figured out that this was a bad thing and he started sticking up for himself. Now, he would kick someone's ass for doing such a thing, but when he was a kid he was easily tricked and turned into a victim.

"I think I am going to go home now," Manson said. "I don't like this. You are a bad man."

"But . . . what about the candy? What about the quarters? Don't you want them?"

"No!" Manson said, firmly. "I don't want nothing. Just let me out of here, now!"

"Fine," Sambo said. "Suit yourself. I'm going to tell your parents you have been a bad boy."

"I don't care," Manson said. "You can tell them, if you want. I'm going to tell them what you did."

Sambo was not happy to hear this; he thought about abducting the boy and locking him in the basement.

"You don't want to do that," Sambo said. "You want to be quiet. You hear? Don't tell anyone about this . . . and I'll let you go. Okay?"

"Okay," Manson said. "I won't tell. Just let me go, now."

Sambo hesitated, pulling on his trousers and zipping up his pants. He tightened his belt and buttoned up his shirt. He smoothed out his hair with his hands, tucking in his shirt to try and look presentable, and then he went to the door and unlocked the deadbolt, and opened the door. There were kids playing in the street outside, a car horn honked loudly as it slammed on the breaks to avoid running the children over. Someone screamed with giddy glee. It was a fine summer day, and Manson could see his escape route right before his eyes.

"Don't you come back here telling anyone lies about me," Sambo said. "You hear, boy? I ain't about to tolerate no lying little shit trying to get me in trouble."

"I am leaving now," Manson said, stepping closer to the door.

"Remember," Sambo said. "Keep this as our little secret."

"Whatever," Manson said. "I don't care. Goodbye."

Manson stormed past Sambo and sprinted out through the door and down the steps. He was running by the time he reached the sidewalk, and he did not look back until he was safely on his porch. Sambo was watching him, a distrustful look in his eyes.

Manson took on last look at the lecherous old black man and then opened the front door and went inside, shutting the door behind himself and locking it tight. This was a terrible turn of events and he just wanted to make it go away. He went into the kitchen and sat down at the table. He needed time to think. Eventually he calmed down, and after a time the memory of the incident faded away, but it changed him forever, and he often wondered what kind of a human being he would have become if he had been molested that day. He narrowly escaped a terrible sexual encounter and he was relieved. Years later he would realize that it was frightening to think about what could have happened. It made no difference, now after so many years had passed, he thought, because he was comfortable with who he was and did not let the past control the present. He was a peace with his past and wiser, too, as a result.

Shortly after the sexual encounter, Sambo, the hustler pimp, ended up getting murdered by some gangsters who shot him in the face during a robbery. Manson was not sad about it. He was not happy, either, but he did not miss the dirty old black man who used to live next door.

Manson had taken on a dark persona after that, and he started wearing gloomy outfits with black leather jacket, denim jeans, and boots, a nose, lip, and tongue piercing, black makeup and painted fingernails.

3

When she was a child, she had a similar incident to Manson, but her sexual encounter involved her stepfather. One day, when Zoey was home alone—the rest of the family were out shopping for cloths and groceries and she had stayed home to catch up on some homework for school sitting at the kitchen table, when Robert came home from work. He instantly went into the kitchen and opened a beer. He took a shot of Old Crow whiskey straight from the bottle and then another, washing it down with more beer.

"Hello there beautiful," he said, looking at her with a sinister grin.

She did not reply. She knew he was a pervert; she just did not know how to explain it.

"You too good to talk to your dear old stepdad?"

"No," she said. "I'm doing my homework."

Robert stood in front of her, staring down at her, a towering figure, looming menacingly. He was holding a bottle of beer, silently observing her.

She grew uncomfortable, putting down her pencil and looking up at him.

"What?" she said, finally.

"I'm just watching you," he said.

"Why?"

"Because you are very pretty," he said. "Do you know that?"

154

"Leave me alone," she said. "You're grossing me out."

He reached down and stroked her hair, petting her like a cat.

"Don't touch me," she said, pushing her chair back from the table. She slapped his hands away, cringing in disgust. "I'm going to tell mom about this."

"No. You won't," Robert said. "There is nothing to tell. I am not doing anything wrong."

"Yes. You are," she said. "You are bothering me."

Robert set his beer down on the table.

"Are you sassing me, you little bitch?"

"Leave. Me. Alone," Zoey said, sternly. "Just go away. I'm trying to do my homework."

"I'm going to teach you a lesson," Robert said. "You need to learn to respect your elders. I pay the rent in this house, and you are under my roof. You belong to me."

"I don't belong to anyone," Zoey said.

"Oh, you are so wrong," Robert said. He reached down and grabbed her by the back of her neck, clutching a handful of her hair. "You listen here, you little cunt. I make the rules. You do as I say. Don't fucking test me. You hear?"

"Please don't hurt me," she said, looking up at him in fear.

"It's too late now, little lady," Robert said. "I'm going to show you something you will never forget."

"No. Don't," she said, struggling to get away.

"Come here," Robert said. He picked her up easily and slammed her down on the kitchen table. Her books and pencils and paper slid off the table and crashed to the kitchen floor.

She screamed at the top of her lungs, pleading for him to stop.

He pulled her dress up and exposed her naked body beneath. He ripped her panties off savagely, leaving her exposed. Unbuttoning his pants, he put his hand over her mouth, and took out his manhood.

She bit his fingers.

"Ouch, fucking bitch," he said, slapping her across the face. "Now you will pay for that."

He thrust his erection forward and penetrated her violently.

It was a horrific and terrible event as he thrust himself into her, violating her innocence and stealing her childhood, ripping and tearing her vagina and drawing blood and inflicting excruciating pain. He pleasured himself and erupted in a climax, his face a twisted agony of orgasm and guilt, rage and hatred, rape and violation. He knew that what he was doing was completely wrong, an atrocity, but his violent nature and narcissistic tendencies far outweighed his sense of right and wrong. His stiff dick had no conscience, and the need to get off was the strongest desire he understood. He was a typical asshole who lived next door to everyone and inflicted this kind of crime on the weak and weary every day around the world; he would then go about his business as though nothing had happened. People respected him and he was considered a pillar of the community, but behind closed doors he was the real monster. They lurk among us, real, tangible, and waiting to prey on their next victim. These are the vampires that need to be hunted and executed—they represent a very real evil, a manifestation of all that is wrong with society today, and they should be put to death, never suffered to live.

When it was over, Robert zipped his pants and buttoned his pants. He was satisfied for the time being. He went to the refrigerator and grabbed another bottle of beer. He twisted the cap, flipped it between his fingers sending it ricocheting across the kitchen, and took a long drink. He burped and sighed contently.

Zoey was quivering and crying on the table. She had no idea

what to do now. She was in complete shock and terror, her mind full of guilt and shame. She felt as though it had been her fault. Her mother would believe Robert, she was sure, and there would be punishment after the fact. She wanted to run away from home and never come back. Never, ever, never come back, she thought.

"Keep your mouth shut about his," Robert said. "If I find out you told your mom I will kill you. You understand me?"

Zoey nodded, sniveling and crying, wiping a bubble of snot from her nose. She was too scared and shocked to do anything other than cower on the table.

"Do. You. Hear. Me. Bitch?"

"Yes," Zoey said. "Just leave me a—a—alone."

"Good. Get out of my sight."

She picked herself up from the table and got to her feet. She wasted no time gathering up her things and leaving the kitchen. She wanted to get as far away from this monster as possible. She would go hide in her bedroom and cry. That was all she could do now, is cry and wonder why this happened to her.

Many years later she would look back on this incident and understand why men were pigs. Presently she was not a misandrist, but she despised assholes and arrogant pricks who were chauvinists and misogynists. If a man treated her like a sexual object, called her baby doll or sweetie, or trivialized her as a possession, she would get furious. What you give is what you get, she reasoned, and if a man was a piece of shit then he deserved to be treated as such.

4

Crandall experienced abuse at the hands of a Catholic priest ... when he was a choir boy and an altar boy in the beginning, way back when he lived at home and was forced to attend Sunday school at the Catholic church.

Every Sunday, his family attended mass, and he would go early and don the robe and attend the priest, Father Donald Price, during the ceremony of the mass. He would hold the golden platter as they served up holy wafers and wine during communion for the congregation. As he was sitting next to the alter in the hard-wooden chairs he would look out on the assembly, see his mother and father and siblings sitting in the penultimate row at the front, stern and reverent looks on their faces. They were devout Christians, and this was serious business. He tried not to make eye contact with the parishioners and kept a solemn expression, remaining detached and holy at the head of the church beneath the tableau of the crucifixion scene on Golgotha. Jesus was hanging from the cross in full detail with nails in his hands and feet, and blood dripping from the wound in his side, the crown of thorns on his head. The icons and construction of the temple behind him was gaudy craftsmanship, and the statues that sat below, Mother Marry, the Saints: Peter, Anthony, Paul, and Christopher.

The smell of candles and incense, and pledge wood polish from the pews, and something else, and old building with musty hymnal books and bibles with moldering pages. The stained-glass windows showing biblical scenes in vivid colors of blue, red, green, purple, white, and yellow, and the pipe organ stacks dominating an entire wall. The sound of the organ on Sundays was magnificent and the organist had been with the church for over fifty years, and she was classically trained and could belt out come classics that were every bit as impressive as anything by Bach, Beethoven, or Mozart. It reminded Chandler of the funerals whenever he heard the music. He had attended too many funerals and it as becoming a habit.

The priest had got him alone, asking him if he could stay for the afternoon and help out with some chores. Since the priest had caught Crandall pilfering dollar bills from the tithing box one day, it gave him some leverage, and he threatened to tell his parents what a bad boy he had been unless he obeyed his every command. Crandall did not want his parents to find out about the petty theft from their coveted church because that would have meant he was going to Hell and his mother would never let him live that down. It was easier to just go along with Father Price and keep him happy. Until it got out of control one day, as they were cleaning up the church and moving some boxes to storage in the basement, things got rather risqué and steamy. Father price brushed up against Crandall as he was bending over to pick up a heavy box and he could feel his bulging erection through the robe, pushing forcefully between his buttocks. For an older gentleman he had an extremely rock-solid cock, Crandall remembered.

"Oh, excuse me," Father Price said. "I believe something has popped up and made a statement."

Crandall was instantly uncomfortable, but did not want to go against the grain, so he giggled and brushed it off as just a coincidence. Maybe the old man was always walking around sporting wood like that. He probably played with his boner under the robe all the time, because that seemed appropriate, considering the tradition and reputation Catholic priests had nowadays.

The situation got worse by degrees. Father price pushed forward, grabbed Crandall by the waste with both hands, and began to dry hump him like a rutting mule.

"What are you doing?" Crandall asked, attempting to get away.

Father price had him by the beltloops and was holding on tight, still humping.

"Why don't you drop your drawers?" Father Price suggested. "If you don't . . . I'll tell your parents about the money you stole from the church. They won't like hearing about that, I'm sure."

Crandall knew this was wrong. He did not want anything to do with it. He also did not want his parents to find out about the theft from the church.

Father Price reached around and fondled Crandall's crotch, grabbing his cock and balls and rubbing them gently. He leaned forward and breathed in Crandall's ear, whispering to him, begging him to just go with the flow and let him have his way. It was going to be alright. He would be forgiven. He would tell God to forgive him for stealing the money.

Father Price was an expert, he had done this before, Crandall could tell, because he quickly had the buttons on his pants unfastened and the zipper down, reaching into his underwear and making purchase on his family jewels.

"That's a nice cock," Father Price said. "Maybe later you'll let me suck it."

Crandall cringed. This was disgusting. There was no one around to call for help. They were alone. He did not know what to do, run, fight, or just go with it and submit to the lecherous old man's whims. In the end, Crandall caved in and let the priest have his way with him. He dropped his pants down to his knees and the priest raised his robe and eased his erect penis in between the butt cheeks and found the anus, penetrating and plunging deep, his tongue sticking from the corner of his mouth and his face an expression of exquisite pleasure. He had sodomized other altar boys in the past, and this was a regular thing for him. Crandall, on the other hand, had never been molested and felt guilt oozing from every pore.

The incident did not last long, for Father Price was excited and reached climax quickly, only after a dozen pumps, and he pulled out and let his semen squirt on Crandall's ass, running down his legs and dripping on the carpet.

"Oh, yes," Father Price said. "That was divine. You will be handsomely rewarded for that."

Crandall pulled up his pants, feeling the wet cum in his underwear and cringing at the thought. He felt terrible. Just terrible. Why had he let this happen?

"Can I go home now?" Crandall asked, unable to look the priest directly in the eyes.

"Yes. But keep this a secret between you and me. Okay? Promise?"

Crandall nodded in agreement. He did not plan on ever telling anybody about this. Ever. Never. He was taking this to the grave, and hopefully he would not burn in Hell for it afterward.

He hurried out of the church building and rode his bike home, in a hurry to take a shower and wash away the dirty grim that was oozing from within. He was disgusted with himself, with the priest, with the church, with God, with his parents for making him part of this church, for being alive and mistreated by a trusted adult. He felt violated. It sucked and he was disappointed in all humanity after that. He might never recover.

Later, when him other forced him to go to the confessional, he was greeted by the familiar smells of the church—every time he went to church, after that he was reminded of and filled with haunting memories of the sexual abuse—and he went into the booth and spoke with the Father Price, thinking bad thoughts about what had happened that day. The priest was pervert and had the audacity to sit on the other side of the screen and speak to him as though nothing had happened.

"Forgive me Father, for I have sinned," Crandall said, thinking deeply about what he had done wrong in life. "I took money from the church tithing box. Can I be forgiven?"

"Yes. You are forgiven," the priest said. "The good Lord sees all and knows all, so before you were born, he died for your salvation. Just believe and you will be saved. Confess your sins in his name."

"Can I still go to Heaven?"

"All who believe will inherit the kingdom of Heaven," the priest said. "Bless you, my son, say three hail marries, the lord's prayer. Now have a wonderful day." He slid the panel shut and was gone, sitting isolated in the booth, waiting for the next sinner to step in and spill their guts in hope of forgiveness.

Crandall sat there for a moment, reflecting on what he had been told, thinking: *Bless you my son, say a prayer, go to church, and then suck my heavenly cock, and you will be forgiven. Amen.* He stood up, left the confessional booth and walked out of the church, still thinking about the incident where he had lost his innocence. *Fucking bullshit,* he thought. *Maybe someday I'll burn this fucking church to the ground. Fucking hypocrites. This is the biggest bunch of shit I've ever see in my life. When I grow up and move out on my own, I'm never going to church again.*

This was a promise he intended to keep.

5

Manson and Zoey and Crandall decided that they would get back at the lecherous perverts of the world and teach them a lesson. They would seek revenge on the assholes of the world for molesting them and other innocent victims. It was all over the news nowadays. The assholes needed to be stopped, including the Catholic priests, Boy Scout leaders, schoolteachers, and anyone else who thought it was acceptable to molest children or rape unwilling humans, period. It was a crime that was deserving of death.

They agreed that any time they discovered one of these per-verts they would take them out in a particularly grizzly and hideous fashion. It would involve castration and stuffing the offending member down their throat and eviscerating them and eating their heart and brains and leaving them in a pile of steaming blood and offal. This was what they planned to do from now on.

They drove around town and preyed on the nightlife, pick-ing out victims, and drinking their blood and eating the flesh.

This was becoming a regular routine. They would leave the mansion and go out and party. It always ended in a bloody romp and pillaging prey.

6

The trio of vampires and a werewolf raced down the Inter-state with death as their avatar. Manson smelled of mint breath drops, Old Spice, and beer. Zoey smelled of fresh Ivory soap, lilacs, chocolate, wintergreen Tic Tacs, and menthol cigarettes. Crandall smelled of licorice, Dial soap, and Sauvage cologne. They were beautiful and deadly and anyone crossing their path might become a delectable treat to eat and end life in a blood bath, ripped apart by tooth and nail.

There was time to chat during the long drives on the high-ways, byways, and backstreets, and they shared much about their past lives, their dreams, their ambitions inside the con-fines of the black Monte Carlo.

Crandall had an interesting story to tell.

After he met Manson and Zoey, he told them something he had never divulged about his desire to be a screenplay writer and perhaps someday a movie director and even a producer.

He wanted to follow in Stephen Spielberg's footsteps, after all, and that was what he intended to do, someday.

"What about the curse?" Manson asked him. "Can you still be all of that and a werewolf too?"

"I don't see why not," Crandall said. "Do you think you can be a rock star musician and a vampire, too?"

"Touché," Manson said, frowning. "I think so. Who has to know the finer details? That's not important. Sinister Fiend will be a household name someday, you wait and see."

"I think it's a great idea," Zoey said, resting her chin on Manson shoulder. "You both should follow your dreams. I wanted to be a tattoo artist . . . maybe I will still do it."

"Can we get free tattoos?" Manson asked.

"Of course," she said, smiling. "I will give you one right now, if you want."

"I've always wanted a dragon tattoo," Crandall said. "When are you going to start your own shop? You could go into business for yourself, you know."

"I don't know, yet," Zoey said, lighting a cigarette. "But I will figure it out someday. I'm still young. I have plenty of time to get started."

"Well, I know this much," Crandall said, flipping through the pages of his movie script. "I am going to go to California someday and visit some directors in Hollywood and pitch this script. That is my destiny."

"That sounds like fun," Zoey said. "I've always wanted to go to Hollywood. We could go with you. Couldn't we, Manson. We could make it into a road trip."

"Let's do it," Manson said. "We'll make plans and go on a road trip. My car will make an excellent coach for the trip."

It was done then. They were going to Hollywood. They just did not have a date set yet. They were still in the control of

Stephanie and they would have to break the news to her that they intended to leave Canada and go to the United States of America, maybe never coming back. They knew that Stephanie would not take the news well because she simply doted on their company and loved the three of them like her own children, despite her wickedly evil streak of vampirism that possessed her with certain demonic spirits at times. They still loved her, despite her manic mood swings.

7

Manson carried his Martin D35 acoustic guitar with him everywhere he went. He worked on his songs and intended to record most of them at the studio when he got a chance. His band, Sinister Fiend, was going to be a smashing success once they cut the first record. He just knew it. The other guys in the band were down with making a record and they planned on independently releasing it on the Internet, selling songs for ninety-nine cents per song. It was the way it was done nowadays and, to tell the truth, Manson did not care about the money. He just wanted to get the music out to the public.

Whenever he had a spare moment, Manson would take out the guitar and strum chords and play riffs, picking leads and melodies that sounded delightful and pleasing. He liked all kinds of music, and even the blues sometimes, but more often than not he found himself entranced by the Grunge musicians from the Pacific Northwest during the 1990s with famous stars like Kurt Cobain, Chris Cornell, Jerry Cantrell and Lane Staley, Eddie Vedder, and recently David Grohl. He liked other bands that had more sinister sounds like Korn, Marylin Manson, Slayer, King Diamond, Megadeth, and Type O Negative, but his heart was stuck on the soggy sound of the rainy-day musicians from Seattle. They were his inspiration, although his own music sounded very little like the three chord thrumming dirges pumped out by the Grunge bands. It was just the movement itself that entranced him. The grunge music changed the face of music and single handedly destroyed hair metal.

CHAPTER NINE

1

Manson and Zoey were at Golden Bean Coffee Shop where she worked one night during her shift as a barista, and they crossed paths with Adrian Burgendorv. He was enjoying a Cappuccino at a table, engrossed in his laptop, blissful and unaware of the presence of the two vampires. He stretched and yawned as Zoey passed by with two cups of hot coffee in her hands, unintentionally bumping into her and causing her to spill the hot beverages directly on his crotch and on the table across his laptop, burning his privates as the scorching brew soaked into his jeans, and threatening to destroy his expensive computer.

"Holy shit," Adrian said, jumping up and fanning his crotch. "You've spilled it on my balls."

"I'm so sorry," Zoey said. She took a towel and blotted his wet pants, which would have been arousing under any other circumstances.

He snatched the towel away from her and blotted himself with it.

"You stupid, twit," he said. "You've burned me. I want to

speak to your manager."

"I'm sorry," Zoey apologized again.

Manson was on the verge of bursting into uncontrollable laughter. He knew that burning your cock with hot coffee had to be excruciating, and he was indulging in some delightful schadenfreude.

Adrian picked up his laptop and shook the wet coffee off the keyboard, using the towel to dry the sensitive electronic device.

"You've killed my computer, too," Adrian said. "I demand to speak to your manager."

He closely inspected the laptop for any damage and that is when he noticed something strange on the LCD screen. The barista had no reflection. He looked at it for a moment and let the new input sink into his mind. What could that mean? He wondered. He looked closely, moving the screen to see if it was an illusion of light, but it was not. The guy dressed in Goth outfit sitting at the table next to them did not have a reflection either. This could mean only one thing: they were vampires.

Manson giggled and squealed with glee. He had to bite his fist to contain his laughter. Zoey looked back at him and scowled, raising her eyebrows and silently letting him know that he was making this worse.

"I'll get my manager," Zoey said. "Are you okay?"

"No. I am not okay," Adrian said. He reached into his pocket and pulled out a small mirror he kept for such occasions. He held it to his face and looked at her reflection; he was convinced now, of what he suspected. She had no reflection, neither did the laughing Goth goofball sitting next to her.

Suddenly, with absolute certainty, he was fully aware that they were vampire and was now alerted to their presence.

He knew that he would be required to make further investigations to determine if they truly were vampires. He would stalk these two now that they were on his radar, and he would perform various tests he conducted without them being aware. He knew what they were, already, and he was now on their trail. He noticed that they did not cast from the overhead lights either. This was the beginning of the end for these vampires, and Adrian vowed to put them to a quick and decisive end. He was a vampire hunter, after all, and this was what he lived for, tracking the hideously foul undead creatures to the end of the earth.

The manager, Terry Kent, a tall and skinny man of thirty years with greasy black hair slicked back over his scalp on a small and misshapen skull on a slim pencil neck with a large Adam's apple, clad in horned rimmed glasses with thick lenses that made his eyes bulge out like boiled eggs came forward from the back office and confronted Zoey.

"What have you done?" he interrogated her. "You are so careless."

"It was an accident," she said, looking at Terry. "He leaned into me and bumped me—"

"Don't blame me," Adrian said, interrupting. "It was your mistake. You should have been watching were you are going."

"I said I was sorry," Zoey said.

"It was his fault," Manson said, defending Zoey.

"Nobody asked you," Terry said, pushing his glasses up on his nose with his middle finger. "I am sorry, sir, for this mistake. I hope you are not injured. How can we remedy this?"

"Well, you can start by employing some better help," Adrian said. "This girl obviously doesn't like being here and it shows in her demeanor and her attitude."

Zoey raised her eyebrows and pouted in surprise at the unfair statement.

"That's not right," she said.

"Zoey is too good for this place," Manson said, standing up. "I should kick your ass for speaking about her in that tone."

"What you gonna do, pretty boy?" Adrian asked, stepping backward and raising his fists. "I'll take you on any time. In fact, nothing would please me more than to kick your ass right now. I know what you are . . ."

Manson and Zoey looked at each other, slightly confused, then understanding what he meant.

"Fuck you," Manson said. "I don't care what you think."

Terry had heard enough. He pushed Zoey and Manson toward the door. "You two need to leave, now. You are fired. Don't come back here, either."

"Yeah," Manson said, heading toward the door. "Fuck you, too! Zoey is too good for the likes of you."

Adrian shook his fist at them as they exited the building. "I'll be seeing you too real soon. I have other matters to attend to right now, but I will find you and you will regret ever crossing paths with me."

Adrian went to the windows and watched as the Goth couple ventured down the sidewalk and got into a black Monte Carlo parked at the curb. He noted the license plate number and committed it to memory. That was all he needed. He had resources and he would be able to locate the owner of the care with ease.

Terry looked at Adrian and said, "I am truly sorry. I don't know what is wrong with the young people in the world today. They have no manners or morals. Their work ethic is . . . shit. Would you like a free coffee on the house?"

"I need to go and change my clothing," Adrian said. "Get into something dry. I will take on to go, however, if that is not too much to ask."

"No problem," Terry said, going behind the counter. "What

170

were you drinking?"

"Cappuccino."

Terry blended up a fresh cappuccino with coffee and cream and ice in a blender that made a loud grinding and surging sound throughout the coffee shop. The other patrons had watched the entire event transpire. He finished the beverage, put it into a clear to-go cup, and gave it to Adrian, along with a free punch card for ten coffees in the future.

"Please do come back soon," Terry said. "You won't have to worry about them any longer. They are long gone."

"Oh, I intend to see them again, real soon," Adrian said, a distant look in his eyes as he took the free coffee. "Spilling coffee on my crotch was only the beginning of their problems with me."

Terry looked at Adrian confused, and a bit frightened; he was talking like a madman with a crazy look in his eyes.

"Okay," Terry said. "Well you do have a good night."

"I intend to," Adrian said, heading toward the door. "Good-night ladies and gentlemen. I hope you enjoyed the show."

He exited out into the night and went back to his van and drank the cappuccino.

2

Adrian Burgendorv's journal.

September 9, 2019. Vancouver—Came back to my van at 11 p.m. I'm creating this journal entry tonight with much anticipation. Although this may be the rantings of a vampire slayer in the twenty-first century, I dutifully require that anyone reading this take heed. I have located two vampires, a male and female couple, in Vancouver, Canada while drinking a coffee at The Golden Bean Coffee Shop. I was busy researching another case and enjoying a cappuccino when I had the serendipitous good fortune of bumping into a real-life vampire. They are a couple, I believe, a young dark-haired woman and a spirited male, both dark and Gothic in nature. They dress in clothing that speaks of an alternative lifestyle, befitting of a vampire, I might ad. They came to my attention when I noticed that they had no reflection in the mirror and cast no shadow in the light. This was enough to pique my curiosity and focus my attention on them. I began to follow them and found that they also only came out at night. I am sure they are vampires and will pursue them to the end of the earth to finish them, once and for all.

I was staying in a room in the Avalon Motor Hotel on the outskirts of Vancouver, in room 219 and am keeping a close eye on this dynamic duo of evil. Now I am staying in my van and following them, closely, but staying out of sight so they don't become aware of my presences.

They have the appearance of a dark and edgy Goth lifestyle, and it makes me wonder where they have come from and why they are here. I will find out. I am a longtime vampire slayer, from a long lineage of warriors of justice out to rid the world of supernatural evil, and I will prevail. I never fail to kill these foul creatures when I confront them. These two will be no exception.

I have sharpened my wooden stakes, refilled my vials of holy water and ampules of herbs and spice of wolfsbane, lunar caustic, wild rose, hawthorn, elixir of garlic, salt, consecrated earth, holy oil, blood of a virgin, sharpened my Bowie knife and kukri knife, gathered fresh clusters of garlic, a pistol with silver bullets—although this is for werewolves, specifically—and a collection numerous crucifixes and rosary beads. I also have several copies of the Holy Bible in different translations and versions, Hebrew, Greek, English, and Romanian. I am prepared for battle.

What does it take to kill a vampire? Stake through the heart. Cut off the head. Sunlight. Holy Water. This, I will do swiftly, and deliver them to the bowels of Hell, posthaste.

I've done my research and know all about them. Manson Stokes is 22 years old, born in Vancouver, British Columbia on January 10, 1997 and he has lived there all his life. Zoey Lavay is 21 years old, born in Winnipeg, Manitoba, Canada, on August 29, 1998, and she moved to Vancouver when she was twelve, after her father died, when her mother met her stepfather, Robert Dillard.

I have pictures taken from their social pages, and copies of documents pulled from various sources, with vital statistics and relevant information that will be useful in tracking them down and putting them to death. I am closing the gap now. It won't be much longer until I confront them and slay them properly.

I am still researching Stephanie Dascălu, the main vampire, as she is proving much harder to find resources for information in detail about her history and record. I expect to learn about her completely very soon.

3

Adrian looked up the license plate number on a website that provided him with the name of the owner of the car, an address, and he was even able to locate a photograph from a Facebook account that belonged to Manson Stokes who lived in apartment number three in the Manor Heights Apartment Building on 33rd Avenue.

Adrian was already on to Stephanie Dascălu and knew that she was a vampire who existed and lived in the castle outside of the city limits of Vancouver. Finding Manson and Zoey was a bonus. He had already made preparations to kill Stephanie, but now the plot had thickened, and he was going to have more evil beasts to dispose of than he had anticipated. His good fortune was smiling on him and he was glad of such good luck.

Once he found out where they were staying in Vancouver, he was able to track down the lead vampire, Stephanie, the evil countess, and hunt her down. Killing her was easy but getting her to the right place in order to do it proved more difficult.

He stalked her until he knew where to get at her with the greatest ease and as few witnesses as possible. She made regular stops at a parking garage downtown Vancouver and he knew that he could set his tarp according to her schedule. She did something strange and mysterious, even sinister and vile and evil, in the high-rise building in the center of the metropolis.

4

Adrian followed Stephanie as she pulled out in her maroon Jaguar from the castle when she left the to go out for a business trip one night—Manson, Zoey, and Crandall stayed behind.

It appeared that she was going to a meeting or something in a building across town, so Adrian followed her into the parking garage. She took her ticket, and he followed suit. He got a parking ticket and kept close behind her but keeping enough distance to avoid her noticing him. She parked her silver Jaguar and got out, walking across parking lot, and went to the elevator.

Adrian parked his van and waited for her to come back.

5

It took several hours of waiting and he was on the verge of falling asleep when Stephanie reappeared, coming out of the elevator and crossing the parking lot in the garage. He got out of the van and crept stealthily across the expanse of the parking garage. He could hear her high heels clicking on the pavement. She walked fast, dressed in furs and an expensive designer dress. Her hair was pulled back in a tight bun. Her face was smooth and creamy, and she had a ruddy and florid complexion, as though she had just consumed blood. Vampires always get flushed when they feed, gorged after they exsanguinate their victims.

Adrian imagined that she may have found a victim in the

building but could not be sure.

She pushed the button on her key fob and the Jaguar lit up, beeping and activating, unlocking the doors.

Adrian chose that moment to confront her at the Jaguar.

"Tonight, is your last night," Adrian said, stepping out from behind a parked car and making himself visible. "You are a vile creature of the night, and I must destroy you."

"What? Who are you?" she said, looking up at him.

"I am your worst nightmare," he said, approaching her with a crucifix held out in his fist.

She smiled and laughed. "You are my worst nightmare? I think that is the other way around."

"Get thee behind me, Satan," he said. "I will send thee back to the chasm of Hell where you belong."

She looked at the crucifix and shrank back, covering her face with her hands.

Adrian reached into his pocket at took out a vial of holy water, sprinkling her with drops of the liquid. He could hear the water hiss and burn as it touched her flesh, causing blisters on her skin.

"Why are you doing this?" she asked.

"It is my job," he said. "I am here to vanquish you from Earth."

"Your job? You are a vampire hunter?"

"Indeed," he said. "And now I am about to slay you—you foul beast!"

"Good luck with that," she said. Her facial features changed, and she displayed an expression of evil with a wretched and stretched serpentine countenance. Her face was morphing into a snakelike being with monstrously hideous and grotesque proportions. Her eyes were yellow and black, reptilian-like, the pupils becoming elliptical black voids in golden-yellow irises, her nostrils tiny openings, her mouth a slit with sharp and jagged teeth, her skin covered with scales.

"You are a hideous beast," he said, holding out the crucifix again and turning away from her hideous glance.

She turned and stepped toward him on tall and spindly legs, reaching out her claws, the fingernails black and variegated, sharp and hooked like talons.

"I will eat you alive," she said. "You are no match for me, vampire hunter. You do not know with whom you are dealing."

"I know full well," he said. "And I intend to see you brought down and put to death."

Adrian jumped at her with the wooden stake, parried, and dodged a swiping blow from her razor-sharp claws. She was fast and cunning and clever. He had to be careful. She growled and bared her teeth, eyes unblinking, watching, waiting for him to make a mistake.

He jumped back, avoid her sweeping blows, and then plunged at her with the stake and mallet, waiting for her to expose a weak spot.

It did not take long, as she turned and attempted to open the car door, obviously intent on getting in and driving away.

He was not going to let her escape that easy. When she was distracted and opening the door, he lunged forward and stabbed her in the chest with the wooden stake, hitting it hard with the mallet. It sunk into the flesh and pierced directly into her heart. She let out a sickening groan and squeal, hissing and spitting, coughing up blood.

"You've killed me," she said. "Vampire hunter. You have killed me after being alive for three hundred years. What a terrible end to such a long and glorious life."

"I'm sorry for you," he said. "But you do not deserve to live."

"And what gives you the authority to decide?"

"I have been chosen from birth for this duty," he said. "Now you must meet your maker. Goodbye, hideous and foul creature. Back to the land of the dead from whence you came."

He hammered the mallet into the stake one more time and felt it sink all the way into the vampire's flesh. She quivered and shook in the throes of death and fell to the ground. Her countenance changed back to that of a beautiful woman; she was no longer a hideous creature; she was just a vampire who had lived a long time and now was dying. She had lived long enough to create two young vampires named Manson and Zoey—who would soon suffer the same fate, if Adrian had anything to do with it.

Adrian turned and hurried back toward his van to get away before the authorities arrived, leaving her dead corpse in the parking garage to be found later by authorities. He drove out on the street and cruised toward Main Street downtown Vancouver.

6

Detective Ethan Pendergrass, wearing a navy wool sports jacket with suede elbow pads, button up shirt, tie, and chewing on a toothpick. He shook his head and breathed a deep sigh as he looked down at the dead woman sprawled out on the pavement in the parking garage. He looked at the wooden stake in her chest. *Who in the world would murder someone in such a fashion? What is this world coming to?* He wondered.

"What in the hell happened here. . . ?" Ethan said, aloud. He looked away from the corpse lying on the pavement in the parking garage, adjusted his Aviator sunglasses with his index finger. "I would not believe this if I was not seeing it with my own two eyes."

One thing was for certain: Stephanie was dead, and although she had turned into a hideous creature upon confrontation with Adrian, upon death she had reverted back to the attractive enchantress that she had been in life. There was a pool of congealing blood flowing from beneath her fur coat, running in a trail down through the parking lot. Her lips and face were ashen gray and her eyes were wide open, staring up at the ceiling, glazed and covered with a white film.

"What a shame," Ethan said. "She was attractive. Whoever did this must have had a terrible grudge against her. Who does that? Kills someone with a wooden stake. Especially a good-looking lady like that."

"Maybe she was a vampire," Detective Byron Hoffmeier said, coughing abruptly into his hand to hide his sarcasm. He was dressed in a trench coat over his suit, a Fedora on his head, also wearing dark sunglasses. "I mean . . . that's what it looks like: somebody staked her through the heart. Why else would that happen?"

"You think so, eh?" Ethan said. "That's pretty funny. Do you really believe in shit like that?"

"I don't," Byron said. "But maybe somebody else does. The killer, for instance. You never know what people are up to nowadays—particularly if they get whacked out on some form of narcotics. From the looks of it . . . I'd say she was staked through the heart because of it."

"Keep a cool head, man," Ethan said. "We don't know if that is true, or not, yet. We don't want something like that getting out to the public. They will think we've gone crazy."

"Sure. If you say so," Byron said. "I'm just calling it like I see it."

7

The two dapperly dressed detectives, Ethan Pendergrass and Byron Hoffmeier, filed a report and insinuated to local police and authorities to be on the lookout for . . . vampires . . . although they said this with much chagrin, not to be taken literally, as no one really believed in supernatural, blood sucking monsters that lurked in the night.

They gave a press conference at the city precinct about what they have discovered.

Ethan stood at the front of the room and addressed all of the officers and press present in the room.

"You are all familiar by now, I'm sure," Ethan said, gripping the podium with both hands, "with the strange case of Stephanie Dascălu . . . the wealthy socialite who owned the mansion outside of town. She was found murdered last night. There are other murders that seem to be involved with this case. It appears we have a serial, or ritualistic, killer, or killers, on our hands here in Vancouver." He paused for effect, took a drink of bottled water, and eyed the men and women in the room. They were all watching him intently, eyes wide, astute, and paying full attention. He continued, "We have obtained some information about the murders, and we have witnesses. There is a rough description and preliminary artist sketches of the perpetrators. Please see your dossiers for copies of all the evidence and notes that we currently have gathered."

Byron moved over and politely pushed Ethan aside, taking center stage in front of the podium. He said, "As strange as this may sound, we have a theory. . . . We surmised that it is a cult or gang of self-proclaimed vampires perpetrating these crimes."

There was a slight commotion in the room as the audience

reacted to what he had told them.

"I know what you're thinking," Byron continued, holding his hand in the air in a solemn gesture. "I am incredulous, too. Vampires. I know what you are thinking . . . how can that be? Right? These are not real vampires, mind you. It is a group of copycats, or pretenders, if you will, and they are only persuading themselves that they are vampires. They have convinced themselves that they are blood sucking vampires of old."

Ethan stepped back in front of the podium, saying, "We have dealt with this before. These cults come and go. And with the Internet and cell phones they have become much more sophisticated. The problem is that they truly believe they are supernatural entities from an ancient lineage of beasts that immigrated over from Hungary from centuries past. This is not our first encounter with these . . . eccentric cult members. I assure you we will shut them down quickly. We will cut off the head of the snake and put this to rest."

Byron spoke, again, saying, "We have it on good authority and reliable information that the cult was part of a following of Stephanie Dascălu, herself, and that she may have been murdered by one of her own followers. She was believed to be the leader of a Satanic cult that worshiped these ancient vampires of old. It was not secret that she was up to strange activities in her mansion . . . however, being strange, peculiar, downright odd is not a crime, in and of itself. It has been suspected for quite some time that she was holding ceremonies and rituals of a dark nature within the confines of her 'castle' know as the Château de Dascălu. Now, we have a reason and probable cause to go and search the premises. We will get to the bottom of this. I assure you of that."

Ethan said, "That is all we have for now . . . are there any questions?"

Hands went up all around the room. Ethan and Byron did

their best to answer all of the questions that arose on the subject, and there were many, mostly concerning the existence of
vampires and how could this be real police work, chasing monsters that is, and why would police even consider such a thing
as a valid case. They told them that it had nothing to do with
'real vampires' and that it was mostly just crimes committed
by a cult.

CHAPTER TEN

1

Manson, Zoey, and Crandall waited for Stephanie to come home to the mansion, but she never arrived, and after several days of waiting they saw the news on the TV about her death in the parking garage downtown Vancouver. The news was shocking to them, and at first, they were instantly in denial. How could that happen? Who would have done such a thing? They had no answers to those questions.

After a few more days, when the police arrived at the Château de Dascălu and questioned them about Stephanie and what they knew about her and her lifestyle. There was not much they could tell the police other than she was a cougar who liked to party and live a wild lifestyle with sex and drugs and alcohol. Who could blame her for wanting to have some fun? How does that saying go: better use it up before you get old? That was the truth.

Soon they realized that they must leave the castle and forget about Stephanie because she was now dead and gone forever; no matter how painful it might be, they must now forget about their gracious host and turn away, keeping fond memories of here close to their blackened hearts—after all, it was she whom had turned them in to vampires. They decided that they must strike out on their own and live the life of the undead, a night breed forever, and honor that Stephanie Dascălu had bestowed upon them.

"What are we going to do now?" Crandall asked, standing in the driveway. He was at a loss for words or action. "I don't have anywhere to go."

"You can come with us," Manson said. "We don't know where we are going either . . . but you are welcome to come there with us. Crazy, perhaps. If you don't mind hanging out with a couple Goth freaks."

"We would love your company," Zoey said

"You two are not freaks," Crandall said. "Far from it. It is the rest of the world that has the true freaks. You guys are just normal people, as far as I can tell."

"You are too kind," Manson said. "I think you may change your mind after you get to know us. And considering this most recent turn of events, I do believe there are some major changes coming our way."

Zoey and Crandall looked at Manson in wonder and curiosity.

"What do you mean, Manson?" Zoey asked. "Are you referring to the transformation?"

"Exactly," Manson said. "Here we are out in the darkness . . . creatures of the night. But we can no longer go about in the day. Don't you think that will change things forever?"

"Yes," Zoey said.

"I know what you are dealing with," Crandall said. "I haven't told you . . . but I too have . . . issues."

"What do you mean?" Zoey asked.

"I am what you would call . . . a werewolf." Crandall said. "I suffer from lycanthropy. On a full moon I am not nice to be around." He kicked a rock with his shoe and then made eye contact with each of them in turns. "I met Stephanie and she took me in . . . she knew about why I was different and she did not care. She was like a mother to me. She treated me like a normal person . . . despite my difference."

"It's okay," Manson said. "We accept you no matter what. You can ride with us. We will travel together and figure out what to do now."

"I do thank you," Crandall said. "I am obliged to tell you that I may have to leave soon, though. Ever since I was changed into this hideous . . . thing . . . I have never been able to stay in one place for too long. I just want to warn you that I may be forced to leave at some point. Don't take it personal."

"We won't," Zoey said.

"Let's go now," Manson said. "It's going to be daylight soon. But I guess that doesn't affect you as much . . . but we should go now."

They packed up their belongings from the castle and got into the Monte Carlo and head for the border of the United States of America.

2

Almost anyone who observed them thought they were a curious yet deliciously strange trio: two Goth lovelies and a golden-haired Adonis. They turned heads wherever they went. The event was never small, and they could always count on some sap falling for their alluring bait of sex and lust, easily enticed into their shocking trap. The black Monte Carlo was the coach of death and always delivered the goods: three freaks with teeth, claws, cock, balls, and pussy, and wet lips that sucked and sucked and sucked blood and cum and alcohol and drugs. The dark menagerie of supernatural death was a magnificent sight to the casual observer; they were real showstoppers; no wonder it was so easy to take in the fools with their perverted lust and cold hard cash.

Tonight was different, however, and they were forced to flee, to run away from their haven. When they left the city of Vancouver, Canada at midnight to avoid prying eyes and questioning stares from onlookers. It always happened that way, for a couple who were dressed in Goth fashion, driving in a vintage black 1975 Monte Carlo. They had to drive at night to avoid the populace at large. People liked to stare, astounded, jaw dropping to the floor as they tried to understand why anyone would dress fully in black, pale faced with darkly painted eyes and lips, dressed like they were attending a party with Nosferatu. Were they going to a funeral? That was a common question.

They listened to the local radio station, WKSB, and an announcement came over the radio that the police are searching for a trio of dark characters in connection with a series of murders downtown, possibly related to the disappearance of Stephanie Dascălu. They were pursued by Adrian, the paranormal investigator, who was driving an old Chevy van.

"That looks like something my grandpa would drive," Zoey said, looking back.

It smoked and backfired and stalled in the intersection.

"I don't think he can catch us in that van," Manson said, grinning from ear to ear. "He is no match for us in that piece of crap."

They were not too worried about the vampire hunter and his piece-of-shit-van. He did not pose much of a threat.

Taking secondary backroads was out of the question, since they had to cross the US and Canadian border at Blane, and all roads going that way connected to the Interstate and funneled traffic through the central checkpoint. There were primitive roads that crossed the border, of course, but that would be illegal and suspicious, and they were not trying to attract any more attention from law enforcement than they already had currently. They had all the legal paperwork and ID required to make a border crossing, but the all-important question was if they were looking for them to cross over: had the authorities posted alerts to border patrol officials to be on the lookout for the three wayward fiends in the black Monte Carlo? Ultimately, they were forced to take the most popular rout down Highway 99 (aka Fraser Delta Thruway) south of Vancouver, and head straight to the border crossing that connected to Interstate 5 in Washington State.

When the lights at the border crossing loomed ahead, they slowed down and got ready for the inspection. They knew there would be questions, and searches, and interrogations due to their appearance.

3

Normal people took exception to the dark look that is associated with an alternative Goth lifestyle, but Manson and Zoey were used to it by now. They had dealt with it so many times that it did not bother them in the least, anymore. After the first meeting with strangers, they would warm their hearts with charm and charisma and good looks, winning over even the most skeptical critic. They were a likeable couple and observers soon found themselves wishing they could go home with them; on the initial first glance, that is, because if they really did go home with them, they would soon find out that there was a literal dark side to the edgy couple.

Crandall was not so dark in dress or demeanor, and had more of a hipster look, although he was guilty by association when he was with Manson and Zoey. He did not care what people thought about him; they could all go eat a bag of dicks, for all he cared.

Together, they made a desirable trio, a ménage à trois. They turned heads everywhere they went, and plenty of observers were drawn with lust and sexual desire when they saw them. This made it easy for them to pick up victims and take their blood, money, and lives. These lovers were only living up to their true nature, that of a vampire and werewolf, and they did what vampires and werewolves do: drink blood, eat flesh, and inspire lust and carnal desire while preying on the innocence.

4

After being out on the road for a few weeks and living in the Monte Carlo, Manson and Zoey sleeping in the trunk—much like their counterparts from centuries past slept in coffins—while Crandall slept in the backseat during the day when they were on the road, with suitcases in the front seat so they could both fit in the trunk during daylight hours, and they kept money taken from their victims. They carried weapons in the form of guns and knives, brass knuckles, nunchakus, throwing stars, and stun guns and a Taser, as well as pepper spray. They were ready for any trouble that may come along.

This much was certain: Manson and Zoey were vampires, and now they were teamed up with Crandall, a werewolf, and they were hell on wheels as they drove a big, black stock 1975 Monte Carlo—except they were being followed at a distance by the

Vampire Hunter. Pedestrians were unaware that death rode darkly and it may be a hazard to their health to carelessly cross the street without looking both ways, because the big black car could appear like a phantom, a giant lurching beast that would bear down on them like a predatory dinosaur and turn them into road mush.

5

The Monte Carlo had two mandatory upgrades: a nitrous oxide kit on the engine for increased horsepower and speed, and an aftermarket stereo, a Kenwood, to play compact disks and connect to their cell phones via Bluetooth. They loved their music, liked the Sex Pistols with Sid Vicious singing "My Way" or "Anarchy in the U.K." and Type-O Negative with "Black No. 1 (Little Miss Scare-All)" and Zoey liked Heart with "Barracuda" or "Magic Man" and anything by the Doors ("Gloria" the dirty version . . . "wrap your lips around my cock . . . eat you . . . rip you in two", Mötley Crüe, or Korn but new music sucked and they both hate Taylor Swift and any Rap or Hip-hop. Another song they can both agree on is "Sympathy for the Devil" by the Rolling Stones. They had a taste for classical music, too, since they had lived through centuries and watched music progress from various forms and styles to the present, so they preferred something a little more modern. The techno, dub step, and club scene music were fine, if you were high on molly and entranced by the laser light show; but for a good variety of music you still had to go back a decade or two in order to get the good stuff. The older musicians knew how to do it better than the new age of uninspired and musically clueless autotune crooners, string breakers, stick whackers, and riff rippers. With house and club DJs and electro beats and synthe-sized sound effects and ripped samples and drum machines it could turn into a massive sonic assault on the senses. It was so mechanical and boring. The whole trance and groove of sonic bass and boom thunder and rap and rhyme was passé. Music was losing cohesion due to the passage of time.

6

Manson and Zoey liked the vinyl interior of the Monte Carlo because it made it easier to clean up the spilled blood when they took a victim inside the car—the swivel seats made it easy to quickly turn and catch a victim in the backseat, unaware. The blood stained the carpet and it made a mess, in general, but they were experts at cleaning it up, most of the time (on one occasion a victim sitting in the back noticed the blood stains on the vinyl, asking what this was all about—before he got bit on the neck). The bench seat in the back was perfect for fucking and feeding, and they could have a passenger sit in the middle and they could both attack the victim from each side, easily.

Manson and Zoey moved from town to town in Canada around Vancouver and outlying areas, preying on the innocent and beautiful, and punished deserving victims, sucking blood, and then moving on the next town. Eventually, they realized that they needed to move on to a new area with fresh blood, and the only way they could go was south. They decided to head to the United States, ultimately to Los Angeles, Holly-wood, the land of the rich and famous and beautiful and rich.

They were natural born killers by any other name and had a legacy and a universal right to pursue their destiny; after all, vampires drank blood, and werewolves consumed human flesh, and they inspired fear and dread in their victims, so it was a matter of course that they should do what supernatural beasts do, really. They were possessed by a paranormal wickedness that came from hundreds of years of history, when they were created by a vampire in Hungary, and bit by a savage unknown beast in the wilderness of rural Main. It was more of a birth than a creation. A becoming. . . .

They were bisexual and shared each other during sexual acts, and they enjoyed the company of either sex during their exciting times of blood drinking, sex, and depravity.

There was only one logical conclusion for them: It was good to be a gay vampire. Life was good and only getting better and they were free, free, free to be the blood drinking sex fiends they longed to be, forever, to eternity.

7

Manson, Zoey, and Chandler lived in hotels and motels, tearing down the walls, and just having one hell of a time. They were dark, sexy and delightfully good looking, and other people found them magnetizing and irresistible. The unsuspecting victims could not help becoming their prey because they exuded a charm and sexuality that was decadently enticing. They were beautiful people that everyone wanted to have sexual intercourse with, and could have been porn stars in another life.

Late one night, they were sitting in a small pub having drinks and playing pool and darts. They were taking it easy. It was a quiet night and the bar was filled with only a few patrons, most of the working stiffs had gone home early to go to bed and get up early for in the morning. Only the devoted barflies, alcoholics, and assorted regulars stayed late on a worknight.

On the TV overhead behind the bar, over the shiny and

colorful bottles of alcohol, where there was a mirror that did not show the reflections of Manson or Zoey—nobody even noticed— the broadcast changed to a live news brief.

"We interrupt the regularly scheduled program for this news bulletin . . ."

A news reporter of an Asian persuasion with a Columbia windbreaker was standing at the scene of the crime, giving a blow-by-blow report on the details of the occurrence. "I'm Chiang Han, and I am standing at the sight of the most recent murder, of what appears to be a string of murders, following the murder of the wealthy socialite Stephanie Dascălu the wealthy socialite

As the patrons of the bar watched the news, drink their beer, and ate their pizza, they were only slightly shocked, since the world was so full of bad news nowadays, and went about their business of eating, drinking, and gossiping about other less important news, laughing at memes on their cell phones, and ordering another round.

8

In their hotel room, the TV was buzzing with news that speculated about the death of Countess Stephanie Dascălu. It was also noted that there were self-proclaimed vampire hunters and vigilantes searching for the vampires as well, and warned that it was inadvisable to take the law into your own hands. Let the police and law handle this issue, the reporter stated in a monotone. Manson had purchased a copy of the current printed edition of *The Vancouver Courier* newspaper and tossed it down on the bed. Zoey read, unsurprised, that their escapades were making headlines. Crandall was looking over her shoulder at the article.

DEATH RIDES DARKLY

BODIES FOUND IN GRUESOME
MURDERS IN VANCOUVER

By Brent Treadwell

The Vancouver Courier

Bodies have been discovered with bite marks on their necks which appear to be the work of vampires . . . it is believed that creatures of the night are running loose in Vancouver, or so some superstitious folks would have you believe. Witnesses claim to have observed them feeding on innocent victims . . . and with the death of Countess Stephanie Dascălu, there is speculation running rampant that a group of vigilantes have taken it upon themselves to hunt down these alleged vampires and put them to death with a steak through the heart.

Manson ran his hand through his hair, perturbed, and looked at the them as he breathed out with a sigh. He said, "That's it then. The cat is out of the bag. They are on to us. This vampire hunter is looking for us now, too."

"What do you mean?" Zoey asked, naively. "They don't know where we are."

"Look at the news on the TV . . . " Manson said, he slapped the newspaper lying on the bed. "You've read this article. We are being hunted by the police, and this self-proclaimed vampire hunter. We can no longer hide here in Vancouver. We must move on now."

Zoey looked bewildered. She knew he was right.

Crandall said, "The secret is out about Stephanie and her mansion. We were part of it, and we are guilty by association.

Never mind the fact that we are vampires and werewolves—which doesn't help our case at all. Mortals will not tolerate us. I know that for a fact. Soon we will be recognized . . . if we stick around here."

"We can make a run for it," Manson said, stroking his chin. "We will drive in my car. Perhaps we will get away unnoticed."

"Where will we go?" Zoey asked.

"I know where," Crandall said, smiling. "We can go south . . . to California."

"Huh?" Zoey said. "Why?"

"Because it is where all the freaks are at," Crandall said. "Haven't you seen the news? Just look at the movie industry. It attracts weirdos from all around the world. We will fit right in. Not only that . . . I can present my movie script to some of the talent agencies in Hollywood."

"Hollywood," Manson said, rolling his eyes. "Isn't that like the modern Sodom and Gomorrah?"

"Precisely," Crandall said. "We will fit right in. Nobody will even give us a second glance."

"I see your point," Manson said. "The music scene is hopping there, too. Maybe I could get my band to move down there with us."

"And they do Tattoos in LA, too," Zoey said. "Some of the best tattoo artists in the world are located in Los Angeles."

Manson looked concerned, and Crandall and Zoey noticed, looking at him and wondering what was on his mind.

"What is it?" Zoey asked, putting her hand on his shoulder.

"My band, Sinister Fiend," Manson said. "I have not told them about my new . . . problem. What will I do? They are my friends and bandmates. We have been through so much together. I can't just abandon them."

"You have to," Zoey said. "They will never be able to understand that you are a vampire now."

"I think they would understand," Manson said. "They are my mates. We've been through everything together. They are not afraid of vampires, or anything."

"Yes, but once they meet a real vampire," Crandall said, "or, a werewolf . . . they are probably going to change their minds."

"I see what you mean," Manson said. "I don't know what to do."

"You have to tell them you are leaving," Zoey said. "It's the only way. You can contact them later . . . but for now, we must leave. We will all be arrested if we stay here."

"She's right," Crandall said. "You have to sever ties with everyone here. At least for the time being. Later, you can get in touch with them."

"It's going to fuck them up, if I just leave," Manson said. "We were on the verge of breaking out. We just got studio time to record our album and we were scheduled to play a bunch of gigs. We were even thinking about going on tour . . . worldwide, eventually. I'm supposed to just leave all of that behind?"

"You have no other choice, now," Crandall said.

"That's the truth," Zoey said. "The police will be—are after us. And that vampire hunter is looking for us, as well."

"You guys are right," Manson said.

"So, we are all in agreement?" Crandall said. "We will go to Hollywood?"

"Yes," Manson said.

"I've always wanted to go to California," Zoey said. "Malibu. Beverly Hills. It's so exciting. I can't wait."

"Okay," Manson said. "So, it's decided. We know it is time to get out of town and head for the border . . . we are decided then. Tonight, we will leave Vancouver and get away, as far away as possible. Hollywood is our destination."

"Let's do this," Crandall said.

"I think we should celebrate and have drinks," Zoey said. "Who's with me."

"Yes," Manson said. "I've got a bottle of Chartreuse chilling. Let's crack it open and have a toast to our new lives."

Manson took the bottle from the minifridge and opened it. He took plastic cups and poured generous amounts in each. They picked up the cups and held them out, touching the rims together, and then making a toast.

"Here is to our new lives in California," Zoey said.

"To Hollywood," Crandall said.

"To vampires and freaks on the Sunset Strip," Manson said.

"Cheers," they said in unison.

They tipped the cups back and guzzled down the green liquor, the burn of the alcohol warming their stomachs. It was invigorating and intoxicating, and soon they would be buzzing from the effects of the liquor.

"This is delicious," Crandall said. "I never knew liquor could taste like that."

"I've been saving this bottle for a special occasion," Manson said. "It was hidden in the trunk of my car for a long time. I thought tonight would be a good reason to crack it open."

"Can I have more?" Zoey said, her eyes beginning to glow with a green hue. The booze was flowing through her body now, and she was getting giddy. "I love it."

"Yes, indeed," Manson said, pouring more Chartreuse into their cups. "Drink up. Tonight we celebrate, and then leave for our new destination."

They were getting rambunctious now, the anticipation and excitement filling them with energy, their libidos rising to a crescendo. Manson kissed Zoey, lovingly, and then he turned and kissed Crandall. Zoey put Crandall's fingers in her mouth and sucked on them, twirling her tongue. It was getting steamy and they were ready to have sex. They unbuckled one another's belts, unfastened the buttons, and zipped down zippers. Swapping tongues and taking turns, each quivering and ecstatic from the sexual encounter. They were naked now and the three of them climbed onto the bed and made enthusiastic love.

9

Later that night, the left the hotel room and drove away. They were determined to get away from Vancouver, to leave the country of Canada completely, and move on to greener pastures. There would surely be a new life for them in the good old U-S of A and they would be able to blend in a seedy and sinfully decadent city such as Los Angeles. The freaks and weirdos flocked to Hollywood in hopes of becoming actors or writers, and many people were hooked on drugs and alcohol there, some living in the streets, some living in the ghetto, some living in highrise penthouses, but all of them getting high and supporting the underground economy by purchasing illicit substances. If two vampires and a werewolf could fit in anywhere, the city of the angels would be a safe bet and they were ready to try their luck. If that did not pan out, there was always Los Vegas, aka Sin City.

The drove away from Vancouver, the city lights fading into the distance behind them, and the highway was streaking by with lines and stripes of yellow and white. Every now and then Manson would run over onto the shoulder and hit the noisy grooves there that were meant to wake up sleepy drivers.

"Stay on the road," Zoey said.

"I'm sorry," he said. "This car likes to drift."

"It vibrates my ass when you hit those things," Crandall said from the backseat.

Up ahead in on the horizon, in the distance, they could see the shimmering lights of the border crossing. They were getting close now. As they approached the Canada-US border in the black Monte Carlo, they were weary . . . and they did not notice the metallic gray 1998 Chevrolet G10 passenger conversion van following behind them, at distance at first, but closing in as they approached the city limits.

10

Detective Ethan Pendergrass and Detective Byron Hoffmeier go to the Château de Dascălu in Vancouver and make a startling discovery inside the castle. There are cadavers and piles of bones in the basement. Lots of them. The find a hidden passage that goes down to a pit with mountains of bones, infested with rats, and dripping from the water in the ceiling, it is a dank and fetid place and it reeks of death.

"It looks like a torture chamber down here," Ethan said.

"You ain't shitting about that," Byron said. "Look at these piles of bones. What the hell? Are those humans?"

"I think so."

"Fuck me running. There must be at least fifty different bodies piled up there."

"This lady, Stephanie Dascălu, was obviously a psychotic—a serial killer," Ethan said, stepping into the dungeon. There were bats flying around overhead. There were fresh cadavers with rotting and fetid flesh swollen and crawling with maggots. The smell was strong and revolting, filling their nostrils with the stench of death and decay. The bloated necks on some of the victims had punctures, like bite marks, where they had possibly been drained of blood.

"Fucking disgusting," Byron said, choking back the urge to vomit.

One thing seemed painfully obvious to both officers: this had all the trappings of vampirism.

"Are you thinking what I'm thinking?" Ethan asked.

"I hope not."

"When I searched her history I found out some astonishing facts . . . she was an immigrant from Hungary, but her records indicated that she was much older than anticipated."

"So, what does it mean?"

"According to this," Ethan said. "She should be almost three hundred years old."

"That's impossible."

"Nothing is impossible."

"The only way she could be that old is if she was a vampire. And I don't believe in vampires, so . . . it has to be a mistake."

"The legend fits the crime, here, I'm afraid. I calls 'em like I sees 'em."

"I refuse to believe this is the work of a vampire. Period. You have to come up with something better than that."

"It's a possibility."

"No. It is not."

"What are we going to say?"

"This is the work of a deranged serial killer. Plain and simple. That's what we are going to say."

"Fine. You're the boss."

"Let's get the CSA in here to clean this mess up."

"You got it."

"I'm getting out of here so I can breathe fresh air."

"Right behind you."

The left the dungeon and went outside, both on the verge of vomiting, and breathing in the clean air, the smell of pine trees and roses never such a welcoming scent.

11

Adrian made a few phone calls and was able to set up a meeting with Ethan and Byron. He paid a visit to the detectives and the agreed to take a lunch with him while they discussed the particulars of this undisclosed case. He told them he had inside knowledge that might be of use to them in solving the crime. They met up at a Cliff's Monster Burgers and ordered food while they talked. The two detectives were listening carefully, anxious to hear what this strange man in the trench coat had to say about the mysterious Stephanie Dascălu.

He had one strategy, and that was to tell them exactly what they were dealing with. He took a bite of his hamburger, chewed on it, and while greasy juice ran down his cheek, he said, "To put it bluntly . . . she was a vampire."

They looked at each other startled. Byron grunted in disbelief. They both obviously thought Adrian was plumb fucking crazy.

"What kind of bullshit whacko nutjob comes in here and says something like that?" Ethan asked, popping a French fry covered in ketchup into his mouth. "You expect us to believe that?"

"How do you know this?" Byron asked, raising an eyebrow.

"I am a vampire hunter."

"What? Are you serious?" Ethan said.

"Who the hell are you, anyway, Mr. Vampire Hunter?"

"My name is Adrian, and I am a paranormal investigator. Vampire hunting is just an offshoot of what I do."

"Really? A ghost hunter, then?"

"Sometimes."

"I think I seen you on TV before. Didn't you used to make shows about paranormal investigations?" Bryon asked.

"Do you have a license and a permit to hunt vampires?" Ethan asked, skeptical. "What a joke. I can't believe you are wasting our time like this."

"Ditto," Byron said. "You should pay for the hamburgers, sir."

"Oh, well," Adrian said. "I figured as much, it is your loss. I was just trying to help your solve the case . . . but since you are not taking me seriously . . . I guess I'll just be on my way. I'll leave you to decided how to solve the problem on your own. The burgers are on me, by the way. Have a nice day."

If there was one thing Adrian knew for sure, it was that police and most law enforcement agencies did not listen to paranormal investigators. That was part of the problem, because anyone who investigated the paranormal or supernatural were automatically considered to be crackpots.

He left the burger joint and went out into the bright daylight, squinting from the blinding sun, and headed for his old Chevy van.

"So much for trying to help the good guys," he said. He chuckled to himself. "Are they really the good guys? Maybe. I don't know. I do know that a bullet travels at two thousand miles per hour and a patrol car travels so slow that it takes them at least fifteen minutes to arrive at the scene of the crime. I believe I will take care of this matter myself. Fuck the police."

PART TWO

KILLERS ON THE ROAD

But see, amid the mimic rout
A crawling shape intrude!
A blood-red thing that writhes from out
The scenic solitude!
It writhes!—it writhes!—with mortal pangs
The mimes become its food,
And seraphs sob at vermin fangs
In human gore imbued.

—Edgar Allan Poe,
"The Conqueror Worm"

CHAPTER ELEVEN

1

Manson stamped down on the gas pedal and revved up the high powered V8 engine, blasting down the highway with a thunderous roar. It was just after sunset, and the night was spreading out before them, twilight giving way to the darkness, the horizon fading away into pitch black obscurity. The gibbous moon waxed brightly in the sky and stars twinkled merrily as they wandered beneath the stars in their hot rod car. The moon had watched over many things that transpired over the centuries throughout history and had witnessed so many vampires coming and going that the astrological signs could tell of the secrets to a diviner of such mysteries. Vampires were real, not mythical, as society would have the world believe, and they roamed the night, looking for victims. It was true, and one could meet their fate at the hands of the undead, if one was not careful and let down their guard. Death was their precursor, and a souped up Monte Carlo was their carriage, carrying them to their destiny, as they road darkly in the night, in search of their next victim. Death was providence that they unmercifully bestowed upon their victims.

In return for the lives of their victims, the trio of mythical creatures earned a living. The blood kept them alive and the money and possessions they liberated from their victims provided loot and lucre that kept them afloat in a world that demanded credits and debits from every soul alive. Like the curse of vampire and lycanthropy, money, too, was a real curse, and death was a release from this evil necessity; Manson and Zoey were simply relieving distressed souls of their misery of existence.

As they approached the border, they grew nervous.

"What if they search us?" Zoey asked.

"The will. They always do," Manson said. "Just relax. We haven't done anything wrong."

"We have guns and weapons. You don't think that will draw their attention?" Crandall asked from the backseat.

"Don't panic," Manson said, looking at Crandall in the rearview mirror. "We've got this."

"You know what to do," Manson said, looking into Zoey's eyes. "You can persuade them to look away . . . can't you?"

"I can," she said. She grinned with a devilish look on her face. Her eyes glittered and twinkled with a fiery brilliance, and her fangs showed slightly. "We can do this."

"No worries," Manson said. "They will let us through."

"I hope you are right," Crandall said, crossing his arms nervously.

Manson pulled the car down the lane past a sign that said keep right, up to the entry lane of zone number 2 with a green arrow, parked behind a line of cars and waited for his turn to pull forward and make a declaration at the border. It was the structure located at the border crossing between US and Canada on the US side. The sign said **U.S. Port of Entry, Peace**

Arch, Blaine, WA. To the left was a cement building with large glass windows with narrowly spaced horizontal white aluminum louvres, and industrial looking complex, well lighted with halogen and fluorescent lights, and branching from that was a massive blue sheet metal canopy overhanging roof with rectangular dormers and vents on top. Below the roof were white pillars and yellow bollard posts, cones, electrical junction box containers with sensors. In green letter, the sign overhead said **LANE OPEN** and below that **DO NOT BLOCK SENSORS.** *Be prepared to show all identification. Declare any articles acquired outside USA.* There were massive orange barricade blocks stopping entry into certain areas. Next to the dull, gray painted booth with solid metal doors and square glass window where the CBP officer was sitting, there were orange delineator posts with black base and white stripes near the booth. There were security cameras pointing in all directions, and they would be watching every move they made, computer screens with information and facial recognition software, and scanners with sniffers for explosive devices, Manson knew.

On the other side of the entryway large alternating white and yellow chevron stripes pointed the way out to freedom. All one had to do was follow those chevrons to the outbound passageway and they were as good as gone. The overpass from the Highway was off in the distance. It was a clear run after that, past Exit 276 that led to Blain City Center and left onto the southbound ramp leading onto Interstate 5, all the way into Washington state.

The Customs agent was dressed all in black, much like Manson and Zoey, but his uniform was official and menacing. He was a display of power and expressed a stern face of control and no-nonsense. He was all business. His badge was gold, a shield over his heart, his patches blue and white with an eagle with wings out, his boots black, his bullet proof vest bulging, a microphone on his radio walky-talky strapped to his chest with spiral cord dangling down to his hip. His utility was leather, black, with service pistol, flashlight, handcuffs, extra rounds. He was prepared for business and would take no shit, from anyone. They dealt harshly with anyone caught breaking the law at the border. His name was on a patch on his chest: **Gonzaga**. Below that it said **CBP** in big white letters. He was a field operations federal officer. His hair was cropped short in flattop, and he had tattoos up and down his forearms. He looked like a military veteran.

He slid the window open in the booth and looked out at the black Monte Carlo. His face was stern, but he had a poker face and it was hard to tell what he was thinking; however, Manson was sure he could figure him out if he thought about it hard enough. People were easy to read, or so it seemed, as there was something, he had acquired lately that made him super sensitive to what people were thinking. It was almost as though he could read their minds.

"Identification please," he said.

"You bet," Manson said, reaching for his wallet. "You got yours, Bee?" He looked at Zoey, and he could tell she was nervous.

"Yes. Of course, I do," she said, digging in her purse. She took out her ID card and handed it to Manson.

"Where are you coming from?"

"Uhm, we are coming from Vancouver," Manson said, rubbing his chin. It was a nervous tick.

"We live there," Zoey said. "We are just going to visit some friends in California."

Manson looked at her sternly. His eyes told her to just be quiet. She was blowing this.

"What is your citizenship?"

"We are both Canadian," Manson said. "Born and bred. God save the queen, eh?"

"Where are you going?"

"I just told you," Zoey said. "We are going to visit a friend in California."

Manson looked at her again, his eyes on fire this time.

"Why are you coming into the USA tonight?"

"Well, uh, we are leaving Vancouver to go into Washington so we can take a little vacation. Visit some friends and family, make our way down to sunny California. You know? Surfs up, eh?"

He could not help throwing the Canadian lilt into the conversation. It just came naturally.

"Do you have anything to declare?"

"I already answered that one: God save the queen."

He was suddenly thinking of Sid Vicious singing the song. It made him want to laugh out loud, but he stifled it, biting his fist.

Has anyone given you anything suspicious?"

"No."

"What is your profession?"

"I'm a, uh, musician," Manson said. "I play guitar in a band, Sinister Fiends. You may have heard of us. Yeah?" *This guy is serious*, Manson thought. *I don't think he likes us.* He looked at Zoey as the though crossed his mind. As if on cue, he heard Zoey's voice clearly in his thoughts.

Zoey: *Just act natural. Don't make him suspicious.*

Manson looked at her, surprised. He knew this was possible, but they had not tried it yet, and this was the first time.

Manson: *You are talking to me with your mind? Can you hear me?*

Zoey: *Yes. I think so. We seem to be telepathic now, too. Neat, huh?*

"Are you transporting anything illegal? Guns? Drugs? Explosives?" officer Gonzaga asked, leaning out the window of the booth and looking down into the car.

"Damn! No. Absolutely not," Manson said. He was lying, of course. They did have guns. No drugs or explosives, but weapons, to be sure. "What do we look like? Fools?"

He regretted asking that question.

Zoey: *Don't blow it.*

Manson and Zoey made eye contact. They were lucid and synchronized in thought and heartbeat. They were a picture-perfect match, a yin-yang symbolizing perfection. They could feel each other breath . . . in . . . out.

Manson: *I think they are going to search us.*

Zoey: *Relax. Breathe. Make them believe. We have control. You can do it.*

"What is your story," Gonzaga said, shining his flashlight into the backseat and inspecting Crandall closely.

"I'm just along for the ride," Crandall said, squinting in the bright light shining directly in his eyes.

"Is that so?" Gonzaga asked. "Do you have identification?"

"Yes," Crandall said, pulling out his billfold. "Here you go."

"Thank you." Gonzaga said, taking the identification card.

At that moment, a second CBP officer, a female with sandy blonde hair pulled back tightly into a bun. Her name patch said: Roland. She approached the vehicle from the passenger side and knocked on the window, instructing Bianco to roll it down.

Zoey complied, rolling down the window with the manual handle.

"Hello," officer Roland said. "What is your name?"

"My name is Zoey," she answered.

"Are you carrying anything illegal tonight?" officer Roland asked, putting her hands on her hips. Her gun was bulging on her belt. She looked menacing and powerful.

"No," Zoey said, timidly at first, and then she looked back at officer Roland and glared deeply into her eyes.

"You have pretty eyes," officer Roland said. "Are those contacts?"

"No. They are real."

Zoey's eyes were the deepest shade of blue, as blue as the sky, surrounded with a silver ring around the iris; there were silver flecks and icy streaks within, just around the pupil. They were the eyes of an angel.

Roland: *Something is suspicious about these two.*

Zoey read her mind. She could hear officer Roland's thoughts.

Gonzaga: *Maybe we should get a dog out here.*

Manson heard this thought, as well as everything else that anyone was thinking at that moment. His thoughts were lightning fast, and his reactions followed. He looked at officer Gonzaga and peered into his eyes, reaching into his mind and twisting his soul, controlling him from the inside.

Manson: *No. You don't want to do that, officer Gonzaga . . . we don't have anything to hide. There is no need for dogs.*

Manson looked up at Gonzaga with piercing eyes and smiled.

Zoey: *We must control them, Manson. Make them do what we want them to do. Make them forget about us. They will let us go. Make them lust for you. Lust for me. Lust for Crandall. Their desire will rule them and make them forget about arresting us for anything.*

Although Crandall could not hear anyone's thoughts, his own internal dialog could be heard by Manson and Zoey.

Crandall: *They're on to us. We're fucking busted.*

"Don't worry, Crandall," Manson said. "We've got this under control."

"If you say so," Crandall said.

Zoey looked deeply into officer Roland's mind and squeezed tightly, making her lose her stern and cold demeanor. There was something sexual there, and Zoey could feel it; this female officer was a lesbian, she could tell, and that meant that she could easily seduce her.

Manson: *This one is straight, but he will still fall for me. Watch him turn and soften right in front of me. I'll have him in my grip in no time.*

They were having fun now as it had become a game to them to control these two CBP officers like puppets and toy with their lust and desire. They would make them want sex in the most incredible way.

Zoey: *You want to fuck me, don't you?*

Roland: *Yes. I do. I would love to. You are so beautiful.*

Manson looked at Gonzaga still inside the booth.

Manson: *You want to fuck her, too, don't you? I can see it in your eyes.*

Gonzaga: *Yes. Yes. I would love to. I would fuck the shit out of her. Fucking slut. I would show her what a real man feels like. I would stick my fat cock in her mouth and let her suck it dry. Oh, yeah, baby.*

Zoey laughed out loud. She was pleased by this, immensely. She loved knowing that she had that control over men. They were mostly the same, if you looked at them just right, and if you just breathed on their dick it would jump to attention and they would instantly expect a blowjob, as if a woman did not have anything better to do with her time. Men were so obsessed with their cocks; however, this was a good thing because it made them easier to control.

Manson: *Not tonight. You cannot do that. But, tonight, is your lucky night. You know why? You don't get to fuck either one of us, but you get to live. How does that sound, eh? We will not kill you. That is better than fucking, any time. Wouldn't you agree?*

Gonzaga just nodded his head. He was in a trance now. He

was agreeing with everything Manson said.

Zoey: *I would love to have this one. She looks delicious in her uniform. I am a sucker for a girl, or guy, in uniform. Truly. It makes me tingle just thinking about it.*

Roland was in the same kind of trance, her mind completely blank now. She was feeling a burning desire in her loin, an itch that needed to be scratched. She wanted to fuck this dark couple in the old hot rod Monte Carlo. It was almost uncontrollable. She was having a vision of them *ripping her clothes off, exposing her breasts, kissing her softly on the neck, breathing with hot breath in her ear.* She wanted to have them *strip her down naked and lick her from head to toe.* They could *probe every orifice with tongues, and cocks, and fingers, and just ravish her* until she was completely exhausted and fulfilled. It was such a pleasurable sensation to imagine these three dark lovers on all sides of her; *their cocks inside her, and the girl with her breasts in her face, and all three squeezing her tightly.* She could feel her warm, wet, pussy throbbing in her pants, and she was close to having an orgasm right on the spot.

Manson and Zoey looked at her and knew what she was thinking. They smiled as they shared in the visions of Roland's fantasy.

Manson: *We must be going now. It was a pleasure meeting you two, though. Really. I've enjoyed it. If we weren't in a hurry, I might consider staying to take you guys out on a date and have you for dinner.*

Zoey: *Are we done here? Can I take this one with us?*

Manson: *Yes. We are leaving. No. You cannot have her. We are on camera. Stay cool. We are almost done here.*

Manson and Zoey began to think the same thoughts together: *You will forget us now. You will not remember this ever happened. Forget us now. You can't remember anything now. You are completely blank. Nothing to see here now. We are leaving. Let us go. Goodbye.*

"Okay, then," officer Gonzaga said. "I guess you want your

ID back." He handed their ID cards back to Manson.

"You three are so cute together," officer Roland said. "I hope you have a great time together on your trip."

"We will," Zoey said. "Thank you for your kind words."

"Absolutely," Crandall said, breathing out with a sigh of relief. "We will have a lively time."

Zoey smiled charmingly at officer Roland, who stepped back and walked around the car toward the booth.

"You guys can leave now," she said. "We are done here."

"Welcome to the USA. Have a nice night," Gonzaga said. "Enjoy your vacation."

The CBP officers were convinced that there was nothing wrong. Little did the officers know that they had just interacted with two fledgling vampires who were on a blood thirty rampage to raise Hell and damnation upon the innocent in their path. As far as the CBP officers were concerned, their identification was all in order and all was well. They were three beautifully dark and delicious Goth sexual beings that would fill their fantasies and their dreams for many nights to come.

The border crossing sight was quiet tonight, but not desolate, and there were quite a few cars crossing over, and despite the outlandishness of this monstrously melodramatic Monte Carlo straight out of a noir film, they managed to get into the USA undiscovered. That was the end of it; they had used mind control and telepathy to get their way. They learned something new that night. They could control people with their minds. This was a new development in their transformation. It was getting better every minute.

"That was too close," Crandall said. "My heart was beating out of my chest."

"No worries," Manson said. "I told you we had it under control."

"You guys took control of them," Crandall said, amazed. "You could read their minds . . . couldn't you?"

"Yes. We could," Zoey said. "This is a new development that was unexpected."

"It will come in handy, I'm sure," Manson said.

"All I know is I cannot take much more excitement like that," Crandall said.

2

After Manson, Zoey, and Crandall crossed the border, they were free to roam the country and find new sufferers to bleed dry and molest indefinitely. The lights from the border crossing station were fading behind them now as they cruised down Interstate 5 toward Bellingham.

Zoey turned on the radio and played a song by Metallica, singing about fading to black. A dark and sad song, but it had the right mood as the cruised down the road, the headlights cutting swaths of light on the pavement, the double yellow lines on the road leading them to their next adventure.

They drove for less than an hour before they reached the city lights of Bellingham. It was time to take care of business.

They did not notice the metallic gray 1998 Chevrolet G10 passenger conversion van fallowing behind them, at distance at first, but closing in as they approached the city limits.

CHAPTER TWELVE

1

Death came to Bellingham, Washington in a black Monte Carlo in the form of two vampires and a werewolf with nothing better to do than stalk the night and exsanguinate some innocent victims. They were riding darkly in the night and looking for some souls to steal. It had been a day since they had taken any blood, and they were starting to feel a hunger, a deep yearning within their immortal core that nagged with an insatiable appetite, an instinctual desire to taste hot blood from a jugular vein of some quivering dupe. There would be a time enough for that later, but first they would find a place to hold up for the night.

It was a beautiful site to see the city of Bellingham. They were next to the airport and a large passenger 747 jet was taking flight overheat into the night sky. The Monte Carlo was running low on fuel, so they needed to stop and get some gas. Manson pulled off the road and into a convenience store, ampm, parking lot and stopped at the pumps.

"We're here," Manson said. "I'm going to fill her up. Do you need anything?"

"I'm going inside," Zoey said. "I need a pack of cigarettes." She looked in the backseat at Crandall, saying, "Do you want anything?"

Crandall pushed the seat forward, saying, "I might get something. I'm coming in." He climbed out and stood up, stretching his muscles.

They stood outside of the car, taking in the night air, the sound of the airport was loud and busy with activity in the distance. An airplane was taking off on the runway and the loud engines blasted the night with a thunderous thrust of jets.

After Zoey purchased menthol cigarettes, Manson bought a copy of The Bellingham Herold newspaper, a six pack of beer, and a tube of spearmint Ice Drops. Crandall was lingering in the back aisle by the beverages, struggling over his choices, finally purchasing a Monster energy drink and three Slim Jim jerky snacks at the counter. Their transactions complete—the clerk, a young man of Indian descent, looked at them skeptically from the corner of his eye as he took their money—they went back outside into the night and got back in the car and drove away toward town.

2

Manson pulled off the quiet street in the Monte Carlo and parked in the lot at the Shamrock Motel on Maplewood Avenue around 10 o'clock in the evening on Friday the 13th in December of 2019. The engine ticked and hissed as rain came down on the hood, covering the windshield and obscuring the view outside. They looked at the motel, lit up at night, and could see into the lobby.

The trio of Gothic vamps, psychos, and fiends got out and

went into the lobby and approached the check-in counter. The clerk inside the lobby was lackadaisical as he watched them enter in through the door, a motley throng of rebels dressed in leather, lace, and denim. He had a nonplussed expression on his pockmarked face, his greasy blonde hair cropped short, large lenses on his glasses giving him the appearance of Jeffrey Dahmer.

"Good morning," Zoey said.

Manson sprayed spearmint Ice Drops in his mouth, because he loved to have minty fresh breath, and approached the counter.

"We need a room," Manson said, reaching in his pocket for money.

"We are exhausted," Zoey said. "It's been a long trip and we need to sleep."

"We need to get some beauty sleep," Manson said, joking.

"Speak for yourself," Crandall said. "I am beautiful no matter what. We don't need no sleep."

"Okay," the clerk said. "Will it be just the three of you?"

"Uhm . . . yes," Manson said. "We are a team. We will be needing the room until tomorrow night, by the way."

They all looked at one another awkwardly. The clerk focused his attention through the window and looked intently at the Monte Carlo parked outside. It was almost sunrise, and the clerk looked at them skeptically, since they were wanting a room for an entire day and night. It was not unusual, however, he eyed them with contempt, unaffected by their gritty charm.

"We require rest after a long drive," Manson said, running his fingers through his hair.

The clerk looked at him, first indifferently, then raising a critical eyebrow.

"You don't have to explain it to me," the clerk said. "I already know."

"What do you know?" Crandall asked, intrigued. "I mean . . . can you read our minds, or something? That would be a good trick, if you could."

Zoey nudged Crandall in the ribs, encouraging him to calm down. "Cool it, hotrod," she said. "Don't get us into trouble here."

"Never mind," the clerk said. "I've seen it all before. I don't care. Nothing is shocking nowadays."

"Aren't you a ham?" Manson said. "Say . . . you remind me of somebody. I can't put my finger on it. Somebody famous. Do I know you?"

"I don't think so," the clerk said, flattered. He had no idea what the Goth man dressed in leather was getting at or insinuating, and if he did know he would have been extremely offended.

"Can we have a double—a room with two king-sized beds?" Zoey asked.

"Either that, or we'll have to share a bed," Manson said. "I think the three of us can handle that. We can have a ménage à trois."

"That sounds lovely," Zoey said, biting her lip in a mocking gesture. "What do you think, Crandall? Are you up for that?"

Crandall was looking at the calendar on the wall, not paying full attention. "I'm sorry," he said. "What did I miss? A threesome, you say? I guess we could do that."

The clerk typed on the keyboard with a perplexed expression, attempting to ignore the sexual innuendos freely expressed in his presence, keeping his focus on the computer screen. His eyes glowed in the backlight from the LCD screen, his lip twitching and betraying his discomfort with this trio of two Gothic misfits and a hipster. The clerk thought they were an odd combination, to be sure.

"I have one room available with two king-sized beds," he said, looking up at them with a quizzical expression. "Would you like that one?"

"We'll take it," Manson said.

"Excellent," the clerk said, typing on the keyboard again. "That will be eighty-nine dollars, please."

"Awesome," Manson said, pulling a wad of crinkled up bills and assorted change from his pocket and setting it down in a pile on the counter. The clerk took their money and gave them a key with a white ball and chain tab with the number 9 printed with indelible ink.

"We only accept credit cards," the clerk said. "No cash." He pointed at a sign overhead that said: Credit only. No cash accepted.

"If you insist," Manson said, reaching for his wallet. "I have a Visa Gold card . . . you know what they say: don't leave home without it. Right?" He pulled out the credit card and handed it to the clerk.

"May I see your driver's license, too, please?" the clerk said.

"My, my, my," Manson said, removing his license from his wallet. "You certainly are thorough, aren't you?"

The clerk smirked and snorted. "It's just policy, sir," the clerk said, inspecting the license card. "Canada, huh? Are you here on vacation?"

"That doesn't concern you," Crandall said. "Just give us a room, already." He was obviously losing his patience with the clerk.

"We won't be requiring made service, either," Zoey said. "We don't want to be disturbed."

"I will make a note of that," the clerk said. "Be sure to turn the do not disturb sign outward on your door so the housekeepers know to let you sleep."

"Of course," Crandall said, rolling his eyes, obviously bored with the clerk.

"Have a nice day," the clerk said, unenthused.

"Likewise," Manson said, turning toward Zoey. "Our room awaits, my lady."

He held out his arm and she put her arm in his and they marched regally out of the lobby and into the parking lot toward their room.

The clerk shook his head as he watched them go on their way.

"Weirdos," he said. He turned his attention back to the TV on the wall and resumed watching the old movie from which he had been interrupted.

3

Manson, Zoey, and Crandall went into the motel room, through door number 9, and Zoey quickly plopped down on the stiff king-sized bed. The room was dingy, definitely not first class, and it had a musty smell of cigarette smoke and spilled beer. The low pile carpet was a dingy beige and cream with stains and worn patches. The furniture consisted of a cheap faux wood desk with a rolling adjustable desk chair, and a brass lamp with a tattered amber paper shade. A coffeepot, a single bag of coffee grounds and a filter, and Styrofoam cups sat next to a digital alarm clock with bright red LED letters showing the time as 10:35 p.m. The bed was covered with a tacky comforter blanket in colors of tangerine, yellow, and chartreuse, in a tropical foliage motif.

"Was it just me, or did that clerk seem like a serial killer?" Manson said, tossing the keys on the desk.

"He was a nerd," Crandall said. "A geek who never got the girl in school. Give him a break. We can't all be beautiful."

"I was thinking Norman Bates, or Jeffrey Dahmer, maybe Charles Manson," said Manson. "He was deliciously diabolical."

"Nice choice of words," Zoey said.

"What can I say? I wax poetic sometimes," Manson said.

"This place is a dump," Crandall said, looking around the room.

"Don't they clean these rooms after guests leave?" Zoey asked, wrinkling her nose in disgust.

"They are supposed to," Manson said. "This one does seem kind of rank, doesn't it?"

"I'm bored," Crandall said, swiping a lock of hair out of his face. "Let's go do something fun. Can we go out and play? Or are we grounded? There is a new day dawning out there and we could explore the town of Bellingham."

"We need to lay low," Manson said, raising his hands to show open palms. "As you may know, we can't go outside in the sun. We must watch out for that vampire hunter, too. He is looking for us."

"I am not afraid of him," Zoey said. She took a 9mm pistol from her waistband, slid the lever back to make sure it was loaded, and held it up to eye level. "I've got this . . . and I will use it on him. No worries. He is just a man. He can die, like the rest."

"He is a hunter," Manson said. "He means to put an end to us."

"We are immortal," she said. "How can he do that?"

"Speak for yourself," Crandall said. "I think everything can be killed . . . including vampires."

"With a stake to the heart," Manson said, stabbing at his

chest to demonstrate. "Perhaps some holy water and garlic and a crucifix. Maybe a knife. We are not truly immortal, you see?"

"Don't forget silver bullets," Crandall said.

"I will shoot him right between the eyes," Zoey said. "I have no sympathy for a vampire killer. Mark my words. I will eat his heart someday."

"You have so much strength and you would choose a gun instead of ripping him apart with your bare hands and teeth?" Crandall asked, bemused.

"Absolutely," she said. "It makes the job that much easier. Why draw it out? A bullet to the head will stop the brain, instantly."

"You are so sexy when you talk like that," Manson said. He crossed the room and sat down beside her on the bed. "Were you always this wicked, or did the change bring this dark side out in you?"

"A little bit of both," she said. "I suppose I've always been dark, but *wicked* . . . that is a new thing. I think I like it.'

"Give me a kiss you dangerous, dark, creature of the night," Manson said, biting softly at her neck. "I long for your embrace."

"You are so romantic," she said, sarcastically. "When you speak like that you make me so hot."

"Kiss me, you fool," he said. "Crandall . . . you can join us, too. If you like."

"I like," Crandall said, moving close to them. It was now a ménage à trois, as promised.

They embraced, fangs exposed, loving kisses, wet and sloppy, and Zoey dropped the pistol on the bed. After a moment, they separated and looked into one another's eyes.

"I love you," Manson said, stroking Zoey's hair.

"I love you, too," she said, stroking his chin with her fingertips.

"I love you both," Crandall said, feeling left out. "Don't forget about me."

"We would never leave you out," Zoey said, rubbing her fingers delicately along the contours of Crandall's sumptuous lips.

"I'm jealous," Manson said.

"Don't be," Zoey said. "There is plenty of me to go around. I will share. Don't worry." She stroked his chin, felt the bristle of stubble, and pulled her hand away. "You need to shave. You will grow a beard soon."

"Then I will look like, Crandall," Manson said, mockingly.

"That's not such a bad thing," Crandall said, grinning.

"It's hard to stay suave when you are sleeping in a car," Manson said. "Sleeping in the trunk, no less."

"Why must we live like this? In hotels and motels. On the road? In an old boat of a car?"

"We have no choice at this point," Manson said. "You know why. We must run . . . as far away as we can get. Now that we have this vampire hunter following us, it makes it even more critical that we stay out of sight and in hiding."

"The vampire hunter is stalking us," Crandall said. "I think he intends to kill us all."

Hickory, dickory, dock . . . Manson was thinking, bored. *The mouse ran up the clock . . . boring!* "I tire of this vampire hunter," he said, looking at his cuticles. "Perhaps we should put an end to him."

"Why don't we just hunt him, instead. Turn the tables," Zoey asked. "We can take him out easy enough. No problem. One bullet should do just fine." She held up the pistol and pulled the slide back, loading a shell into the chamber and cocking the trigger. "He will die easily."

"If I get him on a full moon, he will be toast," Crandall said.

"I know. I know," Manson said. "Don't think I haven't considered our options. The problem is that he is pursuing us right now and we will have to flip the script on him. Turn him from hunter into hunted."

Zoey stood up and stretched, yawning, showing her fangs against her painted black lips. Her makeup was smudged and fading, and she needed a makeover. She set the pistol on the desk and stretched her arms and legs.

"I am going to take a shower," she said. "I feel crusty after being in the car all night."

"Yes. I agree," he said.

"What are you trying to say?" Zoey said, resting her hands on her hips, akimbo. "You agree I am crusty?"

"I meant I agree about driving in the car all night sucks," he said.

"And makes one crusty, too," Crandall said, adding to the conversation.

Zoey laughed at them, rolled her eyes, and then went to the bathroom to take a shower.

4

Inside the bathroom, Zoey turned on the water in the shower. It was cold at first, but then the hot water made its way to the shower head and steam began to fill the room. She undressed and climbed into the hot water, slowly at first, and then all the way in, wetting her hair and closing her eyes.

After showering, Zoey went back out into the hotel room and saw that Manson and Crandall were watching the morning news.

"Whatcha watching?" she asked, a rhetorical question.

"The news, babe," Manson said.

"We're trying to catch up on what is happening in Vancouver since we left," Crandall said, "but this is mostly local news. Not much about Canada here, in the US, I'm afraid."

"Are you expecting to see our pictures on there?" Zoey asked, drying her hair with a towel.

"Maybe. I don't think so, though," he said. "Not yet."

"They know about the murders on Rue Morgue Street in Vancouver," Crandall said, "but they don't know who did it yet."

"We didn't leave any reason for them to think it was us," Zoey said. "Why would they be searching for us?"

"The vampire hunter," Crandall said. "He may alert the authorities. Although I suspect he is a vigilante and will not involve the police."

"Well, I do know," Manson said. "But I do know that we must rest well for the hunt tonight."

"You are right. Let's get some sleep," Zoey said, "while the sun is out and tonight, we will go out on the town."

"Sounds like a splendid plan," Manson said.

"Well, you two heliophobes can stay inside all you want," Crandall said, putting on his coat. "I am going to go out for a walk and see what there is to see in this neighborhood. Mark my territory, so to speak."

"Stay out of trouble," Manson said. "We don't want to have to bail you out of jail."

"Says the pot to the kettle," Crandall said, raising his eyebrows. "I'll be back." He opened the door and let the morning light spill into the room.

"Hurry up and close the door," Zoey said, squinting.

"I shall return," Crandall said.

"Famous last words," Manson said.

Crandall shut the door and ventured away from the hotel.

Inside the hotel room, Manson and Zoey climbed into the stiff bed and pulled the blankets over their bodies, snuggling together, enjoying being close to each other. They nodded off to sleep.

5

Later that night, when they awoke, they were rested but hungry.

"Hurry up and get ready. We will go out tonight and find a mark."

"Indeed. We must find someone lovely to feed on. I am famished."

"We will. We will, my love. We need money, too."

One thing that was certain was that their cash fund was getting low, and they needed to make some money, fast. They decided to find a victim to suck some blood and take some cash. Maybe someone good looking and rich, and if the victim was famous that would be a bonus, but someone with exquisite taste was certainly a perfunctory detail.

"I'm hungry," Manson said. "We need to feed soon."

"Yes. It's almost time," she said. "Let me look for a good hunting place."

"We need to find a bar or club where there will be desirable people. I'm not in the mood for old bar whores and winos. I want someone young and delicious."

"Just wait," she said. "Let me look on Google."

Zoey sat down on the bed again, picking up her iPhone. Her face was lit up by the blue light. She focused on the small LCD screen and quickly typed in something on the simulated keyboard. She searched for restaurants and bars and hotels in Bellingham.

"Here is a good one," she said, after browsing for a moment. "It's called The Halfway Inn & Tavern. Doesn't that sound lovely?"

"What? It sounds like a dive."

"They have karaoke. We can sing and get drunk."

"Maybe I don't want to get drunk tonight."

"Oh, don't be a party pooper. Think about it . . . there will be people there who think they can sing. It will attract wanna be rockers and hipsters. Don't you know anything about that?"

"I suppose," Manson said. "When does it get started?"

"It says they start at ten o'clock," she said. "So, that means they have already started without us."

"Yes. We should go, soon."

"I need to take a shower first."

"But, honey, we need to go now," Zoey said, pleading with him.

"It's not fair that you get to clean up this morning and I must stay in my disgusting cloths, unshaved. I will clean up first, and then we will go."

"Fine. Hurry up. We are already behind. It will be midnight soon and the mortals will go to bed. We will need to find them while they are awake."

Manson went into the bathroom and closed the door.

Zoey heard him turn on the shower, so she waited patiently. She browsed for attractions in the local area that would be of interest to a pair of dark, undead, vampires. She searched for legends and myths, haunted places nearby, and she found something interesting after a short time. It was a website about a spooky legend in a cemetery in Bellingham on a website page named *www.ghostlylegends.com*:

Bayview Cemetery, located in Bellingham, Washington, established in 1888, now contains more than twenty-five thousand graves, and is a serenely beautiful and peaceful resting place for the dead to be visited by the living only during daylight. At night, it takes on a sinister and spooky quality and this is a cemetery where you don't want to go alone after dark, or even at twilight, because strange things happen there in the nighttime hours. It has lore and legend, like many graveyards, and there are a few scary stories that surround it historically: "Angel Eyes" and the "Death Bed" are two of the more common tales.

"Angel Eyes" is a legend that surrounds the fate of a young woman from centuries past who was accused of being a witch. The townsfolk gathered together and killed her, hastily burying her body where the angel statue now stands. She became a restless spirit, and her ghost haunted the cemetery in the dark of night. It has been reported by eyewitnesses that, when the moon is full, blood red tears flow from the angel statue eyes as she weeps in sorrow, and the eyes have also been seen glowing brightly in the dark. This myth has been debunked many times; however, it is still widely shared as a tale of legend and lore.

The legend of the "Death Bed" is another favorite, and it is centered around a tomb that looks like a miniature Roman temple. The story goes that if you lay down on the tomb at midnight you will lose your life shortly afterward. Nobody knows for sure when they will die, so this myth can never truly be confirmed.

There have been reports by witnesses that have walked by the cemetery at night and saw things like ghost, mysterious voices and whispers, orbs and glowing phenomena floating around in the air, and paranormal investigators have taken EVP recordings and videos and pictures that have captured some of these strange events. There is certainly a spooky aura surrounding this graveyard. It is widely believed that the Bayview Cemetery is truly haunted by supernatural entities.

Zoey put down her phone and watched as Manson came out of the shower, fresh and cleanly shaven, in a white towel, his six-pack of abdomen muscled ripped and sexy, his black hairy chest displaying his Devil's eye necklace prominently, his hair mussed and wet. She looked at him and smiled. He was strikingly handsome, built like an elegant and graceful statue carved by Michelangelo, his movements cool and becoming, and she wanted to jump up and grab him right there, and fuck him. He had his little black bag out and was digging through it, taking out a toothbrush and toothpaste.

"A vamp has to keep his teeth clean, eh?" he said, turning and smiling at her. He winked, a dimple forming on his cheek.

"You look good," she said. "And you smell nice, too. What cologne is that?"

"I only use Old Spice," he said. "I got to get my swagger on."

"I could just eat you up, right now," she said. "Too bad we

don't have time for a quick romp."

"There will be time for that later," he said. He put toothpaste on the brush and stuck it in his mouth, brushing vigorously in an up and down motion, the past foaming at the corner of his mouth. His fangs were showing as he cleaned them nicely.

Zoey looked back at her phone. She was drawn back to the website she had been viewing a moment before.

"We have to stop and see this," Zoey said. "There is a haunted cemetery in Bellingham. There is a legend that the dead walk there at night, and an angel statue that weeps blood from the eyes. I want to visit the Angel Eyes statue at midnight—at the dead of night. We can lay down on the Death Bed, too. There is a haunted grave. It's so romantic. Don't you think?"

"Ayah. I don't know," Manson said. He shrugged his shoulders and brushed a lock of black hair away from his brow. "It sounds boring. What is there to see in a cemetery? It's just a bunch of tombstones and corpses."

"Yes. But this one sounds fun," Zoey said. "And since we are here in Bellingham, why not go out there and see? It will be like a field trip."

"You and your cemeteries," Manson said. "I swear. When will you ever get enough?"

"Please," she said. "Just this once. I won't ask again . . ."

"Fine," Manson said. "We'll go there tonight."

"Great," Zoey said. "I can't wait. I just love visiting old graveyards. They are so peaceful and quaint."

"That is because everyone there is dead."

"Well, so are we," she said. "But undead. It's so ironic, don't you think?"

"Oh, yes," he said. "Isn't it? Ironic, I mean. We are dead, but still alive. I see where you are going with that."

"We could dig up a corpse and reanimate it."

"Really? You want to do that? I don't think so. We have enough beasties walking about the Earth without creating more monsters to lurk in the night."

"But it would be so much fun."

"I see. Yes. Maybe. We really don't have time for such festivities, though."

"No. Probably not. It was just an idea."

"We need to go to this karaoke contest and find a sheep to eat."

"Okay, well, I'm waiting on you. Hurry up."

"I'm getting ready as fast as I can."

"I'm going to go out and smoke while you finish getting ready."

"Fine. Don't do anything foolish out there. Leave the neighbors alone. Remember, never kill where you sleep."

"Yes, darling," she said, picking up her cigarettes from her purse. "I'll be back in a moment."

She stepped out of the motel room. Manson dressed in a clean pair of black denim jeans, a white frill lace silk shirt with ruffled cuffs and collar, a black leather vest, and his boots. He was almost ready when she came back inside.

"I think someone was watching me," she said. "It was a gray van, like a camper style van. There was a man sitting in the driver's seat. I could sense him, even from here."

"What do you mean?"

"There was a van parked across the street. I thought I saw someone in it."

Manson went to the window, pulled back the curtain and peered out into the night, looking at the parking lot. He looked across the street and saw the silver Chevy van parked there. It did look suspicious, he thought. He could not see anyone in the van, however, and perhaps it was juts Zoey being paranoid.

They had recently committed murders, after all, and there was a good reason to worry about being followed by anyone, the police, or a vigilante.

"Could it be that guy from Vancouver? He may be following us, still."

"I don't know. But we should be careful."

"Right. Absolutely. We will watch for him," Manson said. He took his leather jacket down from the hanger in the closet and pulled it on, straightening his sleeves and cuffs on his shirt.

Suddenly, there was a knock at the door. It startled them.

"Who is that?" Zoey asked.

"I'm not sure—" He peeked back out the window and was relieved at what he saw. Crandall was standing at the door, grinning. "It's just Crandall."

He opened the door and let him in.

"You scared the holy hell out of us," Manson said.

"Sorry about that," Crandall said.

"Where have you been?" Zoey asked.

"Just roaming about," he said, "checking out the local sights and sounds. A dog must roam, you know?"

"I forgot about you," Manson said, "for a moment."

"See how you are?" Crandall said. "You wouldn't even miss me if I was gone . . . if I never came back."

"That's not true," Zoey said. "I knew you were coming back. You love us too much to leave without saying goodbye."

"True," Crandall said.

"How do I look?" Zoey asked.

"Marvelous," Crandall said.

"Thank you," she said.

"Good, let's get going now," Manson said.

"Can we visit the cemetery after we find our victim?"

"What? Cemetery?" Crandall asked, confused. "We are going to a cemetery?"

"Absolutely," Zoey said, smiling. "It's supposed to be haunted."

"I don't see why not," Manson said.

"Let's go then," Zoey said, primping her one last time. "It's getting late."

"After you, my lady," Manson said, opening the door. "And you, kind sir." He motioned for Crandall to pass through the door so he could lock it behind them.

They left the motel room and went out into the damp and rainy night. It was unseasonably warm for such a night, and there was a warm breeze blowing the dots of rain about in crazy spiraling patterns. They all looked at the van. It made them nervous.

"What could it mean?" Crandall wondered. "I noticed that van when I was out walking. Who is it?"

"The vampire hunter," Zoey said. "He's been following us."

"I figured as much," Crandall said. "What shall we do?"

"Never mind that," Manson said. "Get in the car. We will outrun him if we have to."

"Agreed," Zoey said.

"I will rip his heart out and eat it while it is still beating," Crandall said. "When the time is right . . . he will get what is coming to him."

"Indubitably," Manson said, opening the car door. "Now get in and let's make like ghosts and disappear."

They got inside the Monte Carlo and sat back comfortably, ready for some action. Manson turned on the lights, started the engine with a rumble and roar, and turned on the stereo which was already playing a favorite song by the band Tool. Manson put the car in gear and backed out, turned around, and pulled out on the Maplewood Avenue. They were on their way to sing some karaoke, get drunk, and find a victim to suck some blood and, maybe, eat a beating heart alive, and then they would visit the cemetery where the angel wept and the death bed waited for them to eternally sleep.

6

Adrian was sitting in his van, parked across the street from the Shamrock Motel. He was comfortable in his van, and it served as a second home away from home. It was decked out with a minifridge, a small sink basin, a propane stove with a single burner, pots and pans, real sterling silver wear, HDTV with satellite receiver, a Sony PlayStation, XFM radio, laptop computer, sleeping quarters with a fluffy Eddie Bower down sleeping bag and pillow, shag carpet on the floor, fluorescent lamp on a collapsible desk, and storage space and a foot locker for all his tools and weapons. He kept his clothing in a Samsonite suitcase, his leather coat and suit jackets hung neatly on a hook. His boots and shoes were kept at the foot of his bed.

He had boxes with obscure books about supernatural beings, vampires, werewolves, ghosts, demons, devils, Voodoo, spells, and curses. There were old maps and atlas books that showed routs at certain locations that no longer existed or were not charted on any common, modern map. These were the passages of the dead and the undead, and these roads were traveled by ghostly beings, demons, entities, where no mortal would ever tread. Adrian knew these roads well, and he had fought many battles with malign evil.

Presently, he was eating a Cup Noodles, beef flavored with Tabasco sauce and pepper, and sitting in the back of his van.

He was keeping an eye out for the couple in the black Monte Carlo. They were going to get what they had coming soon. He slurped up the ramen noodles, drank the juice, and wiped his lips on a paper towel.

"Mmm, good," he said. "Best fifty cents I ever spent."

7

Snapping back to reality, Adrian was sitting in the van across from the Shamrock Motel, presently, he threw the empty Styrofoam cup in a trash bag hanging from the cabinet and climbed up into the cockpit, sitting in the driver's seat. He had a pair of binoculars and he used them to peer through the windshield to get closer look at door number 9 where the vampires were currently residing. He knew they would have to come out eventually to feed, and it was getting close to midnight, so he expected them to make a move soon. He decided to make an entry in his journal.

Adrian Burgendorv's journal.

January 1, 2020. Bellingham—I am watching the vampires now, as they are held up in a motel room. They don't know it yet, but I have killed the evil countess who created them. I told the investigators about what I know, but they are stupid cops and wouldn't know the truth if it smacked them in the face. I cannot rely upon law enforcement agencies to help me catch vampires and werewolves. They have never believed in ghosts or boogeymen and I don't expect them to ever change their point of view about that subject. It is hard to believe, after all, but I am unfortunate enough to have experienced these supernatural phenomena, and I know beyond a reasonable doubt that monsters do exits.

With this in mind, I will have to hunt these evil creatures down by myself and put them to rest on my own. I will kill them. Let there be no question about that. I intend to rid the earth of as many of these foul beasts as possible. That is my duty. To uphold the decency of humanity and forever fight against the evils that lurk in the darkness and feed on innocence.

I know where they are going. They are trying to evade me by going to the United States, but I will follow them anywhere, until my job is done.

Law enforcement is completely useless. This is a proven fact. I will have to avoid them unless I want to get arrested for being a vigilante. Note: keep a low profile and do not attract attention from the police. This is a priority at all costs.

Now I will continue to wait and see what these vampires do next. The ball is in their court. I will react to their actions.

8

Adrian watched through the windshield of the van, and all was quiet at the motel, except for a wino passing through parking lot, picking up cigarette butts along his way. The rain was coming down in fits and snatches, and visibility was poor. The neon lights of the sign outside the Motel flickered. The vacancy sign was lit up brightly. This was a seedy motel, and just the kind of place Adrian expected a couple of vampires to choose to hide out. Nobody would question them here, as this was dingy and rundown, and in a part of town where bad things happened to people, frequently.

Suddenly, door number 9 opened, and he saw the pretty girl, a seductive beast, step out into the night. The doorway was lit with a single fluorescent light. She was smoking a cigarette.

"Oh, how nice," Adrian said. "She is observing the no smoking policy. She has manners."

The dark Goth girl vampire was shivering from the cold and damp, and she quickly puffed on the cigarette, in a hurry to get back inside. He knew she smoked Marlboro menthol 100s because he had picked up a discarded butt after he first began following them; he was keeping them for evidence, to get DNA samples if necessary. She looked around the parking lot, then straight at Adrian in the van, as though she sensed his presence. Her blue eyes glittered like diamonds, her evil spirit emanating from within, and she made eye contact with Adrian through the wet windshield and the binoculars. She stared right into his soul. He could feel her evil presence touching him from a distance.

He pulled the binoculars away from his eyes and shrunk down in the seat, hiding away, attempting to go unnoticed. He felt his heart racing in his chest. These creatures were cunning and quick, and if she saw him and knew he was there, she could easily cross the distance in an instant and cause a commotion. He did not want to cause a scene.

After a moment had passed, he peeked over the dash, past the steering wheel and observed that she was stamping out her cigarette with her boot, and then turned and went back inside the motel room.

"Holy shit, that was close," he said.

He did not want to blow his cover or let them know that he was on to them. Not, yet, anyway. The time would come for confrontation, and battle, but for now he just wanted to watch them from a distance.

A moment later, he saw someone in the motel room peek out through the curtain. It was the male vampire, he could see his face, boyish charm and chiseled jaw, and he appeared to be looking over at the van.

Had they noticed him? Was his cover blown? He did not know. No matter, he reasoned, for he would engage them, nonetheless.

The door opened and the trio came out, shutting the light off in the room behind them. They went to the Monte Carlo and climbed inside. The lights on the car flicked on, the head-light lighting up the green wall of the motel. The exhaust from the tailpipe billowed up into the spattering rain, illuminated by the red glow of the taillights.

"It's go time," Adrian said, sitting up in the seat.

The Monte Carlo carrying the werewolf and the dreaded undead creatures pulled out from the motel parking lot and proceeded down Maplewood Avenue at a fast pace. He could see them sitting in the front seat, their pale white faces and black makeup and hair making them look like creepy china dolls, the car like something out of a 1970s horror film. He knew the werewolf was sitting in the back, the normal look-ing one of the bunch, but even he was contemptible, because he possessed the curse of the wolf and was a creature that plagued humanity and must be put our of his misery, for the good of mankind.

He started the engine on his van and waited for a moment before pulling out on the street and following them. This was going to be exciting. He was primed for the kill. This is what he lived for, killing vampires and vanquishing evil.

CHAPTER THIRTEEN

1

It was cold, crisp, night and the stars twinkled brightly in the cloudless sky. Manson steered the Monte Carlo down the avenue and tapped his fingers on the steering wheel to the beat of the music on the radio.

Karaoke in Bellingham would be delightful, Zoey thought. *I would love to sing for a while before I bite someone on the neck. What could be more fun than that?*

It will be spectacular, Manson thought, *and we will have so much fun, it will be legendary.*

Crandall, sitting pretty in the backseat, knew they were communicating with their minds, leaving him out of the conversation, sitting in the all alone and lost in his own thought, which they could also read, and he felt excluded, but that was okay, because he was an open book and he did not care if they knew what he was thinking.

Fuck you both, Crandall thought, intentionally. *No, really . . . I want to fuck you both . . . at the same time.*

They looked back and smiled together.

That would be delightful, Manson thought, wagging his eyebrows.

Indeed, Zoey thought, *I would like that very much.*

"We're here," Manson said, stepping on the brake. "It's time to get it on."

As they approached the tavern lit up against the darkness of the night, the neon sign glowing with green and red light, a welcoming sight, they could sense that this was good place to find an innocent victim. There was blood to spill here, and they could smell it, rich and dark, like a fine chocolate perfume.

"I'm not much of a singer," Crandall said, "but I do love a good dive bar."

"It's just karaoke," Zoey said, looking back at him. "You don't have to be Chad Kroeger."

"Nickelback?" Manson said. "Are they even a thing anymore?"

"I think so," Zoey said.

"Don't expect me to get up there and sing," Crandall said, sitting back and crossing his arms. "That's all I'm saying."

Manson pulled the Monte Carlo up at a stoplight and held the brake pedal down with his foot. He was anxious to get going, his other foot hovering over the accelerator. There was a little old lady hobbling across the street with a cane, and he wondered if she was aware of how close she was to death. *Old people had to know their time was growing short,* he mused. *Not only that, she is passing in front of a massive automobile with enough horsepower to mash her to a bloody pulp in the road.* He would never do such a thing as run over a helpless little old lady—or would he?—and it was just curious how death was stalking her and she continued moving, pursuing her endeavors, despite the fact that the grave was beckoning for her. She passed in front of the headlights and then stepped up onto the sidewalk on the other side of the road just as the crossing light changed from a symbol of a white walking man to an image of a blinking read hand.

"I guess we will never have to worry about that," Manson said.

"What?" Crandall asked.

"Growing old," Zoey said. "We're vampires. We can't grow old."

"We will be forever young," Manson said. "And beautiful."

"Speak for yourself," Crandall said. "I am growing older, even as we speak."

"But you still look good," Manson said. "That's the important part. You have to look good, even when you are old."

"I guess so," Crandall said. "That doesn't make it any sweeter."

The stoplight changed to green and Manson stepped hard on the accelerator, the engine growling savagely, their heads whipping back with the forward momentum. The tires chirped and the throaty growl of the Monte Carlo could be heard for blocks away, announcing that the group of sinister fiends with angst and attitude were on their way and people better get ready for what was coming: decadence, debauchery, and death.

The neon sign of The Halfway Inn & Tavern was glowing with green, red, and white light and it welcomed them in as the marquee said: **Food and Beer, Pool and Darts, Karaoke all Week.**

"What a charming place," Crandall said, looking out the window.

"We shall find some fun inside, I'm sure," Manson said, turning off the main drive and pulling into the parking lot.

"I'm ready," Zoey said. "I need some excitement after such a dull and boring drive."

After parking the car, Manson took out the key, looked at his companions and said, "Let's go, my friends. We have things to do here. Everyone keep it nice. We don't want to attract too much attention, now."

"Whatever," Zoey said. "I just love hillbillies. They are so delicious with their pork rinds and chewing tobacco. I love to see them squirm when they are down on their knees. But, I will be on my best behavior. You have my word."

"Me too," Crandall said, as he grabbed the door handle and opened the door, putting a foot out, ready to go inside. "I only want to reap havoc when the moon is full . . . remember? Otherwise, I am a gentleman of magnificent proportions."

They laughed at his joke. The humor was dark and delightful.

"If there is a problem," Manson said, wagging his eyebrows. "You know what to do. Take no prisoners. If they start some shit, we will finish it. So, let's hope we can all just get along."

They stepped out of the Monte Carlo, regrouped, and then put their arms around one another as they entered in through the door and got their first glance inside.

2

The interior of the bar was seedy, dark, and smelled of cologne and stale beer. They entered and surveyed the scene. There were at least two dozen patrons sitting at tables, at the bar, playing pool at two tables in the back. There was a couple playing darts. Another man was playing a video game, intently twisting the game controller, and cussing at the machine when he failed to score bonus points.

The stage was front and center, and there was a couple dressed like country bumpkins murdering a song by Kid Rock and Sheryl Crow, about a picture. They were out of key and the volume was too loud.

"Ooh," Zoey said. "That is atrocious."

"Let's sit down at the bar and order something to drink," Manson said.

"Don't you want to sing a song?"

"Yes. I do," he said, sitting down. "But first I want something to drink."

They sat down and ordered drinks, three Tequila Sunrises.

There was a young man with a baseball cap sitting alone at a table, nursing a gin and tonic. He was watching the dark Gothic couple across the room. He was attracted to Zoey's magnetic charm, instantly.

"It looks like you have an admirer," Manson said, nodding his head at the man sitting alone.

"I see him," she said.

Crandall was passive and quiet. He seemed out of place in the bar.

"Perhaps he wants some company . . ." Manson said. He looked at Crandall and smiled. "Maybe we could give him what he needs? Eh?"

Crandall smiled, snickered, then shrugged his shoulders.

"In a moment," Zoey said.

The bartender put the Tequila Sunrise drinks in front of them and Manson paid with cash. They each took a sip of their beverage and prepared to assess the victims in the room. Who would be the lucky one tonight? It was always a crapshoot; picking the right blood was important, because not all blood was created equal; some blood tasted terrible, and some was divine, and that was the blood they were seeking.

Before they could make a move, still sipping on their drinks, the man with the baseball cap at the table stood up and walked over to them.

"Hello," he said. "How are you?"

"We are lovely," Manson said. "How are you?"

They could smell the gin on his breath.

Crandall was disgusted and stood up, saying, "I am going to go see if I can wrangle up a game of pool. You guys enjoy yourselves." He stood up and walked over to the pool tables where a group of rough and tumble men were engaged in a heated competition, money sitting on the table. Crandall put down a quarter to signal that he wanted to play. They looked at him cruelly at first, then shrugged indifferently, as they would take his money, too. No worries about that, they thought, as his money was just as good as any other schmuck.

Back at the bar, the man in the baseball cap addressed Manson and said, "I am doing good," the man said. "Can I buy you two a drink?"

"We have one," Manson said. "But another would not hurt. Please sit down and join us."

"My name is Adam," the man said.

"Hello Adam," Zoey said, leaning out to see around Manson. She stuck out her hand for a shake and smiled. "Such a pleasure to meet you."

Adam extended his hand; they shook each other's hands. It was a formality, as old as time.

Adam sat down on the stool where Crandall had been sitting, the seat was still warm as werewolves have an excessively high body temperature, even when they are not in their time of change.

"Ooh, this seat is still warm," Adam said. "Your friend has a hot ass."

"We know," Zoey said, jubilantly. "It is a very nice ass, indeed."

"Well, that's not quite what I meant," Adam said, "but okay. I'll take your word for it." He looked at the bartender and said,

"Bartender . . . please allow me to buy this lovely couple anything they want to drink. It's on me. Drink up and be merry."

The bartender looked at Adam, skeptically, then looked at the dark Goth couple, bemused, and smirked. He had seen this before, and he knew that this was a case of predator and prey. It played itself out frequently in taverns and bars across the world.

Adam looked to be in his early thirties, a working-class stiff, and he was attractive. He was physically fit and handsome.

Zoey looked at him from the corner of her eye. She could see that he was sneaking glances at her.

"Are you going to sing tonight?" Adam asked.

"We are," Manson said. "I am a singer of old. I love karaoke."

"Are you going to sing a song?"

"I already have," Adam said. "But I will sing another one. I'm up next."

The couple on the stage had finished murdering the duet by Kid Rock and Sheryl Crow and the DJ was taking the stage.

"Alright," the DJ said into the microphone. "Let's give it up for Wendel and Rhonda. What a lovely song that was."

"Now, we have a special treat from our friend Adam," the DJ said. He looked around the room and located Adam sitting at the bar with the Goth couple. "There he is. Come up here Adam and sing this song."

Adam got up from his seat, excuse himself, and approached the center stage.

"Here you go, buddy," the DJ said.

Adam took the stage, grabbed the mic and waited for the music to start. The DJ went to the karaoke booth and spun up the track. It was a song by Radio Head, about a creep and weirdo who wanted a perfect soul, so fucking special.

"Are we going to take this guy?" Manson said, looking at Zoey.

"We have to feed soon," she said. "He will do."

"Let's invite him back to a party afterward with us."

"He will be anxious to go, I'm sure."

When the song was over, Adam came back to the bar and sat next to Zoey.

"I guess it's my turn," Manson said. "I will pick a song."

He got up and went over to the DJ and spoke with him in private.

Zoey was watching Adam beside her. He was obviously interested in her.

"You are beautiful," Adam said. "Are you two a couple? If you don't mind me asking."

"Thank you," Zoey said. "And yes. We are a couple. That doesn't mean we don't like other people, sometimes, though."

"Oh, I see," Adam said. "What exactly does that mean?"

"It means exactly what it sounds like. We have an open relationship. Sometimes we like to mix it up."

"Are you swingers, then?"

"No. Absolutely not. We just like to spice it up sometimes."

"I like that."

"I thought you would."

"Do you want to party?" Adam said.

The DJ took the stage and spoke through the microphone.

"Okay, ladies and gentlemen, please welcome Manson to the Halfway Inn karaoke stage. He is going to be singing us a special song tonight. It's not a typical song we hear often, but tonight we are making an exception for our new guest. We are always excited to meet new people. Please give a warm welcome, won't you?"

The audience, and the patrons sitting around the bar,

stopped and looked at Manson. It grew silent for a moment, as they looked at the pale, dark, figure on the stage, glowing in the spotlight.

"Hello," Manson said. "Can someone dim the lights. That thing is blinding me."

The spotlight was turned off, and the ambiance became softer by degrees.

"Sing us a song, there weirdo," a redneck shouted from the pool table.

"Yeah, freak," another redneck pool player said. "Are you a fag, or what?"

"Maybe," Manson said, looking over to the men by the pool tables. He saw Crandall standing with a pool cue, pumping his fist in encouragement, smiling back at him, suggesting that Manson should go for it and rock the mic. "But what concern is that of yours?" Manson asked, shrugging off the rude remarks. "I feel like singing tonight. I hope you all like the song I've picked."

"Just sing the fucking song, ya fag," the first redneck said. He thought he was being funny. The group of pool players were pleased with their attitudes and humor. They slapped one another high fives and strutted around arrogantly.

"I intend to," Manson said into the microphone. "If you'll please allow me to get it started." He looked at the DJ, nodded, and was ready to perform.

The song began to play through the PA system. It was a song by Judas Priest titled "Love Bites."

Manson started singing the song and performed it flawlessly. At first the bar was silent, but then they warmed up and listened intently. It was a hit. The crowd loved it.

After the song was over, Manson blew a kiss to the rednecks at the pool table.

"I love you all," he said, leaving the stage.

There was mild applause from the unenthused masses in the bar, except the for the vigorous cheers and clapping from Crandall, who had thoroughly enjoyed the performance. He put his fingers to his mouth and whistled, then said "Bravo! Bravo! Encore!"

"Thank you, Crandall. I can always count on you, my friend," Manson said, before handing the mic back to the DJ and stepping down from the stage. He crossed back to the bar, and the patrons went back to their own concerns, nursing their beers and mixed drinks.

Manson went back to the bar and sat next to Zoey and Adam, who were now chatting warmly.

Zoey looked at Manson and said, "Adam here wants to come back to our room and have a party."

"That's great," Manson said. "We would love to have you. I'm sure you will be delicious."

"Whatever you say, my friend. I'm down with anything," Adam said.

Crandall came back from the pool tables, a handful of dollar bills in his hand. He had won several games of pool and took the rednecks for their hard-earned money. They were not pleased by this, at all. They stood in the corner watching the strange Goth weirdo strangers at the bar.

"I don't think they like us," Crandall said, putting the wad of bills in his pocket. "It may be a good time to get out of here because I think they indent to retaliate."

"Let them," Manson said. "I could use a little excitement tonight. We can handle them, I think. Don't you?"

Crandall shrugged, finished the last of a remaining Tequila Sunrise sitting on the bar and wiped his lips on his sleeve. "I think so," he said. "No worries. Zero perspiration, as they say."

"I am going to use the little boy's room," Manson said.

He looked at Zoey and nodded, sending her a telepathic thought: *You know what to do.*

She looked back, nodded, and winked.

Zoey: *Yes.*

"Absolutely," Crandall said, winking at them. "We got this."

Manson went to the restroom and relieved himself. When he came back out, Zoey, Crandall, and Adam were gone. The bartender was wiping down the bar with a towel.

"Your friends just left," the bartender said, nodding toward the door.

"I see that," Manson said. "I will have to go and join them."

"Have a good night," the bartender said.

"Likewise," Manson said, exiting the tavern.

The bartender watched him leave, shaking his head and saying, "Poor fools. Some people just never learn."

Manson went out into the parking lot and walked to the Monte Carlo. Crandall was sitting in the front, in the passenger seat where Zoey normally sat, and he was fiddling with the stereo, tuning in a station. He looked bored. Manson looked in the back seat and saw Zoey and Adam there with mouthfuls of tongue, hands full of cock and breast, steaming up the windows. He opened the door and climbed into the back seat to join them. This was going to be fun, and delicious.

3

The rednecks who had been playing pool were gathering outside in the parking lot, now an angry mob, waiting for Manson and Crandall outside the Monte Carlo. They wanted their pound of flesh and meant to take it by force.

"Hey, punk," the redneck with beard said, tapping on the

window. "Why don't you come out here and talk to us? We got something we need to discuss with you. Bring your queer friend, too."

Manson lifted his head from between Zoey legs where he had been licking deep inside her pink parts and grinned. This was going to be good. Adam looked at him, confused, wondering what to do; he was sporting an enormous erection his large cock still bulging with a purple crown, sticking straight up like an exclamation point. Zoey grabbed his shaft, unconcerned about the men outside the car, and stuck it in her mouth and sucked on it lovingly. She liked a large cock and this one was a winner.

"I'll handle this," Manson said. "Just continue without me. I'll be right back. Crandall, would you care to join me while we deal with these assholes?"

Crandall was looking out that the mob in the parking lot, and said, "Sure. I would enjoy it. Nothing more fun than beating the shit out of a bunch of rednecks. Lead the way, muchacho."

Manson climbed between the seats, got into the driver seat, straightened out his hair and jacket in the rearview mirror— had to look good while fighting and fucking, he thought—and then he opened the door and stepped out. Crandall opened the passenger side door and stepped out, too, ready to get it on.

"Well, looky here," a redneck said, spitting tobacco juice. "We got us a couple fairy queers been making out in the parking lot."

Manson and Crandall looked at each other, smiled, knowing that they could beat all of these guys singlehandedly. They had supernatural strength on their side, so it was a no-brainer, they would mop up the parking lot with a few corn-fed Podunk good old boys.

"You sing like a girl," one of the rednecks said. "You a pussy, or something?"

"What?" Manson said, surprised. "I'm not sure—"

They encircled Manson and Crandall made an attack; however, they were much too fast and quickly beat them with his swift and nimble hands. Crandall had the power of the werewolf at his disposal, and Manson was a vampire, a badass, who knew martial arts and was fast with his hands and feet. The rednecks did not stand a chance. The underestimated the Goth and punk appearance of the two skinny looking men and were delivered their asses on a platter.

After they finished kicking the rednecks assess, leaving them in a jumble on the ground to pick themselves up, they went back toward the car, where Adam and Zoey were watching in amazement. The rednecks were beginning to get up, wiping bloody lips and broken noses and limping away, handwaving Manson and Chandler away as a waste of time.

"Forget you," one of the rednecks said. "Faggots. Get the fuck out of here."

"You are lucky, punks," another redneck said. "Next time we're going to kill you motherfuckers."

"Have a nice night, gentlemen," Manson said, wriggling his fingers and smiling at them. "It was a pleasure kicking your asses. Maybe next time, eh?"

"That will teach you assholes," Crandall said, picking up a baseball cap that had fallen off one of the rednecks during the scuffle and throwing it at them. The red hat fluttered like a broken Frisbee and landed at their feet. He kicked a rock at them and spat on the ground. "Maybe next time you'll think twice about fucking with the gay guys. Eh? But, maybe not."

Manon and Chandler went to the black Monte Carlo, opened the door, and climbed inside.

4

"Holy, shit," Adam said, tapping Manson on the shoulder. "You guys handled those men like a champ. I was going to get out and help you . . . but you were already done by the time I could get the door open."

"That's my guys," Zoey said, kissing them each on the cheek. "My heroes."

"Aw, shucks, my lady," Crandall said, feigning a bashful expression. "You are too kind. It was an honor to defend you from the bad guys."

"It was nothing," Manson said, looking back at them in the back seat, still wrapped up in an erotic embrace. "How are you two getting along? I see you have risen to the occasion."

"Hope you don't mind me sitting out here with your girl," Adam said, looking at Manson. "Want to do a line of some badass cocaine I brought with me?"

"Not at all," Manson said. "Maybe Crandall and I will indulge in our own suck and fuck party by ourselves up here in the front seat."

He reached over and embraced Crandall in a full lip lock, they kissed with tongues intertwined, groping for each other's cocks.

"But first," Manson said, pulling back. "We have something to do. Crandall, you may want to sit this one out."

Crandall looked back and winked and nodded. He knew what time it was, and he would enjoy watching.

Manson climbed in the back seat, exposed his fangs, saying, "I will join you, two, first . . . because we have to eat tonight . . . and I'm hungry after the fight."

"What the hell are you talking about?" Adam asked, confused.

Zoey pulled herself up, her fangs now exposed and glittering in the illumination coming in from the sodium vapor lamps mounted in the parking lot and on the bar meant to light up the area and provide security.

Crandall went back to tuning the radio. He was looking for the right radio station to play some music to suit the mood. This was going to be fun and the festivities were about to begin.

"Are you going to join us?" Manson asked, looking at Crandall.

"No. I'll sit this one out, as you said," Crandall replied. "Enjoy. I'll eat some meat later. This is your party now."

Suddenly, the bloodbath was underway, and Adam was taken by surprise as the vampires attacked, biting his throat and ripping it wide open in a bloody, severed mess of flesh and bones and tendons.

He screamed for the last time in his life, loud and piercing, then turning to a gurgle as he choked on his own blood.

The kill was quick. They pulled Adam down in the back seat and sank their fangs into his tender flesh. He never knew what hit him. He tried to fight, screamed and attempted to get away, but they overpowered him and drank his blood.

He was delicious, just as they had anticipated.

After killing Adam, they drove to a secluded backstreet and tossed his corpse into the bushes. It would be found soon, but they had enough time to get away, and by the time it was discovered they would be long gone.

CHAPTER FOURTEEN

1

Manson, Zoey, and Crandall drove to the Bayview Cemetery to take a tour of the legendary Angel statue. The Bayview Cemetery was owned, operated, and managed by the City of Bellingham. It was founded in 1887 after the town of Whatcom purchased a ten-acre parcel adjacent to Lake Whatcom road. They named it "Whatcom City Cemetery" and burials began in 1888. After that, twelve additional acres were acquired in 1889. The rest of the cemetery property was assimilated in 1924, providing Bayview with 234 acres of burial ground. In 1889 human remains from another older cemetery in the Fairhaven community were relocated to Bayview Cemetery. Smaller burial grounds from outlying areas in the vicinity also contributed bodies to the newer, larger cemetery.

They pulled up in the parking lot, thought better of it, and decided to park on an adjacent street a block away from the cemetery. Police and security would be watching for anyone foolish enough to park in the cemetery parking lot.

The cemetery gate was constructed of massive rectangular

pillars with red brick and limestone formed in a Gothic arch motif with crosses at the top. There was a wrought iron arched entry sign overhead between the two pillars with large white letters spelling out **BAYVIEW**. A fence went to smaller pillars adjacent to the main entry gate. It was dark, but they could see the entryway easy enough. The fence was no deterrent and they were able to easily sneak into the cemetery. They were vampires after all, and night vision was one of their abilities, and a werewolf had excellent sight in the dark, too, so they could see things without a flashlight.

The gravestones in the cemetery were a mix of modern and old fashioned stones, some flat granite rectangles in the grass, some of the brass plaques, and others were in the shape of crosses and classic curved shapes, there were obelisks, and pillars, Norman, Gothic, ogee styles stones, square top, checked, raised, square, serpentine, offset, and peon topped, arc or chambered, and every type of headstone available was represented across the grassy graves. The grave markers stood in silhouette against the murky haze lingering in the darkened landscape. The graveyard was beautiful in the dark. The trees stood out against the moonlight and stars twinkling from the night sky.

They sneaked past the gates and entered the cemetery un-noticed.

2

Adrian Burgendorv watched from a distance, sitting his van down the street from the Tavern where they had murdered the karaoke singer in the back seat of the Monte Carlo. He had witnessed everything and new that they killed Adam and dumped him in the woods. He thought about calling the police, but he wanted to put the vampires to death. The police would only arrest them and that would not be good enough. They deserved to die and have their wretched undead vile and evil existence put out and extinguished permanently.

He decided he would attempt to confront them while they were parked at the Bayview Cemetery, in Bellingham, in the middle of the night.

He pulled up next a dark area where trees grew tall and he was concealed by the dark. He shut the engine off and waited. It would be time to strike in a moment.

He had a pair of night vision binoculars and he could watch them as clearly as if it was daytime and the sun was shining. They had strange and sinister looking eyes in the green light.

3

"I want to see this Angel Eyes statue," Zoey said. "It's over there." She pointed in the direction of the statue. "This way, over here."

"This is silly," Crandall said. "I don't believe in ghosts."

"That's funny," Manson said, "considering that you are a werewolf, yourself. You don't think ghosts can exist?"

"Well, since you put it like that," Crandall said. "I guess, maybe."

"Hurry up, you two," Zoey said, moving ahead of them. "Come on and follow me."

They went to the statue and stood beneath the stone angel, looking up, nonplussed. It was not anything special. Just some cold stone statue.

"I don't see anything special about that," Manson said.

"It's kind of neat," Crandall said. "This place gives me the creeps."

"How is that even possible, for you to get the creeps?" Zoey asked. "We are the creeps. It doesn't get any freakier than us. See what I mean?"

"Touché," Manson said. "We are creatures of the night. It is our duty to horrify and terrify the innocent."

"Yes. I see your point," Crandall said. "I'm still getting used to this lifestyle. It takes practice, I guess."

Suddenly, they heard voices in the darkness. There were some kids making out on the slab known as the death bed. They were drinking beer and smoking cigarettes. One of them had a flashlight. He turned on the flashlight and shone it at Manson and Zoey.

"What are you kids doing?" Zoey said, squinting from the bright LED light beam. She was tickled that these young teenagers were out after dark, haunting a cemetery, and making out, drinking and just being bad.

"What are you doing out here?" one of the kids retorted.

"We are here to scare you away," Manson said. "We are here to consume you."

"Are you not scared?" Zoey asked. "You should not trust strangers. Especially in a cemetery at night."

"We are creatures of the night," Manson said. "And our friend here is a werewolf."

Crandall waved and smiled. He looked pale and unassuming, not betraying the beastly nature that lurked within the lycanthropic cells of his blood. "It the moon was full right now you would be frightened beyond belief. I would be tearing you to pieces. Believe that."

"You two don't scare me," the other boy said. "You're just a couple freaks. Why don't you get the fuck out of here?"

"We are here to feed on your fear," Manson said. "You will know fear beyond your wildest imagination."

One of the teenage girls laughed. She said, "Obviously you haven't heard about the wild and crazy old man that lives in the woods out here. He attacks people at night that come to the cemetery to make out and attacks and kills them. That's scary. You two are lame. Definitely not scary."

"Really?" Zoey said. "I haven't heard about the wild old man. I assure you that you will be afraid of us, and if you don't your stupid."

"We are not scared of anything," one of the other boys said. "We do what we want. This is a fun place to sneak away at night and drink and smoke and make out."

"Only pussies would be afraid of something strange happening out here. There is no such thing as ghosts," the other boy said.

"Really?" Manson said. "And what makes you so sure of that?"

"Come on, man," the kid said. "Nobody has ever seen a ghost. All that shit is made up."

"No such thing as ghosts?" Manson said, amused. "What about vampires? What about werewolves?"

"Shall we show you the dark side?" Crandall asked. "Would you believe if you saw it with your own two eyes?"

"Fuck that," the first kid said. "That's ridiculous. Nobody believes in vampires or werewolves, either."

"Then tonight is your lucky night," Manson said, grinning and showing his fangs. "For you are about to experience the sublime."

"Who are you, anyway?" the girl with them asked. "What you going here?"

"We could ask you the same thing," Zoey said.

"We are monsters in the flesh," Crandall said. "Your worst nightmare. You are afraid of the dark because of creatures like us."

"Why don't you go sit on the 'death bed' and see if you die?" one of the kids asked. "Prove that you are a vampire."

"You cannot die when you are already dead," Manson said. "We can prove it. No problem.

"What the hell are you talking about?" the other kid asked. "We are not afraid of you."

"Fuck vampires," the first kid said, spitting on a grave. "I don't believe any of that shit."

Upon hearing this, Manson and Zoey approached them swiftly, Crandall followed closely behind, waiting and watching, as the two vampires moved with superhuman speed, standing close enough to smell the beer breath emanating from the teenagers.

"Who are you? What are your names? Where are you from?" the kid with the flashlight asked. He shone the light in their faces, getting a good look. Crandall stood back at a distance, while Manson and Zoey had wicked expressions of excited malevolent intent, with red glowing eyes, fangs showing, hands out like rakes, pitchforks, with talons. They moved swiftly, grabbing the first teenager, the boy, and hugged him tightly between them.

"What are you doing?" Jimmy asked, confused and frightened as they embraced him.

"Hey, they are fucking with Jimmy," the girl said. "Leave him alone, assholes."

"Now you are about to discover the reality of vampires, friend," Manson said, raising a clawed hand into the air and anticipating the kill.

Manson pulled Jimmy close, breathed in his ear, sniffing his scent and savoring his innocence and fear, listening to the pulse of his heart and the flow of blood through his veins.

With a quick and fierce bite, Manson sunk his fangs down into Jimmy's neck, right at the jugular, grabbing him with his claws and tearing flesh and sinew into ribbons. Blood squirted and dribbled down the boy's neck.

"No. Stop," he said. "You're fucking hurting me."

Zoey spun around quickly, with lightning fast reflexes, and grabbed the girl in a strong and firm embrace. She pulled her close, sniffed her hair, licked her neck, tasting her salty skin.

"You are mine, love," Zoey said. "I will drink your blood and eat your beating heart."

"Leave me alone," the girl said. "Let me go. What are you, some kind of nut, or something?"

"You fuckers are crazy," the other boy said, turning and running away.

Manson and Zoey bit the two teenagers, drawing blood, sucking and draining them dry. They let the bodies fall to the ground, blood on their mouths, the souls of the innocent coursing through their veins.

"Let me take care of this," Zoey said, her eyes filled with wrath and fury.

She stabbed her sharp claws into the girl's stomach, ripping the flesh wide open, letting entrails and offal spill out onto the ground with gruesome, wet, splashes and plops, as the ropes and coils of intestines hit the ground. She pulled her claws upward, firmly splitting the sternum open and grabbing the rib cage with her fingers, spreading them wide open with a sickening cracking and snapping of bone and gristle. She reached into the chest cavity and pulled out internal organs, and grabbed the still beating heart, squeezing it in her fist and ripping it out, holding it up and admiring the bloody organ. She put it to her mouth and ripped into it like a carnivore, tearing meat from the heart. She chewed on it and swallowed the meat. It was delicious.

"My turn," Manson said. He reached with his sharp claws and eviscerated the victim, pulling out the heart. He ate it in big, savage, bites.

The remaining teenagers scattered and ran away into the night, fleeing for their lives, escaping narrowly and living to tell a scary tale about vampires in the Bayview Cemetery.

"Fuck yeah," Zoey said. "I feel so alive."

"This is the life," Manson said. "Now that we have filled ourselves with blood lets depart quickly before they go for help."

Crandall had observed the whole event. He was neither happy nor sad, indifferent, and only thought that when his time came, he would do much the same. His violent nature only came when he was under a full moon, and he had a more pensive mood and relaxed demeanor when he was in his normal state. He even had a conscience that made him feel guilty for what he did when he was under the influence of the moon and lycanthropy.

"What did you think of that?" Manson asked Crandall.

"Quite a site," Crandall said. "I'm bored. Can we go now?"

"Yes. We must leave quickly," Zoey said. "Those kids will certainly alert the authorities that we are here."

"Right you are," Manson said. "Let's go."

4

Adrian had brought garlic, Holy water, a crucifix, and a crossbow and explosive arrows with him as he exited the van and headed toward the gate to Bayview Cemetery. He was prepared to kill these vampires. They must be stopped at once. He saw the flashlight beam flickering by the angel statue and knew that it must be the vampires. They were nearby and he could feel it.

He heard a girl scream and he knew that he must hurry before it was too late. He cautiously sneaked toward the group by the statue, and he could see it was a group of kids and the vampires. They were in trouble. He hid behind a tall, rectangular tombstone, and watched, horrified by the brutal murder he witnessed right then. There were three teenagers running past him, running in fear for their lives. He realized he was too late.

He jumped out from behind the tombstone and confronted the vampires.

"I will take you two to Hell where you belong," he said, shining his own flashlight at them.

The vampire and the werewolf were standing over two dead teenagers. The vampires had blood dripping from their faces, fangs exposed, eyes like evil slits, bloody hands with pieces of meat clutched in grimy fists.

"Hey! Time to die," Adrian said, raising the crossbow.

Manson, Crandall, and Zoey looked at Adrian with surprise. They knew this meeting was inevitable. The time had come for a showdown.

"You will die, too" Manson said.

"Correction," Adrian, said. "It is you who will die. And it will be a good riddance."

"We should run," Crandall said. He was crouched down and prepared to sprint away, his fight or flight response kicking in and urging him to flee.

Adrian fired the crossbow and the arrow hit Crandall in the shoulder, exploding in a ball of fire and sparks. Crandall let out a cry that sounded like a howl of pain and ran away into the darkness, his injury severe and life threatening. He disappeared into the cover of darkness, howling all the way, until he was gone from sight.

Manson and Zoey, on the other hand, were going to stay and fight.

Adrian pulled a vial of Holy Water from his pocket and flipped open the cap, then splashed the water on the two vampires.

The water hissed as it hit their skin. They writhed and squirmed as the water burned like acid.

They tried to use mind control on the Adrian, but it did not work; he was not susceptible to their telepathic power.

He is oblivious to our mind control, Manson thought.

How can that be? Zoey wondered.

Adrian looked at them, knowing what they were thinking.

"Don't worry," he said. "I am not affected by your magic and tricks. My mind is oblivious to your suggestions. I have trained myself in the behaviors of evil entities and have a technique to block your mind control."

"Away with you, vampire hunter," Manson said. "We will defeat you."

"I am wise to your shenanigans," Adrian said. "Do not try to evade me. I have you dead to rights. It is time to end this, now."

"I don't think so," Zoey said.

Manson and Zoey were swift and deceptive, doing a vanishing act and turning into wisps of black smoke, cackling loudly as they disappeared and quickly escaped, outmaneuvering Adrian. They hissed at him in the darkness and disappeared into the night.

5

Back in the Monte Carlo, Manson and Zoey raced away, motor rumbling and roaring with Detroit built horsepower, down the road, taillights fading into the darkness. They drove away and left the scene of the crime at the cemetery. They would stay on guard against the vampire hunter, because they knew that he would fallow them.

Their appetites now satisfied; they required a place to rest through the coming day. They could not go back to the Shamrock Motel because the vampire hunter would be expecting them to return. Instead, they drove away into the night, leaving the city of Bellevue behind and racing down Interstate 5, heading for Seattle. They watch behind them for the vampire hunter and his Chevy van, but they do not see him following, although they were sure they had not seen the last of him.

"What about Crandall?" Zoey asked, holding onto the dash as the car sped at full speed down the road. "We can't just leave him."

"I don't know," Manson said. "We can't go back for him."

"Do you have his phone number?"

"Yes. I do," Manson said. "It's in my contacts. Take my phone out of my pocket and see if you can reach him."

"I will," she said, reaching into his pocket and pulling out his cell phone. "I can try to get in touch with him to see if he is okay."

"Good," Manson said. "In the meantime, I am going to get us as far away from this place as possible. We must be cautious of this vampire hunter. He means to kill us."

Zoey found Crandall listed in the contacts and dialed the number . . . there was no answer.

"I'm worried about him," she said, hanging up the phone. "He is not answering."

"He is a big boy," Manson said. "I think he can take care of himself."

"What if he is injured?" she asked. "He was struck with an arrow . . . and it exploded. You saw that, too, didn't you?"

"Of course, I saw it," Manson said. "I was standing right there when it happened."

"I'm afraid he might be terribly injured," she said, saddened by the thought.

"Just hope for the best," Manson said. "We have no choice but to keep moving now."

"Poor Crandall," she said. "I am going to miss him."

"We may meet again."

"I hope so."

"Now worries, love," Manson said. "Keep confident. We have more to worry about than that."

"I guess you are right," she said.

They drove into the night down the Interstate without speaking further after that and listened to the sound of the engine revving like a locomotive as the needle hovered at 120 mph. The headlights were like spotlights illuminating the concrete landscape before them, the yellow and white lines like ribbons stretching out before them. It was a risk to drive so fast, Manson knew, but he also knew that they could talk their way out of a speeding ticket, if necessary, with gentle telepathic persuasion.

CHAPTER FIFTEEN

1

Adrian was astounded at the defeat he experienced in the cemetery. He had planned to kill the vampires and the werewolf, but it did not turn out as he expected. Although, he had scored a direct hit on the werewolf, and possibly his injuries would be severe enough to end his miserable life. *One could only hope,* Adrian thought.

Now, he was back in his van, and he regretted the fact that they had slipped away from him, gaining a head start. He knew where they were going, however, because he had placed a tracking device on their car and now, he could simply follow them with the GPS locator with pinpoint accuracy.

He watched on his tablet as the map showed their progress down I5 and he knew where they were going. They were heading directly toward Seattle. He would meet them there and confront them again. Only this time, he intended to finish them completely. They would not be so lucky to escape next time, he vowed, and their luck would certainly run out eventually.

He put the van in gear and drove after them, taking his time because he could easily track their location at his leisure now.

2

Manson and Zoey stopped and picked up a hitchhiker thinking he might be fun and gave him a ride. He might turn out to be a tasty treat, too, they thought. After a short distance they knew that he was not an average citizen. He was a killer.

His name was Bertram Holland and he was cold and tired and strung out from the road.

"You can just call me Bert for short," he said, sitting comfortably in the back seat.

"You can just call me Manson and she is Zoey."

"Nice to meet both of you," Bert said. "How far are you going?"

"All the way to Hell if we don't change our ways," Manson said.

"Ah, ha," Bert said. "I hear that. I'm right behind you."

"I got that impression," Manson said. "How far are you going?"

"I'm on my way to Seattle," he said. "I'm hoping to run into some old friends out there."

"I see," Manson said.

"Isn't it scary to be hitchhiking out here with so many weirdos on the loose?" Zoey said, joining the conversation. "I mean . . . it isn't safe, you know?"

"I'm not too worried about that," Bert said. "I can take care of myself."

They talked for a while during the ride . . . and they came to the conclusion that he was an odd individual, even by the standards of vampires. They did not know what to make of this guy, Bertram, the grungy hitchhiker. They knew he was different and they would leave him alone . . . he was probably not all that tasty anyway, they reasoned.

I can read his mind, Manson thought, looking at Zoey. *He's a fucking hot mess. We don't want to fuck with this guy. He's death in disguise, worse than we could ever imagine.*

What do you mean? Zoey asked in her mind. *I'm not getting much from him other than random, crazy thoughts. I detect bipolar disorder, maybe schizophrenia. He's definitely whacked in the head. I know that much. Maybe we should be rid of him quickly.*

You might be right, Manson was thinking.

Burt was the famous serial killer the police had been tracking for months. He had killed hundreds of people and he was still on the loose. He kept jewelry and teeth as trinkets from his victims and carried them in his travel bag. He was down on his luck right now and needed to come up with some money and material possessions. This could be a fortunate serendipitous ride, and he had fully intended to take advantage of anyone dumb enough to stop and give him a ride. He would try to kill anyone if it suited his purpose, and it just so happened that he liked the Monte Carlo and thought it might be a nice acquisition.

There's a killer on the road . . . his brain is squirming like a toad . . . The lyrics to the Doors song suddenly crossed Manson's mind.

"This is a nice ride," Bert said, looking around the interior of the car. "This is a Monte Carlo, right? What year is this?"

"It's a vintage seventy-five," Manson said, looking in the rearview mirror.

"Very nice," Bert said. "I like it. Did you fix it up yourself?"

"With my own two hands," Manson said. "Cost a pretty penny, too."

"That's coo, man," Bert said. "Kids nowadays just don't appreciate a classic car like this. This was made for comfort and cruising. They really knew how to make a car back then."

"I agree," Manson said.

"I think I might like to have a car like this," Bert said, leaning forward and showing the blade of a sharp butcher's knife. He put it up against Manson's throat, saying, "How about I just take it from you?"

I knew it, Zoey said with her mind. She looked at Manson from the corner of her eye. *I knew he was a freak.*

I'll deal with this asshole, Manson said, looking back at her from the corner of his eye. *Hold on tight and watch how I roll.*

"Pull over and get out," Bert said. "I'm taking your shit. You'll be lucky if I let you live. Understand? I might even fuck your girlfriend too, before I kill you both. And then maybe afterward, too. Sounds like fun, huh?"

"Yes. I understand," Manson said, looking in the rearview mirror, feeling the edge of the knife against his throat.

Hold on, Zoey, he thought, *it's going to get hectic now . . .*

Without hesitation, Manson slammed on the brakes at 120 mph and threw Bert into the front seat, unexpectedly, and grabbed the wrist of the hand that was clutching the knife.

"What the hell?" Bert said, looking up from between the seats. He saw the faces of the vampires with fiery red eyes and sharp fangs, monstrous creatures, more frightening than anything he had ever encountered. He was used to being in control, and now that he was in a vulnerable position he was reduced to a simple coward. Manson plucked the knife from his hand, brought the Monte Carlo to a complete stop on the side of the Interstate and the tore into the sad little serial killer with viciousness and gnashing teeth and ripping claws.

Bert did not stand a chance. They ripped him limb from limb, and then discarded him on the side of the road, stopping at a rest area to clean up the mess before heading into the city of Seattle.

"That was a strange one, there," Manson said, back inside

the car. "But he is no longer a threat to anyone.

"You are one to talk," Zoey said, hitting him on the shoulder. "We are killers, too."

"Not like that," Manson said. "That was an entirely different situation with that guy."

"We are all death incarnate," Zoey said. "We become death, and we ride darkly in the night, seeking out our prey."

"You are a poet."

"I know."

"I love you."

"Ditto."

They pulled out of the rest area and drove darkly through the night toward Seattle.

CHAPTER SIXTEEN

1

Bright points of lights were dotted across the cityscape of Seattle which loomed ahead in a brilliant mosaic of neon, fluorescent, incandescent, and diodes emitting radiance in multicolored hues as they sped toward the heart of the city. The Space Needle was lit up brilliantly with a red beacon light at the very tip. The skyscrapers towered over the streets below, with rectangular windows illuminated internally. The tallest building blotted out the skyline, and soon they were driving down the inner-city toward First and Pike street. Pedestrians were out in force, crossing the street carelessly at the stoplights, bustling past one another with straight and focused faces, eyes ahead, no-nonsense, in a hurry and all business-like as seems to be the standard mode for most city dwellers. There were some miscreants, to be expected, who were standing on the street corners and making a spectacle, drinking beer from cans and smoking marijuana directly in public. There were ladies of the night walking down the street, flashing their goods, sultry and strutting as they ambled along, hoping to find a date.

"I just love being in the city," Zoey said.

"It is splendid," Manson said.

"Let's park and get out and explore the nightlife," Zoey said.

"It's late," Manson said. "And we must find a hotel room or someplace to sleep for the coming daylight."

"I guess you are right," Zoey said.

Manson drove the Monte Carlo down the street and arrived at 211 Dexter Avenue North, noting the Holiday Inn building to his left. He drove up his block pulled into the Diamond Parking Services garage #A872 on 220 8th Ave N, South Lake Union at 7 a.m. and paid for a ten hour stay until 5 p.m. that evening.

They walked back to the hotel, entered the lobby, and booked a room in the heart of Seattle to sleep through the daylight hours—a jackhammer is heard breaking the cement outside all day long while they are trying to sleep.

"What the fuck?" Manson said, peeking out through the curtain and down to the street. "What luck we have. A jackhammer. I would love to shove that up his ass."

"Speaking of jackhammers," Zoey said, sprawling out naked on the bed. "Why don't you come over here and fuck me. I'm waiting . . ."

Manson turned from the window, saw her lovely naked body on the bed, and instantly copped a boner. He went to her and stripped off his cloths, his erection stiff and solid as a rock. He dove onto her and entered her in one fluid motion, driving in deep, thrusting his hips, and stroking to the beat of the jackhammer outside.

2

Again with the strange dreams . . . they both shared the dream through some type of ESP connection, a lucid and vivid imagery that flowed through their minds during their sleep. They were old, aged and wrinkled, sitting on a porch in rocking chairs. Zoey was knitting with colorful yarn and Manson was whittling a stick with a sharp Buck knife. There were chickens, piglets, and bunnies in the yard. There were children playing in a tree in the yard. This was their future selves, but how could that be if they were now vampires and immortal? They could never grow old. This was impossible.

There was a loud explosion from somewhere behind the house, the ground shook like an earthquake had struck, and the clouds in the sky began to roil, leaves and debris picked up in a cyclone.

The ground fractured through the yard and large rift was exposed, deep and jagged cliffs that appeared to go straight into the bowels of Hell. There was fire and smoke and the smell of brimstone.

Everything began to be sucked into the chasm. First the little animals, squawking and squealing on the way down, then the children and the tree, screaming and flailing for their lives. The cars in the driveway, the sidewalk, the telephone poles, all sucked downward, the crag like a giant mouth eating everything, like massive sinkhole.

"Zoey, we are going to get sucked into that hole," Manson said, reaching over to hold her hand.

"What is happening?" she cried, holding his hand tightly.

"This is a dream. It has to be. We can stop this."

"What does it mean?"

"I don't know."

They fell into the hole and went down, down, down into the darkness. The smell of the acrid smoke burning their eyes, nostrils, throat, making them choke.

"Help," Zoey cried.

"Hold my hand," Manson said.

They were pulled out of the rocking chairs in the descent. The house behind them was sucked into the chasm and the sound of cracking boards and ripping and tearing of the fabric of time and space could be heard clearly.

They were descending into the pit of Hell and they knew it.

How could that be? How could this be happening? Was there really a place such as Hell?

At the bottom they could see a dragon looking up at them, breathing fire and smoke from it nose, mouth open and teeth exposed. It had a serpent's tongue and it licked at them, tasting them, preparing to devour them whole.

Stephanie was riding on the back of the dragon and she was laughing hideously, grinning with a mouthful of jagged teeth, blood running down her chin and neck. Her eyes were alighted like fiery coals and her skin was covered with scales and boils, weeping, oozing, pus flowing from the open sores. Crandall was nailed to a crucifix below the dragon, his head was hanging down to his chest and he was wearing a crown of thorns, blood trickling from the thorns piercing into his forehead. He was unconscious, clad only in a loincloth, appearing much like the famous image of Jesus Christ on the cross.

"You've come home to me, my children," Stephanie said. She cackled insanely. "I've been waiting here for you."

They were falling feet first into the dragon's mouth . . .

Manson and Zoey screamed in fear . . .

3

They awoke from the dream with a start, both sitting up, sweating, eyes dilated and wide in terror.

"What the hell was that?" Manson said.

"Did you have the same dream?"

"It was a nightmare."

"What does it mean?"

"I don't know," Manson said, running his hand through his hair. He got up and went into the bathroom and poured water from the tap into a disposable plastic cup. He took a long drink. He poured another cup full and then took it out to Zoey. "Here, drink this."

She took the water and sipped on it.

"I don't want to go to Hell," she said, looking up at him with sorrowful eyes.

"There is no such thing."

"They say the same thing about vampires, you know?"

"Yes. I suppose that is true . . . but there is no Heaven and there certainly is no Hell."

"How can you be so sure?"

Manson put his hand on her shoulder and looked at her sincerely. "Life is hell. That is all there is too it. It cannot be any worse than being born and living life in this world today. Anything is better than this. Don't you think?"

"I don't know."

"You are a vampire now," Manson said. "Be strong. You are immortal. Don't worry."

"What was Stephanie doing in the dream?"

"It is our subconscious playing tricks on us."

"What was with Crandall on the cross?"

"It was a strange dream. But it was only dream."

"I don't want to think about it. What if we are in danger?"

"We are in danger," Manson said. "We are being pursued by a vigilante. The police are looking for us. This may not turn out well. You have to be prepared for the worst."

"And what is that?"

"A stake through the heart . . . left out in the daylight to blister and burn to ashes . . ."

"I don't want to think about it."

"Then we won't," Manson said. "We will forget some stupid dream and get drunk. How does that sound?"

"But, this is not the first dream . . . remember?"

"They are reoccurring," Manson said. He pulled a pint of vodka from his jacket pocket and twisted the cap. "We may have more dreams to come . . . but we will deal with them. Life is stranger than any dream, if you ask me." He put the bottle to his lips and took a long drink, his Adam's apple bobbing up and down as he chugged the clear alcohol, the air bubbles glugging inside the glass bottle. He sighed contentedly and handed the bottle to Zoey.

"Here's to life on the run," he said, "a salute to vampires and outlaws that we've become."

"Thank you," she said, taking a dainty sip. "I'm not a criminal."

"Not a criminal. But a creature of the night. You had better drink a bit more than that if you want to forget about the dream."

She tipped the bottle back and guzzled deeply.

4

As soon as the sun set, Manson made a quick trip to the liquor store and purchased a box full of booze and cigarettes. Zoey stayed behind at the hotel room and took a long shower, wanting to wash the grime from the road and the guilt she felt from the dream. She was overcome with grief and sadden by the current state of events. She wanted to be a good human being, but now it seemed impossible since she had been turned into a vampire. She was quickly losing touch with her good conscious and morals, overwhelmed with a dark sensation that felt almost evil and benign. She used to be such a nice girl, and now she was becoming calloused and dark and had a sinister look in her eyes. The lust for blood and flesh and carnage was becoming a second nature to her now.

When Manson returned from his shopping trip, he came inside and locked the door behind him. His eyes were wide, and his expression was on of bewilderment.

"I saw that vampire hunter guy sitting in his van in the parking lot at the liquor store."

"Are you sure?"

"I am certain it was him."

"What shall we do."

"Keep that pistol out and ready."

Zoey took the pistol out and pulled the lever back, placing a live round in the chamber, and then set it down on the bed. "Is that better?"

"Yes. I'm afraid he is going to sneak up on us. We have to be ready for him."

"I will eat his heart for breakfast."

"That's my girl," Manson said. He took a fifth of Jim Beam bourbon from the box and cracked it open, took a guzzle, and then wiped his lips. "Tonight we drink . . . alcohol . . . and blood."

"Did you get my cigarettes?"

"In the box, dear."

"Thank you."

She took out a pack of cigarettes and lit one, ignoring the no smoking policy of the hotel.

"I do miss Crandall," Zoey said, in deep thought.

"I do too," Manson said. "He is doing his own thing. I can't say I blame him. A werewolf has a rough life, not able to control himself when the moon is full. It is like being a psychotic with turrets and amnesia all rolled into one."

"I guess that makes sense," she said, taking another drink of booze from the bottle. "I just fell in love with him in such a short time. It was like I had known him forever."

"I know what you mean," Manson said. "He will be alright, I think. He is smart, good looking, and strong. Maybe we will see him again someday."

"I hope so."

Manson raised the bottle and said, "Here is to our good friend, Crandall. Drink to his memory and good health."

After drinking two bottles of bourbon and a bottle of wine, they were getting good and drunk and ready to go out on the town. Seattle awaited them. There were victims to stalk, blood to be drank, hearts to eat. They were getting hungry and their newly discovered vampire traits were becoming more demanding and controlling them with malevolent urges and desires. They were ready for a night of action and fun. Seattle would be their playground and they prepared for the festivities with a zeal and ardor that displayed their anticipation of blood and horror.

CHAPTER SEVENTEEN

1

On the Waterfront Park at pier 57 on Elliot bay, Manson and Zoey walked along the boardwalk beneath the city lights. It was beautiful. There were people milling about, even late in the evening, and restaurants and bars were bustling with activity. They took a ride on the Great Wheel, a giant Ferris wheel that was just over 175 feet tall with 42 fully enclosed gondolas. It was the largest Ferris wheel on the West Coast. The Seattle cityscape and Space Needle were prominent in the background.

They went to the Pike Place Market with its massive square lettered red neon sign and white circular clock overlooking the brick road. They observed the sights and sounds, street performers, quaint curio shops and seafood vendors, and stopped at a pub for a quick drink. Later, during their walk along Pike Street, they saw a photoshoot with cameras, bright lights, and a gorgeous model posing for glamor shots.

"Look at that," Zoey said. "She is hot."

"I wonder who she is?" Manson said.

"Let's find out," Zoey said.

They stood by, watching as the photographer snapped shots of the pretty model laying on top of a sapphire blue Corvette. It was exciting and sexy. The model noticed Manson and Zoey watching her as she posed, and she felt even sexier as a result of these two beautiful dark souls observing her while she did her fashion shoot.

After the model was done posing, the cameraman began gathering his gear.

"Great shoot, Cynthia," the photographer said.

"Thanks, John," she replied.

Cynthia, the glamour model, approached Manson and Zoey.

"Hello," she said. "Who are you? I saw you watching me while I worked."

"Yes," Manson said. "You are amazing."

"What are you posing for?" Zoey asked. "I mean, where will these pictures be published."

"Ah, yes," Cynthia said. "I'm doing a shoot for Penthouse magazine. I'm sure you've heard of it."

"Oh, indeed," Manson said.

"Really?" Zoey said. "That is awesome. I would love to do that."

"You are certainly pretty enough, honey," Cynthia said. "You would look good in a nude spread, I'm sure."

"You are too modest to do that," Manson said.

"No, I am not," Zoey said. "I could do it. I have this body and men would kill to have me."

"I'm not disagreeing with that," Cynthia said. "Maybe I could get you an interview with my people. I have connections, you know?"

"Maybe," Zoey said. "I might like that."

"Tsk-tsk," Manson said. "You dream too much."

"Oh, you hush, now, Manson," Zoey said.

Cynthia looked at Manson and said, "And you, my dear, are delicious enough to do a shoot for Playgirl. What do you think about that?"

"I daresay I've never really thought about it," Manson replied. "But it might be fun."

"You two are an adorable couple," Cynthia said. "Would you like to join me for a drink?"

"Absolutely," Zoey said. "That would be lovely."

"Great. It's a date, then," Cynthia said, gathering her possessions from the photoshoot. She picked up her clothing and shoes and placed them into a duffel bag, slung her purse over her shoulder and kissed John, the photographer, goodnight. She told him that she was going out for a drink and that she would contact him later—do not worry if she stayed out late because she might be busy for the rest of the night.

2

After stopping at a quaint cocktail lounge and drinking several drinks, they did some cocaine and molly, and things started to heat up; they were all getting horny and wanted to fuck one another right there, but they kept modest and waited to get back to the hotel room.

They took Cynthia back to the Holiday Inn and the three of them fucked for hours. It was fabulous. Cynthia grabbed her cloths and left later, not one for long goodbyes, right before the sun came up, and Manson and Zoey let her go without killing her or drawing a drop of blood. She was too good and lovely to kill like that; they liked here and chose to let her live. They closed the shades and blinds to block out the daylight after she left. They would sleep through the night and bask in the glory of their sexual encounter with a Penthouse centerfold. What a serendipitous night it had been, and they were pleased. It would get better when they had some victims to exsanguinate.

3

They left the Holiday Inn the following night and went downtown Seattle looking for some souls to steal and victims to kill. They wanted someone tasty, with a long, supple milk white neck and exquisite taste. The roamed the city streets, passing urchins and vagabonds, pimps and whores, thieves and hustlers, and panhandlers begging for spare change. They needed somebody to kill, some worthy people to slay and eat their hearts out of their chests. They walked up the hill and stood beneath the Space Needle, looking up at the towering structure. It made one dizzy to look at it too long, Manson realized, and he had to look away.

"There goes one, right there," Zoey said, pointing at a young man walking alone. He had Skullcandy headphones over his ears and he was shuffling and grinding to the beat of some hip-hop tunes. He was wearing a blue waxed canvas jacket from Duluth Trading Company, an orange t-shirt, and blue skinny jeans rolled up to the shins, and leather boat shoes. "He looks delicious."

"Fabulous," Manson said. "Let's follow him and see where he goes."

The stayed at a safe distance until they knew the coast was clear and then they pounced on the unsuspecting victim. He tried to fight at first, but they overpowered him and dragged him off into a nearby cluster of ornamental shrubs and hedges that concealed their activities. They made a quick kill, ripping the prey into shreds as they sucked the blood from his severed and ripped neck. They ripped out his heart and shared it together, a delicious and tasty morsel to be savored.

"We need one more," Zoey said. "I have an appetite tonight and want more blood."

"Then you shall have your heart's desire, my love," Manson said. "Let's leave this one here and go find another. It should be easy picking on a night like tonight."

They left the body of the victim bleeding and pulverized into a steaming pile of flesh and bones in the bushes. The wiped their faces clean to look presentable and changed their demeanors back to a nice and warm, friendly appearance. They looked fabulous and trustworthy and beautiful and other unsuspecting innocent and naïve superficial individuals would easily fall into their snare, allowing them to spring the trap and take their lives and drink their blood.

4

They found more victims, this time two girls out walking down the sidewalk, and when they passed by a darkened alley, Manson and Zoey struck quickly, taking down two victims for the price of one, and dragged them back into the dimness of the alley and killed them, consuming flesh and blood and taking their fill.

It was a grizzly and bloody mess, and the bodies were left scattered in the streets. The authorities were alerted, and these murders were attributed to the Goth City Killers—that is what the media has labeled the dark duo.

They went back to the Monte Carlo and decided it was probably a good idea to get out of Seattle and head somewhere new, with fresh victims and uncharted territory.

5

Seattle Police Department—Briefing 8:00 a.m., December 16, 2019 just after sunrise.

Captain Snidanko was at the front of the board room in the Seattle Police Department. He had a clipboard and folder on the podium in front of him.

"We have a team of murderers running loose in our city. There is a national manhunt underway," Snidanko said. "They have been dubbed the Gothic City killers due to their clothing, makeup, and lifestyle. They prefer killing at night and hiding during the day. We know very little about them, but a few witnesses have been located who claim to have observed the couple committing crimes on a spree that is taking them along Interstate 5 in a southbound direction. We do not know their destination, but we think they may be heading for Mexico. It appears that they have entered the country from Canada and are moving from town to town murdering innocent victims. They have killed enough people to be considered serial killers now.

They are considered armed and dangerous. Witnesses claim to have seen them driving a black sedan, perhaps a GTO or Impala, but nobody is sure yet. All we know is that it is a big black car and has been spotted near the murder scenes on numerous occasions. They started in Bellingham, and now they have made their way here to Seattle. We suspect that they may flee, as they are transient, and may be heading south, but they could go in any direction, so we must watch closely for them. We are working with law enforcement agencies in Portland and Vancouver to track these merciless killers and bring them to justice."

Snidanko took papers out of the folder on the podium and

produced Xerox copies of photos of Manson and Zoey. He held each one up for the officers in the room to see and then clipped them to the white board behind him.

"We are passing around copies of these images, so you can familiarize yourselves with the physical appearance and features of these criminals.

In an additional development, we suspect that they were involved in the shooting incident that involved our own officers over the weekend, but we cannot be sure. Investigators are currently looking into the connection and we should know soon if this involved the Gothic City killers.

The MO of these killers is to completely mutilate their victims and leave an eviscerated corpse that has been completely exsanguinated. For those of you who don't know what that is, that means they have been drained of blood. Why? We don't know for sure. It has been theorized that they may think they are vampires and are drinking the blood. Whatever the case may be, they appear to be cannibals and are consuming human flesh during the murders, because teeth and bite marks are present on the flesh of the victims.

So, now you know what we are dealing with and you are all to be on the lookout for these perpetrators. They are priority number one and we need to stop them immediately. They cannot continue this rampage any longer.

Any questions?"

The officers in the room looked puzzled and perplexed. They could not believe what they were hearing.

"They think they are vampires?" Officer Smith asked.

"Yes. It appears they do," Snidanko replied.

"We think they are involved with the shooting that occurred with are officers? How do we know that?" Officer Smith asked.

"Witnesses say they observed a large black sedan at the

scene prior to the shooting," Snidanko said. "They were also seen fleeing away from the scene said vehicle. We are certain they are connected."

"Is there a task force involved yet?" Officer Pinkerton asked.

"Yes. We have a full-fledged investigation and task force currently pursuing leads. We expect to apprehend the perpetrators soon."

Snidanko looked around the briefing room, raised his eyebrows and sighed, and leaned on the podium, saying, "If there are no further questions . . . this meeting is adjourned."

The officers stood up and left the room.

6

Adrian was hot on the trail of the vampires in the black Monte Carlo. He had followed them to Seattle and was prepared to confront them. He had witness the male vampire, Manson, going into the liquor store but there were too many witnesses around for him to have a confrontation. He wanted to get both vampires together, a twofer, a multiple bonus, killing both of them at once.

He had followed Manson back to the hotel and parked down the street. The time was coming soon. He knew it would not be long before he had his moment. He would trap them in a dark alley or some other secluded place and finish both of them off for good.

Tonight, would be the night for the ultimate showdown. Adrian did not know where it would take place, but he did know that he was determined to bring this chase to an end as quickly as possible. He followed the vampires on foot as they walked through Seattle on rampage, and he observed them from a distance as they attacked their victims. His trigger finger was itchy and he had to resist the urge to run up on them in the open and start the fight in view of so many witnesses.

It made him angry to watch the vampires killing the victims, but he did not want to risk exposing himself.

CHAPTER EIGHTEEN

1

Manson and Zoey were caught unaware when a police patrol car began to follow them through downtown Seattle.

"Oh, shit," Manson said. "We have company."

"What?" Zoey said, turning around and looking through the rear window. "Oh, no. What are we going to do?"

"Just act normal. Don't panic," Manson said. "We can deal with this."

Manson pulled the car onto Elliot Avenue and proceeded left, trying to shake this police car, in hopes that he was not really following them. Unfortunately, the police car sirens erupted, and the bright red and blue lights began to flash, lighting up the night.

"He's pulling us over," Manson said. "What shall we do?"

"Well, we can't outrun the police in this car," Zoey said. "We have to stop. Maybe he is just checking us out."

"He's checking us out, alright," Manson said. "Count on that."

"Just stop the car," Zoey said. "We will deal with him. He is not match for our power."

"Right. Good call."

Manson pulled the Monte Carlo over to the side of the road and put it in park. The railroad tracks were to the right of them, and a wooded and grass landscaped area, Kinnear Park was to the right. Cars passed by with blindingly bright headlights in both directions, motoring by in a whoosh of whirring tires and revving engines, but the traffic was sparse, overall. This was a somewhat secluded area in the city. They watched in the rearview mirrors as the police officer stepped out of the patrol car and approached the driver's side door. Manson rolled down the window.

"Good evening officer," Manson said. "To what do I owe this pleasure?"

"Turn off the ignition," the police officer commanded. He was standing at a safe distance, flashlight pointing at the Monte Carlo, hand hovering over his sidearm on his hip. He was ready to act at on reflex and at notice if anything peculiar should happen with the driver of the car.

Manson complied, turning the key off in the ignition. The engine immediately stopped running and began emitting a tick-tick-tick. The sounds of the city flooded in through the open window: honking horns on nearby streets, an ambulance siren wailing in the distance, a train rumbling down the tracks, a foghorn from a passing ship in the Puget Sound.

"I've stopped you because you were exceeding the speed limit," the officer said. "Can I see your driver's license, registration, and proof of insurance."

Manson produced all the required documents and handed them to the officer.

"Here you go, sir," Manson said, looking at the officer's name tag pin on his uniform. "Officer Wiggins, I believe you will find everything is in order."

"Sit tight while I check this out," the officer Wiggins said, turning and going back to his patrol car.

The officer Wiggins was suspicious of their strange visage and demeanor, and after he had read a bulletin in his patrol car on his laptop he was alerted to their identity. They fit the description of the Gothic City Killers who were at large and wanted for multiple homicides.

Officer Wiggins called for backup units, and when the extra patrol cars arrived, he attempted to make an arrest and take the suspects into custody at gunpoint, but it was of no use. Manson and Zoey used their mind control to overpower the police officers. He took a defensive position behind the safety of his patrol car door and aimed his gun at the driver's side door.

"Driver," officer Wiggins said, loudly. "Step out of the car with your hands up in the air. Do not make any sudden movements."

Manson looked at Zoey, and they met each other's gaze, knowing what they had to do; this situation called for the use of their telepathic powers.

"Okay," Manson said. "If you really want me to. So be it." He opened the door, stepped out into the night air, and raised his hands above his head.

"Now turn around and walk backward toward me," officer Wiggins said. "Follow the sound of my voice."

Manson was sending his thoughts to Zoey. He spoke to her within his mind, commanding her to get out and act now, before it was too late. She got opened the door and stepped out, turning and looking at the police cars and the officers hunkered down in shooting positions, guns pointed and aimed at them with deadly intent.

"Passenger!" another officer screamed. "Do not get out of

the car! Stop, now! Put your hands in the air and turn away from us."

Officer Wiggins knew this was going to get ugly.

Manson: Do it now, Zoey. Put them under your control.

Zoey: Yes. I will. I will make them freeze in fear. You must take care of officer Wiggins.

Manson: Leave that to me. I've got this. When it is over . . . get back in the car and get ready to get the hell out of here, fast.

Zoey: Let's do this.

Manson turned around swiftly, before officer Wiggins had a chance to realized what was happening, and with their combined telepathy, they took control of the situation before any of the officers could react.

Manson: *Officer Wiggins, you will take your weapon and shoot the other officers now! Don't waste any time. Kill them all!*

Zoey: *Yes. Do it. And you other officers will drop your weapons and stand tall, so he has a clear shot. Maker yourselves into easy targets. Goodbye. So long. Farewell.*

Officer Wiggins turned and pointed his weapon, a 9mm Glock handgun, at the other officers, who had dropped their weapons and stood looking dazed and confused, even surprised as they were shot dead in rapid succession. They never knew what hit them.

Wiggins: *What have I done? What is happening to me?*

Zoey: *Yes. That's it, Manson. Finish him now.*

Manson: *Officer Wiggins . . . now you will your gun on yourself, putting a bullet into your own head. Lights out my friend.*

Wiggins: *No. I can't do that.*

Zoey: *Yes. You can. Do it now.*

Manson: *Shoot yourself, Wiggins. Obey!*

Officer Wiggins raised his gun to his temple and pulled the

trigger, blood and bone jetting out the hole in his head as the bullet passed through his brain and out the other side. He collapsed and fell over dead.

"Perfect," Manson said. "Now let's get the fuck out of here before more cops come."

"Where will we go now?"

"I know where we can hide the car," Manson said. "I got this. Just get in. Let's go."

They climbed back into the Monte Carlo and pulled away, free to run riot for another night, at least until their next encounter with law enforcement. Now that they knew the law was after them, they would have to be more cautious. They both had a sickening felling that time was running for them out since they were now wanted for murder and being pursued by a vampire hunter.

2

Manson drove to a secluded spot outside of the city and parked in a treelined lot at a public park on the shore of the Puget Sound. This seemed like a safe place to stay for a while, at least for a moment to let the heat cool down. It was going to be daylight soon, too, so they required sleep and shelter from the sun's deadly rays.

"They won't expect us to be hiding the car here," Manson said. "We are hiding it right in plain sight."

"What if they find it?"

"They won't. Trust me. We'll be long gone by the time they think to look for us here."

They climbed in the trunk and prepared to sleep through another day, hiding from the sun.

They knew they were again being followed by the vampire

hunter, and they were planning to ambush him this time—as well as the dealing with any foreseeable incidents with the police. The police were closing in and it was just a matter of time until they crossed paths with the vampires again. Manson and Zoey would not go down without a fight.

3

Adrian knew this was his chance, to catch them while they were vulnerable, sleeping in the trunk of the car. He waited until they were inside the trunk and then made his way toward the vehicle. As he was preparing to pry open the trunk, suddenly from behind a pack of feral dogs moved out of the bushes and came into the opening. They growled at Adrian, and when he moved, they showed their fangs.

"What the hell is this?" Adrian said. "This is not possible."

He thought it was as though the vampires had some control over the animals from within the trunk. These dogs were acting as protectors.

Adrian stopped, stood stone still, and waited. The dogs slowly closed in on him. The had foaming mouths and snapped at him viscously, making intimations that they would bit him if he came any closer. He decided that the best thing to do was turn and walk away, for now, the vampires were safe because the dogs were guarding them.

After Adrian made it back to his van, he turned and looked to see the dogs circling the black Monte Carlo, lying down in the dirt and grass and waiting for darkness. He would have to catch the vampires another time, because he was not match for a pack of rabid and wild dogs.

4

Following behind the dogs was a solitary figure. It was a were-wolf and he was controlling the dogs. He was horrifically terrifying with the appearance of a man-wolf, and he approached lurking with a menacing gate, claws outstretched and feet kicking up dirt and rocks in the gravel lot. He had come to save his friends who had given him a ride. It was more than mere coincidence, for the moon was full on November 12, 2019, and he had been in the area, hiding in the trees and bushes as he transformed into a werewolf. Before the change, he had observed the black Monte Carlo from a distance and knew it was them, and as the lycanthropic blood pulsed through his veins and turned him into a beast, he still had enough wherewithal and humanity to come to their rescue and save them from the vampire hunter.

5

As the sun set and twilight approached, Manson and Zoey awoke in the trunk, opened the lid on their makeshift coffin, and happily greeted a new night. The dogs were still there, and they were not surprised to see them. It was a mutual gladness, for the dogs were happy to see the vampires.

"Look at that," Manson said, pointing toward the Chevy van parked across the field in the distance. "He has been waiting there for us."

"That dogs protected us from him," Zoey said. "We must hurry and get away."

They petted the dogs on the heads, wished them goodbye and said thanks, and then climbed inside the Monte Carlo and sped away in an attempt to allude the vampire hunter.

Back on Interstate 5 they headed south toward Olympia and put the city of Seattle behind them in the rearview mirror.

CHAPTER NINETEEN

1

Olympia, The Capitol City, was ravaged by bloodlust for a weekend when Manson and Zoey arrived in the black Monte Carlo with the vampire hunter hot on their heels.

Located at the very extent of the Puget Sound in Washington state, Olympia is the hub of political legislation and liberal proliferation. Free thinkers thrive there. There used to be a world-class brewery located there, the Olympia Brewing Company, which made the city's namesake beer. It was popular back in the 1960s and 70s, sponsoring such great names as Evil Knievel and appearing in many popular movies, including a few made by Clint Eastwood—he seemed to have a preference for the beer. The brewery created many jobs, and the logo became a mark for the original "Oly lifestyle" from that era: a laid back, relaxed and mellow attitude with a fine appreciating for life, liberty, and art. The beer was good, life was good, and it was only getting better for the "hippies" in the late 1960s and into the 1970s. They grooved to songs like "Incense and Peppermints" by Strawberry Alarm Clock and congregated on the streets of Olympia in a movement that spanned the Vietnam War era. It was a microcosm of Hate-Ashbury, and life was good.

The next big thing to happen in, and around, Olympia, was the emergence of the band Nirvana, fronted by the legendary rocker, Kurt Cobain in the late 1980s and early 1990s. He lived downtown in Olympia for a while before he became a huge and popular rock star and moved north to Seattle, and afterward the city of Olympia was caught up completely in the grunge movement with Cobain wannabes and slackers wearing long hair, ripped up jeans, flannel shirts and Converse high top sneakers. They rode skateboards, smoked marijuana, and drank wine from bottles concealed in paper sacks, sitting on the corners downtown playing guitars and drums and having a swell time. It was a good fit for Olympia, and people were happy back then. In April 5, 1994 the grunge music movement lost one of its founding members when Kurt committed suicide in his Seattle home, and the grunge movement itself began to lose dominion over to the encroaching and unstoppable influence of hip-hop music that was gaining popularity and influence on the youth. Olympia was now only a remnant of its glory days from the previous decades.

One day in 2003, the Olympia brewery closed, purchased by MillerCoors and the popular beer was relocated to Irwindale, California. Along with the beer, Olympia began to lose most of its musical presence and artistic pizzazz, and the local scene was giving way to mediocrity. Rap music didn't translate well to street music, and the street musicians themselves were not partial to rap music, so the street music scene in general didn't survive well—although it didn't vanish completely. The youth were now wearing baggy pants—or the complete opposite, skinny jeans—flat billed baseball caps, tank tops, tattoos, gold chains, and scrubby beards. The hooded sweater, known as a "hoody" was their favorite overcoat, and they roamed around in groups or packs with skateboards or on BMX bicycles. Smoking marijuana was still popular, but now they were adding copious amounts of methamphetamine and heroine to the mix, and they were sleeping anywhere they could find in an alley, under a bridge, or on the sidewalk. Homelessness had become rampant, and an entire generation was now living on the streets, uninterested in working for a living, and wanting to do nothing but party every day. Olympia was now known by the locals as a complete "shithole" and nobody really wanted to go downtown anymore. When the brewery closed shop and left town, there was nothing left but politicians, locals, and homeless miscreants.

Over the decades, the different churches in Olympia, have served the public and cared for the homeless. On Saturdays, in particular, they serve a free breakfast to the homeless population downtown in a parking lot across from the Olympia Transit Center. I see them while I'm waiting for my bus to go to work on Saturdays. They look like they are recovering from a wild Friday night and gathering strength for another round again, tonight. Saturday night is alright for fighting, just like the song by Elton John states, and it is true. He could have been singing about the local riffraff downtown. They are a motley throng of vagrants, old bums, young punks, and smoked out freaks, yelling aloud, whooping it up, and just having an overall good time with their carefree lifestyle. I'm on my way to work and I wonder if I am really the one who is the butt of the joke. Are these individuals that live on the fringe of society on the public's dime really living the "good life" on the street? Is it possible? They look like they're enjoying themselves.

They got to have a hot breakfast passed out by a local church that consists of biscuits and gravy, scrambled eggs, sausage and bacon, toast, juice and milk. They get little Ziploc bags with hygiene items: toothbrush and toothpaste, deodorant, dental floss, shampoo, and soap. They get a bag lunch in a brown paper bag with a cheese and bologna sandwich, a piece of fruit, potato chips, a candy bar, and a Capri Sun juice pouch. There is a box with donated clothing so they can find something to wear. This is a festival that spreads out into the streets and lasts into the night. That is why some of the locals called it the "Festival Breakfast," because it was festive, and they were getting a free, hot breakfast to fuel them for further fun on the mean streets of Olympia on a Saturday night.

They sure know how to live out there on the streets, and boy are they having fun. The nightlife and riffraff were not prepared for the vampires that arrived late on that Saturday night.

2

Manson pulled the Monte Carlo into the parking lot on second avenue, across from the Intercity Transit center. It was dark and the tweakers and freaks were out in force.

"Let's get out and walk," Manson said. "This looks like a perfect place to find an innocent victim."

"I don't know about innocent," Zoey said. "Look at them."

She nodded her head at a group of miscreants gathered on the street corner in front of a small Asian convenience store.

"They are whacked out of their minds."

"We are not looking for street urchins," Manson said. "They are common flotsam and jetsam. We are going after the innocent, not the sickened and wasted souls on the street. We shall find the bar of choice where they congregate. Come now. The hour is getting late."

They walked past the weirdos and winos, the meth-heads and heroine junkies lying in the street, past the homeless pan-handlers and vagrants. Just as they were passing around a cor-ner near an alley, they were accosted by a random weirdo. This guy was pushing a shopping cart, dressed in an assortment of clothing culled from dumpsters and the Goodwill. His coat was tattered and torn, a beige bomber jacket with dingy white fleece lining. On his head was an Urban Pipeline cap with ear-flaps covering his ears. One of his stained and faded Hilfiger pantlegs was rolled up to the knee, exposing his tube sock with red stripes beneath. His shoes were old worn out sneakers with duct tape holding the soles on and covering the holes. He smiled and exposed a mouthful of rotten teeth and diseased gums.

"Good evening, beautiful," the man said. "What brings you out on such a night?"

"I'm sorry," Manson said. "Do I know you?"

"I wasn't talking to you, friend," the man said. "I was talking to your pretty lady friend."

"She has nothing to say to you," Manson said, stepping in between the man and Zoey.

"Fuck you, asshole," the man said. "The real question is: do you have any money?"

"Not for you," Zoey said.

"She talks," the man said, licking his lips and wiping them on his sleeve.

"Listen here," Manson said. "We are just passing through. We don't want any trouble. Just step aside and let us pass . . . and we will forget this whole thing. Yes?"

"No. Not even," the man said. "I want some money. You're going to pay me to go away. How about that?"

"You think so?" Manson said.

"I do," the man said. He reached into his shopping cart and pulled out an ax, testing the blade for sharpness. "If you don't give me some money . . . I'm going to hit you with this. Maybe even cut your heads off. How does that sound?"

"Touché," Manson said. "However, you have chosen the wrong people to rob tonight."

"Oh, yeah?" the man said, grinning. "Says who? I am known on the streets as Big Smoke. I kill people. You get it? I will kill you, too."

Zoey laughed aloud. She was amused by this disheveled and menacing street vagrant.

"You never know who you may cross paths with," Zoey said. "Sadly, for you, you have underestimated your opponent tonight. Have you ever heard of vampires?"

"Huh? What? Vampires?" the man said, dumbfounded and skeptical. "The hell you say?"

"We are vampires," Manson said. "You have chosen to rob the undead. What a terrible mistake on your part."

"That's some funny shit," the man said. "And I am Batman."

Manson looked at Zoey and nodded his head, sending her a mental note.

Manson: *Let's scare the daylights out of this fool.*

Zoey: *Agreed. He is making me nauseous. Let's be done with him and go on our way.*

The man sensed something was about to happen and he raised the ax and swung it at Manson.

"I told you I'd kill you, fucker," the man said. "You didn't believe me."

"Observe," Manson said, catching the man's hand holding the ax. "Watch closely and pay attention."

Manson and Zoey changed their demeanors into the hideous undead creatures that they truly were, showing their faces as fiendishly evil vampires with fangs and dark, bloody read eyes with no sclera, streaked white and black hair, bony fingers with claws like razor sharp talons. They grew taller, menacing, looking much like a creature from an early 20th century vampire horror film. Their faces were the countenance of a corpse and a devil, stretched into facades of cruelty and wickedness, nostrils only slits, lips thin and black, teeth prickly and sharp like jagged spikes. These were not the faces of beauty, but faces of fear and terror, horrific to observe and inspiring dread in all who looked upon them.

"Holy shit," the man said, dropping the ax and attempting to back away.

Manson still had a firm grip on his wrist, and picked him up, feet dangling above the ground.

"You are a miserable wretch," Manson said, voice growling and evil.

"Let me go," the man said. "I'm sorry. I won't bother you again. Just let me go."

"You are lucky we don't eat scum like you," Zoey said. "Although we should kill you, spill your guts right here to rid the world of such vermin." She stroked his cheek with her claws and smelled his fear. "You stink of foul death, anyway. Your time is short. We don't need to kill you. You will do that by yourself."

"Run for your life, little man," Manson said, letting go of the filthy wrist and letting the man drop back to his feet on the ground. He hit the ground in mid-stride, sprinting away.

"Shoo," Zoey said. "Run. Run away before we change our minds."

The homeless man turned, looking back over his should as he ran, oblivious to his shopping cart with all his worldly possessions, and fled around the corner and down the street, running away in fear for his life. The only thing on his mind was getting away from these evil monsters that called themselves vampires; perhaps, he thought he would go to the police and tell them his story—although the police would not believe a homeless drug addict with such a spectacular and bazaar story.

"He won't be back," Manson said.

"What if he tells someone about us?" Zoey said.

"No one will believe him," Manson said. "He's a vagrant and a drug addict. His word is shit."

3

Manson and Zoey transformed back into their beautiful visages, their alter ego, and looked around to see if anyone had observed them making the change from fiends into lustful objects of desire. Once again, they were attractive and handsome, and spectators would jump through wrath and fire to get next to them, to have a chance at a sexual encounter, to love and be loved by someone so painfully pretty and desirable. They were like supermodels dressed in Gothic attire, and the world would once again lust after them, glancing audaciously and approaching with nonchalant pickup lines. They started walking and took the opposite path in which the vagrant robber had fled.

Farther up Fourth Avenue they found a quaint and popular little establishment known as Jack's Pub. This was a bar for anyone curious about counterculture, gay and lesbian, cross dressing, drag queens, and curious bystanders interested in how the other side lives. You could be whatever you wanted to be there.

The music was loud as they approached the entryway to the Jack's Pub. The city smelled of comingled food, greasy, salty, and car exhaust, and the rank Puget Sound, and the hot dog stand next to the pub. There was also a lingering aroma of urine, feces, and body odor, and worse, the smell of dying dreams and hopelessness from the city dwellers who lived on the street, endlessly.

"Let's hurry and get inside," Manson said. "This city has scurvy, I think."

"I agree," Zoey said. "I might be afraid to drink blood from this cesspool."

"We will find a nice and lovely quarry in here, I am sure," he said, pulling the door to Jack's Pub open. The music within blasted out into the street. It was the sound of dubstep and hypnotic beats, with techno synthesizer and warbling bass riffs and samples from psychotronic film clips featured in the background.

Inside there were a variety of patrons, some dressed in drag, some in jeans and flannel, some in Gothic gear and makeup. It was a pleasant mix of diverse cultures, style, taste, and fashion, with a flamboyant flare.

They went to the bar and sat down. The bartender was a young, androgynous sprite with neatly cropped purple hair and lip and nose piercings.

"What can I get for you?" the androgynous bartender asked.

"We'll have two Crown and Cokes, please," Manson said.

"What? No Tequila Sunrises?" Zoey asked.

"Not yet," Manson said. "We are just getting warmed up."

He looked around the pub, taking in the ragtag patrons. There was a pool table, dart boards, a pinball machine, a stage with a DJ and a dance floor. A couple of outlandishly dressed queens were dancing on the floor, having a wonderful time together. Their costumes were colorful and bright, rainbow themed, and cheerful. They simply radiated pride and exuberance.

"I like this place," Manson said. "It's quaint and cozy."

"It's not bad," Zoey said. "I've seen better."

"This is a perfect place to hunt," Manson said. "We will have no trouble procuring bleeding hearts here."

"Sounds delightful," Zoey said. "I do love a salty blue-blooded libertarian . . . literally. They have such delicate skin and discriminating taste."

They spotted their next victims: a group of ambiguously gay ogresses in rainbow colored clothing and hair, giggling and laughing at one another as they joked and poked fun at the other oddball patrons in the bar.

"I am in the mood for something sweet tonight," Manson said. "What do you think?"

"I say bravo, Manson," Zoey said, looking at the table of queer folk. "We shall follow them and take them quickly."

One of the colorful and flamboyant fleshy mortals at the table looked over and noticed they were being watched by Manson and Zoey.

"What are you looking at, freaks?" the rainbow haired butch girl said. She was wearing a flannel shirt with cut off sleeves, her sheered, closely cropped hair colored with three hues of florescent dye. Her ass was tightly packed into a pair of bib overalls and as wide as a dump truck, engulfing the seat beneath her, and her feet were clad in Birkenstocks. She sucked on her straw in a fruity mixed drink and smacked her lips in a pouty gesture, saying "We are not your type, honey."

"I'm sorry," Manson said, raising his eyebrows. "I'm not sure I understand . . ."

"Oh, you understand, sweety," the butch girl said. "You don't stand a chance with us. This merchandise is not for the likes of you."

"Ouch," Zoey said. "That has got to hurt."

Manson sat back in his seat and crossed his arms. His face was an expression of startled bewilderment.

"Now, you honey," the butch girl said, pointing at Zoey. "You are welcome anytime, dear. We would just eat you alive, precious. You can join us anytime. You are a fine motherfucker, if you don't mind me saying. Catch my drift?"

The butch girl used her hand to trace her full-figured features as if displaying the goods like a prize on the Price is Right. She finished by rubbing her crotch and then blowing Zoey a kiss.

"Like what you see?" the butch girl asked.

"You can come home with us," one of the other sexually ambiguous individuals at the table said. "You'll have to lose your boyfriend, though. No dicks aloud at our parties. We have dildos to take care of that."

The group of gay, butch ladies laughed heartily at their crude witticisms.

"Oh, my," Manson said. "I'm not sure what to say."

"You've just been told," Zoey said. "This is a clear case of misandry."

"A case of what?" Manson asked.

"Man haters," Zoey said. "They don't like penis. Get it? But, on the upside . . . they love me. And why not? I have a magnificent vagina . . . and they would love to see it."

"You are so modest," Manson said. "Perhaps you should go home with them while I go about and play tiddlywinks with myself . . . and my penis."

"Perhaps," Zoey said. "The only problem is they are not my type . . . unless, of course, you consider them as sustenance. Everyone bleeds red where they are cut. Do they not?"

"I see your point," Manson said. "Why don't you go and make friends while I flirt with some of the fellows in here. This does seem to by that kind of place. Maybe I'll find a boyfriend for the evening. Perhaps someone else will enjoy my penis."

"Ha! You are so funny," Zoey said. "I simply adore your penis. What are you worried about?"

"Thank you dear," Manson said, turning a whiter shade of pale. "You've made me blush. Now go lure these plump and gay trollops outside so we can ravage them."

Zoey stood up from the table and went over to the coven of butch women and introduced herself. They all cheered merrily when the beautiful Goth girl came to their table. They were victorious and had ousted the dirty man from the Amazonian tribe and homosexual cleansing ritual. Death to all men and pigs, they chanted. She sat down and joined them, laughing with them and entertaining their sexual innuendos; after all, Zoey was partial to men and women, so it did not make much difference to her one way or the other.

4

Manson was amazed at who walked through the door and sat down at the bar. It was Crandall, the long lost third part of the original ménage à trois. He smiled, heart brimming over, as stealthily strolled over to the bar and sat down next to Crandall, sitting silently and waiting to see how long it would take for him to notice.

Manson observed that he had changed cloths, and now he was dressed in hipster clothing with a brown vest, green button up shirt, tight fitting beige pleated slacks and shiny burgundy leather dress shoes. He wore rounded spectacles much like those worn by eccentric scholars, artists, writers, and musicians. On his head, a gray Fedora. He was drinking a craft beer from the bottle, something fancy and local, made by Fish Tail Brewpub; it was an organic pale ale, named Wild Salmon, and had the logo of a fish tale on the label.

Crandall sensed his presence, felling that he was being watched, and turned and looked at Manson, with sudden recognition, his eyes wide in startled amazement.

"Holy smokes," Crandall said, leaning forward and taking a good look. "Is that you, Manson? I don't believe it. What a coincidence running into you here."

"Crandall, my man," Manson said, leaning over and giving him a hug. "Yes. It's me. And I am just as surprised to see you here. You are a sight for sore eyes. What the hell happened to you?" Manson was overjoyed and extremely happy to be reunited with him after losing him in Bellingham after the incident with the vampire hunter in the cemetery.

"As I live and breathe," Crandall said, patting Manson on the shoulder. "I am so happy so see you and know that you are still alive." He knew that Manson did not know about the confrontation with the vampire hunter last night in Seattle, or how he had saved their lives as they were sleeping in the trunk of their car, and he decided to keep it to himself, as there was no need to brag about his heroism. "I've missed you and Zoey."

"You're telling me. I thought you were dead. What a coincidence meeting you here," Manson said, taking a second look and doting on his friend. He grabbed his face with his hands and gave him a big kiss on the cheek. "I love you, brother. Man. I don't believe it. It's really you." He shook his head in bemusement. "We lost track of you in Bellingham, after the . . . hunter attacked us in the cemetery. Where did you go?"

"Yes. I know," Crandall said. "I had to get away quickly. He hit me in the shoulder with the arrow, and I was severely injured. I feared for my life, so I kept running and hid away in the woods. When I found the courage to go back and look for you and Zoey, you were already gone, and daylight had arrived, and I knew I would not find you after that."

"Why didn't you call us?" Manson asked. "You had my phone number."

"First, I had to seek medical attention," he said. "I had to go to the emergency room and get stitches and bandaged up. It was pretty bad. I was lucky to avoid surgery." He unbuttoned his coat and shirt and showed him the bandage beneath, a layer of white medical tape and gauze patches stuck over the wound on his shoulder blade. "After I left the hospital that night, I decided I needed some time alone, I guess," Manson said. "I've been hitchhiking in order to get here, knowing I could meet you in California someday. I intended to call you soon . . . just felt like waiting for a bit. I did not want to impose on you two. I felt like a third wheel."

"You are always a welcome third wheel to us," Manson said, waving his hand at the silly statement. "Remember that. By the way, what's up with the fancy clothes? You look . . . dashing. Are you trying to change your image?"

"No. I am not," he said, looking at Manson coolly. "Just felt like changing things up. Is that so wrong?"

"Not at all," Manson said. "I just never took you for the . . . well-dressed hipster type. You seem more like a dark and edgy kind of guy, to me. But, hey . . . if it makes you happy, who am I to complain?"

"It's just outward appearance," Crandall said. "Our fashion makes a statement about us that leads people to believe certain things. It may not be true, of course, because inside we might really be a savage beast. See what I mean?"

"I do," Manson said. "Indubitably, so. First impressions can be misleading." He waved to the bartender to get him a beer, saying, "I'll have what he's having." He pointed at the beer Crandall was drinking. The bartender acknowledged his request with a nod of the head.

"Apropos of nothing," Crandall said, adjusting his shirt cuffs. "How's life treating you?"

"I am feeling absolutely marvelous," Manson said. "Couldn't be better, to tell the truth. Life has given me a new outlook and purpose that I did not have before. I am alive, now, and loving it."

"That's nice," Crandall said. "I assume you are talking about being a dark rogue. Dressed in musty black leather. An angsty vamp. It's a classic look."

"Rogue?" Manson said. "Hmm. I suppose. And I like your hat. *That* is a classic look."

Crandall took off the Fedora and spun it around on his finger.

"Thanks. It's just a hat," he said. He took a drink of his beer and then nodded his head toward the table where Zoey was cutting up with the rainbow lesbians. "Is she recruiting the lesbians for an orgy, or what?"

"Uh, yeah," Manson said. "She's working her magic."

"Why is she sitting with the LGBTQ social justice warriors?"

"I'm sorry? I'm not sure I follow," Manson said. "Is there something wrong with that? You are not exactly a straight shooter yourself."

"No. Hardly," Crandall said, tipping back his beer and taking another swig. "Just curious what she's up to."

Manson looked over toward the direction of Zoey and grinned. He looked back at Crandall, and said, "Girls will be girls, you know? She just wants to be with the sweethearts for a bit. I'm fine with that. It can have its benefits, if you know what I mean."

The purple haired bartender walked over and gave Manson a beer. He accepted gracefully.

"She prefers the company of lesbians. They will try to convert her, you know?"

"Oh, I see where you're going with that," Manson said. "Listen, you cannot steal what you already have. Zoey likes it both ways—I'm down with that. Who am I to deny her that pleasure?"

"You two are comfortable sharing each other?" Crandall asked.

"I guess you could say that. You should know the answer to that by now. I don't know if I would use the term 'comfortable' though," Manson said, taking a drink. "More like friendly and free with a mutual agreement. We do what we like and see whom we choose. No restrictions. Dominance is so last century. But we are exclusive to each other."

"Ah, I see," Crandall said. "That explains how we met in the first place."

Without warning, Zoey walked up and put her hands lovingly on Manson's shoulders, resting her chin on his shoulder.

"Hello, love," she said, looking at Crandall and her eyes opening wide. "Crandall. What are you going here? How did you find us here? It's good to see you . . . and know you are still alive."

"Hello, Zoey," Crandall said, raising his beer in a salute. "I'm happy to see you, too. I'm happy to be alive, as well. Thank you."

"Imagine the luck," Manson said, smiling at Zoey. "We've got our friend back, even after we thought he was lost for good."

"Well, I just came over here to see if you would like to join me and my new friends for a drink. We don't want you to feel left out."

"What do you think, Crandall?" Manson asked. "Shall we?"

"I'm game," Crandall said. "Let's bless them with our presence."

"Well, let's go then . . . move like somebody," Zoey said, ushering them toward the table where the rainbow lesbians were waiting anxiously.

They went back to the table and formed a group of intermingled styles, tastes, and genders that warmed the heart. After numerous drinks and much flirting, they all decided a walk around Capitol Lake would be just what the doctor ordered. They could smoke some marijuana, count the stars, and make out like kids at a high school dance. Zoey and Manson thought that sounded like a wonderful idea. Crandall was not so sure because tonight was going to be filled with a full moon. This could turn out bad, he knew, and perhaps he should go a separate way again, at least until the change came and went and he was over it and he returned to normal.

"It's cold outside," one of girls at the table said. "I need my coat.'

"Oh, don't be a wet blanket," the big girl with the rainbow hair said. "It's not that bad. Put your coat on, already."

"Fine. Let's go," the girl said, putting on her coat.

The entourage left the bar and walked out onto the city streets of Olympia at night, the bar flies, thugs, hipsters, street musicians, freaks, and tweakers out in force.

5

They left the bar in a group and walked through the city of Olympia and went down to Capitol Lake, walking around the trail that skirted the circumference of edge of the water. There were black lampposts with lighted white orbs, wrought iron benches where they could sit and smoke and drink from a bottle of peppermint schnapps.

The rainbow haired girls were happy and talkative, infatuated with Zoey.

"Oh, poop," one of the girls said. "It's cloudy tonight. We can't see the stars."

"Bummer," Zoey said. "Hopefully it won't rain."

"That would suck," the other girl said.

Crandall was quiet and distant. He pulled back, catching Manson by the arm.

"Listen," Crandall said. "I have something to tell you."

"What?"

"I'm going to be in trouble soon," he said, stopping and holding Manson. "Unlike you . . . a vampire . . . I cannot control myself."

"I'm sorry. What are you getting at?" Manson asked.

"As a vampire you crave blood. My condition is worse than that, because I can't control it and I crave flesh and blood and go into a rampage."

"So, what is the matter? I know you are a lycanthrope. Big deal."

"Because I am disgusted by my actions when I am under the spell—the curse," Crandall said, looking to the sky. "The moon is full tonight. I have a keen sense and I can smell you— you reek of death and blood. I may try to harm you, too."

"You are a werewolf," Manson said. "Deal with it. I can handle you. You worry too much."

"I am. That's the point. What if I injure the wrong person . . . you or Zoey?"

"What are the odds of that? I mean . . . you should just relax."

"I'm warning you now, soon I will transform . . . and it is nothing pretty."

"I don't know what to say," Manson said. "Just go with it. Act natural. Be yourself."

"Just beware," Crandall said. "I know what you are going to do to these girls. You are going to feed on them. You're a vampire, after all and that is what you do. I don't care. You must do what you must do. And so shall I—I will join you in the feast. But beware of my inner beast. You have not seen anything like it before. I promise you that."

"So be it," Manson said. "Come. Let's take advantage of this glorious night."

They walked back to the group of girls giggling gayly and sat beside them on the bench.

Manson and Zoey looked at each other and nodded. It was time. They would take their victims now, under the cloudy sky by Capitol Lake.

Manson communicated with Zoey with his mind.

Manson: *Our friend, Crandall, is a afraid of us seeing him as a werewolf. Just so you know.*

Zoey: *Really? I'm eager to see him transform. I've never met a werewolf before. Are you sure he will change? He looks normal to me. Will he feed with us, too?*

Manson: *Yes. He is going to transform since the moon is full. Just watch out. He will be dangerous. Stand clear.*

Zoey: *Okay. Duly noted.*

"And now, boys and girls," Manson said. "Let the fun begin."

The girls giggled, unaware of what was about to transpire.

Manson approached from behind the bench. Zoey was sitting next to the girls.

Crandall was standing to the right, looming patiently.

Overhead, the clouds miraculously parted and the moon

shone through, beaming brightly, illuminating a fog that hung over the lake in a sinister mist. An owl hooted from the nearby woods. A shiver of horripilation fell upon the girls and their skin raised in gooseflesh.

"I think it's time to get out of here," the rainbow haired girl said. "I'm not having fun anymore."

"So soon?" Manson asked, sarcastically feigning disappointment. "We just got here. What's the rush?"

The girls stood up from the bench and that was the signal that the three creatures of the night needed to usher in the attack.

Crandall growled, the lycanthropic chemistry in his blood began to react to the moon, and his flesh bubbled and writhed, swelling, hair growing from his face, fangs protruding from his mouth. His nose stretched and become elongated, whiskers sprouting from his lips. He leaned his head back, howled as he transformed into a werewolf. His clothes were ripped and torn and tattered.

The victims screamed in horror. The feeding frenzy began in earnest, blood and gore flying and spilling on the cobblestones, splattering the white orb lamps overhead. The panicked girls cried out in blood curdling screams of terror as they were bitten on the neck, jugular veins severed, tendons and sinew snapping apart, meat and gristle ripping sickly as bones and cartilage separated. The screams stopped and only the sounds of sucking of blood, teeth gnashing and macerating meat, and the snapping of bones crunched between wölfen jaws. There were contented growls and groans and grunts as the meat and blood was consumed completely and the feeding was finished.

The trio of bloodthirsty beasts ran away into the night and disappeared from the scene of the grisly murder. Crandall ran away in a different direction, into the woods to hide from sight, and Manson and Zoey hurried back to the Monte Carlo, drove out into the Capitol Forest, and found a quiet place to park and sleep it off for the daylight hours. It had been a tumultuous night, and they were worried that they may have attracted too much attention.

6

The vampire hunter, Adrian Burgendorv, was hot on the trail of Manson, Zoey, and Crandall. He had used his tracking locator to find them after they slipped away in Seattle.

He watched from the woods as the vampires and the werewolf attacked the victims in a savage bloodlust. A tempestuous storm of wet and sticky meat and blood flew in a horrendous blast that rained down on the ground, spattering the white globe lamps with crimson and pieces of flesh.

Soon he would bring them to their miserable end.

The police would arrive soon, and he did not want to be anywhere near the murder scene. He got in his van and followed the vampires and the werewolf . . . where were they going now? After staying in a hotel room he follows them to Interstate 90 and sees them dropping of the werewolf.

Where is he going?

This was a random and strange shift in activity . . . they were splitting up. He could not follow them in different directions, so he decided to stick with the Monte Carlo and as they were heading back south, he sped up and let his presence be known. He followed them closely, tailing them, ready to fight them at the next stop.

1

The next night, Crandall called Manson and Zoey on his cell phone and they regrouped at the Tumwater Falls Park Trail.

He was waiting for them when they pulled into the parking lot. He got into the car and sat in his place in the backseat.

"So good to see you again, old friend," Manson said. "I thought we may have lost you."

"I'm okay," Crandall said.

"Where did you go?" Zoey asked.

"I went and hid in the woods," Crandall said. "I did not want to take a chance on anyone seeing me during the transformation. I slept in the cold . . . but I was safe."

"That makes sense," Manson said.

"We should get the hell out of here," Crandall said. "They are going to be looking for us . . . for sure."

"I agree," Manson said.

"Where are we going?" Zoey asked.

"Tacoma," Manson said. "It is in the wrong direction . . . but it is a safe place to hide out for a while until things cool off."

"What are we waiting for?" Zoey asked. "Let's get out of here. I'm ready."

"Indeed," Manson said, putting the car in gear and pulling out of the parking lot.

"I fucking hate this shit," Crandall said, drumming his fists on his knees. "I'm cursed." He was not happy with his lifestyle. "I'm thinking about making a change."

"What do you mean?" Manson asked, looking in the rear-view mirror.

Zoey turned and looked at Crandall, resting her chin on her hands.

"I am thinking about breaking away," Crandall said. "Maybe

going to Europe. I read on the Internet that there is a doctor in Paris who can cure werewolves. It sounds like a good idea to me."

"What? Are you crazy?" Manson said.

"You are unhappy?" Zoey asked.

"Yes," Crandall said. "I did not ask for this curse."

There was a moment of silence. They drove along Interstate 5 out of Olympia, heading north, arriving in Tacoma in a matter of ten minutes.

"I think your nuts," Manson said, pulling off on the exit and driving into the city of Tacoma. "But, that's just my opinion, I guess."

Zoey struck him on the shoulder, saying, "Don't be so insensitive. He is having a crisis. You should be supportive of him."

"Meh," Manson said. "I think being a werewolf is a wonderful gift. You should be grateful, Crandall."

"So, you say," Crandall replied. "If it were really happening to you . . . you may have a different opinion."

"We are vampires," Manson said. "I'm not unhappy." He looked at Zoey. "Are you?"

She looked back, a blank look on her face, it was obvious that she was struggling to agree. "I don't know," she said, wringing her hands in her lap. "I'm not completely convinced I like it . . . but, it's not the end of the world."

"Well, I am not happy," Crandall said. "It is like being bipolar and emotionally distraught all the time. I cannot control myself . . . and that is the part that scares me."

"Just go with it," Manson said. "You are a beast. It is your nature now . . . don't fight it."

"I'm not so sure it's going to be that easy," Crandall said.

"Whatever," Manson said. "We need to find a place to hide

out for a while. I think this hotel up ahead looks marvelous. What a fabulous name."

"I love it," Zoey said.

"Perfect," Crandall said, slapping his knees again, frustrated. "I guess it will have to do."

Manson pulled the Monte Carlo into the hotel parking lot, the marquee sign brightly lit, THE HIDEAWAY INN blazing in neon. They went inside and they rented a room for the night. The hotel clerk did not even give them a second glance, as this was Tacoma and nothing was shocking in that city anymore.

Inside the room, they peeked out through the curtains, watching out for the vampire hunter because they knew he was on their trail.

"I don't see that piece of shit van out there," Manson said. "We must have lost him."

"I don't care anymore," Crandall said. "If he catches us and kills us, what does it matter?"

"Lighten up, man," Zoey said. "Keep a positive frame of mind."

"Sure, whatever," Crandall said, plopping down on the bed. "I'm exhausted."

"What about your movie script?" Zoey asked. "I thought you wanted to go to Hollywood with us."

"I do—I did," Crandall said, sighing. "I can't live like this any longer. I want to go to Paris. I'm sorry I won't be making the trip to Hollywood with you. You can take my script there with you and see if you can pitch it to a producer."

"I don't know much about pitching a script," Manson said.

"It's no big deal," Crandall said. "Once I find the cure I can come back."

"You don't like being a werewolf?" Zoey said, stating the obvious.

"That's what he's saying," Manson said.

"No. It's a curse," Crandall said, rubbing his eyes. "I don't like not having control of my rage. The moon owns my soul. I want it back."

"Let's get something to drink," Manson said. "We can have a party. Enough of this depressing banter."

"Fine," Crandall said. "Whatever. Let's get drunk."

"I'm down," Zoey said, lighting a cigarette.

Manson dug in his pockets, pulled out wads of dollar bills, counted them, and said, "I'll be right back. The liquor store is right down the road." He was gone for only a few minutes and came back with arms loaded with beer, whiskey, and wine. It was time to get drunk and forget about things for a while.

8

The following night, Manson was morose and saddened, Zoey sitting sullenly in the passenger seat of the Monte Carlo, driving down the highway, moving east in order to drop Crandall off so he could go home to Main.

"I hate to see you go," Manson said. "Having you along has been a riot."

"I know," Crandall said, crossing his arms in the backseat. "I just have to go home now. It is time. I feel the end is near and if I don't try to do something different, I will fail miserably."

"Never say that," Zoey said. "You can do whatever you set your mind to."

"Not with the curse," Crandall said. "I will never be fully in control of my fate or destiny so long as I suffer under a full moon. I can't control myself . . . and that is the worst feeling in the world."

"You are a creature of the night," Manson said. "You should embrace it. Imagine the possibilities. If you go to Hollywood with us you could be so much more . . . you could be discovered with your movie script and be famous."

"I don't think scriptwriters have such a glamorous life," Crandall said. "I will never be able to enjoy a normal life so long as I suffer from this curse."

"I think it's awesome that you are a werewolf," Zoey said. "A few months ago, I would never have believed that they even existed. And now I know one personally. I feel privileged."

"Well, I am glad to know the both of you, too," Crandall said, leaning forward and patting her on the shoulder. "I feel the same way about vampires. Who knew? They really do exist. Don't you feel strange . . . a different life-form now? I mean, do you miss being . . . normal?"

"No. Not at all," Manson said. "I am happy with my new life. I have strength and blood . . . and Zoey. I feel alive." He looked at her and smiled—she looked back and returned a smile with alluring eyes. "That's all I need now."

"I guess I see your point," Crandall said. "I will miss the two of you. I must go my own way now. It saddens my heart to leave in the middle of this adventure, but I must follow the path toward my destiny. I have always wanted to go to Europe. I think visiting France will be a lovely adventure."

"I agree," Zoey said. "It's so romantic there. I'm jealous."

"We could go there someday," Manson said.

"We shall," Zoey said. "After we go to Hollywood and reestablish ourselves . . . we will come visit you in France."

"That's a lovely idea," Crandall said. "I don't know what I am doing yet. I just know I must find this scientist fellow who holds the cure to my . . . what ails me."

A green sign that said **Auburn 6 Miles** whisked by on the side of the road.

"Were almost there," Manson said. "You sure we can't change your mind?"

"No. I'm set on my mission now," Crandall said.

"I'm going to miss you," Zoey said.

"I'm going to miss you guys, too," Crandall said.

"Well, keep our numbers in your phone," Manson said. "Keep in touch. Let us know how things go for you."

"Of course," Crandall said. "I will do that."

They drove the remaining miles in an awkward silence.

The exit sign appeared up ahead and Manson pulled the car off of Interstate 5 and slowed down and followed the side street that led to the small town of Auburn. There was a stoplight and an intersection up ahead. He turned right and followed the road down to where there was a small convenience store lighting up the night. The store parking lot was empty.

"Okay, here we are," Manson said. "Are you going to be all right?"

"Yes. I got this," Crandall said. "This isn't my first rodeo."

"Do be safe," Zoey said. "It's dangerous . . ."

They all made eye contact and idly laughed at the statement, realizing the irony of the fact that they were living monsters and that mortal man was still evil, nonetheless, requiring no supernatural source or curse to make them a malignant blight. Mankind was evil of course, and there was no cause or reason other than they could be the most foul and wicked creatures on the Earth. Humans were the real monsters. That much was obvious. Some of the biggest atrocities in history were brought about by mortal men, not supernatural or mythical beasts. It was true.

"I will make it, just fine," Crandall said. "Now let's not be making this long goodbye. We will meet again, my friend."

Manson climbed out of the car and leaned the seat forward so Crandall could get out, and he climbed out and stretched, feeling a bit stiff after the drive. Zoey climbed out and came around toward them.

"Give me a hug, you big galoot," she said, reaching her arms around Crandall and squeezing him tight. "I'm going to miss you so much."

"It's going to be okay," Crandall said, and he squeezed her tightly, a single tear forming at the corner of her eye.

Manson patted Crandall on the shoulder and then they hugged.

"You take care, brother," Manson said.

"You two just get back in that car and drive away now," Crandall said. "I can't take this drama. Don't look back."

Zoey wiped the tear from her eye.

"Fine. Take care, my friend," Manson said, shaking Crandall's hand. "We shall meet again."

"Yes. Absolutely," Crandall said.

"Let's go, Zoey," Manson said. "Get in the car. We are just going to stand here and feel sad forever."

"Goodbye, Crandall," Zoey said.

Crandall raised his hand and smiled. He had nothing left to say. He was not much for long goodbyes.

Manson and Zoey climbed back into the car and shut the doors. They took one last glance at Crandall, who had moved to the sidewalk near the store. They waved goodbye as Manson put the car in gear and backed up, turning around and pulling out of the parking lot.

"I'm going to cry," Zoey said.

"Don't do that," Manson said. "He'll be fine."

"But I'm going to miss him."

"I know, babe. Just be strong. He's a big boy. He can take

care of himself."

"Yes. I know."

They pulled out onto the road and drove away, heading back south down Interstate 5 on their way toward their destination in Hollywood.

9

Manson and Zoey tricked the vampire hunter when they pull into a rest area—southbound on Interstate 5 (8.1 miles South of Woodland, Washington) just miles away from the Oregon border—and using stealth and invisibility, they are able to sabotage the vampire hunter's van and leave him stuck behind, unable to pursue them, while he changes the flat tire with a spare.

CHAPTER TWENTY

1

After Crandall decided to go his own way and Manson and Zoey dropped him off in Auburn, he went inside the store and purchased a package of Jack Link's beef jerky and a bottle of water. It was not much, but it would have to be enough to sustain him for the beginning of his journey. He was low on cash and did not have much to spend on his trip, so he would have to ration his funds and live lean and mean along the way . . . although there was the curse, and that would bring a feeding rampage where he would get fresh meat, and a full moon was coming soon, only a week away, and he knew that he would eat well then, even though it sickened him to thing about the implications of eating human flesh. The thought strengthened his resolve to find a cure for the lycanthropic curse tainting his blood.

When he thought about the carnage, he had taken part in over the past few months, he was sickened and saddened. He suddenly knew that he no longer wanted to be part of the killing spree on the road with the vampires. He knew that he must separate from them and go his own way to find the cure he had read about. He hoped to be rid of the curse of the werewolf. His desire was to find a way to fly to Europe, his destination, Paris. He longed to find a rumored mad scientist who could cure the lycanthropic malignancy flowing through his veins. He just wanted to live a normal life and not be controlled by the tendencies to be a Dr. Jekyll and Mr. Hyde.

He planned was to go back to Main, get his passport, visit his parents again, and borrow the money to go to Paris. He left the parking lot of the convenience store and walked down the dark and deserted street. It was a quiet night. The sky was overcast and it was on the verge of rain, a slight drizzle coming down in the streetlamps, and he zipped his coat up all the way and raised his collar to shield himself from the bitter and stinging wind that came in gusts and blasts when a car would blast by on the road, now that the rain was beginning to come down thicker and heavier by degrees, until the large, stinging droplets were falling on his face. Fall and then winter were coming close, he could feel it, and with those seasons would come death. The seasons always reminded him of dying.

He braced himself against the onset of the dismal weather and set out to hitchhike home along Interstate 90 that split away from Interstate 5 in Auburn. He could see both paths spread out before him to the left and to the right, and it was symbolic, two roads diverging in the night, and they represented the two paths he could travel.

His heart was saddened, but he knew that he must take the right road, literally to the right, and leave the other path behind. He was a good person at heart and being a beastly menace to the world did not sit well with him. He did not want to harm others, but when he was under the influence of the full moon it was out of his control, and he literally became a different person, and was unable to make good moral choices.

Sitting in the weather for a short time with his thumb out, only a few cars passing by on the Interstate, he knew that he was making the right choice. It was inevitable. He longed to see his family again, too, for they had parted on bad terms and he wanted to make amends. They were not pleased with his recent behavior and they wanted him to make something of his life. He knew that he could go home now and have a chance to make amends. He could explain to them what he planned to do in Europe. Naturally, he could not tell them about the curse of the werewolf, but he could give them hope that he would travel abroad and make good choices in life. He would tell them that he was planning to attend college soon, but first he wanted to travel and see the world. They would not be happy to hear that he was not ready to settle down, yet, but he thought they would be behind him no matter what decisions he made. They just did not want the trouble like before when he was living at home. That is why he had to leave. The police had come to the house and there had been terrible crimes committed in the town. Fingers were pointed and insinuations and accusations began to fly around, and they were leading back to Crandall. There was never any evidence to prove anything, but the rumors and suspicion were enough to cause bad blood between he and his parents.

It would be different now, he knew, because he wanted to make a change in his life for the better. He had learned his lesson and wanted to be a better man. He would tell his parents as much and try to make amends. What else could he do?

In the distance, bright headlights were coming his way as a semi-truck pulled slowly up alongside and came to stop. The diesel engine was rumbling and chugging, the smell of the acrid exhaust strong and rich in his nostrils. The truck door opened, and the driver wearing a red baseball cap and a green flannel shirt looked down at him.

"Where you headed?" the driver asked.

"I'm going back to Main," Crandall said.

"Main? Holy shit, son," the driver said. "You're a long way from home."

"Well, yes," Crandall said, moving toward the truck. "But I've got to get back there to take care of business."

"I'm going to Butte, Montana," the driver said. "I can get you that far."

"That's a good start," Crandall said.

"Jump in," the driver said. "We've got to make good time. I don't want to be late."

"Okay," Crandall said, climbing up into the cab of the truck, shutting the door.

The driver put the truck in gear and pulled away down the Interstate. Crandall was glad that he caught a ride with the truck driver. This would be a good start on the first leg of his journey.

2

Butte Montana, Crandall had a run-in with some local yokels who did not like his looks or his smell. They were big guys with cowboy boots, belt buckles, ten-gallon hats, and mother-of-pearl snaps on their colorful western style shirts. They were outside the bar having a cigarette by their pickup trucks when they saw the stranger, Crandall, pass by, all heads turned and looking intently at him.

"Hey, there, son," one of the cowboys said. He was wearing a large black Stetson. His lip bulged in a lump with a wad of chewing tobacco. "What you doing around here?"

Crandall glanced over at them, kept walking.

"You hear me, boy?" the cowboy said again. He was chewing Copenhagen snuff, and spit a stream of tobacco juice onto the dusty ground. "I'm talking to you."

Crandall stopped, pointed his finger at his chest, and said, "Me? You're talking to me?"

"That's right," the cowboy said. "You look like one of them sissy queers I keep seeing on the Internet. You ain't from around these parts, are you?"

"You are correct," Crandall said. "I am only passing through."

The other cowboys laughed and brayed at the response.

Crandall could tell right away that they were a particularly rambunctious group of hecklers looking to stir up trouble.

"He's an educated queer, Leroy," one of the sidebusters, a short and squat man in a straw cowboy hat and snakeskin boots—probably boa constrictor—with silver tips said, cigarette dangling from the corner of his mouth. His five o'clock shadow looked like it was painted on with lampblack. His shirt was a faded shade of red brick with white cord piping, floral embroidery, and pearl snaps. His stretch denim jeans were so tight it gave him a bubble but and his large, silver belt buckle looked like a superhero shield above his zipped-up bulging package. "I bet he's got a P-H-D in homosexuality."

They all laughed, snorted, and yucked it up at this comment.

"You got something to say, punk?" Leroy asked, tipping back his hat.

"Nope," Crandall said. "I'll just be on my way. You gentlemen have a lovely day."

"He said lovely," the cowboy in stretch pants said. "Don't that just beat all. Can't you come up with something better than that . . . queer boy? What's on your mind. You must have something to say."

"Gee, I don't have much to say," Crandall said, putting his hands down to his side. "But, if you must know . . . I was just thinking that your pants looked so tight that maybe they were cutting off your circulation."

The cowboys looked at each other, bemused and irritated, then back at Crandall.

"You looking for trouble," Leroy asked. "Because we can give you some trouble."

At that moment, a group of three cute cowgirls walked out of the bar. The stopped and admired the handsome stranger, approving of his hipster look, and making comments about how they thought he was cute.

That was enough to send the cowboys into a frenzy.

"Get him, boys," Leroy said, jealousy arousing his anger. "Let's kick his lily ass."

Crandall made a run for it, but it was too late, the five cowboys were faster than he anticipated in their tight pants and tall bootheels, the souls of their feet clomping on the pavement as they surrounded him and closed in for the kill.

He had to fight his way out of this mess, and although he was physically fit and healthy, he was no match with odds of five against one.

Leroy pulled a fist the size of a Christmas ham back and blasted it forward like a piston, hitting Crandall square in the face, causing a brilliant display of multicolored sparks to appear in his vision, a thunderous pain exploding in his head as the blow hammered into his the face. The smack was loud and clear, and that was all the other cowboys need to ignite the fire and provoking the attack. They dogpiled onto Crandall in a rain of fists, elbows, and knees, pummeling and pelting him savagely. He could taste blood in his mouth, and with each blow he felt a new lump, bump, and welt developing and swelling, instantly. He knew this was going to leave some visible damage, and all he could do was tuck and roll and try to absorb the blows with as much cushion and padding as he could produce, blocking them with his arms and legs and tucking up into a fetal position. In the back of his mind he was wished that the moon was full, because if he could change into a werewolf right now, these idiots would get a good dose of comeuppance. Unfortunately, the next full moon was still a few weeks away.

The girls on the veranda were not surprised at the fight, but they did not want to see this handsome stranger get injured, so they called the police, immediately. The called to the cowboys to stop, but it was useless.

"Leory, leave him alone," one of the girls screamed. "You're nothing but bully."

"Yeah," another girl said. "He didn't do nothing to you."

Leory looked back, mid-swing, and said, "Shut up, bitches. Why don't you mind your own business?"

"You're gonna kill him," the first girl said. "Just let him go. Right now!"

The cowboys kept on hammering with their fists and gave Crandall a damn good beating.

It took about five minutes for the local police to respond, and they pulled up in a black sedan and a white SUV, and two officers, one heavyset and the other tall and skinny, jumped out of the vehicles. They pulled the mob of angry cowboys off Crandall, picked him up, and slammed him against the SUV, face first, lips cracked and bleeding.

"You got some identification?" the heavyset police officer asked. His nametag identified him as: **Torrance**.

The tall, skinny officer held Crandall's arms behind his back, patting him down and looking for anything out of the ordinary, guns, knives, needles, or anything else suspicious. His nametag identified him as: **Stearns**. "Well, do you?" He asked, pulling up on the suspects arms, intent on inflicting pain. "The cat got your tongue?"

"I've got ID," Crandall said, licking his cracked and bleeding lips. "It's in my wallet."

"That's better," officer Stearns said. "I'm going to remove your wallet. Don't move . . . or I may have to shoot you. Am I making myself clear?"

"Perfectly," Crandall said. "Crystal clear."

Stearns kicked Crandall's feet apart at the ankles and reached into his back pocket and removed his wallet. He took out the ID card and looked at it closely.

"Washington state, huh?" Stearns said, snorting. "What you doing over here?"

"I'm on my way home," Crandall said.

"Yeah, really?" Officer Torrance said, stepping closer and peering into his face. "Where might that be? You a smart ass, or something?"

"I'm going home to Main," Crandall said. "That's in New England, if you don't know."

"We got us a wise guy, here," Torrance said.

The cowboys all laughed and cheered at the officers.

"Hey, there Leory," Torrance said. "What seems to be the problem?"

"This dumbass was giving us some shit," Leroy said, pointing his fat finger at Crandall. "We were out here having a chat in the parking lot and he walked by and started fucking with us."

Torrance looked over at the girls standing on the veranda where a crowd of spectators was now gathering in cluster of ogling and gawking men and women. He recognized the girls.

They were regulars at the bar. "Donna Sue, you the ones that called us?"

Donna Sue nodded, affirmative. "That guy didn't do anything," she said. "Leroy and them jumped on him for no reason."

"That's not true," Leroy said. "He started badmouthing Vince."

Vince, the cowboy in the tight stretch pants and snakeskin boots stepped up, saying, "Yeah. He did. I was minding my own business and he called me a redneck."

"I never said that," Crandall said, cringing in disagreement. "I was passing by and they started calling me names."

"Okay, no matter what happened," Torrance said, turning and looking at the cowboys. "We got a disturbance here. You folks go inside. The shows over. There's nothing to see here."

Officer Stearns was on his radio calling in the name and numbers from Crandall's identification card. The dispatcher came back and said there were no warrants.

"Looks like he's clean," officer Stearns said, looking at Torrance. "We gonna hold him?"

"Well, I think we should take him down to the station," Torrance said, wrinkling his nose. "I don't like the looks of him. I want to hear his whole story. Something isn't right. We can hold him on disturbing the peace . . . at least for now."

He was a troublemaker, a stranger in town, a peculiar liberal looking fellow galivanting about and messing with the local boys and causing a ruckus. The women at the bar all turned their heads to look at this handsome stranger. He was not typical, dressed in a style that screamed that he was an outsider. They knew he was either queer or a hippy, and they did not care for the likes of either, so they took him to jail and locked him in a holding cell.

After a long night for Crandall, sleeping on the cold metal bunk and looking at the stainless-steel toilet, he woke up and ate a terrible breakfast of oatmeal and toast. The officers opened the cell door and told him to come out. They were letting him go because they did not have a reason to keep him.

Torrance and Stearns were at the front desk as the deputy processed the inmate for release. They looked at Crandall in contempt. They were not pleased with his appearance or his story, but they had release him with no legal cause to hold him, and against their suspicions and gut instincts, they opened the door and sent him out into the free world to be on his way.

"Just get out of my town," Torrance said. "If I have to deal with you again . . . I'm not going to let you go so easy, next time. Understand me?"

Crandall nodded. "I'm as good as gone," he said, grabbing his shoes and the Ziploc bag that contained his wallet, comb, Bic lighter, and a few miscellaneous legal papers he had signed.

After Crandall was let out of jail and free to go on his way, he quickly walked through the center of town, all heads turning and staring as he crossed the street, and hurried to the exit ramp onto Interstate 90 and stuck out his thumb.

The police cruised by to let him know they were watching him and that his welcome was worn in Butte, but they just passed by, a warning that it was time for him to be on his way.

Crandall did not care, and he was ready to get down the road anyway.

Soon, a brown Ford F-150, older than dirt, pulled over on the side of the road, rumbling and sputtering, belching clouds of obnoxious carbon monoxide into the air.

He ran up to the truck and opened the passenger side door. Inside was a young man, early twenties, blonde hair in a spiked mullet and sleeveless jean jacket and studded leather collar and wristbands, looking like someone who had jumped right out of a Billy Idol video from the 1980s, reminding Crandall that style and fashion sense were something that seemed to be recycled from generation to generation.

"Hop in," the driver said.

"Awesome," Crandall said, climbing in and shutting the door.

"Where you headed?" the driver asked.

"I'm on my way to the East Coast," Crandall said.

"Cool, man," the driver said. "I'm going to Chicago . . . so I can get you that far."

"That would be great," Crandall said. "Just get me as far away from this town as possible."

The driver laughed. "Yeah, I grew up here," he said, looking at Crandall. "You don't want to be an outsider and scare the locals. They don't like strangers too much around here."

"What's in Chicago?" Crandall asked. "I mean . . . it's none of my business. Just curious."

"I'm going there to see my relatives," the driver said. "My grandma is sick with cancer and I have to go over there and take care of everything. It's my duty. So . . . here I go."

"Oh, well, I'm sorry to hear that," Crandall said, as he looked at the interior of the old truck and wondered if it was capable of making the long drive across the badlands and the grassy plains without breaking down.

"My name is Billy," the driver said.

"Nice to meet you. I'm Crandall."

They shook hands. It was cordial. Crandall felt comfortable with Billy, he of the mullet beat up truck driver kind of guy.

"Alright," Billy said, steeping on the gas pedal. "Let's get rolling, then."

They talked off and on during the trip and became acquainted, as riding in a car will make happen, and they stopped for coffee and food at the last gas station for miles before crossing South Dakota and on to the promise land.

3

The beat-up old truck survived the trip and Billy dropped Crandall off on the south side. Suddenly, he found himself downtown south of Chicago, Illinois, at the Greyhound Bus station, deep in the ghetto in Gary, Indiana, where he walked carefully past gangbangers and drug dealers and made his way to the exit ramp heading toward Ohio and onward to his final destination. He stood out in the city, but nobody bothered him, and little did they know that if it were a full moon they would be dealing with a werewolf, which would undoubtedly not turn out in their favor. They had guns and numbers (but no silver bullets), but Crandall had fangs, claws, and lycanthropic rage coursing through his veins, so during a full moon, if a conflict came to a boil, he would be able to destroy the inner-city punks, easily. Fortunately, it did not come to that. They were not interested in the skinny white boy passing down the street, for they had better things to do like selling drugs and chasing prostitutes, and they ignored him as he walked through the hood.

Just before sunset, he managed to make his way across the dangerous neighborhood and find the exit ramp onto the Interstate that would take him back toward his family in Main, where he longed to have just one normal day, like it used to be way back when. The nostalgia was painful when he thought about this childhood and now mundane and normal it was back in those day. Now, everything was all mucked up and complicated.

As he walked across the city and found the exit ramp leading back out toward Interstate 90, he realized hitchhiking in this area was going to be hard. He thought about catching the bus, but he was low on funds, and could not buy a ticket. He had about twenty dollars in bills and change to his name, and that was not enough to get far on the bus. So, he gathered himself together and walked up to the exit ramp, standing next to signs that warned of no pedestrians or hitchhiking, and he ignored them, sticking out his thumb and hoping someone would take sympathy on him and stop and offer him a ride.

After more than an hour of standing on the exit ramp and trying to flag down a ride, finally a car, a blue Honda Accord, pulled over and hit the brakes, the taillights bright as the sun was setting over the horizon.

Crandall ran up to the car and peered in at the driver through the window. Low and behold, it was a cute young girl, blonde and pretty, wearing a hoody and denim jeans, and she was smiling back at him. He opened the door and jumped inside.

"Hello," he said, sitting down and shutting the door.

"Hi," she replied. "This is a terrible place to be hitchhiking."

"I figured that out," Crandall said. "Thank you for stopping."

"No problem," she said. "How far are you going?"

"I'm going all the way to Main," Crandall said.

"Wow," she said, pulling the car away from the side of the road and merging into traffic. "That's a long way to go."

"Yes," he said. "I'm trying to get home."

"Well, I just happen to be going to New York," she said, smiling at him. "So, your in luck. I can get you that far."

"That's awesome," Crandall said.

"My name is Leslie," she said, gripping the steering wheel.

"I'm Crandall," he said, looking at her and taking in her features. She was pretty, and he was pleased to be sitting next to her and getting a ride all the way to New York. "It's nice to meet you, Leslie."

"Likewise," she said. "I don't normally pick up hitchhikers . . . but you look harmless. No offense. I could use the company, too, for such a long drive."

"Well, no offense taken," Crandall said. "And I am glad you stopped . . . because that part of town was certainly unsafe. I was feeling a little out of place."

"For real," she said. "You're safe now . . . for a moment. Until we get to New York."

"I don't think New York can even come close to that craziness back there."

"You might be right," she said.

He sat back in the seat and relaxed. Things were looking up for him and he could let his guard down for a moment now that he was out of the danger zone in the murder capital of the world, Gary Indiana.

Leslie was on the run from a troubled relationship and off to meet her friends in the Catskills where she would start over.

She could give him a ride as far as Albany, New York.

He is happy to have such good fortune, and the best part was . . . there would not be another full moon for a month.

They shared stories during the drive and got acquainted. Crandall was feeling human again, and he knew that there was hope for him after all.

When they arrived in New York he was relieved to be back on the East Coast. He did not have much farther to go now, and he was feeling relieved.

Leslie dropped him off in Albany, and they parted company. He was sad to see her go as she drove away in the Honda, but he knew that some things were ephemeral and not meant to be forever, much like life, in general.

4

A series of short rides from Albany got him all the way East, when he finally arrived in Boston, Crandall knew that he was on the last leg of his journey, at least to get back to visit his family in Bangor, Main, anyway. He stuck out his thumb and caught a ride North, into Main and all the way to Bangor. That was it, then, he had made it and he was in familiar territory. He called a cab and paid the fifteen bucks to get him out to his parent's house.

He was not sure how they would react to his sudden appearance out of nowhere, but he braced himself and prepared for the worst. They still loved him, he knew that much, and he was ready to suck it up and go in and listen to what they had to say. He would explain everything—within reason, that was, because being a werewolf was not easy to explain—and he would plead with them to understand that he needed to go to Paris to find himself, and he knew that they could load him the money . . . it was just a matter of if they would, or not.

He opened the gate to the white picket fence and stepping inside the yard. It had been a long time. He was nervous as he stepped up on to the porch—the thought about knocking because he felt like a stranger now—and turned the doorknob and opened the door.

CHAPTER TWENTY-ONE

1

Portland Oregon welcomed Manson and Zoey at sunset. The drive was short, but after saying goodbye to Crandall, they were ready for another night of blood and gore.

Dante's Inferno was a music club with a mural painted on a black cinder block wall in the parking lot that says **KEEP PORTLAND WEIRD**. They featured bands with dark and sinister themes, death metal, and Gothic music. Manson and Bianco went inside the club on the prowl, looking for a soul to steal.

Up on the stage a band comprised of middle-aged men in all dressed in black outfits was murdering the song by Type-O Negative, "Black No. 1 (Little Miss Scare-All)"

. . . loving you . . . loving you . . . love love loving you . . . was like loving the dead.

"I love that song," Manson said.

"Yes, it's wonderful," Zoey agreed. "They wrote a song about me. Who would of thought?"

Manson and Zoey went to a table and sat down. This was going to be good.

The club was full of a ragtag mix of patrons dressed in leather and spiked collars, trench coats, engineer boots, black hair spiked and flowing, piercings, makeup, and some lumberjacks sitting in the corner, as well as some skateboard buffs, jocks, rockers, Goths and Emos, queers and freaks, every demographic and style was represented and present and the mood was festive. The smell of beer and body sweat, angst, and sex was strong. It had the energy of a rave mixed with the doom and gloom of a funeral. What an exciting atmosphere in which to stalk prey.

The bartender, a young girl in Emo garb, walked up and frowned, filled with angst, her nose and lips pierced with hoops and studs. He hair was streaked with purple and red dye, her eyes lined with thick black eyeliner, her lips black, her demeanor pouty and solemn. She looked like she wished she was somewhere else, anywhere else, anywhere but here, her eyes pleading for mercy.

"What do you want?" she asked, standing in front of them with her arms crossed.

"We'll have a drink, dear," Manson said.

"What kind of drink?"

Manson looked at Zoey, questioning expression, raising his eyebrows, shrugging his shoulders. He was at a lost. This little dark waif had thrown him a curve. He looked at her and was surprised by her appearance. She reminded him of a minified version of Zoey, only . . . *angstier*. Was that a word? If not, it should be . . . he thought.

"Aren't you just the sweetest thing," Zoey said, looking at the bartender. "I love your hair. Your just a peach."

"Whatever," the bartender said. "Are you going to order something to drink? Or what?"

"We'll have two beers and a shot of vodka as a chaser,"

Manson said.

"Great," the bartender said. She turned and opened the refrigerator and brought out two bottles of Budweiser Light beer and set them on the counter. She took two shot glasses from the counter and set them down on the bar, grabbed the Smirnoff Vodka from the plethora of shiny and colorful bottles shelved on the wall, and poured the drinks with a deft and practiced hand, right to the top without spilling a drop.

"That's going to be seventeen oh five," the bartender said, putting the bottle of alcohol back on the shelf.

"Damn," Manson said. "That's steep. You're proud of your drinks, here, eh?"

"It is what it is," the bartender said. "You want drinks . . . they are not free."

"Yes, I see your point," Manson said, pulling a crumpled twenty-dollar bill from his pocket and placing it on the bar.

She plucked the bill off the bar and held it out with her fingertips like a diseased specimen, a disgusted look on her face. She put it in the cash register and put the change, two ones and some coins down next to the drinks. She was done here, so she turned and left, moving down the to the other end of the bar to deal with other thirsty customers.

"She's adorable," Manson said, picking up the shots of vodka. He handed on toe Zoey, then raised his own and said, "Cheers. To life . . . and blood."

"Cheers," Zoey said.

They clinked the shot glasses together and drank the clear liquor down in one gulp.

"Ah, yeah," Manson said, a grimace on his face. "That's what I'm talking about."

"I would love to fuck that bartender," Zoey said. "She just gets me so hot."

"Let's invite her back to our place," Manson said, waggling his eyebrows.

"You mean the Monte Carlo?"

"Precisely."

"I don't think she'll go for it," Zoey said, grabbing her beer and taking a sip. "I think she is on to us. We may not be her type."

"What is her type, then?"

"She probably likes hardcore porn stars with big dicks," Zoey said. "She's Emo. She's probably into being submissive and dominated. And not that I can blame her . . . because I just adore a stiff cock wrangler, all tattooed up and full of muscles. A masochist who likes to choke and donkey punch in the face. Ooh, makes me hot just thinking about it."

"You can't be serious."

"No. I'm not," she said, taking another drink. "I fucking hate those kinds of pricks. They always want to fuck you in the ass, shoving their massive cocks right in there until it bleeds. I would cut their dick of and stuff it down their throat before I would give them the time of day. What a waste of skin, to tell the truth."

"They are just doing their job," Manson said. "You are getting me all hot and bothered with this dirty talk."

"I'm just saying," Zoey said, ripping the label from her beer bottle. "I can't stand abusive men. I like being dominated too, sometimes, but some of the assholes in those porn movies deserve to die . . . miserable deaths."

"We could suck them and fuck them," Manson said. "We could make a vampire porno video where we have brutal sex and then drink their blood . . . live action."

"I would not drink their blood if I were starving to death. Even a vampire has better taste than that."

"Not all porn stars are disgusting."

"No. But I'm talking about a particularly hideous sort," she said, finishing her beer. "These guys are monsters. They treat women—and men—like pieces of meat."

"Touché," Manson said. "Isn't that the truth. Don't we do that, too. We are vampires, after all."

"Yes, but what we do is different," Zoey said. "We are supposed to kill and drink blood. It is what we do."

"So, we are just porn stars by another name."

"Not necessarily," Zoey said. "I'm talking about monsters that fuck people and inflict pain for pleasure. They would fuck a corpse, if given the opportunity. I'm sure some of them have actually done just that."

"Yes. I agree. Oh, but I do love a big dick from time to time," Manson said, picking up his beer. He took a swig, then looked around the bar, turning back and saying, "This is a seedy joint. One could catch death of disease, here, I think."

"It's quaint," Zoey said. "I just love it."

"Where is that bartender?" Manson said. "I'm ready for another round. How about you."

Zoey shook her head, affirmative.

"Hey, bartender," Manson said, waving his arms to get her attention. "Come here you sexy little thing. We need more drinks."

The bartender turned and looked at him, scowled in contempt, wrinkled her nose, and pouted, rolling her eyes, then walked briskly over and stood at attention.

"What do you want?" she asked, crossing her arms. This was her regular posture, apparently.

"We'll have another round of the same, please," Manson said. "And be nice. We love you."

She rolled her eyes and got the drinks.

Manson paid her with another wrinkled twenty, realizing that funds were getting low.

The bartender quickly went away, not interested in Manson or Zoey, which was intriguing, because most bystanders were enamored with the couple.

"We need to come up with some cash," Manson said. "I think we should find someone who is loaded and invite them out for a night of fun."

"I think you are right," Zoey said. "Do you want me to pick . . . ?"

"If you like," Manson said, guzzling his beer. "Or, we can just grab someone and take them down against their own will."

"I like the subtle approach," Zoey said. "But, if worst comes to worst, that will have to do."

They looked around the room, sizing up the patrons, deciding who they would select for their next victim. Someone with money. Someone with looks. Someone delicious. That was the ticket.

This was a scurvy crowd, and the pickings were slim. It did not appear that many wealthy customers patronized this establishment, and that was going to make their mission difficult.

"Perhaps we should choose a different venue," Manson said, leaning back on the bar. "This looks doubtful, here."

The band on the stage were dressed in outlandish outfits, dark makeup, the drummer wearing a Leatherface mask, the bass player wearing a mask with a zipper running down his face, stitches across eyes and mouth, dreadlocks like giant strands of rope sprouting out of his skull. The lead singer looked like a spitting image of Marylin Manson, pale faced and blacked out eyes, with black circles of makeup painted around the sockets, his lips were black, his leather pants so tight they looked like they were fit to bursting. He was wearing a white silk shirt with ruffles and lace, buttoned down and exposing his hairy chest, collars loose, cuffs opened, gold jewelry on his neck and wrists. He was a dark and menacing figure on the stage. The guitar player was wearing a top hat and a velvet trench coat, tall heels on his leather boots with spurs, a leather belt with silver conchos. They were a motley crew and had stage presence. The lights glaring and strobing and pulsing to the rhythm. They were finishing a song by Five Finger Death Punch.

When the song was over, the singer said, "We are Black Static, and we love you all. Thank you for coming down to Dante's Inferno. We are going to take a short break and get some refreshments. Be sure to tip your waitress or bartender. Thank you again, and we will be right back."

The singer stepped down off the stage and walked toward the bar, directly to where Manson and Zoey were seated.

They watched as he came . . . taking a seat right next to them at the bar.

2

The lead singer sat down at the bar after finishing the set and he was sweaty and exhausted from his stage performance. The bartender brought him a drink in a snifter, amber liquor sloshing around as she set it down, and was unaware of the vampire couple sitting next to him, watching him intently.

Manson walked over and introduced himself.

"Hello," Manson said. "My name is Manson. I love your band . . . your sound is fucking amazing."

The singer looked at him, and said, "Yeah? So . . . I'm over it."

Manson was slightly taken aback by the reply.

"Excuse my rude manners," the singer said. "I just don't

car anymore. Anyway, my name is Trenton and I am a freak. I am the lead singer of the band Black Static. Nice to meet you Manson. What can I do for you?" He glared at Manson, then at Zoey, then back again. He looked straight out of a scary movie or graphic horror novel, the villain, a real sinister fiend. Manson was pleased by this; however, Zoey was not so sure, although, she was fascinated by his makeup and outfit. She was enamored with this wild and weird looking singer with multi-colored contacts. He had one bright blue eye and one red eye, and it gave the most sinister effect to his facial expressions.

"Well, okay then," Manson said. "Whatever floats you boat. No worries. It takes all kinds to make the world go around. I really like your show, though. I'll tell you that much."

Trenton shrugged, sipped his drink, scratched his chin.

"This is Zoey," Manson said, introducing her, putting his hand on her shoulder. "She is freaky, too . . . so you have something in common."

Trenton looked at her, sized her up, snorted.

"Nice to meet you," Zoey said, putting out her hand. "I love your music."

"Whatever," Trenton said, rolling his eyes. "It's a living." He left her hand hanging in midair, then took it in his own hand. "Forgive my rudeness." He took her hand and kissed it in a simulated sign of chivalrous mockery. "So nice to meet you, my lady. How's that? Better?"

"You are a sharp one, aren't you?" Zoey said. She pulled her hand back and wiped the area where the kiss was pulsing with fire and electricity. It was strange but she felt something from the kiss, an attachment, a kinship. There was a magical connection in that kiss, and she could not put her finger on it. Something familiar . . .

"How long have you been playing gigs here?" Manson asked.

"Too long. I'm bored with it."

"I'm in a band," Manson said.

"I bet you are," Trenton said.

"It's called Sinister Fiend."

"That's original."

"He's really very good," Zoey said, coming to Manson's defense.

"I'm sure he is," Trenton said, finishing his drink. "Look . . . I don't give a shit about your band. I've been doing this so long it's lost its appeal. If I could be anything else in life, I would. I just play music because it is all I've ever known."

"You've got a bad attitude," Zoey said.

"Bah," he said, raising his glass. "I'm just jaded. Forgive me for being so rude." He waved to the bartender and said, "Lucrecia, give me another drink . . . please."

The bartender, Lucrecia, she of the purple hair, came over and refreshed his Grand Marnier in the empty snifter. She put it in the microwave for a few seconds to heated it up, then placed it in front of Trenton.

"Thank you, dear," he said. "Just like I like it."

"Your name is Lucrecia?" Zoey said. "What an interesting name."

The bartender looked at her and rolled her eyes, saying, "Yeah. So what?"

"I'm just saying . . ." Zoe said. "I think it's a wonderful name."

"Okay," Lucrecia said. "It's what they named me when I was born. I can't help it."

"It's a lovely name," Manson said.

Lucrecia was completely angst ridden and marched away, sulking, and gloomy, uninterested, as though she would rather be anyplace else than inside the seedy bar known as Dante's

Inferno.

"You want to come back to my place?" Trenton said. "I throw a wonderful afterhours bash every night. It's tradition."

"We would love that," Manson said.

Zoey looked at him, anxious and giddy, and nodded her head.

"Okay," Trenton said, finishing his drink and standing up. "You are cordially invited to the most freaky and wild party in town. I assure you—you won't be disappointed."

"We would love that," Manson said. He was getting sucked into the animal magnetism of this dark and strange musician.

"When we finish our performance, you can follow us out to my place, and we will party into the breaking hours of the dawn."

"I'm so excited," Zoey said.

"Excellent," Manson said.

"I am giddy with anticipation," Trenton said, in a mocking tone of voice. "I have to get back with the rest of the band now and finish the set."

"We will be right here listening and waiting for you," Manson said.

"I will come back when we are done," Trenton said. "You can follow me out to my place."

"We wouldn't miss it for the world," Manson said.

Trenton was an extremely cynical and sarcastic, brooding and moody, fellow Manson realized, but he liked the guy for some unknown reason. He turned and quickly walked away, moving back toward the stage where the rest of the band was already in place, strapping on guitars and bass, the drummer spinning his sticks and then tightening ups loose mounts.

3

After Black Static finished their show for the night, they passed by Manson and Zoey and went out through the door, uninterested in the new vampires in town. Trenton was the last to leave and he motioned for them to follow. They did. They went out through the door and into the parking lot.

"That's my car over there," Trenton said, pointing to an old 1965 Hearse.

"You drive a Hearse?" Manson asked, amazed.

"Yes. Why not? It's a fabulous car," Trenton said.

"Okay, then," Manson said. "Very impressive."

"Just follow me to my place," Trenton said. "We can talk about it later."

Manson and Zoey got into the Monte Carlo and followed the Hearse back to Trenton's place, a large and lavish house that had all the resemblance of a haunted house befitting of the Adams Family. It looked just like the mansion out of the movie Psycho with Norman Bates.

"This is your house?" Manson asked as they pulled up.
. . . and have a fuck fest with the band and a bunch of groupies, getting loaded on fistful of pills and drugs and mixed assortments of alcohol.

"Come here," Trenton said, leading them to a back room.

Manson and Zoey followed down the hallway.

They are vampires too, it turns out, and perhaps Manson and Zoey have met their match.

"Did you think you were the only ones?" Trenton asked, sitting back, sipping on his wine. "We have been here for a long time."

"How long have you been . . . vampires?"

"I am over two hundred years old," Trenton said. "I've lived in Portland for more than a century. This is my home."

Zoey was frightened. Other than Stephanie in Vancouver, and Manson, she had never met a real vampire before. This was new to her. Manson was not so easily frightened.

4

Portland Police Department—Briefing 9:00 a.m., December 17, 2019

Sergeant Birnbaum stood at the front of the room at the head of a large wooden table. The other officers were seated around the table. He had a stern expression on his face

"We have a serious issue on our hands, folks," he said. "It appears there is a set of serial killers, a male and a female, on the loose and heading toward our city. We have been informed by the Seattle Police Department that they have been in pursuit of a couple dubbed the Gothic City killers who have left many victims in their wake. They think they are vampires."

The officers in the room all murmured and groaned at the announcement.

"That is ludicrous," a rookie said. "There is no such thing."

"We don't believe they are really vampires, Officer Johnson," Brinbaum said, rolling his eye. "It is just what the assailants believe. *They* believe they are vampires, and that is what makes them so dangerous."

"How have they eluded capture so easily," Johnson said, tapping his pen on the table. "With today's technology . . . we should have captured them already."

"Good point," Birnbaum said. "They are slippery. Somehow they manage to get away from law enforcement. We have a make on their vehicle, a black Monte Carlo, and a description of what they look like. A dark couple, dressing in Gothic cloth-ing, makeup and black hair. It should be easy to catch them. But, alas, they are eluding capture."

"I'll catch them," Johnson said. He looked around at the other officers. "We can nail these creeps. Easy. Right?"

The other officers agreed, saluting and high-fiving with him. They were ready to catch these alleged vampires and put them in jail where they belonged.

"Calm down, Johnson," Birnbaum said. "Everyone just calm down. We need to keep order and remain vigilant. They are considered armed and dangerous and should be approached with due diligence and extreme caution."

"I'm not afraid of Goths or vampires," another rookie, Officer Chadwick, said. "I'll take them out in second. Some wimpy skinny punks are no match for me."

"Do not underestimate them," Birnbaum said. "That is the first mistake. Always a rookie who makes it, too. They are to be dealt with carefully and with extreme caution. Am I clear. Do not approach them without backup. Am I clear?"

"Yes sir," the officers replied in unison.

"Good. Now get out there on patrol and find the scum-bags."

"Will do, Sergeant. Their joy rid is over," Johnson said.

"Excellent," Birnbaum said. "this meeting is now adjourned. Get out there and make some arrests."

The officers gathered up their belongings and went out to their patrol cars and hit the streets.

5

After the festivities of blood, guts, and gore, feeding on the meat and offal of their murdered victims, Manson and Zoey found a secluded area in an overgrown vacant lot with trees

and bushes and parked. It was almost daylight, and they needed to get in the trunk fast. They were exhausted and needed
sleep. Manson pulled into the lot and turned off the engine.

"This will have to do," he said.

"Okay," Zoey said. "I'm tired. Let's get some sleep."

They got out of the car just as the first rays of sunlight were
creeping over the horizon, and climbed in the trunk of the car
and pulled it closed. Concealed neatly in their makeshift coffin,
and tucked neatly into their blankets, their vampire bed, they
felt somewhat safe. They were still vulnerable, and they knew
it; especially, if the police were to come upon them while they
were sleeping, they would be proverbial sitting ducks and their
goose would be cooked. At least they would be protected from
exposure to the daylight.

It was quite comfortable in the trunk . . . to a seclude patch
of woods on the outskirts of town and pulled into a dirt road
that led to a vacant lot. The sun was beginning to rise, and they
were short on time. They would need to be concealed away
before the sun began to creep over the horizon.

They parked in a hidden spot behind bushes and trees and
climbed into the trunk. They had blankets and pillows they
kept for comfort. They laid down and went to sleep. They were
completely satisfied and ready to dream.

6

The next night, when they arose from their slumber, they
crawled out of the trunk and climbed inside the Monte Carlo.
Sitting behind the steering wheel, Manson was in his element.
He now was back in control of things. This was where he ex-
celled. He could drive anywhere, do anything, fuck anybody,
and he was obliging to no one . . . except Zoey, maybe, he
thought. Even then, there were no restrictions, and he could

do whatever the hell he wanted to do, and that was a fact.

"What are we going to do now?" Zoey asked. "We are low on cash."

"I've got a plan," Manson said. "I was dreaming last night and it occurred to me . . . we just need to relax. Things will come our way. It is serendipity. We can make it without resorting to petty crime."

"Huh? Are you crazy?"

"No. Absolutely not. I'm completely sane and serious."

"We are vampires . . . don't you know? It's a crime to kill people and suck their blood, if you haven't considered that."

"I know. I know. All I'm saying is just go with the flow. We can get what we want. Money isn't everything. It comes and it goes. Just enjoy the ride. That's all I'm saying."

"You are such a dreamer," she said, "you know that?"

"I do. I do. Now let's go get something to drink and find a good hustle."

The drove back to the seedy bar and parked, went inside and greeted the same Emo bartender, Lucrecia, they had talked to the night before. They ordered a drink and were excited now that they had a plan to earn some extra cash from a potential victim whom might be sitting in the bar tonight, and they could then cushion their expense account. They could then afford fuel, food, alcohol, cigarettes, and breath mints after that.

While having a drink, Manson was unaware of the dark figure lurking in the far booth, just out of sight through dim lights. Zoey was aware of the looming presence, however, and she looked closely. She sensed it was an impending conundrum, and something bad was about to happen . . . she could feel it.

"Who is that?" She said, squinting to see through the dimly lit room.

"I don't know," Manson said.

Zoey said, "Look over there."

Manson looked and noticed Adrian sitting at the booth, trying to blend in, hoping they would not notice him.

"Look over there," Manson said, pointing his finger. "That's the vampire hunter . . ."

Adrian was sitting in the back of the bar, at a booth by himself, watching their every move. He was waiting for the opportune moment. Drink in hand . . .

7

The party was of extreme and decadent proportions.

The band members, all with strange nicknames of Kerf, Bentley, Scrog, and Diablo, were all present, as well as a dozen other misfits, male and female, all dressed in garish and wild fashions from Victorian periods to modern bondage and fetish motifs constructed from plastic, PVC, and leather and lace.

The stereo was blasting out beats from some surreal modern band that was cross between dark metal and trance music that defied classification or logic. It was part pipe organ and funeral music and part heavy metal guitar and bass, machine gun drum rhythms giving way to syncopated rhythms like rap music tracks, then hellish sound effects of people screaming and writhing in agony. The music gave one an unsettling feeling, almost like vertigo, and was pumped through massive speakers situated around the room strategically to produce the most sound and ambiance possible.

The partygoers were sitting on a mishmash of furniture, from sofas to easy chairs to wicker and even three swings that hung from the ceiling and doubled as sex devices. It was a playground of sin and vice and the carpet was plush and carmine red, there was a heart shaped bed in one corner with black and red lacy blankets, sheets, and pillows. There were a group of five, two men, three women, piled on the bed, kissing and exchanging tongues, fingers, toes, and deeply involved in making love.

After introductions were finished, Manson and Zoey stood timidly in the doorway, watching the festivities, unsure just what they had gotten themselves into. They looked at each other. Manson raised his eyebrows in surprise; Zoey bit her lip, uncertain, wiping her sweaty palms on her blouse.

Kerf, an ogre, built like a brick shithouse, wearing thick leather with studs and chains, his long black curly hair hanging down to his shoulders.

Bentley, a scarecrow, was tall and skinny and looked like a skeleton dressed in lace and frilly clothing with designer boots with tassels.

Scrog, was a massive and muscular man, a bear, and he was dressed in tight jeans, a leather jacket, and hair cropped short into a Mohawk.

Diablo, a devilish looking man, had studs and hoops and piercings in every part of his face, a long split tongue extended from his mouth with a barbell in the tip, and his eyes were those of a serpent. He smiled and exposed sharp fangs.

Over on the heart shaped bed in one corner the group of five lovers continued to pile drive one another, a bystander with a camera filming the festivities, coaching the entwined fornicators like a pornstar director.

The dozen other misfits and loose ends that were hanging around snorted some cocaine, drank deeply of the alcohol, and passed around a large joint of some aromatic ganja that smelled of skunk and pine boughs. They were beginning to get randy and making out with one another, grabbing for sweaty bulges in jeans and slippery parts beneath skirts, kissing with lips wet and rife with booze, fangs gnashing, tongues and fingers probing. It was going to be fuck fest and the air was charged with a sexual electricity.

Trenton looked knowingly at Manson and Zoey, still standing awkwardly by the door, and laughed aloud. He gestured for them to come nearer with his arms, waving them closer, closer, closer.

"Make yourselves at home," Trenton said, holding out his arms in a gesture of hospitality. "You will find drinks at the bar . . . drugs on the tables . . . and sex everywhere."

"Thank you," Manson said. "I'm not sure where to begin."

Trenton laughed at their uneasiness. He leaned back his head and howled over the music. "This is the life we choose," he said, licking his lips. "You are one of us . . . I already know. I can smell you. So, don't be bashful. Come in and make yourselves comfortable. We will drink blood and fuck and enjoy our immortal selves."

"Sounds delightful," Zoey said, still unsure.

Manson grabbed Zoey by the hand and led her to the bar across the room where they made themselves drinks of scotch whiskey, neat, in large cut crystal glasses.

"Are they vampires?" Zoey asked, whispering to Manson.

"I think so," Manson said.

"Well this is awkward," Zoey said, sipping from her drink. "What are we going to do?"

"Enjoy the fun," Manson said. "We'll just roll with it and see where it takes us."

"Look at them on the bed over there," Zoey said, nodding toward the group on the bed who were fully engulfed in sexual activities, penetrating one another's orifices and secreted fluids and moaning and groaning in the throes of ecstasy.

"Looks like fun," Manson said. "Should we join them."

"I don't know," Zoey said, wrinkling her nose. "Maybe. I guess."

"Don't be shy," Manson said. "You are so daring and outgoing . . . why have shame now?"

"I see your point," Zoey said. "I'm not ashamed . . . just curious . . ."

They went back across the room and sat down next to Trenton.

"The fun is getting ready to start," Trenton said. "I'm awaiting the arrival of more guests . . . and you will be invited to the feast. We will quench our thirst for blood. I'm sure you two are thirsty . . . are you not? It is not secret. You are vampires. We are vampires. We are about to partake of a great bloodletting . . . and you have been cordially invited."

Manson and Zoey looked at each other, taken aback, feeling an inward hunger within, a longing for blood.

"Yes," Manson said. "It has been a while since we've fed."

"I'm starving," Zoey said. "I was worried we would go without tonight."

"Rest assured," Trenton said, "I will take care of you tonight. You are my guests and, in a moment, you will be rewarded handsomely for our acquaintance."

8

Without warning, the front door burst open and Lucrecia, the Emo bartender entered the room in a hurry. She was frantic and apologetic.

"Sorry I'm late," she said, wiping her brows from her eyes.

"There you are, my lovely," Trenton said. "I've been expecting you. What took you so long?"

"I had a hard time gathering up the . . ." she said, trailing off, looking suspiciously at Manson and Zoey. "Oh, you guys. I forgot about you two."

Manson waved and wriggled his finger, saying, "So good to

see you again."

Zoey smiled, saying, "Hi. How are you?"

"I'm fine, thank you," Lucretia said, looking back at Trenton. "Are you going to include them?" She was referring to the new vampires, Manson and Zoey, who she did not really like or trust.

"They are fine," Trenton said. "More importantly, did you get what I asked for?"

"Of course," Lucretia said. "I got stuck at work, longer than expected," she said, coming in and setting down her purse on the table. "I had some trouble finding them . . . but, yes. I got your . . . things."

"Excellent," Trenton said. "Hey, Kerf . . . you and the other guys need to go out and bring in the party favors. Lucretia has them in the van."

"Okay, Trent," Kerf said, looking at the others. He motioned for Bentley and the rest to follow him outside.

When they came back inside, they were leading shabbily dressed teenage boys and girls who were blindfolded, six in total, four girls and two androgynous boys.

"Ladies and gentlemen," Trenton said. "Our nubile guests have arrived."

There was an eruption of cheers and applause from the usual guests.

The vampires in the room looked upon the teenage victims with delight, licking their lips and showing their fangs. This was going to be wonderful. Their eyes were alighted with lust and longing for the feast.

The young victims had been rounded up from the streets, offered cash to partake in the filming of a pornographic video, but duped because they were going to be more than just sexual props in an X-rated movie. They were going to be the victims of a feeding by vampires who would not only fuck them but eat them, and if any of the newbies were lucky they may be turned into vampires themselves, but more often what happened was that they wound up discarded as corpses along a vacant street somewhere to be found and counted as more cases of homeless vagrants, runaways and deviant delinquents, lost and forgotten to the world. They were undesirables anyway and the world would never miss them, so the public at large did not necessarily care what happened to them. When they were found dead and discarded most of the people in the city thought it was a good riddance.

They entered the room, nervous and uneasy, and the blindfolds were removed. Kerf, Scrog and the other band members stood close by, blocking the doorway so they could not run away.

"Welcome friends and fiends," Trenton said. "So nice meet your acquaintance. Welcome to my humble abode."

"Where are we?" one of the girls asked. She was dressed in light Goth with piercings and makeup.

"When are we going to get paid?" another of the teenagers asked.

"Are you going to fuck us in the ass?" the first girl asked. "Because I don't do anal."

Trenton laughed aloud, raising his hands in glee, saying, "Oh, my sweet, sweet, young children. You have no idea . . . anal sex is the least of your concerns, I'm afraid."

"I just want my money," one of the boys said. "I don't care . . . I'll suck your cock, take it in the ass, or whatever you want. I just want my money, now!"

"Yeah, you promised to pay us," another of the teenagers, dressed in a hoody with a rap star face printed on the front.

The atmosphere was growing hot by degrees, and the room

grew silent, even the lovemakers on the heart shaped bed stopped and watched anxiously, midstroke.

"Easy, easy," Trenton said. "You will have your money . . . and there will be plenty of sucking . . . in due time, my child."

The vampires were anticipating a feeding frenzy, they could smell the blood and pheromones of the teenagers, and the expectation of salty blood and sex was beginning to tempt them beyond control, and they inched closer to the group of victims huddled in the middle of the room.

"You're not going to do anything weird, are you?" the first teenager, the light Goth girl, asked. "I'm not interested in anything weird. I'll do regular sex, or whatever, but nothing kinky like sadistic shit. No hitting or biting."

"Blah, blah," Trenton said, rising from his chair. "Where is your sense of adventure. No biting? You take all the fun out of it. You will do whatever we want. You are in no position to bargain at this point."

The teenagers looked at each other, unsure, frightened, despite that they were street urchins and had experienced rough treatment living out in the rugged and hostile homeless encampments of the city, this new environment was making them uncomfortable. They could sense that something unusual was about to happen.

"Ladies and gentlemen," Trenton said, raising his hands like a musical conductor about to signal the striking of a diminished chord. "Let the games begin."

The teenagers knew they were in trouble and they turned to run for the door, however, Kerf and Scrog and Bentley and Diablo were standing in the way and quickly grabbed them and ushered them back toward the group of hungry vampires.

"Allow me to start the fun," Trenton said, moving swiftly forward and grabbing one of the androgynous teenage boys firmly by the shoulders. "I'll have you, my boy." He pulled the boy close and licked his neck, tasting the salty skin, relishing the pulsing jugular beneath the pale skin. He could smell the boy's fear, the blood, the angst, the sexual energy, and he felt his loins stirring in anticipation of the kill.

"No, don't," the boy said.

"Help," the light Goth girl said. "Don't hurt us."

"You have played with death, tonight," Trenton said. "And you have lost the game, I'm afraid."

He opened his mouth and exposed sharp and jagged fangs. He quickly chomped down on the boy's neck and sunk his fangs into the meat and veins, drawing blood, the boy screaming out in pain and pleasure all at once as Trenton sucked his blood.

The other teenagers were crying out in fear now, begging for mercy, trying to escape. It was too late. The vampires would have their feast of blood and sex. It would be an orgy of blood and necrophilia and evil desire fulfilled.

Manson and Zoey watched in amazement. This was a new event for them, as they had never partaken of a vampire feeding en masse before.

The other vampires fell into the feeding and they swarmed the victims, biting and slashing, grabbing and groping, sucking their blood. It was a grizzly feast. Manson and Zoey could not ignore their desire to feed and they fell in with the rest of the vampires, including the nude vampires that had been fucking on the bed, and it was a giant pile of biting and blood sucking and fucking and fulfilling of the flesh and desire to satiate a hunger for all things evil and vile that involved being a vampire.

They had to eat, after all, and that is what vampires do . . . suck blood and fuck the dead.

When they were finished, there was a pile of six cadavers,

exsanguinated, and lying dead and pale in the middle of the room. None of them had survived, and none of them had been converted into vampires; tonight was not their lucky night, although Trenton did reach into his pocket and pull out a wad of cash, in large bills, and tossed it on the pile of corpses.

"Here is your money, you poor fools," he said. "Not that you will be needing it where you are going . . . to the grave."

Manson and Zoey were covered in gore, their faces smeared, their eyes glittering and glimmering, their flesh florid and vibrant from the fresh blood. They felt satiated, but out of place, and uncomfortable in the presence of the recently discovered vampires.

"I want to go outside and have a cigarette," Zoey said.

"An after-dinner smoke?" Manson said, grinning.

"Yes," she said.

Trenton overheard them, saying, "I don't mind if you smoke in my house."

"That's okay," Zoey said. "I want to get outside and get some fresh air."

"That's funny," Trenton said, "Go out and smoke and get some fresh air . . . but I understand, completely."

"Come on, Manson," she said.

He followed her to the door, and they stepped out into the night. They walked down the driveway and looked up at the gibbous moon hanging brightly over their heads.

"That was a rush," Manson said, stepping clumsily on the gravel drive, kicking rocks.

"I feel like I should be ashamed," Zoey said, lighting her cigarette. "I don't know why . . . but I feel nothing. That was not right . . . what just happened in there."

"We are vampires," Manson said, his eyes twinkling in the moonlight. "It is our nature to consume the lives and blood of mortals."

"I understand that," Zoey said. "It just feels . . . strange. I have some kind of internal conflict that makes me feel . . . guilty?"

"Fuck guilt," Manson said. "Guilt is for pussies. You are no longer a mortal . . . and you cannot live by their standards any longer."

"I suppose you are right," Zoey said, taking a deep drag off the cigarette and then exhaling the smoke with a sultry expression. "Let us go for a walk. I want to clear my head—get away from this strange place for a moment. I'm struggling with this . . . this new life."

"Fine, then," Manson said. "It is a lovely night. We can walk down this road . . . but hopefully we don't get ran over by a passing car."

"It's so deathly quiet and still out here," she said, as she reached the pavement, stepping off the gravel and moving down the shoulder of the road, along the ditch. "There isn't a car within miles of this place."

Manson tilted his head and listened. He looked at the dark country road leading away and around a corner into the trees.

It was a brisk and chilly evening, but for a vampire the cold has little effect since they are already dead, and the circulatory system does not work in a completely logical fashion as with lizards, bats, or humans, and they existed somewhere in between, able to transcend death to immortality and escape such unpleasantries as cold weather. They were more comfortable on a chilly night than a hot sunny day, and that was a fact.

9

While Manson and Zoey were away on their walk, they did not notice the nondescript white Chevy van pulling into the gravel driveway leading up to the haunted house where the band,

Black Static, lived.

Trenton and his gang of vampires were inside, unaware, as they finished the feeding frenzy, relishing the meat on the bones of the dead teenagers, picking through the delicate parts, licking here and biting there, nibbling the sweetbreads and licking the bits of offal from their fingers. They had no idea that in an instant they would be in a confrontation with a vampire hunter . . .

Trenton was mildly surprised when Adrian crashed through the door, kicking it open with a leather boot, his trench coat fluttering behind him like a cape, strapped with weapons of vampire destruction.

"Who are you?" Trenton said, nibbling on a severed finger, looking up at the stranger clad in a trench coat, only slightly startled and by the sudden appearance of the strange man holding a crossbow.

"Your worst nightmare," Adrian said, raising the crossbow. He fired an arrow directly at Trenton, aiming for the center of mass, directly for the blackened heart that resided in the vampire's chest.

"I doubt that," Trenton said, catching the arrow in mid-air with a deft and swift hand, snapping the shaft int two. "I think you have that backwards. I am your worst nightmare." He looked over at his band members and nodded his head, motioning for his mates to take action. "Get this pathetic little man out of my house." He threw the broken arrow on the ground. "You think you can come into my house and shoot me with an arrow? How stupid are you, mortal?"

Kerf, the ogre, leather creaking, fists clenching, closed in for the attack, black curly hair whipping wildly while reached out his clawed fingers and grinned with a mouthful of sharp and jagged teeth.

Adrian notched another arrow in the crossbow, pumping it with his hand quickly, arrow in place, and fired, sending it straight into Kerf's forehead. It was a perfect shot, bullseye, right between the eyes, and the sound of the bone splintering as the tip of the arrow penetrated was like a ripe melon falling from a wagon and splatting on the ground. It set Kerf down to his knees and made his eyes cross. He reached up and grabbed the arrow with both hands and tugged fiercely to dislodge it from his skull. It was stuck fast.

Bentley, the scarecrow, lurched toward Adrian on skinny legs, arms outstretched, eyes glowing evil and red, his lacy and frilly outfit fluttering as his boots and tassels clopped and clinked on the floor with each long stride. "I'll get you, fool," he said, drooling, fangs exposed.

"Not today," Adrian said, reaching into his pocket and bringing out a bottle of Holy Water. He splashed large dollops and drops of the water, like acid, onto Bentley, sizzling and spattering like hot grease in a wet skillet. "Take that, fiend."

"Argh," Bentley cried, covering his face, smoke wafting in wisps from the burned areas. He was blinded and stifled, buckling over in agony. "My eyes. I can't see."

"Good," Adrian said. "And you shall die, too."

Scrog, the juggernaut, roared like a bear, jumped up and sprinted across the room, his muscled buttocks bulging in his tight jeans, flexing and clenching with each step, the musty leather jacket creaking with his motions, arms raised in a V, fangs exposed, as he dove like a professional football player making a game saving tackle. His Mohawk was like an exclamation point across his glimmering bowling ball shaped head. He attempted to grab Adrian, hitting him like a wrecking ball, but was quickly thwarted as the vampire hunter stepped aside, spinning around, trench coat flapping and swirling like a skirt on a dervish. He ducked, dodged, and jigged and whacked Scrog across the back of the skull with the butt of the crossbow, making a solid connection with a whack that sounded like knocking on a wooden block with a mallet.

"Bah! Mother fucker," Scrog said, hitting the ground and rolling over, crab crawling backward.

Adrian was quick. He let the crossbow fall to his side, suspended by a strap around his shoulder and chest. He pulled a fistful of garlic from the clove necklace that was also dangling around his neck. He reached down and stuffed the garlic into Scrog's mouth, force feeding him like a giant baby.

Scrog tried to speak, choking, smothered by the garlic cloves. He began to flop and buck, kicking his legs and grabbing at his face in a spasmodic jerking motion.

Adrian looked over at Trenton who was watching with a twisted face, his head swaying side to side in disgrace. The leader of the vampires could not believe his mates were failing so miserably. "You fools," he cried. "There is only one of him and many of you. How can you let him defeat you? You are all pathetic."

Diablo, the devil faced vampire, licked his lips, running his pierced and split snakelike tongue over the studs and hoops sticking from around his mouth. He licked his fangs, grinning stupidly. He snickered and cried out like a hyena as he circled and moved in for the attack. Moving from side to side, shifting his weight to the left then to the right, reaching out with snatched and grasps of claws and knuckles, fingernails painted black. His piercings glittered and glimmered in the fluorescent light coming from the glowing gas filled tubes overhead.

"Bring it, bitch," Adrian said, pulling a wooden stake from a cluster of bundled sticks hanging from his belt at his hip. The point of the stake was sharp and true.

"What are you going to do with that?" Diablo asked, raising his eyebrows curiously.

"What do you think?" Adrian said. "Figure it out, dipshit. You are a vampire . . . this is a wooden stake. Get it?"

"Shit! You bring sticks to a deathmatch," Diablo said, snickering again. "You are indeed an idiot."

"Come and get some, then," Adrian said, motioning with his fingers, wriggling them like a magician summoning a wristwatch from a handkerchief.

"Die, asshole," Diablo said, lurching toward Adrian.

"Nope. Not today," Adrian said, lunging and stabbing the stake into Diablo's chest.

"Oof," Diablo said, then coughed, sputtered, and staggered backward, clutching at the stake protruding from his chest with both hands. He fell to the ground and died slowly in a jerking dance of death on the floor.

Trenton looked at the other vampires in the room who had only sat watching the fight. "Well, come on . . . what are you waiting for?"

Trenton had seen enough. "I guess if you want something done right you have to do it yourself," he said, stepping up and moving in quickly. He was an experienced vampire having lived for centuries, and he had battled with vampire slayers before, and won, and he would not be taking out so easily now. "I will kill you, vampire slayer."

"I'd like to see that," Adrian said, stepping backward toward the door.

He transformed like a shapeshifter into a giant demonic beast with horns and fangs and claws and red glowing eyes. He looked like Satan himself.

Adrian was shocked by the sudden transformation.

Trenton leaned back, laughing aloud, pleased by his frightening appearance. He spoke, and his voice had changed, too, into a deep, growling baritone that boomed and bellowed like the quaking and sputtering of an erupting volcano.

"You dare to kill me?" Trenton said, reaching out with a massive arm, grasping Adrian by the throat. "You don't stand a chance." He lifted Adrian up from the floor; his feet dangled, hands clutching at his throat, choking, and struggling to breath. He was able to reach into his pocket and find the bottle of Holy Water, spin the cap off with his fingers, and bring it up in a swift and sudden arc of his arm and splashed Trenton in the face. The water was like hydrochloric acid, hissing and smoking as it hit the demonic beasts face.

"No, no, no," Trenton said. "That was a cheap shot." He wiped his red and blistered beastly face with his massive devilish clawed hand. He turned and looked again at the rest of the vampires. "Everyone . . . kill this asshole, now!"

They sat back in a stupor, eyes wide, abashed and stuck on stupid. This was not going to happen, the vampire slayer was too strong, too fast, too well equipped, and the other vampires in the room were leery, standing back at a safe distance. The wanted no part of this fight.

Adrian jumped away, spun around, and held up the giant silver crucifix hanging from a chain around his neck. He held it out and pointed it at the other vampires. They shrunk back, hissing and spitting, afraid of the symbolic cross with the crucified Christ king. He moved toward the door and reached back and found the doorknob with his searching hand. The door was open and ajar. His escape was imminent.

"And now, for the coupe de grace," he said, pulling another item from his coat. It was a bottle of Ronsonol lighter fluid. He flipped the nipple tip on the cap of the bottle and squeezed, squirting streams of the fluid out and dousing the curtains, the carpet, the sofa. He took out a red road flare from inside his trench coat and struck the tip into a red glowing sputtering jet of fire.

"What's that?" Trenton asked, but he already knew the answer. "Don't do that."

"Too late, asshole," Adrian said. He threw down the flare and it hit the carpet with a thump, the flame sputtering and spitting out sparks, igniting the liquid lighter fluid and bursting into flame with a *whump*.

"Good day, scumbags," Adrian said, opening the door and stepping outside. He dashed to his van, climbed in, turned the key, and started the engine and stepped on the gas, ripping down the road at a high rate of speed. He would look for Manson and Zoey later, but as for now he just wanted to get across town to avoid being caught by the police. They could charge him with arson and he would have a hard time explaining why he had set the house on fire.

Behind him the house began to glow with flames inside out through the windows in the darkness as he drove down the road. He could see it in the rearview mirror.

The vampires exited in a commotion, spilling out into the night, their refuge now aflame, and they would be forced to seek a new place to hide.

Trenton was furious. He watched the gray van disappear down the road into the night.

"I will get you for this," he said, shaking his head. "Someday, I will get you. I promise this from the bottom of my blackened heart."

10

For Manson and Zoey, when they came back and saw that the house was on fire, they were shocked, and amazed.

Trenton was running down the driveway toward them.

"We've been had," he said. "There is a vampire slayer trying to kill us."

"Huh?" Manson asked, but he knew the answer already. "What happened?"

"We've been attacked by a trench coat wearing vampire slayer," Trenton said. "I know the type. Over the years I have met them and done battle."

"I think he followed us here," Zoey said.

"What do you mean?" Trenton asked.

The house was now a blazing inferno, lighting up the night.

"He has been pursuing us," Manson said. "He's been on our trail since we left Vancouver."

"You know this guy?" Trenton said, dubiously.

"Sadly, yes," Trenton said.

The sound of fire engine sirens could be heard looming in the distance.

"You did this to us?" Trenton asked. "You brought this curse upon us?"

"We didn't mean to," Zoey said. "He had been after us . . . but how were we supposed to know he would do this?"

"I don't care," Trenton said. "Take your miserable selves away from here. I want to speak to you no more."

"That's it then?" Manson said. "You are dismissing us just like that?"

"Yes! Go! Now!"

"Fine then," Manson said, looking at Zoey. "Let's go. We don't need these people anyway."

Manson and Zoey turned and walked to the Monte Carlo and climbed inside. Manson started the engine and pulled away, driving slowly, reflecting on what had just transpired.

When they were safely away at a good distance, the pulled over onto the side of the road and parked, looking back and watching as fire engines raced by in a furious and loud shriek of red flashing lights, hurrying toward the flaming house.

They watched for a moment, the flames rising high into the night, the vampires scurrying about in the yard and driveway. It was chaos and pandemonium.

"Too bad," Manson said. "I never expected that to happen."

"Well, it's over now," Zoey said.

"Let's get out of here," Manson said, putting the car in gear and pulling onto the road.

As they drove away, suddenly from behind, a set of headlights shone brightly in through the rear windshield.

"It's him," Zoey said, looking back, seeing the white fan following closely behind at a high rate of speed. "It's the vampire hunter."

"Great," Manson said. "Just great."

He stepped on the gas and sped away, hoping to elude Adrian, and it was possible because the old Chevy van was no match for the Monte Carlo.

The chase ensued and they sped away down the road into the night hoping to get away and lose the vampire hunter.

The gray van was parked outside, and it was obvious that Adrian the vampire hunter had been following them, and was waiting for them, but he had missed Manson and Zoey while they slipped away on a nature walk . . . it was a close call, but they managed to outwit him once more, and while he was distracted fighting with the vampires of the Black Static tribe, they took off and hit highway 101 in the Monte Carlo, cruising fast and loud toward their final destination, Los Angeles, but that was still a long way away and there would surely be trouble in between.

They raced away down Interstate 5 and found a secluded area to sleep. They turned off onto a side road and followed a sign that led to a secluded park, The Mission State Park along the Willamette river, where they found a parking spot that was out of sight. They knew they needed to get some rest, and they did not want to be observed by any passersby, so they quickly got out and climbed into the trunk to sleep away the daylight and refresh themselves for a new day.

Tomorrow they would try to make up time, but for now they needed rest.

CHAPTER TWENTY-TWO

1

After sleeping the day away in a wooded camping sight along the river, Manson and Zoey climbed out of the trunk and got into the car, pulled out from the desolate gravel road and pulled out onto Interstate 5 and drove into Salem, Oregon.

As they drove through town they were looking for something to do, something to keep them entertained before the twilight gave way to midnight and the hunt would begin. They needed to feed on blood, and they were famished, not having had any blood for some time. So, they drove up and down the streets of the town, looking, watching for entertainment, with a hunger and thirst . . . and that is how they wound up watching a vintage horror movie, *Nosferatu*, at the haunted cinema and performance center known as The Elsinore Theatre located in downtown Salem.

The building was opened in the 1920s and was rumored to be haunted by ghosts, a young boy allegedly murdered in the men's restroom . . . blood mysteriously appearing on the mirrors . . . a ghost walking across the stage during movies . . . the upper balcony haunted by the ghost of the owner's daughter who fell to her death and now resides there and scares the daylights out of patrons.

The building itself was built to look like the Elsinore Castle immortalized in Shakespeare's tragedy, Hamlet, and was constructed of Gothic style architecture with a modern flare, painted in yellow with white trim, spires and arched windows with stained glass taken from a cathedral in Germany that was bombed in World War II and appropriated and relocated specially for the theatre. The interior was also adorned in rich Gothic decorum with the stained glass showing a scene from the play, Hamlet, and with Portia and Lady Macbeth. There was a large Wurlitzer pipe organ that is played during screenings of old silent movies on the second Tuesday of every month at 7:00 p.m. and that was when Manson and Zoey arrived in time to watch a viewing of *Nosferatu* with the pipe organ blaring.

They arrived just as the sun was setting across the horizon, pulling into town, and observing the bright lights and signage of The Elsinore Theatre.

"What a fortunate find this is," Manson said, as he read the signage that proclaimed tonight was a special screening of the silent movie, *Nosferatu*. "We could not have picked a better time to pull into town."

The movie was a bout a vampire, Count Orlok, who shows a keen interest in a new arrival in town taking up residence, the wife of a real estate agent, Hutter. The move was directed by F. W. Murnau, starred Max Schreck, Greta Schröder, and Ruth Landshoff. The movie was a cult classic and famous to all horror movie buffs across the world, inspired by *Dracula*, an unauthorized reproduction of Bran Stokers novel that was changed and rearranged to become a successful story in and of itself.

"I love that movie," Zoey said, sitting up and looking out

at the theatre building. She looked at the clock on the radio and saw that it was almost 7:00 p.m. and she was giddy with excitement. "It's going to start soon. We need to go inside and get a seat."

"I agree," Manson said. "Let me find a parking space."

He pulled the car over and parked at a meter down the street, stepped out and put coins in the meter.

2

Ebony, Oregon, a small town just off Interstate 5 halfway between Portland and Eugene . . . home to the legendary state penitentiary known as "Big Blue." As they drove into town the prison was a dominant feature as it loomed like a fortress, lighting up the night against the dark of night in the distance.

"That's gloomy," Manson said, nodding at the prison.

"What is it?" Zoey asked.

"It's a prison," Manson said.

"How do you know?"

"Truest me," Manson said. "There is no mistaking that place. I would recognize a prison anywhere."

"If you say so," Zoey said. "Have you ever been to prison?"

"No," Manson said, looking at her intently.

"Then how do you know so much about it?"

"I've seen them on the Internet before," Manson said. "Sheesh . . . it is the twenty-first century, for crying out loud. I've seen pictures and watched movies."

"Okay, okay," she said. "You don't have to be so defensive about it. I was just asking."

"Fine," he said, turning the steering wheel and pulling down onto Main Street. "We need to find a place to stay. It will be morning soon."

The found a hotel at the end of town and rented a room and

decided to stay a while.

They both agreed that Ebony was a perfect town to haunt for a while and have some fun and create some carnage.

Inside the hotel room, Zoey did some research on her cell phone, getting on the Internet and searching for information about the town of Ebony.

"Look at this," she said, thumbing through the pages on the LCD screen. "The prison is affectionately known to the prisoners and correctional officers as 'Big Blue'. . . what a strange name for a prison."

"That's nice," Manson said. "Are we going out tonight?"

"Hold on," she said, intensely reading the content on the cell phone. "There is more . . . it says that back in nineteen ninety-eight there was an earthquake that broke down some of the walls and fences and allowed a prisoner to escape— his name was Jack Lucas Cheery—and he is still at large to this day."

"Well, good for Mr. Cheery. I'm sure he is long gone by now," Manson said. "And I should care about this because . . ."

"I don't know," Zoey said. "I just thought it was interesting. This town has a fascinating history."

"If that's what you thin, I guess," Manson said, shrugging. "I'm more interested in going out and getting something to eat. My stomach is growling."

Zoey put the phone down on the bed and sat back, leaning on her elbows. "You are a growler."

"And you are as cute as a button," he said, leaning over and touching the tip of her nose with his index finger. "I could just gobble you up whole."

"Would you like to eat me?"

"Indeed."

"Well come here, big boy," she said. "I am yours for the taking. Ravish me."

Manson could not resist. Hunger aside, he was also aroused, his groin stirring and rising to the occasion.

"There is always time for a good fuck," Manson said. "Take off your cloths and allow me to plow your field, my dear."

"You are so romantic."

"I do my best," he said, unbuckling his belt and unzipping his jeans. He had a grin on his face. He took off his boots and soon was naked, an Adonis, a statuesque figure like a Michelangelo carving from marble.

Zoey took off her shoes and jeans and spread her legs and lay back on the bed, her sex exposed, pubic hair glistening in the light. Her vagina was magnificent and perfect, like a pink flower. She reached up and ran her fingers across Manson's lips, lovingly, caressing his cheek.

Manson ripped Zoey's blouse open and exposed her perfect breasts, like two round orbs of soft and silky flesh, milky white, nipples protruding like two buttons. He grabbed his throbbing shaft and moved forward, easing down onto the bed on his knees and inching toward her, slowly sliding into her moist and soft folds of flesh, pushing his long rod all the way into her wetness, all the way, deep, until he was in all the way to his balls.

They fucked hard, wild and passionate, making grunts and groans, rutting in the throes of ecstasy. He pulled her legs up and put them on his shoulders, her ankles next to his ears, running his tongue along her perfectly manicured toes, the black nail polish glittering in the light. He pushed in hard, full, pounding her with all of his might; she cried out for more, more, more.

"Yes. Yes. Yes," she said. "Give it to me baby."

He stuck his fingers in her mouth and she sucked on them.

The rhythm was building in a crescendo to a climax.

She moaned.

He groaned.

Release was on it its way. Manson could feel his balls tightening and preparing for the final act.

"Cum inside me," she said, biting her lip. "I want you to shoot your cum deep inside me."

"I will," Manson said, gritting his teeth and groaning in delight. "Oh, you little tramp. I'm going to . . . here it comes . . ."

His face contorted and twisted. Zoey thrust her hips up to meet his pounding loin, wrapping her legs around his back and squeezing him tightly.

"Cum for me baby," she cried out.

Manson pounded, plunging deep, his body beginning to quiver. His face was locked into a grimace of exquisite pleasure, his lips in a sneer, his nostrils flaring. There was a bead of drool building at the corner of his lips. His eyes rolled back in the sockets and his brow raised in elation.

"I'm going to cum," he said, thrusting faster and faster.

They reached orgasm at the same time. It was magnificent. Sparks, pops, and crackles lit before their eyes like fireworks as they climaxed together.

He groaned and cried out in pleasure. His balls released and pulled together tight in his sac, releasing their payload of semen in jets and streams, pearls of love, as he emptied his load deep inside of Zoey. He drained his balls completely, and the sensation was almost too much to bear.

They clung together like a single goosepimple, intertwined, becoming one, momentarily the beast with two backs, a single unit, quivering and quaking in the throes of orgasm.

3

After the lovely sex, they sat back on the bed and basked in the glory and glow of the lovely sexual jaunt. Manson was pleased with his performance. Zoey was pleased, too. The lay on the bed naked, for moment, savoring the afterglow.

She rolled over and took a cigarette from the nightstand, lit it, and smoked it with satisfaction. The smoke rose in fluttering wisps toward the ceiling. She exhaled and licked her lips.

"That was fucking awesome," she said. "I'm tempted to do it again."

"You're telling me," he said, grinning. "I don't know if I can go again so quickly, though."

"Are you kidding me?" she said. "You are a stallion. I just love your fat cock."

"Why thank you, my lady," Manson said, waggling his eyebrows. "I aim to please."

"You were blessed," she said. "I can tell you that much. You have a beautiful dick."

"Gosh, you're making me blush," he said, reaching for his pants. "Now I'm all bashful and have stage fright."

"You have no reason to be bashful," she said, touching his pale white buttocks. "You have more than most men could ever dream."

"Well, I don't mean to brag," Manson said, rising to his feet and pulling up his pants, zipping up and putting on his belt.

He leaned over and turned on the radio.

On the radio, a song was playing . . . *Where you going for tomorrow?* The song was "Plush" by Stone Temple Pilots. *Would you even care? . . . When the dogs begin to smell her . . .*

Manson could not help but think about how other men were indeed like dogs and came around sniffing Zoey, itching to fuck her, not making any effort to conceal their carnal desires. Sometimes it pissed him off, but he was not jealous or possessive, and he knew that Zoey loved him and would never leave his side, so he was confident in her loyalty. They belonged to each other and they both knew it was true.

"I love that song," Zoey said.

"Me too," Manson said, turning up the volume.

"Are we going out now?" Zoey said, rising up from the bed and putting on her cloths. The cigarette dangled from the corner of her mouth, sliding her pretty feet into the pants legs and pulling them up, zipped, then fastened the button. "I'm hungry after that."

"Yes," Manson said. "I believe we should go find someone to eat."

"Let me look for a good place to go," Zoey said, picking up her phone.

"I think we should just go drive around and see what we can see," Manson said. "Let's just wing it. We can pick someone or someplace at random."

"Okay, let's do it," Zoey said.

"Let's go."

"I want to take a shower first," Zoey said.

"You don't want to go out with that freshly fucked look?"

"Not that," she said. "I don't care about that. I just feel like freshening up."

"Can I join you?"

"Absolutely."

"Let's do this."

They walked together into the bathroom, undressed, and she turned on the shower, feeling the water with her hands to make sure it was warm enough to climb in, waiting, until it was just right. She stepped in and he followed. They washed each other's backs, hair, kissing and caressing lovingly. It was a beautiful and intimate moment. They were truly, deeply, and undoubtedly in love.

After the shower, they quickly dried, dressed, and left the hotel room and went to the Monte Carlo.

"This is a beautiful night to be alive," Manson said, opening the door and climbing in, pulling the keys from his pocket.

Zoey climbed in and shut the door behind her.

The engine rumbled as it started.

The black Monte Carlo crept out of the parking lot and rolled casually down the street toward the center of town.

4

Inside the car the radio was blasting out a song by Nirvana, "Negative Creep" and the speakers were thumping to the grunge rhythm and gravelly voice of Kurt Cobain.

"That's me," Manson said. "I'm a negative creep."

"No, you are not," Zoey said. "You're a vampire, a creep, maybe . . . but definitely not negative."

"You are too kind," Manson said, steering the car down the street.

They passed by a small tavern with a billboard sign that said Jake's Tavern. It was cattycorner to a Safeway grocery store. The night was quiet, however the tavern looked to be active with more than two dozen cars parked in the lot.

"This looks promising," Manson said. "Why don't we go in here and see what we can come up with."

"Let's do it," Zoey said, looking in the mirror and making sure her makeup was done right.

"You are beautiful," Manson said.

"Thank you."

Manson parked at the far end of the lot and they climbed out of the car.

There was muffled music coming from inside the bar. The neon beer lights in the window glowed brightly with red, green, white, and blue light, one of them humming and flickering as it failed and faltered, the P in Pabst Blue Ribbon going out and then flickering and coming back to life, the neon gas inside sputtering and flickering like a tongue of flame inside the glass tube.

The door swung open and two husky men in baseball caps and flannel shirt burst out into the night in a drunken commotion. They were laughing and staggering as they came out. The saw Manson and Zoey and stopped to stare.

"Well, looky there, Jed," the man in the red baseball cap said. "Them's some of the fairy queers we been hearing about."

"I don't know, Deek," Jed said. "I think I'd fuck both of them. They are kinda purty."

"You two got a rainbow flag, do ya?" Deek asked, leaning over on Jed's shoulder.

Manson and Zoey veered around the two drunk men.

"Too good to talk to us," Jed said.

Manson looked back as he opened the door, glared, thinking how he could just tear these two homophobic assholes from limb to limb, but realizing that he did not want to make a scene in public where everyone inside would see.

Zoey raised her hand and flipped the two rednecks off with her middle finger displaying her fingernail that was painted black. She winked and blew them a kiss.

"In your dreams, assholes," she said, sliding her hand across her breasts. "You couldn't handle me."

"Whoa," Deek said. "You are a little whore, aren't you?"

"Fuck off," Zoey said.

"Come on, Zoey," Manson said, pulling her in through the door. "We don't want any problems here."

"Listen to your fag boyfriend, honey," Jed said. "You two could get yourselves hurt around here looking like that."

"Never mind them," Manson said.

The went inside, leaving the two asshole rednecks to stumble across the parking lot outside, and stepped into the dingy and dimly lit tavern.

There was a country song playing on the jukebox. The sound of pool balls clacking in the back. All heads turned as the Goth couple entered and made themselves comfortable at the bar.

Manson knew the men in the bar would be sniffing around like dogs when they caught a whiff of Zoey and decided that she might be worth a good fuck, if they could have their way.

The bartender, a heavyset woman in jeans and a black T-shirt with saggy breasts, came over and stood in front of them, eyeing them skeptically, knowing that they were not from around the area.

"What can I get you?" the bartender asked.

"We'll have a beer with a whiskey chaser," Manon said.

A man in a leather vest, bandanna over his bald head, and a pool cue walked up to them and spit on the ground. "We don't like people like you around here," he said, wrinkling his nose.

"It's a free country," Manson said, looking up at the tall man peering down at him with a hooked nose and scar above his eyebrow.

"Leave them alone," the bartender said to the big man.

"Maybe it is a free country," the man said. "Just not around here. Not for the likes of you. Why don't you get the fuck outta here before me and my friend fuck you up real good."

Zoey was concerned and watched, knowing that Manson was just cocky enough to stand up to this asshole. "Come on," she said, grabbing Manson's arm. "Let's just go. We don't need any trouble."

Manson resisted, standing up, still a head shorter than the man, but standing his ground, nonetheless.

"Why don't you listen to your pretty lady friend, you fucking freak?"

"Another time and place," Manson said, "and I would deal with you accordingly. Lucky for you, I don't feel like fighting tonight."

The big man looked at his buddies and they all laughed loudly, slapping their knees and yuk, yuk, yukking as they elbowed one another in the ribs. This was just too rich.

"Let's go, Manson," Zoey said, pulling him backward toward the exit. "We can stop somewhere else. This is a dive anyway."

The bartender was looking at the phone. She was concerned and might call the cops. Manson saw the look in her eyes and knew he did not want any trouble wit the police.

"Fine," he said. "We will leave now. Have a good night."

Manson and Zoey exited the musty bar and went back to the Monte Carlo.

"What a bunch of redneck assholes," Manson said, starting the car.

"No shit," Zoey said. "That was ridiculous."

"Bunch of inbred fuckers."

"Hurry up," she said, pleading with him. "Let's get out of here before they decide to come out into the parking lot. I have a feeling these guys are bad people and would try to hurt us."

"I think it would be the other way around," Manson said. "But, I agree. We don't need any trouble."

He put the car in gear and pulled out of the parking lot and onto the main drive.

Back on the road, leaving Interstate 5 and veering west on Highway 20 heading directly through the city of Corvallis, then onward toward the Pacific Ocean, they were racing against time because the gauntlet of law enforcement and the vampire hunter seemed to be closing in, tightening their fists.

Next, arriving in the city of Newport, the city lights were

fabulous, and they drove to the beach to take in the ocean at night, the waves crashing against the sandy surf. The wind was blowing through their hair as they sat on the hood of the Monte Carlo, listening to the wind and the surf, smelling the salty Pacific Ocean, seaweed and something fishy, and the lights of the city off in the distance behind them. It was peaceful and serene.

CHAPTER TWENTY-THREE

1

Inside the house, Crandall heard his mother take a deep breath, shocked by his sudden entry into the room through the door . . .

"Hello, mom," Crandall said.

She was standing in the kitchen with a dishtowel in her hands.

"Crandall, I don't believe it," she said. "Where have you been?"

He went to her and held out his arms to give her a hug. She had a disconcerted look on her face, her eyes beginning to water. He embraced her; she was reluctant at first, then she relaxed and fell into his arms.

Her name was Sandy, and she was a headstrong, wiry woman with gray dark brown hair, starting to go gray—and she used hair color to keep the silver strands of hair at bay—and wrinkles around the corners of her eyes and lips. She was in descending from middle-age to old-age and she was wise from all her fifty-nine years on Earth. She was a gentle and compassionate woman, and she loved her children—Crandall being one of three, two sons and a daughter—and they had all gone to college or moved out now, and Sandy and her husband, Mike, were empty nesters and moving into the retirement phase of their lives.

"I've missed you, Mom," he said, holding her tightly in his arms. "Where is Dad?"

She pushed him away, grabbed his shoulders and looked deeply into his eyes. "Your father is out, at the moment." She said, wiping her hands on the dishtowel. "He will be home soon. He's at the store buying some things for a project he has around the house. He might be upset when he sees you . . . so be prepared for that. You should have called first."

"I understand," Crandall said. "I thought about calling . . . but I wanted to surprise you."

"Well, you certainly succeeded in that," she said.

"I have so much to tell you," he said.

She put her fingers to his lips, saying, "Wait. I'm sure you do . . . but first, I bet you are hungry."

"I am," he said. "You know how to make me happy. Feed me first . . . then get to the details." He smiled. She always wanted to feed him. He loved her.

"Exactly," she said. "You can tell me all about it over a nice breakfast. I will make you pancakes. You always loved them. Does that sound good?"

"Yes. I would love that," he said.

They went into the kitchen.

"Sit down at the table," she said. "Do you want some orange juice?"

"Please," he said, realizing that he was thirsty and parched.

She served him orange juice in at tall glass, setting it on the table in front of him. He took a long drink, feeling the cold juice flow down his throat, hitting his empty stomach and causing a growling reaction there, the acids reacting with each other.

"I better make you something to eat fast," she said. "You stomach sounds like it is eating itself."

He laughed.

She took the contents from the cabinets and refrigerator to cook his breakfast.

"So, tell me all about it," she said, turning on the stove and putting a frying pan on the burner. "Where have you been? What have you been doing since you left us?"

"I've been all over the place," Crandall said, setting down the glass of orange juice. "I traveled to South Carolina, first," he said, running his fingers through his hair. "I wanted to see the land of my early years. It was not what I expected. So, I did not stay there long. I then went west, wound up in Louisiana where I attended Mardi Gras and took in the sights and sounds and food. After that, I then went to Texas, Arizona, California . . . to try and pursue my scriptwriting career."

"Is that so?" she said, rolling her eyes. She was not a huge fan of the elusive dream of being a bigtime Hollywood movie writer. That was a dream that she thought would never see fruition.

"Sounds like you had quite an experience," she said, she smacked her lips and shook her head, sighing with exasperation. "That's a lot of traveling. I don't understand why you left in the first place."

"I had to go," he said. "Dad was not making it easy for me to stay here . . . as you know, he was being too overbearing."

"Well, that's just how he is," she said. "I tried to get him to calm down."

"He wanted me to take a job at the factory," Crandall said. "I just wasn't interested. I know he has made a career out of it, but I did not want to be company man, like him. I'm glad for what he has accomplished, but I crave something different from life. I want to be somebody. I want to make a difference in the world."

"That's nice, dear," she said. "I want you to be successful, too. But, you also have to be realistic. There are so many people wanting to be famous, to make a difference, to be stars . . . you just have to accept that maybe you are just an ordinary man. There is nothing wrong with that."

"I don't want to just be *ordinary*," he said, finishing his juice. "I aspire to be great. That is what I'm going to do with my life."

"I'm not disagreeing," she said. "Please understand, you have my full support. I just want you to be realistic. Everybody has dreams . . . but are they capable of achieving them?"

"I'm perfectly capable," Chandler said. "I'm going to go to school and get a degree. You wait and see. I'll show everyone that I've got what it takes. You'll see."

"Okay," she said. "If you say so. I support your ambitions, son." She sighed and stood with her arms akimbo. "Enough about all of that. Let me make you breakfast. You look like you will wither away." She mussed his hair and gave him a hug.

He held her arms and hugged her back from his seated position. It was awkward, but he was glad to be with her, sitting in the kitchen, the familiar smell of the house, the smell of dish soap and laundry fabric softener, onions and celery, lavender from a Renuzit air freshener, and sandalwood candles, greeting his nostrils. They held each other in an embrace for a long moment, he could feel her heartbeat from her breast against him and feel her pulse in her hands touching his head. She as warm and alive and he was happy to be home, at least for the time being. She kissed him on the forehead, a wet kiss, the kind that always embarrassed him when he was a young boy, and he always had to wipe it off with his sleeve.

"Jeeze, Mom," he said, blushing. "I'm not a little kid anymore."

"You'll always be my little boy," she said, pinching his cheek.

She cooked pancakes and bacon and eggs, humming softly as she completed the tasks, banging pots, pans, and utensils together, completely in her element. Overjoyed in motherhood, she felt complete when she was tending to her children's needs and having Chandler home again made her feel complete. She finished cooking and put the steaming food on a plate and set it on the table in front of him.

"Thanks," he said. "I'm starving." He grabbed the fork and dove into the food, shoveling it into his mouth with ardor, practically inhaling, wolfing it down like a starving dog because he was famished from the long trip. He had not been eating well on the road and he had lost weight. It was obvious as his eyes were sunk in and his face was hollow.

She watched him eat, amazed at his appetite, and smiled with pleasure. Her prodigal son was home and she could stop worrying about him, at least for the time being.

Outside, they heard a car engine rumbling and ticking as it pulled into the driveway.

"It's your father," Sandy said. "Just let him blow off steam."

"Dad's home?" Chandler said, peeking out the window. "He's going to hit the roof when he sees me."

"Don't worry," Sandy said. "Just let me handle him."

She went to the door and waited for it to open. She knew this was a volatile situation and she was ready to intervene and defend her son.

The suspense was coming to a boil and they waited, the second hand on the clock ticking loudly, as they watched the doorknob and waited for Ashton to come through the door.

2

Ashton Smith Hanson, and he was a strict and demanding man. He stood just over six feet tall, had a full beard, wore flannel shirts, often with zip up hooded sweaters, Carhartt denim jeans held up with red suspenders, and Sorrel boots. He was a tried and true New Englander, born and bred, whom chopped his own firewood for winter, owned an old Ford pickup truck he kept in the garage, and had a thick accent that betrayed him—when he spoke it was obvious that he had lived in the North Eastern part of the united states for most of his life. The only reason he moved to South Carolina was because he was stationed there in the Army and he had been forced to make a move. When the time came, he took his then young and burgeoning family and moved them back to his homeland. He was content and happy to live in the colder climate and he believed that home is where the heart is, specifically in Main. He liked to have things done his way, and if you were in his home under his roof, you would march to the beat of his drum. That was the way it was, and anyone who knew him understood this fact.

He came through the door, stood in the doorway like a towering lumberjack (Paul Bunyan came to mind) and looked at Sandy and Chandler. His face was a blank slate, at first, and then color filled his face in degrees, turning from rose to florid crimson, his demeanor glowing hot and radiant until it appeared that steam would blow out from his ears like a teakettle at full boil.

"What's he doing here?" Ashton asked, pointing a thick finger. "I thought we said he was not supposed to ever come back here again?"

"Calm down, honey," Sandy said. "How can you act like that toward your own son?"

"Hello, Dad," Chandler said, standing up, a cheeky grin on his face. He felt like he was a little kid again and his angst filled attitude was coming back full force. "I'm happy to see you, too."

"I didn't ask for your smart-ass comments," Ashton said, stepping inside and shutting the door. He took off his jacket and hung it on the hook.

"Can't we all just get along?" Sandy said.

"It's okay, Mom," Chandler said. "I got this."

"I thought you were gone for good?" Ashton said, crossing the room and standing in the kitchen.

"Me, too," Chandlers said. "But, alas, I'm back. I had to come home. I need help. Is that too much to ask? Can't a child come home to his parents and ask for help?"

Ashton smirked and grunted, crossing his arms.

"He's right, you know," Sandy said. "He should be able to come home . . . if he needs help."

"I'm not sure about that," Ashton said, going to the cabinet and taking out a coffee cup. He poured a cup of coffee and leaned back against the counter. "You crossed me for the last time, Chandler. I told you I was done . . . and I meant it."

"You're still mad that I didn't go to college?" Chandlers asked, shrugging.

"You guessed it, buster," Ashton said. "I had plans. I saved up money for you to go to school and you just pissed it away. And then you went to jail . . . my son, the convict. What was I supposed to do? When you got out of prison you ran away like a coward. What do you expect me to do? The community thinks I've raised a criminal."

"I told you I was sorry," Chandler said. "I didn't mean to get into trouble. It wasn't really my fault. You have to believe me. . . ."

"Can't we just let bygones be bygones?" Sandy asked, stepping between them. "Why are we reliving the past?"

"No. We can't," Ashton said. "I'm still mad. It won't just go away."

"It's been over two years, now," Chandler said. "I've been gone a long time. I would think you could find it in your heart to show a little forgiveness."

"You embarrassed me," Ashton said.

"So, your pride is hurt," Chandler said. "Get over it. Shit happens. I'm a different person now. I made some mistakes and I apologized. That's not good enough?"

"Just let it go, honey," Sandy said, intently. "Can't we just be happy that he is home? Isn't that the most important thing?"

Ashton breathed a heavy sigh and scratched his head, throwing his hands in the air in defeat. He turned away and looked into the living room. He was completely flabbergasted.

Sandy looked at Chandler, raised her eyebrows in a hopeful expression, knowing that the worst was over.

"What are you going to do now?" Ashton asked, turning back around. "You've been gone so long . . . and now you expect to just come back and everything is going to be normal again?"

"I didn't say that," Chandler said. "I have a plan. I came back to ask for help."

"With what?" Ashton said, grilling him. "We've done everything we can. Don't you think? Your mother has cried so much that you've given her gray hair. You've been gone, but you were still a burden to us . . . no matter what."

"Can't we just hear him out?" Sandy said. "He is our son, after all. I think we owe him that much."

"Fine, sure . . . why not," Ashton said, entering the kitchen. He sat down at the kitchen table. "Let me get comfortable. You can tell me all about it, now. You have my undivided attention. Speak your mind."

"First off," Chandler said, sitting down across from his father. "I would not come her and ask for help unless I really needed it. I want to make a change . . . I want to be a better person."

"Well, that's good to hear," Ashton said.

Sandy went to the sink and started washing dishes, listening intently to the conversation. She was silent for the moment, but she knew that she would get involved if Chandler needed her help, because that was her way. She always protected him, no matter what, coming to his defense when his father became to stubborn and obstinate and overbearing. She had stopped many a confrontation in the past, and, presently, she was ready to jump in at a moment's notice. She poured a cup of coffee and put it on the table in front of Chandler.

"Thanks, Mom," Chandler said, picking up the coffee. He sipped it then continued, saying, "I'm sick and tired of the life I've been living. You were right, Dad. I should have gone to college with all my friends like I was supposed to . . . but, fate intervened. You have to understand that things that were beyond my control . . . happened."

"What things are you talking about?" Ashton said. "That's the part I've never understood. You've always eluded to this *thing* that caused all your troubles . . . but you never state specifically what *it* is . . ."

Crandall shrugged, rolling his eyes to the ceiling, and blowing a lock of hair out of his eyes.

Sandy put her hands on his shoulders, holding him close, comforting him. "It's okay, son," she said. "You don't have to talk about it . . . if you don't want to." She knew that he was sensitive about the subject—whatever it was—and she always allowed him to keep his private matters private. She had a suspicion that he may have been involved with molestation or something of that nature with neighbors in the past, but she was not certain, and she did not want to jump to conclusions. It was a sensitive subject matter, and she thought that he would divulge the truth eventually, on his own, when the time was right.

"Something happened," Crandall said. "I never told you everything . . . because you wouldn't believe me. But it all started when we went camping out at the lake that summer. The time I got bit by the wild animal. You thought it was a dog, or wild animal, a wolf."

"I remember," Ashton said. "You had to go to the emergency room and get over fifty stitches. How could I forget?"

"I was so scared," Sandy said. "I thought for sure we were going to lose you." She hugged Crandall tightly in her arms.

"The truth is," Crandall said. "Something happened after that. I don't know what . . . and you would not believe me if I told you what I think it is, so I have to pretend it is something else. I was cursed . . . after I was bitten. It was an evil thing that bit me."

"I don't understand," Ashton said. "We've been over this a hundred times. What is this nonsense about? Are you saying you were bitten by the Devil? You need to talk to a priest about that."

"Yeah, like that would do any good," Chandler said, remembering how he had been molested by the Catholic priest in the basement of the church so long ago. "Not the Devil. I was bitten by a . . . some *thing* . . . a monster."

"Stop, Chandler," Sandy said. "I can't hear this story again. I fear for your sanity when you talk that way."

"See, that's the problem," Chandler said. "You two always think I'm crazy when I talk about it. You tell me to go to church. Like that would solve anything. If you only knew about your beloved priests and the church. It's ludicrous."

"What do you want from us?" Ashton asked, sitting forward, and glaring into his eyes.

Chandler hesitated, then said, "I want to go to Paris. I think I can find a new life there and start over. I want to move there and go to college, to start over. I think the change will do me good."

Ashton and Sandy were startled beyond words.

"What are we to do?" Sandy asked.

"I want you to buy me a ticket to Paris," Chandler said, finally.

"So, you are going to waltz in here and ask us for money?" Ashton said.

"Precisely," Chandler said.

"Well, we are going to have to think about this for a minute," Sandy said. "This is a lot to take in all at once."

"I promise if you help me out this time," Chandler said. "I will make everything right. You'll see. I'll make you proud."

Ashton was silent and ruminating. He looked at Sandy, bit his lip, then ran his fingers through his hair. "That's your plan?" he asked, after a moment. "You're going to run away to France and everything will be different?"

"Yes. That's it," Chandler said.

"Who do you know in Paris?" Sandy asked.

"No one," Chandler said. "And that's the beauty of the

whole thing. It's a brand new and fresh beginning. A new chapter in my life."

"Have you looked into any of this?" Ashton asked. "I mean . . . you can't just run off halfcocked."

"I think it's a wonderful idea," Sandy said.

"How will you live?" Ashton asked. "You can't just be a bum in Paris. That's not cool."

"I'll get a job," Chandler said. "I'll go to college. I have a plan."

"I like it," Sandy said.

Ashton was set aback. He was not convinced.

"Just think about it," Chandler said. "You won't have to deal with my problems. I'll be in clear across the Atlantic."

Ashton looked at Sandy, and they made eye contact. This was a big decision.

"I don't know what to say," Ashton said. "You run away from home . . . disappear for two years without so much as a single phone call . . . and now you expect us to just give you a handout? Doesn't that sound ludicrous to you?"

"I guess," Chandler said. "I see your point. I'm only asking for enough to get a ticket and a place to stay for a while when I first get there. I will take it from there. I will promise."

"I think we should do it, dear," Sandy said. "It sounds like a good idea."

"Alright," Ashton said. "We'll do it. But, don't expect us to support you. You have to make it on your own."

"I don't. I will. I won't," Chandler said. "You'll see. I can do it."

"Okay, I guess that settles it then," Sandy said. "When are you planning on leaving?"

"As soon as possible," Chandler said.

"I will go to the bank in the morning," Ashton said. "That's the end of the whole mess. I can't keep bailing you out all your life, son. You must know that."

"I do, Dad," Chandler said. "I am grateful for everything you've done for me. Believe that. I haven't always shown it, but it's true."

"Make sure to send us an update. You can text us or send an email. It's not that hard to stay in touch. At least send us a postcard every now and then," Sandy said. "We want to know how you are doing."

"A postcard?" Chandler said, incredulous. "This is the twenty-first century, Mom. Nobody sends postcards anymore."

"They don't?"

"No."

"Whatever . . . you know what I am saying."

"Yes."

"That's the end of that, then," Ashton said, as he finished his coffee. He turned to Sandy, saying, "What's for dinner?"

Chandler was giddy with delight. He had succeeded. He knew that his parents would back him up, it just took a little convincing. He was going to Paris, France. How awesome was that?

"Awesome!" Chandlers said, aloud.

Ashton and Sandy looked at him curiously.

"Sorry," he said, shrugging. "Just excited, that's all."

3

They ate dinner, a roasted chicken with all the trimming of mashed potatoes and green beans and biscuits and gravy. Chandler could not stop talking. He told them all about his adventures hitchhiking and living in Canada. Then he talked about his plans for his trip to Paris. He had great dreams and aspirations. They listened intently.

After dinner they cleaned up the dishes and retired to the living room to watch TV until it was late enough for everyone to go to bed.

Chandler stayed in his old bedroom. It was left just as he remembered it. His old posters were still on the walls. It was a welcoming room, but it brought back some memories that were uncomfortable.

Sandy came into the room and wished him a good night. She tucked him into bed, just like when he was a little boy, and she kissed him on the cheek. It was a wet kiss, just like he remembered, and he wiped it off with his hand.

"Good night, Mom," he said.

"Sleep well, son," she said, turning off the light, shutting the door.

The glow in the dark crucifix on the wall was still there from long ago when his mother had placed it there when he was just a little boy. She had said it would protect him from evil spirits. He never bothered to take it down, even when he grew older and did not believe in such things as evil spirits, but not that he was older and cursed with lycanthropy he knew that there indeed were evil things that lurked in the dark and that the world was not always a safe place for mortals or beasts. He looked at the crucifix as it lit up the darkness with a chartreuse glow.

His mind was racing. He could not stop thinking about Manson and Zoey and wondering how they were fairing on their trip to California.

He picked his phone up from the desk and tapped the screen. He could send them a text message and ask how they are now, as he had not communicated with them for a while and he felt guilty for remaining silent on his end. He felt that it was time to make contact and ask them how life was treating them.

Somewhere in the small hours he drifted off to sleep.

4

He dreamed about Manson, Zoey, and Stephanie. They were having a party. Drinking and getting high. He was happy to be with them. Everything was going great until he saw the full moon shining brightly in the night sky outside through the window.

Suddenly he felt the transformation begin, his skin was crawling and sprouting hair, his face was morphing into a wolfish expression, his fingers became knobby and grew sharp claws. His friends saw him morphing into a werewolf and they had shocked looks of dismay on their faces. They were frightened.

He growled and jumped up onto his springy legs. He howled and beat his chest. Rage filled him and an insane and uncontrollable desire to tear everyone to pieces wracked his mind. Out of control, he went after his friends, grabbing them and ripping them limb from limb, their heads severed from the neck, blood spurting out in gouts and streams, bones and sinewy snapping and popping as joints and skeletal structures splintered and separated.

His mind was racing as he created a macabre pile of flesh and bone from his beloved friends.

No, no, no, please God, no. Don't let this happen . . .

Behind him, his parents were watching him in disapproval and shock. They had no idea their son had such murderous and psychotic tendencies.

He looked back at them, ashamed, claws clutching with bits of blood and bone sticking to the claws.

"What have you done, son," his mother asked. "What has become of you?"

He groaned, cocked his head, howled and moaned in grief.

He could not help himself. This curse was beyond his control.

"You are a bad boy," his father said. "I am disappointed in you."

"Now we will have to disown you," his mother said. "We have no son like you. You do not belong to us."

He wanted to beg for mercy, to ask for their forgiveness. Suddenly, the rage filled him like thunder and lightning coursing through his veins, and he lost control.

He dashed toward his parents and sunk his claws and teeth into them with a savageness that only a wild animal could muster. The kill was quick. He severed his mother's throat, blood spurting out in streams, the head dropping to the floor with a plop and clunk. His father tried to back away, but it was too late . . . he was on him with speed and agility of a ferocious beast and he sunk his teeth into the jugular veins, tasting the hot salty blood as it squirted out into his mouth. His father groaned and gurgled as his esophagus was ripped out hole, like a rope from bucket of guts and gizzards.

Yes, yes, yes, death and destruction. Kill, kill, kill. It let's you know you are still alive. I am alive. I am alive. I am a hideous beast, but I am alive . . .

The blood was dripping from his mouth and hands. He was insane. He was a monster. He was cursed to live his life like this forever. There was not cure. He would have blood on his hands always and innocent people would die. He could not control it.

Fuck the innocent people. They deserve to die anyway. I am a monster. I will kill and murder and destroy . . . I am evil.

"No. No. No," Crandall said, rolling back and forth in his bed. He cringed in his sleep, biting his lip in his nightmare. "I don't want to be a monster. Please . . . somebody help . . ."

He awoke with a start, seeing the first rays of the sunrise

coming in through the window.

"It was a dream," he said, rubbing his face. "A terrible dream. A nightmare. Oh. My. Fucking. God. What have I become?"

He pulled off the covers, sat up and put his feet on the cold floor, and rubbed his eyes, shaking his head to wake up. He tried to forget the dream as quickly as possible. All he could think about was that his friends and family were still alive and safe. He had not killed them.

"Thank God," he said, getting up and going to the door.

He went downstairs to see his mother and father and he could smell the familiar aroma of bacon cooking in the kitchen.

5

Breakfast with the family was beautiful. He felt like a kid again, juts like when he was growing up and his mother always made him bacon, eggs, pancakes, and hash browns on Saturdays. The sat down at the table and prepared to dive into the food. Crandall poured an extra splash of syrup on his pancakes, as that was how he always ate them.

His father looked at him and said, "Somethings never change, Huh? You and all that syrup."

"It's how I like my pancakes," Crandall said, defensively. "You always gave me a hard time about it."

"It's fine, dear," his mother said. "Would you like some orange juice?"

"Yes. For sure," he said.

She filled a cup for him and slid it over in front of his plate.

"So, I know you will probably not like what I have decided to do," he said, breaking a piece of bacon in half. "I am planning to move to Europe."

"What?" his father said, startled. "What in the world for?"

"Really?" his mother said.

"Yes. I am going to Paris, France," he said, shoving the bacon in his mouth. "I plan to live there and be student abroad. I will go to school there. Make something of myself."

"Paris is a lovely city," his mother said.

"What are you going to do? School? What can you study in Paris that you can't study here in Main, or any other university in the United States?"

"I just want the cultural experience. I want to see things from a different perspective that the capitalistic ideology of America."

"That sounds lovely, son," his mother said.

"I'm not sure I am convinced," his father said.

After much arguing, they were persuaded that his idea was sound and they were supportive, standing behind his plan, and even suggested that they would buy him a ticket and give him money to travel and live when he first arrived, until he could get a job and support himself.

6

At the Logan International Airport in Boston, Ashton and Sandy saw Crandall to the plane. They wished him well and watched him go through the security checkpoint as he got on the plane . . . waving goodbye, they held each other tight. They were happy for their son, but anxious and worried.

Chandler looked back and smiled, waved, and adjusted his backpack on his shoulder. He is only slightly aware that maybe it would be the last time he would ever see them again. He turned away, feeling tears welling in his eyes, and walked toward the boarding area. Passengers were gathering around at the gate in the terminal, and they would soon be boarding.

1

The Delta Boeing 747 departed at 5:15 p.m. Monday, January 2020 Logan International Airport. It was going to be a seven-hour flight and Crandall was tired from all the recent traveling. He was excited about his new adventure, and all that it had in store and what the future foretold. He was relieved and leaned his head back and tried to rest, but his mind was racing.

He thought about Manson and Zoey. He wondered how they were doing, and how they were faring on their way to California. He missed them already. Someday, he wanted to see them again, maybe go back and visit them . . . but for now he had to get away. He had to find the cure for the lycanthropic curse that ebbed and flowed through his veins.

He nodded off and slept soundly, only waking up when the captain announced that they were preparing for a landing, and everyone needed to buckle up their seatbelts. He shook his head, rubbed his eyes, and looked out the windows at the clouds and tiny landscape below. They were making a descent now and his ears were popping.

Without incident, the plane landed at the Charles de Gaulle Airport in Paris at 6:15 a.m. Tuesday.

CHAPTER TWENTY-FOUR

1

It was just after sunset, and Judy Holmes was pissed.

"You can go to Hell," she said, screaming at her boyfriend, Eric Clark. "You're such a jerk."

"Man, shut up, bitch," Eric said. He made a disgusted face and smacked his lips. "Shit. You ain't special. Who you think you is? Bitch?"

The gang of skateboarders and BMX bicycle riders were all hanging out down at the park, under the pavilion, passing around a bottle of Captain Morgan rum and a meth pipe, and Eric was making a scene; he was intentionally embarrassing her and making sexual innuendos. He was talking about her breasts and how big they were and that she should take off her shirt and show them to everyone. She did not want to do that.

"Why should I do that?" she asked. "I don't want to show everyone my breasts. Are you crazy?"

She did not like the fact that he was being an asshole. Her mind was made up; she had decided to leave him forever; she just needed to make good on the decision.

"Leave me alone, Eric," Delilah said.

"Come on," Eric said. "Just show everyone your tits. You know you want to."

Delilah was humiliated. She hated this jerk. She did not know what she had ever seen in him in the first place. To make matters worse, he was embarrassing her in front of his friends, treating her like an object. All she knew was that she wanted to leave Coos Bay for good, not just the city, but the entire region of the Oregon, farther than that even, to get away from the Pacific Northwest. She didn't care where she was going, just as long as it was away from the trash filled city of Coos Bay, and hopefully to another state, or even better, another country.

The black Monte Carlo pulled up in the parking lot, engine idling, music bumping from within the interior.

"Look at that," Eric said, nodding at the black car. "Who do you suppose that is?"

"I don't know," one of the BMX kiddies with a blue flat brimmed baseball cap with white letters, NY, stenciled on the front, sitting sideways on his greasy hair. He said, "I like that car, though. That is fresh, yo." He had a large marijuana leaf tattooed directly on the right side of his face; it obscured the entire cheek on that side of his face, reaching from the chin all the way to his eye. He was clad in a black hoodie and skinny jeans with white Nike skateboard shoes. He had two gold upper front teeth, wide gauge hollow ear plugs, and a large rope style gold chain hanging limply around his neck, down the front of his chest to his abdomen.

"Man, what are they doing here in my space?" Eric said. "This is my turf."

"You don't own this place," Delilah said.

"Oh yeah," Eric said. "Who asked you?"

"Just saying. This is a public place. You act like you're a king, or something," she said.

"I am a king," Eric said. "I'm a pimp. Don't hate the player—hate the game."

"Whatever," Delilah said. "You are such a cliché."

"Man, fuck off, bitch," Eric said. "Why don't you just get the hell outta hear. I'm tired of looking at you."

"Fine," Delilah said. "I'm leaving. I'm sick and tired of you treating me like shit. Goodbye, Eric. Hope you rot in Hell." She spat at him and quickly turned away, storming down the sidewalk, past the black Monte Carlo and toward the entry way to the park. She was getting the fuck out of dodge, and it was about time. She did not bother to look back.

The music stopped inside the black Monte Carlo and the passenger door opened. Zoey, a beautiful dark-haired Goth girl stepped out, smoking a cigarette, and looked at the group under the pavilion. She took a long drag off the cigarette, and squinted, looking directly at the group of troublemakers with piercing blue eyes.

"Holy shit," Eric said. "Who the fuck is that?"

"I don't know, yo," Blue Hat said. "But she is fine as a motherfucker. I'd do her."

"Yeah, but would she do you?" Delilah asked, sharply.

"Yes. She would," Blue Hat said.

"I doubt it," Delilah said.

"Man, shut up," Blue Hat said. "Nobody asked you for your opinion."

Eric was beside himself. He wanted to know more about this girl and the black car.

"Hey, what you doing?" Eric said. He parked his bicycle, leaning it against the picnic table, and took a few steps in the direction of the car. "Who are you?"

The Goth girl looked back at him and said, "Who are you?"

"I asked you first," Eric said.

At that moment, Manson, the driver, a mysterious man with black hair and leather and badass boots, got out of the car. He was a tall, dark, and handsome man who had the resemblance of a musician with black hair and Gothic attire.

Crandall chose to stay in the car, watching the festivities from the comfort of the back seat.

"Who the fuck is that?" one of the other kids, wearing a white bandanna tied like Aunt Jemima over his head and a red, loose-fitting tank top, said. He stood up from the picnic table, flexing his muscles. "You can't just come around here unannounced, man. This is our turf."

"Yeah. You looking for trouble?" Eric said, in agreement with White Bandanna man.

Manson and Zoey stood side-by-side in front of the car, looking back at the group.

"You do look like a festive bunch," Manson said, loudly enough to be heard across the parking lot. "Are you looking to start a part?"

"Not with you, asshole," Eric said. "What are you doing around here? We don't like your type here. Don't you know that?"

The dark couple crossed the parking lot, slowly, methodically, approaching the group of troublemakers. When they were within a stone's throw, they stopped and looked around, considering the surroundings. It was a secluded and quite place; perfect for a murder or horrendous crime to occur and go unnoticed for a time.

"What a lovely night," Zoey said. "I do love when the stars first come out. I love to wish upon the first shining star. Don't you think that is just so quaint?"

"What are you talking about?" Eric said. "Nobody gives a shit about that."

"Yeah, man," Blue Hat said. "Fuck your lucky star. And fuck you, too."

"You have a dirty mouth, son," Manson said. "Do you have any class, whatsoever?"

"Fuck class," Red Hat said, grabbing his crotch. "I dropped out of school a long time ago. I ain't got no need for class."

"That is rich," Manson said. "How I do envy your scumbag skate-punk lifestyle."

"Look who's talking, Goth man," White Bandanna man said, laughing aloud. "You look like you just stepped out of fuckin carnival freak show."

"Says the white wannabe gangster with a Tupac Shakur head dress," Zoey said, sternly. "Have you forgotten what side of the tracks you were born on?"

"Man, fuck you," White Bandanna man said, spinning around in a circle, snapping his fingers and reciting a verse of rap-rhyme. "You can't fuck with this. Eminem was a white rapper, motherfucker. Watchu think about that?"

"I do adore Eminem," Manson said. "However, that being said. What are we going here tonight, children?"

"Children?"

"You heard me, boys and girls," Manson said. "Do your parents know where you are?"

"This motherfucker is clowning on us, yo," Blue Hat said, rocking back and forth like a chimpanzee, arms swaying to the left and to the right. He flipped his hat straight, the flat brim in its proper place, displaying that he was serious now. "Man, you guys looking for a fight. Cause I'm ready. I'll fuck you up. You want some? Bring it, bitch." He stepped back in an Ulitmate Fighting Championship stance and put his fists out. He was ready for a brawl.

"Calm down, friend," Manson said. "We don't want to fight you. We came here to bight you."

"What? You stupid, or something?" White Bandanna man asked. "You gonna bite us?"

"That's right," Zoey said.

"Let the party begin," Manson said.

At that moment, both Manson and Zoey transformed into their true shape, shifting into the monsters that they truly were: vampires. Unlike traditional or modern tales, these two were human, but when they transformed, they changed into a visage of something far worse and sinister than Nosferatu or Satan himself. They were truly frightening and terrifying to look upon. They were no longer the beautiful creatures that walked the night in dark, slinky leather and lace, but instead became monsters with rows of sharp teeth, solid black eyes with a red tinge in slanted slits with blackened sockets, their nose collapsed inward like a bat, and their hair becoming coarse and matted. Their skin took on the tinge of tallow and wax, their fingernails becoming long black claws. They were not beautiful; they were dreadful and frightening.

"What the fuck is happening to you?" Eric asked, stepping back.

"You is ugly," Blue Hat said, snickering. "You looked good at first, but now you's ugly as fuck."

"It's time to feed," Manson said, grinning with sharp fangs and evil eyes. "And you are on the menu."

"Man, fuck this shit," White Bandanna man said, grabbing his bike and attempting to make a quick exit.

"Where do you think you are going?" Zoey said, moving so quickly she was invisible for a moment, and then she reappeared in front of White Bandanna man. She grabbed his bike by the handlebars and yanked it out from underneath him. He fell backward. She discarded the bike over her shoulder, and it flew across the parking lot and crashed against the asphalt with grinding metal and cracking plastic. She snatched him up by his pants, grabbing him just above the groin, and picking him up, and then slamming him back down firmly on the ground.

"Let me go," he cried. "Don't hurt me."

She wasted no time, quickly biting his neck with her wickedly sharp teeth, removing a mouthful of flesh. The chewed and swallowed the meat, putting her mouth back to the wound and drinking the blood that was spurting from the severed artery in jets and streams. The blood tasted delectable and salty and she drank her fill of the warm, sticky, live giving fluid.

Manson made quick work of Eric, tackling him and pinning him to the ground. He quickly grabbed his head and jerked it from left to right in a snapping motion. His neck was instantly severed at the spine, and he died with one last breath.

"Are you crazy?" Eric said. "What are you doing? Is this some kind of joke?"

Blue Hat had seen enough. He took off running, beating feet across the pavement toward the park gate. He did not want anything to do with it.

Manson moved with supernatural speed, like as streak, as he closed the distance between himself and Blue Hat. He stood in front of the punk as he ran away, looking over his shoulder, unaware that Manson was now in front of him. When he turned around, he ran headlong into Manson and it was like hitting a granite slab. Blue Hat was stopped dead in his tracks, literally, as Manson grabbed him, spun him around upside down, and chewed half of his neck of in large, chomping, bites. Blood spattered and spewed in squirts and gouts, flowing onto the ground and across Manson's hands. He bent down, lifting the lifeless body, and drank the blood oozing out from the nasty gash in the flesh. He ripped flesh loose and chewed it with a ravenous hunger. He raised his claws like talons stabbed them into Blue Hat's stomach, gutting him from groin to sternum, reaching in and pulling out innards, offal, intestines, organs, until he reached the heart. He pulled out the heart and smiled. This was the *pièce de résistance*. The sweetbread was delicious, but the heart was simply divine, especially while it was still warm and beating, dripping with blood.

After he finished feeding on his kill, he went back to Zoey and helped her gut her victim. They ate their fill, licking the blood from their fingers, and savoring the moment. The kill was always the best part, and then after that it was anticlimactic. They would need to get away now and put distance between themselves and the scene of the slaughter.

They jumped into the Monte Carlo and Manson fired up the engine with a roar.

"Nice work," Crandall said from the back seat, patting Manson on the back. "That was exciting to watch."

"Yes. The blood has been spilled," Manson said. "Not the blood of the innocence, either I'm afraid. These fools deserved everything they got."

"Agreed," Crandall said.

"They tasted like shit," Zoey said, spitting out the window. "Their blood was polluted with poison and wretchedness."

"Let's go get the other girl," Manson said. "She is getting away."

Manson put it in gear, stomped on the gas pedal, and peeled out with smoking squealing from the rubber tires. They were ecstatic and jubilated. They had taken out some punks who the world would never miss, and now the world was a better place as a result of it. Someone should award vampires a prize, they thought. Would that not be appropriate? They thought it would be not only appropriate, but that it should be mandatory. Rid the scum-fucks from the world. That was the ticket.

2

They left the scene of carnage behind and drove away from the park fast and loud. When they got a few miles down the road, they saw Delilah walking with her thumb out.

Manson pulled the car over and rolled down the window.

"You need a ride?" he asked.

"Yes. Please," Delilah said.

"Where are you going?" Zoey asked.

"I don't know. Anywhere but here. That's all I care. I'm sick of Coos Bay . . . and those fuckers back there."

"Understandably so," Manson said. "I don't think they will bother you any longer. I have a funny feeling." He wiped the last traces of blood from the corner of his mouth with his fingers, licked them clean, turned and smiled at Delilah.

Delilah didn't notice his fangs, at first.

"Why don't you get in," Manson asked. "We'll give you a ride."

Delilah looked into the back seat and saw Crandall. He waved back at her. He was handsome and not scary looking at all, so she felt comfortable getting in the back seat with him.

"Okay," she said. "I just live a few miles from here."

"We'll take you home then, darling," Manson said, opening the door. "Hop in. Don't mind Crandall back there . . . he won't bite you . . . not hard, anyway."

Delilah snickered at the remark, climbing in and sitting in the backseat by Crandall.

They liked her. They wanted to fuck her. They were all pretty and beautiful again. Manson was his old sexy self, and Zoey was again a ravishing beauty to die for, and Delilah instantly felt a chemistry with the three sexy strangers in the hotrod.

They pulled over on a backroad, near a grove of trees and a small creek where the streetlights were sparse and there were no houses, and they stripped of one another's clothes. The sex was delicious, all tongues and cocks and pussies and wet, moist, slippery holes and cracks and pink fleshy folds of lip and crevice. It was another orgy of splendid performances by all involved and they rocketed to climax, shooting cum all over the car. If they could not have blood, they could have come, and it was just as good in the long run. They licked each other and sucked and fucked in the backseat again, and again, and again, the black Monte Carlo bouncing and jumping on the shocks, jouncing the suspension, and causing the wheels to dig ruts in the gravel and dirt where it was parked.

They did not want to kill Delilah, as she was such a sweet girl, so the let her go.

Manson said, "Tonight you have slept with death and lived to tell about it."

Delila, sexually gratified and glowing, her eyes twinkling with admiration and enamored with the dark trio of sexual deviants, longed to run away with them.

"I want to go wherever you are going," she said. "I know what you are."

"What do you mean?" Zoey asked.

"I see your teeth," Delilah said. "I know you are vampires. I'm not stupid. I know what you did to my asshole boyfriend, Eric and his friends. I watched from a distance. I saw what you did. And I don't care."

Manson and Zoey and Crandall looked at on another.

Should we take her with us? Manson thought, sending his thought to Zoey. *She is beautiful and would make a great addition to our motley crew.*

No. Absolutely not, Zoey replied with her thoughts. *She is too innocent and we would destroy her life.*

We can turn her into one of us, Manson thought.

"I think you should go home," Zoey said. "You have a family that misses you, I'm sure. Go home and live your life. Be a good person. Don't do drugs. Grow up and make a difference in this world. You don't want to become one of us. Trust me. It's not for you."

"But, I'm old enough to decide for myself," Delilah said, pouting. "Please. Just let me come with you. I don't want to live at home with my parents anymore."

"You should cherish your parents," Crandall said, putting his hand on her shoulder. "I loved my parents . . . and now I can never go back. They have disowned me. That is the worst thing that can happen to a child."

"We would love for you to come with us," Manson said, turning, gripping the steering wheel with white knuckles. "It seems that you are better off going a separate way. Our destiny is not for you. Trust me. You don't want to be like us."

"What if I just don't get out of the car?" Delilah said. "What if you are just stuck with me?"

"Then we will have no choice but to eat you alive," Manson said. "Consider your life a gift. Normally we would have ripped you to pieces, but you are special . . . you will be something someday. I can sense it."

Delilah was disappointed. She sulked and crossed her arms. She looked at Crandall and he returned her glare, raising his eyebrows in an expression of ambivalence, unable to offer her any support. He obviously liked her, too, but he was in agreement with the others. They could not support another waif on the road. She would have to go her own way.

Manson opened the car door and said, "You have to go now, sweetheart. It's nothing personal. We are looking out for everyone's better interest now."

"Fine," Delilah said. "Just fuck me and dump me off on the side of the road like a common whore. Whatever. I don't care. Go to hell." She climbed out of the car and stood looking at them. "I'm sorry I ever met you guys."

"You have to admit the sex was wonderful," Manson said. "You've always got that to look back on."

"Yeah. Okay. Whatever," she said, turning and walking away. "Thanks for nothing." She stopped and sobbed into her hands. She really was infatuated with the trio of dark riders in the car and she longed to travel with them, to hell, or wherever it may take her, but, alas, it was not meant to be, so they started up the car and pulled away, leaving her standing on the side of the road, only a short distance from her home.

She walked home, crying, freshly fucked and still alive, but saddened by the whirlwind love storm that had been the three creatures of the night.

They sped away in the Monte Carlo and left town quickly, not wanting to attract the attention of local law enforcement, afraid that Delilah may have a change of heart and report them to that authorities.

3

They stopped at a convenience store in Crescent City to get some refreshments. Zoey went inside to buy beer, cigarettes, and breath mints while Manson refueled the gas guzzling Monte Carlo. As he was pulling the car up to park in front of the

7-Eleven he received a text message from Crandall. The phone buzzed in his pocket and he pulled it out to see who could be contacting him. When he saw the name on the message, he was excited. His face was lighted by the bright blue light from the LCD screen. He read the message coming through hand smiled as he replied to the text.

"You son of a bitch," Manson said aloud, thinking fondly of Crandall. "I wondered when you were going to get in touch with me."

Zoey was still inside the store, speaking with the clerk. Manson could see her through the glass, past the ATM and the sunglasses in the rotating display.

He types quickly on the cell phone, responding to Crandall, anxious to know what was happening with his werewolf friend. He smiled at the text messages coming through. It was good news. Crandall had made it home and was now over in Paris, France, on his way to finding the legendary doctor who had professed his knowledge of a cure for lycanthropy.

Zoey came out of the star with a paper bag holding all her goods. She looked into the Monte Carlo and smiled at Manson. He put his cell phone back in his pocket and reached over to open the door for Zoey. He pulled the latch on the door and pushed it open.

"What took you so long?" he asked, looking up at her as she climbed into the car.

"I was buying a lottery ticket," she said, sarcastically. "What do you think took me so long?"

"You bought a lottery ticket?"

"No. I was kidding."

"Then what?"

"The clerk was on the phone and taking his own sweet time."

"Really?"

"Yes," she said, taking the breath mints out of the bag. "Have one of these . . ."

"Thank you," Manson said. "Is my breath that bad?"

"No . . . but seriously . . . I think that clerk was flirting with me."

"Is that any surprise?"

"I guess not."

Manson started the car, put his hands on the steering wheel, then looked at Zoey.

"Guess who I just got a text message from . . ."

"Who? Your band mate, Skipper Buzzwhacker, or whatever his name is."

"Skeeter Dinglewood," Manson corrected her. "You're so silly. No. That's not who. Take another guess."

"I don't know," she said, taking a beer out of the bag and cracking it open, taking a long drink. "Do you want a beer?"

"Certainly. Why not drink and drive? What's the worst that can happen?"

She handed him a beer. He opened it and took a drink.

"I got a message from Crandall," Manson said.

"Oh, really?" She was surprised and excited. "What did he say? Is he okay?"

"He's fine," Manson said, burping and wiping his lips on his sleeve. "He said he made it home and he is now in Paris."

"France?"

"Yes. That's where Paris is located."

She hit him on the shoulder. "I know that, you goof," she said, sipping her beer. "What is he doing over there?"

"He's looking for that doctor with the cure."

"I see."

"Sounds like he is doing well."

"Good. I'm glad. I miss him dearly."

"I know you do."

"Is he going to come back?"

"He didn't say. You have his number . . . you can ask him, if you want."

"I might do that," she said, reaching in the bag and pulling out a pack of cigarettes. "Can I smoke?"

"Well, you know I don't like it in the car," Manson said. "But would I ever tell you 'no?' I would do anything for you and the answer is always 'yes' isn't it?"

"Depends," she said, opening the cigarettes and lighting one. "Not always."

"Depends on what?"

She exhaled seductively and looked at him with a knowing glare.

"If you agree with me or not."

"I see your point."

"Can I have a man for breakfast?"

"You can have me?"

"I mean a stranger. Can I eat someone alive . . . maybe that clerk in there?"

"Huh?"

"I think I would love to go in there and rip his throat out and drink his blood."

"What are you waiting for?" Manson said. "He is alone. It is late. No one would know. There is nobody around to see it. Go in there and kill him, if you like."

"Really?"

"Absolutely," Manson said. "Finish your cigarette and beer and then go eat his heart. I'll wait. See . . . I told you I never say 'no' . . ."

"Just this once," she said.

"Go for it."

Zoey finished her beer, put out her cigarette and went inside and quickly ripped the clerk's throat out with her clawed fist. He did not see it coming and did not stand a chance. The kill was quick, the blood flowed in streams. She ate his heart. Her cheeks smeared with his blood as he lay on the floor in a pool of crimson. She hurried out of the store and got back into the car, wiping her bloody face on her sleeves.

"All better?" Manson asked.

"Yes."

"Good," Manson said, putting the car in gear. "Let's get the hell out of here before someone shows up."

"Go!"

Manson put the car in gear, revved up the engine, and peeled out from the parking lot leaving smoking streaks of rubber on the road.

CHAPTER TWENTY-FIVE

1

Crandall landed in Paris and took in the sights and sounds of Paris, France, a patriot abroad . . . he was reminded of Ernest Hemingway and how the great writer had loved Paris, spent much time there with his wife and contemporaries, drinking coffee in the cafés and writing letters and books that would be of historical and literary significance. He loved "Papa" and adored his work. This was going to be his place to pursue a new life, a new beginning, a fresh start to follow in the footsteps of great artists that had gone this way before. Most importantly, this was the place where he would find the scientist who had the rumored cure for lycanthropy.

When Crandall stepped off the plane, carefully walked down the exit ramp, and passed through the massive Charles de Gaulle Airport he was astounded by all the travelers from around the world and the sheer size of the terminal. It was shaped like a giant tube, the vaulted ceiling rising high above, making an echo chamber that was filled with the sights and sounds of busy travelers, staff, and custodial workers. Outside through the giant picture windows on the runway jets were taking off and landing and inside tourists were moving back and forth. The glass on the windows rattled as jets hit thrusters and made massive booms and blasts from the engines. Overhead the giant domed roof spanned the terminal like a massive Quonset hut. There were escalators spanning the long passages past checkpoints and boarding areas and docking bays where passengers gathered in waiting areas, lounging on seats and looking at their cell phones, laptops, or engaging one another in conversation. The air smelled of exotic locals and perfumes and anticipation. It was invigorating and exciting to be in a foreign airport amongst world travelers. It was a new beginning.

Crandall walked through the terminal in an effort to find his way to an exit where he could locate a cab. The workers in the airport, dressed in professional attire of suits, vests, skirts, and ties and hats, were busy at different flight companies behind the counters assisting customers and selling tickets, the security personnel were busy checking bags and watching for illegal or hazardous materials through the checkpoints on X-ray machines. Workers were driving through the terminal on buggies with passengers loaded with baggage weaving in and out of the crowd, careful not to run anyone over. It was alive with excited and hurrying passengers and travelers coming from destinations across the globe, and there was a hustle and bustle that was exhilarating.

Crandall was so happy to be away from the United States of America and Canada, finding a new country to explore. He stepped on an escalator and rode it past shops selling food and clothing that said Buy Paris Duty Free and coffee shops and restaurants and jewelry kiosks and electronic devices with cell phones and laptops and video cameras. He passed by the colossal walls of LCD monitors that displayed flight times, departures and arrivals, screens stacked in grids, white text on blue backgrounds, a sign that said **Correspondances - Flight Connections** and **Lounge Instant Paris** and **Airport Hotel** with Chinese characters and arrows pointing which way to go, and he followed the signs, walking down the passageway until he found an exit where he passed through the secured gates, nodded to the attendant on duty at the door, and passed through the large doors and stepped out into the welcoming morning air of Paris.

He clutched his travel bags and stepped to the curb, locating a waiting taxicab, a sporty black Mercedes Benz, and hailed the driver. The driver, dressed in a black suit and chauffeurs' hat, stepped toward him, reaching for his bags.

"Good morning, sir," the driver said with a French accent. "May I take your bags?"

"Hello," Crandall said, handing the driver his bags. "Yes. Please."

"Where would you like to go?"

"I need to find a cheap hotel," Crandall said, not really knowing where he was going, necessarily. He had googled cheap hotels, but the figured the taxi driver would know the best places in the city.

"Ah, yes," the driver said, opening the trunk and placing the bags inside. "I know many places. You say cheap . . . no? I can help you. Paris is an expensive city, but . . . there are some places you can go that are not so costly."

"I like your style," Crandall said.

"Please," the taxi driver said, opening rear passenger door and waving him over. "Come and get inside. I'll take you there and show you."

"That would be most excellent," Crandall said, remembering the line from an old movie. "Most excellent indeed, good man."

He climbed inside and the driver shut the door. The cab smelled of clean leather and new materials. Crandall loved the smell of a new car, and a Mercedes had the most pleasant smell of all. It was an intoxicating aroma. He wished he could afford such a luxurious vehicle. Maybe someday, he thought, after I sell a movie script and hit the big time, I can cash some royalty checks and get a mansion on the hill with my own personal driver, just like the heavy weights in Hollywood. *Wouldn't that be great,* he mused. *Yes, that would be wonderful. And I can do it. I am a great writer. I am going to be a star. But, I am a werewolf and I must find the cure or it will never happen. I will never be normal as long as I am vexed by this curse.*

He sat back in the plush seat and relaxed, pleased to be on his way, closer to finding the cure, and watched as the driver climbed into the front and pulled the car away from the curb, heading toward the heart of the city.

He thought about his parents and how they had supported his decision to travel to Paris. He loved them, and he did not want to disappoint them, however, this was a terrible mess that had become his life, and now he had to change everything. He thought about Manson and Zoey and wondered how they were doing. He decided he would send them a text message and see if he could get in touch. It had been a while since he had heard from them and he was concerned about how they may be faring on their trip to California.

He took out his phone, tapped the screen with his thumb, and hit the contacts icon. He found Manson and hit the message tab. He hesitated . . . unsure of what to say . . . it was an awkward moment and he felt like a stranger all of the sudden, as though he had never known Manson or Zoey at all, and it had only been a few weeks since he spoke to them last. He loved them so much, but the distance had made them seem so far away and out of reach. Why had they not responded to his earlier message when he had tried to contact them? He hoped they were alright and that everything was going well for them. Hopefully, they had not had a bad experience with the vampire hunter who had been stalking them.

His phone had an error message, a roaming issue, and he could not send a message. This was just his luck. He would have to have the issue fixed, somehow, or buy a new phone with a carrier from France.

He decided he would wait until he was at the hotel to contact Verizon and inquire into why he as having an issue sending the messages. Something struck him as odd, a strange premonition, as though Manson and Zoey might be in trouble, and he was curious and anxious to find out.

"How much do you want to spend?" the taxi driver asked, looking back at him in the mirror. "I can help you, but I must know what is your spending limit."

"I have a Visa card," Crandall said. "And some cash. I want something affordable, but not so cheap or rundown that I wind up in an unsafe area." His parents had loaded a prepaid Visa and stuffed a large wad of cash into his hand. They had some money saved and they could afford to make sure their number one son would travel abroad in style.

"Perfect," the driver said. "I know just the place."

"Where is that?"

"It is on the Rue De Vaugirard," the driver said. "It is affordable but not lacking in all the amenities. It is right in the heart of things so you can explore all the wonderful attractions of the city."

"Is it close to the Eiffel Tower?"

"Everything in Paris is close to the Eiffel Tower," the driver said. "It is visible from everywhere."

"Fine," Crandall said. "Take me there. I'm ready to check in . . . and I'm hungry."

"Sure, yes," the drive said. "I will drive fast to get you there right way."

The driver was not joking, accentuating his statement by stepping hard on the accelerator, causing Crandall's head to jerk back, and raced down the city streets, weaving in and out of traffic, taking corners like a race car driver, and maneuvering through the busy and crowded roadways.

"I knew I liked your style," Crandall said, fastening his seat belt. "You drive like Mario Andretti."

"Bah! He is Italian," the driver said. "Alain Marie Pascal Prost was the greatest race car driver to ever live. He was French, you know . . . and he was the best."

"I see your point," Crandall said. "Viva la France."

"*Wi monsieur,*" the driver said, pulling up in front of the building. "We have arrived. I will get your bags and escort you inside."

"Lovely," Crandall said, handing the driver a hundred-dollar bill. "Keep the change, friend. That ride was worth every penny."

"Nice, and thank you," the driver said, plucking the bill from his hand.

They got out of the car and grabbed his bags.

Crandall looked at the sign on the building that read **Hôtel Paris Vaugirard**. The doorway was adorned on each side by potted trees and flowers. The building was tall and made of limestone and polished marble, wrought iron railing with Gothic motifs and flourishes on each balcony.

He went inside and checked in at the lobby desk. The taxi driver put his bags down at the counter and wished him well, giving him a handshake, and then turning and quickly exiting through the doors. The receptionist behind the desk was polite and very French. He asked him all the relevant questions and pertinent information. Crandall put his passport and Visa card down on the counter.

"Perfect," the clerk said. "How long will you be staying?"

"I don't know yet," Crandall said. "Just give me the room for a week."

"We have a few vacancies now," the receptionist said. "I will make all of the arrangements and have you in your room in no time."

"That would be great," Crandall said, looking around the lobby. He was still amazed that he had actually made it to Paris. He had wanted to visit the famous city for most of his adult life, and now he was standing in a posh hotel in the heart of the city.

The receptionist typed away on the keyboard, printed some paperwork, grabbed a key, and handed it to Crandall.

After he paid for everything, Crandall went to his room, assisted by a bellhop who carried his bags for him. He used the keycard to open the door, the light blinking red and then green, and the lock clicking as it unlatched in the internal mechanism. He pushed the door open and looked at the wonderful hotel room. The furnishings were modern, tasteful, and perfect.

He tipped the bellhop with a twenty and then let the door close.

He put down his bags and went directly to the window looking down over the city . . . he looked out at the cityscape and saw the Eiffel Tower in the distance and was smitten with the iconic tower outlined against the horizon.

He could feel the ghost of Ernest Hemingway hovering over the city. It was magical.

He emptied his pockets on the nightstand and plopped down on the comfortable bed, propped up the pillows behind his back, and leaned back and smiled. He had made it the Paris. It was actually true. This was going to be fucking fabulous. He could feel it. Something great was about to happen.

2

Crandall picked his cell phone and decided it was time to get in touch with Manson and Zoey. He would send them a text message or call them or both, but he felt like he needed to establish contact since it had been so long now that he had communicated with them. After that he would search for any information he could fine on the legendary doctor (what was his name? Jaques Le Griswold? Something like that. He could not remember, so he would have to Google it) who had the rumored cure for lycanthropy.

He searched through his contacts, a list that was getting shorty everyday since he had contracted lycanthropy and become and unwitting introvert and recluse—having friends and being around people during a full moon had become a liability. What good was having friends if you would rip them to pieces in a heightened state of mania during a lunar induced insanity and psychosis? It made more sense to isolate and avoid people altogether to save them from personal injury or death at the hands of a madman under the tidal influence of the moon. He found Manson's clicked on the contact link.

The heads-up display at the top of the LCD screen showed that he had four bars was **47%** charged. The hotel provided free Wi-Fi, so roaming was not an issue now, and he was sure he could get through by using Facebook Messenger to make a conference call. First, he would send a quick text, establish contact, and then do a video call so he could see them face-to-face.

He punched the send icon.

Crandall: Hey, what's up?

Manson: Is it really you?

Crandall: Yes.

Manson: How are you? Did you make it home?

Crandall: I did.

Manson: How did it go with your parents? Good, I hope.

Crandall: It's all good. They understood my situation.

Manson: So, what are you going to do now? Still looking for that Dr. Whats his name?

Crandall: Dr. Griswold. Yes. In fact, I'm in Paris right now, as we speak.

Manson: Really? That's great. How did you get there so fast?

Crandall: My parents gave me some money to take a trip to Europe.

Manson: Must be nice to have rich parents, eh?

Crandall: Yes. Of course it is. Anyway, I just wanted to see how you guys are getting along. How is Zoey?

Manson: We are doing OK.

Crandall: Tell her I said hello, and I miss her.

Manson: Will do, bro.

Crandall: Good. Well, I'm sitting in a hotel room in Paris right now and getting ready to go on my mission to find Dr. Griswold.

Manson: I am sitting at a 7-Eleven waiting for Zoey to buy me some beer and breath mints.

Crandall: LOL. You and your breath mints. Wint-O-Green?

Manson: You know it. Got to keep the breath fresh.

Crandall: You so crazy. Well, gotta go. Just wanted to let you know I'm still alive and well. I'll contact you later when I figure out what I'm going to do.

Manson: Great! I look forward to it. Zoey and I are on are way to Hollywood. We hope to be there in a few days. We still have your movie script . . . do you want us to give it to a producer?

Crandall: If you want. I'm not too worried about it now. I've got more important things to do right now.

Manson: Sure. I understand. I'll see what happens when we get to LA. Maybe I can give it to an agent or something.

Crandall: That would be great, if you can. I'm going out on the town in a minute, so . . . take care and keep in touch.

Manson: Will do, broskie doskie.
Thanks for getting in touch with
me. I was worried about you.

Crandall: No worries, man. It's all good.
I'm going to take care of business.

Manson: Sweet. Be careful.
You never know what kind of
trouble you can get into over in
a foreign country.

Crandall: You be careful, too. A vampire
isn't safe in this world, you know.

Manson: Yes. That's true. Thank
you. Be good.

Crandall: OK. Peace. Over and out.

Manson: TTYL.

Crandall closed the messenger app and sat back on the bed and reflected on the conversation.

3

After the conversation with Manson and Zoey he felt better. They were still alive and making their way to California. He was pleased immensely by this news. It made his heart glad. He felt better now that he had at least established some contact with his friends back in the Unites States. He was worried about them. He knew they would have a hard time adapting to life in Hollywood, but he hoped for the best for them.

Crandall felt compelled to locate this Doctor Griswold. That was his primary mission and he was ready to track this guy down. A full moon was coming soon, and he did not want to be alone in a foreign city and become a werewolf in such an unknown land. Who knows what could happen? He had watched the movies, *The Werewolf of Paris*, in particular, and that was quite a story. Could it really be like that?

He opened up Google Chrome and typed Doctor Griswold's name into the search dialog box.

The search engine provided several entries for the name, and one in particular caught his attention. He clicked on the link and went to the website. It was a homepage for Doctor Griswold and his clinic. His image was in the upper right-hand corner. He was wearing round rimmed spectacles, hair neatly trimmed and combed, wearing a white smock. He was a specialized physician with an MD in general surgery and Ph.D. in neuroscience. His website said he pursued the study of special cases of disease, disorder, and malfunctions of the nervous system as well and deformities as a result. He was actively recruiting test subjects for studies on experimental medications that were supposed to be used to remedy spinal injuries such as spinal column injuries that resulted in subjects becoming paraplegic and sufferers of sclerosis and Lou Gehrig's disease. He also researched mutations of brain cells and spinal column structures for cures and reparative properties. He professed to have a cure for psychosis and dementia with holistic medications and certain questionable surgical practices that were only available in Europe and not in the United States. Although the website hinted about the strange phenomena of human nature being affected by the lunar periods and tidal shifts imposed by the Moon, it did not give outright information about a cure for lycanthropy.

Crandall was happy to have found the website and he clicked on the contact link to see what was available on that page. It had a contact form, a phone number, and an email address.

This was too good to be true.

Crandall quickly dialed the number and waited for someone to pick up on the other end. When the assistant answered the phone, she sounded nice and gentle in tone, and instantly Crandall knew that he had hit paydirt. He set up and appointment, telling the assistant that he was in urgent need of care, and they scheduled and appointment for the following week on Monday. This was the soonest Dr. Griswold could see him.

That was good enough, and Crandall was happy to have made the connection.

"Thank you so much," Crandall said. "I will be there with bells on Monday morning at eight o'clock."

4

"The truth is," Dr. Griswold said, sitting back in his chair and tapping the tips of his fingers together. "There is no cure for lycanthropy."

The doctor was dressed in a white smock. He was wearing horned rimmed glasses, the lenses making his eyes bulge liked boiled eggs, the irises the color of hydrangeas. His black hair was neatly combed, and his smile was crooked beneath a neatly trimmed mustache.

"You're kidding, right?" Crandall sat up straight, looking at the plaques and degrees on the wall behind the doctor. "This has to be some kind of a joke."

"Nope," the doctor said, shuffling papers on the desk. "I'm afraid this is not a joke."

"I thought you were working on a cure . . . for it."

"That is the rumor that I cannot seem to get away from," the doctor said. He adjusted his tie. "But it simply isn't true."

"I don't get it," Crandall said, sighing. "I read on the Internet that you were experimenting with a cure and having success with your efforts."

"That is how the story goes," Dr. Griswold said. He picked

up a pen and looked at it coolly. "You think you are a werewolf, right?"

Crandall shook his head in the affirmative. "I don't think—I know. It's true. This is a bunch of B-S. How can I be wrong when I know it is real?"

"Allow me to elaborate. It is a psychological disorder, really. It's all in your head. Plenty of people are affected by the moon. It creates the tides. The wolves howl at night. It is mythical and magical. Legendary, you might say. Humans have active imaginations. We are affected by lunar gravity on Earth. But not by much . . . it does have a mild force, but not much more than these books on my shelves have. Now, for some reason, humans tend to get a little crazy during a full moon. It's all in our heads."

Crandall was disappointed. He had not come all this way to hear this vagary. "I don't believe you. How can you say this . . . I am a werewolf and I know it's true."

"That is what they all say," Dr. Griswold said. "I know a psychologist who may be able to help you more with this issue. Would you like his card?"

"No. I don't need a shrink," Crandall said. "What I need is to be rid of this curse."

"I'm afraid I can't help you. I wish I could, but I have no cure for which you seek."

Crandall was flabbergasted. He ran his hands through his hair, took a deep breath, regained his composure, dug his fingernails into the faux leather on the handles of the chair in which he was sitting. "I guess that's it then. I'll be going now. Thank so much for your time."

"No problem," Dr. Griswold said. "I hope you find a solution to this issue you are having. You can show yourself out."

"Of course," Crandall said, standing, turning and going to the door. He turned and looked at the doctor. "I'm curious . . .

why did you get placed on the Internet as the man who cured lycanthropy?"

Dr. Griswold smiled, tapped the pen, then said, "Have you ever read a tabloid paper?"

Crandall shook his head to signal that he had not.

"Well, if you know about 'fake news' then you will understand."

"Fake news?"

"Yes. Just like your president Trump is always talking about. It is made up by someone sitting in a room somewhere with nothing better to do than start trouble. I have opposition to my work . . . liberals and radicals who protest my studies with animals. It happens. They have crated rumors about me in an attempt to make me look . . . less than desirable. I hope you understand."

"I think I understand," Crandall said. "I just was optimistic. I thought I could be rid of this . . . problem. Alas, I must go and deal with it on my own."

"So sorry. I wish I could help you."

"No worries. I'll be on my way now."

"Have a wonderful day."

"You too."

Crandall went to the door and exited the office, walking down the hall past the receptionist, and out through the front door into the afternoon sunlight. The sun as warm on his face and he breathed deeply of the fresh Parisian air.

5

Outside, there was a beatnik smoking a cigarette. Crandall looked at him curiously, thinking he looked like a throwback from a 1950s movie about Jack Kerouac and the beat poets that stood on street corners reciting verse and rhyme in broken rhythms. He was apparently a French hipster wearing a black beret, striped shirt, and skinny jeans rolled up in cuffs above black patent zipper boots. They made eye contact, and it was an odd moment, uncomfortable and awkward.

Crandall was preparing to hail a taxi when the hipster spoke to him in a thick French accent.

"You are here for the cure, no?"

"I'm sorry," Crandall said. "What do you mean?"

"I mean," the hipster said, stamping on the cigarette beneath his foot. "You came here to find the cure for lycanthropy." The words were thick on his tongue, his accent affecting his English like a magnet to steel.

"How did you know that?"

The hipster rolled his eyes and stroked his chin. "I know many things . . . and I can tell you are a werewolf because I can smell your scent. This is the office of Dr. Griswold, the infamous, the notorious, the legendary snake oils salesman who pedals pills and potions to the downtrodden. He is like a fakir who makes his living solely on the alms of the sickly and the poor. He has cures for cancer, for AIDS, for the common cold, but nothing truly works. He has no cure for lycanthropy."

"How do you know this?"

"Because, I too, am a werewolf," the hipster said. "That is how I can detect you. I smell you. I know my own kind."

"Interesting, to say the least."

"Allow me to introduce myself," the hipster said, extending his hand. "My name is Alonso François. I am the leader of a pack of werewolves who live here in Paris. We are always on the lookout for others of our kind. We like to keep order amongst ourselves."

"Really? There are more of you—us?"

"Yes. We are many. We live in a commune just outside of the

city in a rural area, but we are in trouble . . . as there are those who do not like our kind."

"I've seen the movie *An American Werewolf in Paris*," Crandall said, cracking a grin. "Is it anything like that? I am an American, you see, and I cannot help but make the connection."

"Bah! Nonsense," Alonso said, waving the statement away. "That is all Hollywood. We are much different than that. We are of noble blood, princes and scholars and knights of old, with honorable endeavors. We long to be accepted by mankind, but it may never come to pass. We are being hunted by mercenaries."

"A hunter?" Crandall was taken back to the incident with the vampire hunter in Vancouver, who had followed Manson and Zoey and he in the black Monte Carlo across the border into the United States. "There are hunters of werewolves here? In Paris?"

"Yes. There are hunters. We have battled with them on many occasions. They are closing in and making it hard for us to survive. And they have involved the local authorities, too."

"What will you do about it?"

"We must move away," Alonso said, to a safer place.

"I see," Crandall said. He was skeptical of what Alonso was telling him, but he was also intrigued. "I am curious about all of this. I would like to meet the others you speak of . . . in your pack. I have never met any other . . . werewolves."

"You are welcome to come to our estate and join us, if you like," Alonso said, lighting another cigarette. "I have a motor car parked just around the corner."

"Just out of curiosity," Crandall said. "Why are you here at Dr. Griswold's office building?"

"I am one of the voices of reason," Alonso said. "We are on a crusade to expose these lies propagated by the media and hoaxers. I am here gathering information to further our cause. We must always keep our ear to the ground. I happened to see *you* coming out and I knew right away why you were here."

"Interesting," Crandall said. "This is all too strange. I am intrigued, though."

"Come with me," Alonso said. "I will show you the way. You can join us. My pack will welcome you with open arms."

"I would love that. I have a hotel room . . . I will need to gather my belongings."

"Sure. Sure. I will take you there. Follow me to my automobile and I will give you a ride."

Crandall did not know why he believed what Alonso was saying, or why it rang true, however, he knew that he felt comfortable in the man's presence and he felt an unexplainable kinship. He wanted to meet others like himself, and this was a perfect opportunity.

They went around the corner to a small red Fiat parked at the curb.

"This is my car," Alonso said. "Climb in. I will drive you wherever you need to go."

They got into the car and pulled away from the curb, merging into traffic, and speeding away from Dr. Griswold's office, never to return.

6

The countryside on the outskirts of Paris was picturesque and delightful. It was like a scene from an impressionistic painting by Renoir. The trees lined the sides of the road and there were grassy fields and pastures with cottages and farmhouses on vineyards and cattle ranches. The rolling hills with humped backs green and expansive. The red clay roofs on white stucco buildings lining alleyways and streets. It was hard to believe that they had only recently been in the busy metropolis and now were in the countryside where rural living dominated. It was breathtaking and beautiful.

When they got to the secluded drive that led back into the trees, Crandall could see a farmhouse at the end of the gravel path . . .

They got out of the car and stretched. There was a young man standing on the porch of the house looking at them intently. His arms were crossed. He was smoking a cigarette.

Alonso put his hand on Crandall's shoulder and ushered him toward the house.

"Hello, Winton," Alonso said, hailing the man standing on the porch. "I have brought a guest."

"I see that," Winton said, scowling. "You have brought a stranger to our haven. Why would you do this?"

"He is one of us," Alonso said.

"Hi, my name is Crandall." He extended his hand.

Winton ignored the gesture and continued to scowl. He was not impressed.

"I told Crandall he would be our guest and that we would welcome him with open arms," Alonso said. "Are you going to make me into a liar? Winton. Mind your manners."

"Yes. Whatever you say, Alonso," Winton said, turning away and going inside.

"Never mind him," Alonso said, patting Crandall on the back. "He is just cantankerous. He does not trust strangers. He will come to like you, in time. Take my word."

"Okay, if you say so," Crandall said. He was skeptical.

"Let's go inside," Alonso said. "I want you to meet the others."

"I would love that."

They stepped in through the door and Crandall was greeted by the smell of baking bread and red wine. A group of men and women were sitting around the living room drinking beer and wine and watching a large screen LCD TV where two teenagers engaged in playing a video game. It was a captivating sight to watch them lean from side to side, lifting the controllers up and pressing the buttons madly, during the action. They were in the middle of a heated battle on the screen, a war of beasts and armored knights fighting legendary demons and monsters. The volume was cranked up and the speakers blasted out sound effects of clashing swords and guttural grunts and groans, growling and howling, explosions and breaking glass as vials of potion broke on the ground, and a haunting musical score with a sinister melody, discordant harmony, and wicked theme.

"That is Vance and Nathan," Alonso said, pointing to the video game aficionados. "Meet Crandall, you two . . . if you can pull yourselves away from that game long enough."

They made a token gesture, waved, said "nice to meet you" but never looked away for more than a quick glance, riveted by the game and the intense graphics on the TV screen.

"It is a pleasure to meet you," Crandall said.

They continued to play their video game and ignored him.

"Boys will boys," Alonso said to Crandall. "What can you do? Do not be offended by their rudeness . . . they mean no insult you. They are just so self-absorbed that they do not know how to great a guest in the house of the wolves." He said the last part loud and clear to drive the point home to the youths.

"It is okay," Crandall said, handwaving them away. "I understand. I like to play video games too."

There was a couple sitting on the black leather sofa against the wall, drinking beer and smoking cigarettes, kissing and rubbing each other amorously. Another man, with a beard and long curly brown hair was seated in a La-Z-Boy recliner, reading a book, a novel by Stephen King. He was dressed in a long sleeve shirt with red suspenders.

"That is Janette and Pierre," Alonso said, pointing at the kissing couple. "They are madly in love, as you can see . . . and over there, reading a book, is Ronald."

"Say hello to our new friend, everyone," Alonso said.

They all stopped—including those playing the video game, if only momentarily—and looked at Crandall, waved, said "hello," then went back to what they were doing, kissing, reading, panting and breathing hard. Ronald picked his nose, examined a booger, then rubbed his feet together, wearing heavy wool socks where he deposited the nose nugget, and sighed, setting the book aside.

"To what do we owe this pleasure?" he asked, dubiously.

"Crandall will be staying with us for a while," Alonso said. "Am I right, Crandall?" He looked at Crandall with a questioning stare, raised his eyebrows, waiting for a response.

Crandall caught the cue and said, "Yes. Of course. I will be staying."

"We want to give him the warmest welcome and make him feel right at home," Alonso said. "He is one of us . . . he belongs."

"Not if we don't want him," Vance said, still tapping the video game controller.

"It is not up to you, son," Alonso said. "You are not the Alpha in the pack. Remember that."

"Whatever you say," Vance said, sticking his tongue out of the corner of his mouth.

"And you," Alonso said, looking at Ronald. "Mind your manners. You have the hygiene habits of a lumberjack."

"I am an ax man, after all," Ronald said. "I cut wood for a living and like it."

"You chop firewood for the stove," Alonso said, sighing. "That does not make you a logger, by any means."

"I disagree," Ronald said. "I am a tree feller and have honor. The only good tree is a stump."

"Anyway, mind your manners, won't you please?" Alonso said. "I expect you to be on your best behaviors and how our guest every courtesy he is entitled to while in our home."

"And you two," Alonso said to the couple on the sofa. "Can't you go to your room and conduct your . . . promiscuity?"

"Okay, Dad," Janette said, sarcastically. "Is the lecture over?"

"Indeed," Alonso said, taking Crandall by the arm. "We will go into the kitchen and meet some other lovely werewolves. What do you say?"

"Most definitely," Crandall said, going with him anxiously and willingly.

"Follow me."

They went into the kitchen and there were three women, a red head, a brunette, and a blonde, busy cooking and cleaning as they prepared for the evening meal.

"Ladies," Alonso said, entering the kitchen with Crandall in tow. "Meet our new house guest. He is a werewolf if you can't discern that already. His name is Crandall, and he will be staying with us for a while . . . isn't that right?" Alonso put his arm around Crandall's shoulders and looked at him eagerly while he spoke the last interrogation.

"I guess so," Crandall said. "I have nowhere else to go right now, so, yeah."

"Don't make it sound so dismal," Alonso said. "We are your friends here. You are welcome. Isn't that right ladies? Say hello, why don't you?"

The women stopped mid-task and looked at the two men who walked in the door unexpected.

"Yes. Hello," the blonde girl said cheerfully. Shew was pretty, Crandall noticed immediately. "My name is Leona." She wiped her hands on a dishtowel and then stuck it out for him to shake. "Nice to meet you . . . Crandall."

They shook hands.

"Charmed, I'm sure," Crandall said.

"This is Maria," Leona said, pointing to the woman with shoulder length red hair and freckles. "She is our chef in residence. She is very shy and bashful."

Maria smiled and said hello, waving instead of shaking hands.

"And this is our lovely maid, Jennifer," Leona said, pointing to the brunette woman who was busy emptying the dishwashing machine and stacking plated in the cabinet. "Say hello, to Crandall," she said to Jennifer.

"Hello," she said, stopping her chores for a moment. "Nice to make your acquaintance."

"Likewise, Jennifer," he said, awkwardly.

"Oh, you can just call me Jen for short. I prefer the condensed version."

"I will remember that," Crandall said.

"Okay, now that our introductions are over," Alonso said, "we shall show you to your quarters. We have a lovely room upstairs that you can share with Vance and Nathan. They are quite nice once you get to know them. I'm sure they won't mind sharing a room with you."

"Sounds lovely," Crandall said.

They walked out of the kitchen, through the living room, and up the stairs toward the bedrooms.

"There are others you will meet," Alonso said, looking

speaking as they went down the hallway, his voice echoing off the walls. There was a smell of old wood and paint. "They are outside tending to the crops and animals. A ranch like this takes a lot of work to keep it running in tip top shape."

"I can imagine that it does," Crandall said.

"We will figure out what you are good at and assign you a set of chores, too," Alonso said. "That is part of living here. We must all chip in and make sure everything gets taken care of . . ."

"I understand," Crandall said.

Alonso opened a door and ushered Crandall into a small room that had three beds all made nicely. There were posters of musicians, video game characters, swords and daggers hanging on the wall, and oil paintings of lovely landscapes. It was obviously the room of teenagers, and Crandall thought he might be out of place there, but he was willing to give it a try. He could get along with them, he was certain of that.

"Make yourself at home," Alonso said. "That is your bed and desk over there. I will leave you to get settled in and then you can come down and enjoy a nice dinner with us shortly."

"That sounds wonderful," Crandall said.

"Fine then," Alonso said. "Give me a shout if there is anything you require. A toothbrush, shower, soap, clothing, whatever it is you need . . . I am here at your disposal."

"That is very kind of you," Crandall said. "I appreciate your hospitality."

"No worries," Alonso said. "I am glad to have made your acquaintance and bring you home to meet others of your kind."

"I've never met other werewolves before," Crandall said. "I do appreciate it. I already feel as though I belong here. As though it is meant to be."

"That is perfect. Now you can put your personal effects in

that desk and drawers over their by your bed. Take a load off. I'm sure you are tired from you travels."

"I am exhausted."

"Jet lag will get you every time."

"Yes. Tell me about it."

"Dinner will be served precisely at five o'clock," Alonso said, looking at his watch. "Be sure to come down and join us at the table. Tonight, we will be serving ribeye steaks with all the trimming."

"Sounds delicious."

"It is."

"Fine."

"And now, for the time being, I will leave you to your privacy and bid you adieu."

"Thank you."

Alonso quickly left, shutting the door behind him.

Crandall sat down on the bed, bounced up and down and felt the softness of the mattress, thought about taking a nap, but decided to put his belongings away instead. He did not want to fall asleep and miss dinner. He was happy to have met Alonso and the others and the thought that perhaps this new place on the ranch might become his home.

Only time would tell, and he was extremely interested in the cute blonde girl, Leona, and wanted to learn more about her, get to know her better, and find out what she was all about. This was new territory for him, and he was extremely curious what a female werewolf might be like.

He had an hour to kill, so he put away his belongings and sat down and looked out the window at the ranch. He could see others outside in the fields and at the barn doing chores. This was a lovely environment. He liked the quaintness of the rural living and he thought this could turn out to be a great thing: living with a pack of werewolves.

1

Crandall was introduced to everyone and soon Dinner was served, and the twelve members of the pack sat round the table with ravenous appetites, eyes wide as they looked at food spread out before them. Ribeye steaks, rare, with baked potatoes loaded with butter and sour cream, Brussels sprouts, and French bread. Large bottles of Bordeaux were passed around, the red wine poured into tall glasses with medium bowls, the aroma and taste were exquisite. Candles were lit and the lights were dimmed.

"So, what is your story?" Alonso asked, looking across the table at Crandall while holding up fork with a bloody piece of meat stuck to the tines. "I mean, how did you become a werewolf? Where are you from? Who are you? I'm sure everyone would be delighted to know."

Crandall chewed on a mouthful of food, looked around at all of the others—they were looking back intently, eyes glittering and glimmering in the candlelight—and swallowed hard, a lump if meat getting partially stuck in his windpipe. He wiped his lips with a napkin, took a drink of wine, then cleared his throat. He took a deep breath and gathered his thoughts, wanting to make sense of his story, despite how odd and crazy it might sound. He turned and looked at Leona ~~as she was~~ sitting next to him at the table; she looked back at him with bright and amorous eyes, completely entranced by the newcomer.

"I guess you all want to know more about me," Crandall said. "That is to be expected."

Winton glared and scowled across the table and said, "The only thing I want to know is: are you an impostor? I don't like the way you smell."

"Winton mind your manners," Alonso said. He chewed

thoughtfully, methodically, on the tender meat. "Do not be disrespectful to our guest."

"He brings the change that we have feared," Winton said. "He is fulfilling the prophecy."

Crandall looked at them in bewilderment.

"Nonsense," Alonso said. "That is all superstition and conjecture."

"No. I believe the prophecy. It is true," Ronald said. "An interloper will arrive bringing death and suffering to our pack."

"It is written in the stars," Winton said. "The old witch had read the future for us and said that a newcomer would signal the end of our life here."

"You two should stop visiting the doomsayer prophet," Alonso said. "She is a crackpot, and old crazy lady who consults with Tarot cards and drink hallucinogenic tea. She cannot be trusted."

"You bring us misery and death," Winton said, pointing at Crandall across the table. "We do not want you here. You should go away."

"He is our guest," Alonso said, sipping on his wine. "You will welcome him here and leave your silly speculation out of the conversation."

"What makes you think you can boss us around?" Ronald asked, raising an eyebrow at Alonso while chewing on a piece of meat. "Why should we listen to you?"

"Because I am in charge," Alonso said, suddenly becoming serious and stern. His eyes glowed in the candlelight and he showed his teeth, a subtle growl coming from his throat.

Ronald and Winton ducked their heads in submission. They knew that Alonso was the Alpha wolf and they did not want to challenge his authority.

"What is this all about?" Crandall asked. "I don't want to

cause any trouble."

"These two have been talking with a witch," Alonso said. "She had poisoned their minds with here nonsense."

"The hunters will come," Winton said. "You watch . . . you'll see. They are going to come for us on the next moon, right after the newcomer arrives. The interloper—" he pointed at Crandall. "—You have come and signaled the beginning of the end for us."

Crandall sat motionless, shocked, unsure how to respond or what to do in the current circumstances.

The other members of the pack watched and listened closely. They were tuned into the conversation, because they, too, had heard of the prophecy, and they were slightly frightened by the prospect of the future and what uncertainties it may have in store for them.

"A full moon is coming the night after tomorrow," Vance said. He had been sitting quietly next to Nathan at the end of the table. "We have to perform our ritual. What if they come? We have to be ready . . ."

"I will deal with this," Alonso said. "Do not concern yourselves with this prophecy. We will have our ritual as usual—"

"But, what if they do come for us?" Ronald asked. "What will you have us do?"

"We will flee to the motherland," Alonso said. "That has been the backup plan all along. You know this. If there is any trouble, we will leave through the mountains and flee back to Poland and hide in the refuge."

Crandall was taking all of this in, but he was clueless as to what it was all about.

Alonso looked at him and said, "On the next full moon we will all transform, and we perform a ritual of eating raw meat and mating. You are invited to join us. It is a tradition, every month, and we invite you to attend our ceremony."

"I don't know what to say," Crandall said. He looked around at the others, nervous, unsure, the interloper.

They looked back at him with mixed expressions of acceptance and disdain, and when he met Leona's eyes, they connected for a moment, a twinge of lust and desire crossing between them. It was an amorous moment; they were attracted to each other; one thing was certain: they would join together during the ceremony.

"Now, enough," Alonso said. "We will go on as usual."

"What of the hunters?" Winton interrupted. "What will we do?"

"I told you," Alonso said. "We have an escape plan. We will flee to the refuge in Poland . . . they will never follow us there, nor will they be able to find us."

Crandall was curious what this refuge was in Poland and what all of this meant. He had so many questions. He intended to ask Alonso about all of this later.

"Now, enjoy your meal and then we will convene and do our nightly chores," Alonso said. "The rest of you know the drill. If anyone threatens our existence . . . we are to follow the path to enlightenment and return to the old country. Is that clear?"

They all nodded in agreement. They knew that eventually their existence on the ranch in the countryside of France would be threatened and they would have to flee. It was inevitable. They had planned for it. Now that Crandall had arrived it made the prospect of leaving and going back to Poland even more tangible now.

Crandall could not help feeling guilty somehow for the change that was blowing in the wind. He pushed his food a way, no longer hungry, and suddenly felt tired and exhausted.

"I think I need to sleep," Crandall said.

Alonso looked at him with a long and considerate glance. "Yes. You are tired. I am sure. You may be excused and go to your quarters. We will take care of the chores tonight. You must get your beauty rest. We have many things to do tomorrow."

"Okay, I am bushed," Crandall said, pushing himself away from the table. "Thank you for the lovely meal."

He looked at Leona and smiled. She smiled back. The other women watched in admiration because they knew there was a connection and they wished that they could be a mate with the newcomer. He was fresh blood, a replenishment of new genetics for the bloodline of the werewolf pack, and he was essential and necessary to bring strength and longevity to the future offspring and prosperity of the pack.

"Everyone say goodnight to Crandall," Alonso said.

They all said goodnight in unison.

Crandall waved a hand and turned and sauntered off up the stairs, his feet dragging, his eyes drooping, suddenly tired and ready to go to sleep.

When his head hit the pillow, he was out in an instant, drifting into a dreamy state where he would have nightmares and images of things to come.

CHAPTER TWENTY-SIX

1

Manson and Zoey pulled into Eureka in the Monte Carlo just before sunrise. They needed to get ready for the day. Either they would find a place to park and sleep in the trunk or check into a hotel for the day and get some rest. It had been a long night. They had been driving since twilight and they were both exhausted from the long trip.

"Are we going to get a hotel room?" Manson asked.

"I think we should," Zoey said. "I need to take a shower."

"Yes. We should wash the stench of blood and sex off. I agree."

They stopped at the Laguna Inn, located just off Highway 10. It was a gray, two story building constructed of cinder blocks and it looked cozy and quiet, just the kind of place for two vampires to sleep through the day unnoticed.

Checking in was the usual affair, with an indifferent and uninterested clerk behind the counter, this time he was Asian and seemed to be in a hurry. He gave them the key assigned to room 13—this pleased the two vampires immensely—and they went out of the office and into the night, parking the

Monte Carlo in front of the dingy building next to their room.

The numbers on the door were crooked, and this was an omen that did not go unnoticed.

"Look at that," Zoey said. "The numbers are crooked."

"Thirteen," Manson said. "How fortunate for us. I feel lucky tonight. Do you?"

"You don't believe all of that superstitious stuff, do you?"

"If you don't know me by now," Manson said. "Yes. Absolutely, I believe in it. I didn't believe in vampires, either . . . but here we are . . . in the flesh."

"I see your point," Zoey said. "Hurry up. It's going to be daylight soon. Let's get inside and out of the light."

"Agreed."

They went inside and shut the door behind them, just as the sun was beginning to creep up over the horizon.

"What shall we do?" Manson said. "We have so much time and little money."

"We can find someone tonight. I'm sure there are some high rollers in Eureka."

"You are right. We will go out tonight and paint the town red."

"Most definitely."

They climbed into the bed and slept through the daylight hours, as vampires are wont to do, and dreamed of sinister things lurking in the shadows, chasing them, meaning to do them harm.

2

Adrian was watching them closely from the comfort of his van. He grew weary of this chase. He wanted to bring it to an end quickly, but they always seemed to elude him at every opportunity. This was frustrating, to say the least. He thought about invading the hotel room and catching them while they were sleeping, trapped inside, and he could just end it all right now.

But, it was not going to happen like that because the parking lot was well lighted and there were surveillance cameras everywhere. He would be caught in the act for sure, and even though the victims were vampires, he would still go to prison for murder . . . because no court of law or police department in the world would justify murdering people suspected of being vampires.

So, he waited in his van and watched, turning on the TV and watching the news, flipping through the channels.

He caught a program that told of the vampires in the black Monte Carlo, and he knew that the time was growing short. The police would soon apprehend the suspects. *What would become of them in prison,* he wondered. *Surely a vampire cannot survive in prison. It was impossible. Maybe I should just turn them in and let justice be served by law enforcement and the judicial system . . . but then again, no. I want to kill them with my own hands.*

He would wait. There was still enough time to get them on his own. He was a vampire killer, after all, and it was his duty to drive a stake through their undead hearts.

3

When they awoke, it was dark outside, and Manon and Zoey were well rested but famished. They would need to feed right away, so they required a quick kill, somewhere nearby, where they could just take a victim quickly and dispatch them to quell their hunger.

They opted to catch a prostitute who was standing on the corner outside the hotel. They had seen her standing out there earlier and knew she was a prime target. Nobody would ever miss her, except for her pimp, and they could easily lure her into the car and bring her to a quiet and dark place in town to drink her blood.

She was dressed in a skirt, high heels, a light jacket, her purse handing from her shoulder.

The pulled up and asked her how the night was going.

She was smacking on a piece of chewing gum.

"Good," she said, leaning down and looking into the car. "How are you? What do you want? Are you looking for a date?"

"Yes," Manson said. "We are, in fact, looking for a date."

"You two are kind of cute," she said. "What do you need me for?"

"We like to get freaky," Manson said, "If you know what I mean."

"Well, it's your money," she said. "I don't care what you do. It all cost the same, no matter what."

They let her into the car and drove to a secluded spot by the park.

"What's your name?" Manson asked, cursorily.

"Maddy," she said. "What's your names?"

"I'm Manson," he answered, "and that is Zoey. We are creatures of the night."

"Nice to meet you," Maddy said, ignoring the rest of what he said. She did not get it, or did not care. "Pull off over here." She pointed to a dark and shady parking lot beneath some trees near a vacant lot.

"You got to watch out for the cops here," she said. "We have to be quick."

"Is that so?" Zoey asked. "No worries. We'll make it real quick."

"Indeed," Manson said.

They turned and showed their fiendish vampire faces, wicked devilish eyes, fangs, slits for nostrils. Maddy was caught unaware, shocked and frightened when she saw their wicked faces. They attacked without relenting and tore Maddy to shreds, eating her heart and drinking all her blood until she was completely exsanguinated.

Afterward, they tossed the remainder of the corpse out the door and drove away.

"We have to clean the car out now," Manson said. "Let's find a car wash."

"Certainly," Zoey said, looking on her phone for the nearest car wash facility. "There is one right up ahead."

"It has to be a quiet place," he said. "We can't wash out the blood just anywhere."

"Duh, I know that," she said, flipping and scrolling on the phone. "This isn't my first rodeo, cornholio."

"Ha ha," Manson said, looking at her in frustration. "You are so very funny."

"At least I'm not hungry anymore," she said. "Be thankful for that because you know I can be bitch when I don't have something to eat."

"True that," he said, turning the steering wheel and pulling into the car wash, the sign said **SOAP AND SUDS CAR WASH** *open 24 hours.*

They washed out the car quickly and made plans to go to a bar and get a drink. They were now in need of money, so they required a rich victim they could take to the bank. They picked an upscale bar and parked in the lot, getting out and going inside to see what they could conjure up while there was still time. It was getting late and the prime hours were slipping by fast.

CHAPTER TWENTY-SEVEN

1

Crandall quickly became well acquainted with Alonso, Winton, and other friends on the farm. They had horses, cows, goats, pigs, rabbits, and chickens. There were crops of corn, rutabagas, potatoes, green beans, tomatoes, and tobacco. There was also an orchard with apples, plums, pears, and cherries trees. A vineyard with red, green, and purple grapes covered a nearby hillside. It was a self-sustaining farm in the countryside and Crandall was in heaven. He had found his own people and they welcomed him with open arms.

There was a woman named Leona out in the stable amid her daily routine of feeding the animals. She was giving hay and grains to the horses and Crandall walked up behind her, startling her out of her peaceful and necessary task.

"Hello," Crandall said, stopping and leaning against the stable wall.

"Oh, you startled me," she said. She turned and looked at Crandall. "You are the new one . . . aren't you?"

She was young and beautiful with sandy blonde hair and green eyes, and she was bashful. She was holding a galvanized grain bucket in her harm. A black stallion was leaning over the gate and insisted on having some of the grains, sticking its nose down inside and picking up the oats with its lips.

"I'm sorry," Crandall said. "I didn't mean to scare you."

"It's okay," she said, blowing her bangs out of her eyes.

"My name is Crandall," he said.

"It's so very nice to meet you. My name is Leona." Her French accent was strong, but her English was proficient.

"That's a beautiful name."

"It's the one I was born with." She looked at him with a sultry glance from the corner of her eyes. "You are an American? No?"

"That's right. Born and bred in the good old U-S-A."

"I heard about you from Alonso and Winton. What are you doing in France?"

"I came here to find a cure for my disease."

"Disease?"

"Yes. The curse of the . . . lycanthropy. I heard about a doctor who might have a cure. I came here to find him."

"You are speaking of Dr. Griswold. I've heard about him. It is nonsense. Fake news, as they say on the Internet. You silly Americans."

"We did not invent fake news. You have it here in France too."

"America invents everything. Pornography. Drugs. Rock music. Rap music. Movie stars. Suicide. It all comes from decadence inspired by the American way. You don't think so."

"Maybe. But I don't take responsibility for any of that. It is a personal choice to do anything wrong. Crime is worldwide."

"I was told you are a smart one."

"Who told you that?"

"Alonso told me about you, already. I know you are a werewolf and that you are ashamed of it."

"I'm not ashamed. I just don't like losing control of my . . . anger."

"It's not anger. It is passion."

"Is that what you call it?"

"Yes. Precisely."

"What is with that Winton guy? He seems so . . . hateful."

"Don't be intimidated by Winton. He is a horse's ass sometimes."

"Oh, I see. I noticed he did not like me very much."

"He is just a buffoon. His pride is too much for him sometimes. He is really an omega."

"What do you mean?"

"In the wolf pack, there are alpha, beta, omega, and others. The alpha is dominant, the beta is submissive, and the omega is a loner, the lowliest of the pack, somewhat of a coward, who stays on the outside and cowers to the others."

"Interesting," Crandall said. "And how do you know so much about wolves?"

"You don't really know yourself, do you?"

"I know a little."

"Well, since you are a . . . lycanthrope . . . you should know these things. You are essentially a wolf by blood and lineage."

"Wolves?"

"That's right," she said. "We are all werewolves here. We are family. You have been invited to our pack."

"I am grateful."

"Don't thank me. Thank Alonso. He is the beta. He leads us all. He is very wise. You should listen to him. He will never lead you in the wrong direction."

"That's' good to know."

"Winton, on the other hand, you can disregard his stubbornness," she said, looking into Crandall's eyes again with her intense eyes. "He might try to trick you, or make fun of you, but in his heart he is not a bad . . . wolf."

"I will keep all of this in mind."

"Good. Now. Do you want to help me feed the animals?"

"Yes. Of course. I would love to."

Crandall walked over and patted the black stallion on the head. The horse whinnied and pulled back, wrinkling its lips and baring yellow square teeth.

"Whoa," Leona said. "It's alright, Pogo."

"I don't think he likes me."

"Pogo is a strong male," Leona said. "He is leery of strangers. Once he gets to know you he will be your best friend." She patted Pogo on the head, scratching behind his ears. "Isn't that right?"

The horse nodded its head as if in response, agreeing with Leona.

"He can understand you?"

"I think so."

"Kind of like Mister Ed."

"Who is Mister Ed?"

Crandall had watched Youtube videos and old black and white reruns on TV of the Mister Ed show staring the talking horse that was a popular sitcom back in the 1960s. His father got him hooked on the old classic black and white shows from that era, shows such as Leave it to Beaver, The Andy Griffith Show, Gilligan's Island, and Happy days were a few of his favorites. It was odd for someone his age to know about these shows, but he was an odd young man, so it was fitting for his character.

"Uh, it's a TV show from back in the sixties."

"You are not that old," Leona said. "You watch ancient TV shows?"

"Sure, why not?"

"Hello, it is the twenty-first century," Leona said.

"How old are you?"

"Don't you know you are not supposed to ask a lady that question?"

"Yes. But . . . I just wondered . . ."

"It's fine," she said, smiling. She peered at him intently with her brilliant green eyes that glinted like rubies in the sun. "I don't mind. I am twenty-one for your information."

"So young and very beautiful." Crandall noticed that she wore no makeup and that her beauty was all natural.

She blushed and looked away, patting Pogo on the nose again and offering him more oats from the bucket. The horse snickered and the stuck its nose back inside the bucket. Pogo's jaw worked, grinding, chewing, his tail swishing as he delighted in the taste of sweet grains. The smell of the oats and horse breath was strong and intoxicating. Flies were buzzing around and one tried to land on the horses eye. Another flew around Chandler's head and he swatted at it, ducking down to avoid the invasive insect.

"I'm sorry. Did I say something wrong?"

"No. Not at all," she said, looking back at him. "I bet you say that to all the girls."

"Not all, but some of the girls."

"You are funny," she said. "And how old are you? Since we are getting to know each other intimately."

Crandall was caught on the spot, now, and it was his turn to blush. He was not ashamed, however, to tell her his age. "I am old." He laughed and ran his finger through his hair. "I am twenty-three, for your information."

"Oh, you are so old," she said. "I don't know if I can even talk to you now." She laughed and showed her perfect teeth, a dimple in her cheeks when she smiled.

"I feel older than that. I think I am almost over the hill."

"What is an old man, such as yourself, going to do with his life?"

"That's a good question. I don't know. I wanted to write screenplays for Hollywood . . . but that may never be a reality."

"Movies? Hollywood? That is very American."

"I guess so."

"Well, why don't you do it?"

"Because I am now in France and I don't know if I will ever go back to America."

"Why not? Are you running from something?"

Crandall thought back to his time spent with Manson and Zoey and Stephanie in Vancouver, the drive south in the black Monte Carlo, the blood, the carnage, and the wretchedness of consuming blood and human flesh. It was something that made him feel guilty and ashamed. He realized that he missed the vampires, but he did not miss their activity. He did not want to kill humans any longer.

"What are you thinking," Leona asked. "I see a distant look in your eyes. You are remembering something . . ."

"Yes. I was thinking about my past. I don't want to go back there."

"You are obviously ashamed of who you are. You should be proud. Accept yourself. It is liberating to just be . . . just be free . . . just be yourself. We all accept you here. You are welcome here. Let down your defenses and relax. We love you already."

Crandall was taken in by her kind words. He always wanted to belong somewhere. Even though he had felt like he belonged with the vampires, he felt even more kinship to the werewolves because they were his true kindred spirits and biologically, organically, chemically, they were the same. He felt at home with his new family in Paris.

"Come on," she said, taking him by the hand. "Follow me. We have to feed the rest of the animals."

Her hand was warm and soft in his palm. He could feel her heartbeat pulsing in rhythm with his own. He was attracted to her. She smelled like Ivory soap and sweet perfume, a floral fragrance with spicy undertones. He looked at her and knew that he was going to fall head over heals for her if he was not cautious.

She looked back, smiled, meeting his stare, and her eyes told him everything he needed to know. She was available and she seemed to have an interest in him. Why would she not have an attraction to him? He was an extremely handsome young man. In her mind and heart she had already decided that she would like to get to know him better.

They walked hand in hand down to the creek than meandered through the property and stopped at a pen that held a dozen pigs. There were goats running freely in the pasture. They were gathered together blatting and bleating, seeing Leona and Crandall and knowing that it was feeding time. They came closer and surrounded the two werewolves as they fed slop to the hogs.

It was going to be a wonderful day. Crandall was home. He was welcome. He had found a new love interest. Life was good.

"The goats like you," Leona said.

"Good, because I like the goats."

She laughed at him. They smiled together. The sun was warm and bright and sensational on their skin.

They fed all the animals and then made their way back to the house.

Crandall was ecstatic.

2

That night, in the news, on TV, the pack sat in the living room and watched a story about the legendary mad scientist, Dr. Griswold was displayed on the TV with a French newscaster sharply dressed in a suit and tie. He was telling of how Dr. Griswold was brutally murdered outside his office building by attackers who savagely killed him with sharp knives, leaving him in a pile of meat and offal on the sidewalk, blood running into the street.

"They've killed him," Alonso said. "It's over. We are no longer safe here. They will come for us now."

"What do you mean?" Crandall asked.

"We have been the target of a group of vigilantes who want to murder us," Winton said. "It has been prophesized by the witch."

"Tonight, we will feed and fuck," Ronald said. "It is a full moon. Are you ready?"

Crandall was taken back by his boldness, and said, "I guess so."

"Good," Alonso said. "We will meet out in the meadow just at twilight to transform and eat our livestock raised just for this purpose."

3

The night fell and the group of werewolves gathered in the meadow near where the pigs and goats and sheep were all kept in the pens and corrals. The moon was full in the sky, the stars twinkled. There was a large bonfire burning in the meadow and the entire pack of werewolves were present. Leona stood close to Crandall, holding his hand. The others were gathered close together. The animals in the pens were nervous making squeals and blats and moving about with skittish and jerking motions. The chickens had all roosted by now and they were safe from the slaughter that was about to happen.

At first there was a calm wind blowing and there was the sound of the fire crackling. The smell of livestock wafted on the air. The pig pen smelled of shit and the sheep smelled of fear and distress. The trees, grass, flowers, and crops smelled delightful. The night was cool and damp and refreshing against their skin. The pack sniffed the air. There was chaos on the horizon. They knew it was coming. It was about to begin, and they were all giddy with excitement.

Alonso was the first to transform into a werewolf. His face changed into wolf-like features, nose extending, teeth elongating with canines, whiskers sprouting out of his lupine nose. His should hunched and his legs grew long and inverted into sharp angles, obtuse and acute angles, claws sprouting from his long and knobby knuckled fingers.

Suddenly, all of the members of the pack began to transform, including Crandall, and there was popping of bones and joints as fingers turned into claws and teeth into fangs, hair sprouting out of the skin and eyes changing to bright yellow orbs with cannonball pupils. There were growls and grunts and groans, and sniffing, and licking, and smacking of teeth on lips. Tongues extended and drooling. They changed into werewolves and sniffed one another intimately.

They howled at the moon in unison. They were hunchbacked beasts standing tall on two legs, raising their noses to the wind and looking up at the full moon. Against the horizon they looked like sinister fiends, hunched backs like Quasimodo, the twilight a background a fading shade of darkened lavender, their hackles up as they circled and closed in on the animals for the kill.

The attack was vicious and brutal. The penned in animals screamed in fear as the werewolves descended, grabbing the prey and ripping the flesh from the bone, fur flying, bones snapping, blood spattering wölfen faces and fur. The pigs squealed loudly as they were eviscerated. The sheep blatted in distress as the werewolves sunk claws and fangs into their tender innards, ripping out the guts and offal, spilling the warm and steaming meat and fat to the ground in piles of dripping gore.

Crandall was fully transformed and joined in for the kill. The blood and meat tasted delightful and the fell of flesh ripping beneath his claws was exquisite. They danced around the bonfire, werewolves in the throes of the kill, eating until their stomachs were full and their ravenous hunger satiated. After the feeding was finished, they turned their attention to one another and knew that it was time to mate.

Leona, now full transformed into a beautiful werewolf, went to Crandall and offered herself to him. He sniffed her, grunted with satisfaction, and mounted her in animal lust. The other werewolves found their mates, Alonso took his pick of the pack, Maria, was his first choice. Then he mated with Jennifer. He was the Alpha male so he could have any of the females he chose. He did not want to be greedy, though, as some of the other males deserved to mate. He allowed Crandall to have Leona because he knew that this was good for the pack. Janette and Pierre were an obvious couple and they mated by the fire light. Vance and Nathan chose Ellie and Sarah, two available females who were still new to the pack. It was an orgy of magnificent proportions. They ate. They fucked. They danced around the fire.

The festivities lasted long into the night by the light of the moon.

4

Alonso came back to the ranch in a panic.

"Everyone listen," he said, frantically. "We must leave at once—because the authorities are coming for us. They have linked our pack to the murder of Dr. Griswold. We must flee the country right away. Does everybody understand what I am saying?"

The pack of werewolves looked back at him in earnest, taking in his word and digesting them thoughtfully, with deep consternation.

"We understand," Winton said. "We have been exposed. Now they will try to kill us all."

Outside, there were cars pulling up at the gate. It was the police and vigilantes. They could see the men in the vehicles as they got out and prepared to breach the barrier. The gate was no match for the rugged vehicles and methods they used to knock it down. The police and werewolf hunters had arrived en masse to arrest the murderers of Dr. Griswold. They were in the act of surrounding the ranch, ready for a fight and they set up defensive and offensive positions in an attempt to corral the pack in and keep them from escaping.

"Hurry, everyone, run," Alonso said. We must escape through the woods and follow the hidden trails to safety. They will kill us if we do not hurry."

Outside, there was the sound of guns erupting rapid reports, bang, bang, bang, *rattatatttat*, with silver bullets flying to the left and to the right, streaks of tracer rounds like golden threads stretching across the property, some of them hitting the mark. There were casualties, and some of the bullets killed members of the werewolf pack as they ran away into the woods for cover and safety and a rout of escape.

Winton was mortally wounded . . . they had no time to save him, and it is too late . . . when the authorities closed in and the bloodshed was over, there were three dead werewolves: Winton, Randal, and Vance were killed by the silver bullets. Alonso and the rest of the pack had already fled into the woods, barely escaping the gunfire, and the house was empty.5

Alonso led them to the train station downtown, Paris, and they were able to procure tickets to the motherland, Poland. They made their way across the border by train, traveling through Germany, then into Poland. Their destination was a connection in Warsaw who could help them disappear. Then they would head to Czestochowa and then on to Krakow where there was a safe haven, a refuge on another sprawling farm in the country where they could safely hide away.

Once aboard the train they were able to relax and wind down from the excitement of the previous night.

"Who were those men who attacked us?" Crandall asked Alonso, sitting across from him in the seat.

Outside the train, the landscape rolled by in a whisk and blur of trees, hillsides, and rivers as they passed from town to town and small villages.

"Those were the werewolf hunters," Alonso said, "and they have been after us for quite some time."

"Why do they want to kill us?"

"It's been this way for thousands of years. Werewolves have never been able to coexist with humanity in a peaceful way."

"That sucks," Crandall said.

"I have to make a call," Alonso said. "Please excuse me."

He pulled out his cell phone and dialed a number. He spoke to someone on the other end and they disused the issues at hand: they required a safe place. The person on the other end was amicable and seemed to agree that they could help the werewolves with a place to escape from the killers who pursued them.

After the conversation was over Alonso told Crandall, and the others, that they would meet with their source in Warsaw and everything would be alright after they arrived. It was all taken care of, and they could now concern themselves with staying alive.

5

Arriving in Warsaw, the trains slowed as it entered the city and stopped at the main station

"This is where we get off," Alonso said. "Everyone just follow me and keep as quiet as possible. We do not need to expose who we are, and we will hurry to get out of town. No time to waste."

They all agreed with him and followed close behind as they exited the train and stepped out into the dank and foul-smelling city air.

There was a man standing to the side with sunglasses, trench coat, black Fedora. He was holding as sign that said "Alonso" on it.

"There is our man," Alonso said, approaching the stranger. "I am Alonso."

"Very good," the man's said in broken English. "Follow me. I will take you to the safe house."

"Excellent," Alonso said, looking at the others.

There were two black Mercedes vans waiting for them out on the street.

The man in the trench coat hurried them inside the vans and whisked them away down the street to an undisclosed location.

They went inside and were given items that they would need,

like clothing, toothbrush and soap, a shower, shoes, money in the form of Zlotys. After a brief meeting with a group of rough looking men, they were then led back to the vans and driven through the countryside, heading south toward Czestochowa, where they would stop and refuel. After that, they headed to Krakow and drove down a backroad to a driveway that led down a long driveway into a farmhouse secluded in the woods.

"This is it," the man in the black trench coat said. "This is your new home. You will be safe here. There are others like you. There is a militia that will protect you."

"Thank you," Alonso said. "We are forever in your debt and afford you every gratitude."

"Not to worry," the man in the black trench coat said. "You owe us nothing. This has all been prearranged for you. The Master has seen to it that all of your needs will be met."

"Wonderful," Alonso said.

Outside, the werewolves regrouped, gathered together and then were led inside the country house.

It was good to be out of France and in the safety of the borders of the motherland, Poland. They would stay there as long as they needed and make new lives for themselves.

Crandall felt right at home with them, and he held on to Leona's hand as they sat down in the living room of the farm house and were instructed on the particulars of where their quarters would be and the sleeping arrangements.

It was going to be alright. That was all that mattered.

Crandall knew that it was going to be alright.

He trusted Alonso. As they laid down in the dingy little room on the small mattresses, they knew that tomorrow would bring challenges and they would have to support themselves by working on the farm, but that was the way that it had always been, even back in France, and they were prepared to work hard and make a living.

They shut their eyes and went to sleep.

Tomorrow was going to be a new day, a new beginning, a new way of life.

CHAPTER TWENTY-EIGHT

1

Manson and Zoey went to a cozy cocktail lounge and found a well-to-do wine salesman.

"My name is Warren Jamieson," he said, shaking hands. "If that matters to you."

"Yes. It is good manners to introduce yourself," Manson said, shaking his hand, noticing that the palm was wet and sweaty, but his grip was firm.

"Nice to meet you," Zoey said, sitting down at the bar.

"What are you drinking?" Warren asked, beaming at her. She was attractive and seductive, and he wanted a piece of whatever she was offering. the sexual chemistry was instantaneous, and his libido was running hot tonight.

"Whatever you are," Zoey replied, looking at him indifferently. She knew what he wanted. It was obvious. She made a sultry expression and looked at him with come-fuck-me-eyes, the kind of look that can make lesser men shoot their load right in their pants. She knew she could work this man for whatever he was worth, if she wanted to, but she would play it easy and slow. It was not always about taking advantage of people—or was it—but a vampire had to feed on blood and there were not too many volunteers, unless you counted the blood bank, and they were not giving the blood away for free.

"Okay, good," Warren said, waving to the bartender. "Barkeep . . . give these two a shot. This stuff right here." He pointed at his own shot glass. "Chivas Regal. The good shit. Make it a double and refill mine while you're at it." He slapped a platinum Visa card down on the bar and said, "Let me start a tab, too. I think we're going to need one." He looked at Manson and Zoey and smiled, showing his straight white teeth, a dimple in his chin and cheek as he grinned brightly. He obviously had money, or so it was supposed to look, and he as ready to spend some tonight treating them to a party.

He looked at Manson, still standing, and said, "Sit down, son. You're making me nervous. Sit down and make yourself comfortable. Your drinking on my tab tonight."

"Alright, then," Manson said, sitting down on a barstool. "I won't argue with you about that."

"Where you two coming from?" Warren asked, looking at them as he took a sip of whiskey. "Or, should I ask where you are going?"

They looked at each other blankly, not knowing exactly how to reply to the question.

The bartender brought over the drinks, set the shot glasses down.

"Go ahead and leave the bottle," Warren said, reaching out for it greedily. "I'm thirsty . . . and I think my new friends are too."

"We are going to Hollywood," Manson said, at last, winging it. He would just make up some shit on the fly, because he was a pretty good bullshitter, after all. "We're on our way to write movie scripts and become actors."

"Is that so?" Warren said, grinning. "Writers, huh? You know, I've always wanted to be a writer. As a matter of fact, I'm working on my memoirs right now. It's one hell of a story. Maybe you could give me some pointers on how to spruce it up a bit."

"Sure. Why not," Manson said, bluffing. "I can show you whatever you need to know."

"Is she going to be the movie star?" Warren asked, pointing at Zoey. "I can see it. She has that star quality, for sure."

Zoey looked back and smirked, unphased by his flattery.

"Yes. Yes, she is," Manson said. "Isn't that right dear?" He looked at her and winked, signaling for her to go along with the charade.

"Of course," Zoey said. "I am auditioning for a feature film about vampires. I will play the wicked countess and prey on the innocent in the dark of night."

"I'd buy it," Warren said. "Not that I'm into that kind of thing, mind you. But if you are staring in it . . . then I'll watch it. You've got it girl."

Zoey was disappointed with the tired and jaded pickup lines of lecherous middle-aged men. She was thinking that if she had a dollar for every old creep that looked at her with perverted thoughts and tried to whisk her off her feet, trying to woo her with cars, money, and diamonds, or big dicks and fat wallets full of credit cards, she would be wealthy by now. Dirty old men were just too easy, and too abundant, and it was getting old, too.

"How would you like to join me for a little get together tonight?" He asked, beaming merrily at them. "I'm staying in a hotel room at Waldorf Hotel, and I would like to invite you both back for a drink . . . and maybe a little a blast of the white stuff. A blow for your nose, if you get what I mean."

"We would be delighted and love to come," Manson said.

Zoey was not looking so impressed by the proposition, but Manson looked at her and willed her with him mind to go with the flow, do not rock the boat, because this guy could be a jackpot.

"Sure, why not," Zoey said. "I would love to come to your room and keep you company."

"Lovely, then, friends," Warren said. "Let's rap this up and get on our way."

The finished their shots and left the bar without incident.

2

Back in the room the middle-aged wine salesman named Warren took off his jacket and offered them a seat at the table.

"Please," he said. "Be my guests. Make yourselves at home."

Zoey knew what this man really wanted. He was setting up a scene where they would talk about sex. It always came down to that. Men could be pigs when they wanted to, and this man was no exception, she could tell. She was good at reading people.

"I need a rest," Manson said, plopping down on the bed. He laid back on the bed and stared at the ceiling. "This has been a long trip. I got to tell you."

Manson was fatigued and strung out from the road. All the driving and running under the cover of darkness was beginning to take its toll, on both he and Zoey. Although they were creatures of the dead and immortal and not exactly susceptible to the regular rigors of physical exertion and exhaustion induced by extraneous activities and long marathon activities that would wear a mere mortal down like a dead battery; nevertheless, they were growing bored and disenchanted with running away and longed to be done with their journey, it was growing a bit long in the tooth, so to speak.

"Have a drink," Warren said, lifting a bottle of Chivas Regal and holding it out for them to see. "This is a fine blended Scotch whiskey. It will cure what's ailing you." He took three plastic cups, unwrapped the plastic protective film from reach, put ice inside the cups, and then poured generous plashes of the liquor, filling them better than two thirds full. "Here, have one," he said, passing them to Zoey and Manson. "Let's have a toast. Drink up. What do you say?"

"Thank you," Zoey said. "I can use a stiff drink."

Manson took the cup, but he was unenthused, looking at it glumly. "I hope it cheers me up a bit, because I'm not feeling too enthused right now."

"Cheers!" Warren said, enthusiastically. "To long life and good friends."

"Cheers!" Zoey and Manson refrained.

They all tipped up their cups and took long drinks, the hot liquor burning in their throats and stomachs as it sunk down to the bottom.

"Ah cha cha," Warren said. "That's good. Now, for a line of some fine Peruvian flake . . ."

They thought that finally arriving in Hollywood they would afford them the luxury of rest and relaxation, as it was an location where they thought they would fit right in, living right next to movies stars, rock stars, celebrities of every stripe, and no one would be the wiser that two vampires had moved into the neighborhood. In other words, they would not have to work so hard to hide the fact that they were vampires. The problem was that they required money, lots of money, mountains made of money, to live the lifestyles of the rich and famous in Beverly

Hills.

And then . . . they saw the money . . . because this man, Warren, was apparently a wealthy drug dealer. He had a suitcase full of crack, meth, molly, heroine, paraphernalia like needles, spoons, straws, and pistols and knives. He was a walking pharmacy for the strung-out addicts everywhere. He was a big fish and did not deal on the street. He was only here to sell to the soldiers who bought his goods in quantities. Next, they discovered he had stacks of illicit cash in a suitcase under the bed. That was all they needed to see . . .

Manson had been right. They truly had hit the jackpot. This guy was a windfall and they would be loaded after they took him out.

Then they . . . dupe him easily. Manson agreed to sit back and look the other way while Warren took advantage of Zoey. She knew exactly what to do. She used her sexuality to get him naked and in the shower. He was a potbellied, hairy and balding man, with gold chains around his neck, and a Rolex watch. He was loaded. When they got in the shower, he had a raging boner and was ready to fuck the shit out of her, but that is not how it went down. When he was taking a drink—he had the bottle of Chivas Regal in the shower with him—and when he was at a vulnerable position, in mid-guzzle, his Adam's apple bobbing as he gulped down the booze, Zoey struck with lightning speed. She bared her fangs and sunk them into Warren's neck, drawing blood that trickled down onto the white tile basin on the floor and swirled around into the drain.

He screamed, and she bit out his Adam's apple, squelching the cry in his throat. He gagged and gargled on his own blood, then fell to his knees clutching the gaping wound in his throat. She spit out the flesh that was hanging from her mouth.

Manson came in through the door, having heard the commotion, and looked through the foggy glass shower door.

"Is he dead?" Manson asked.

"Almost," she said.

"I want some blood."

"He tastes terrible," she said, spitting again. "He's sick and poisoned. You don't want any of this one . . . he is disgusting."

"If you say so," Manson said. "Then let's get the hell out of here. He made a lot of noise. Someone might have heard him screaming. Hurry up and get dressed. Let' go."

"Okay," she said, stepping out of the shower.

Warren was lying dead and bleeding on the floor. She left the water running to wash the blood down the drain completely.

Manson gathered up the drugs and money and weapons while Zoey dressed. They hurried out of the room, down the hallway, and back across the parking lot to the Monte Carlo. Inside, the put the suitcases in the backseat, started the engine, and revved up the engine, taking off easy so as not to attract any unnecessary attention.

Down the street they drove, loaded with drugs and money and ready to hit the streets of Hollywood. They would have a good start in the city of the Angels.

Daylight was coming fast, and they would need to hide someplace. Manson drove the down a backstreet until he noticed an enclosed lot with and old loading ramp that was well out of sight and looked abandoned. This was a perfect place to pull in and hide behind the buildings. They could sleep through the day and make the trip to Hollywood in the morning. The ignored the private property signs that said KEEP OUT and pulled in behind the chain-link fence that skirted the lot with old pieces of machinery and equipment that had been discarded and gone to rust and ruin. This was a forgotten area and it was perfect for them to avoid detection by law enforcement of anyone else because there obviously was no one around to notice them parked in the hiding place.

Manson pulled into the parking spot and turned off the headlights and the engine.

"We'll stay here for the day," Manson said. "Then in the evening we can make the drive into Hollywood and find a place to stay."

"Do you think it's okay to park here?" Zoey asked.

"I think we'll be alright."

They looked at the suitcases with the drugs and money in the back seat. It was a mixed blessing. They knew it would bring them a significant amount of money to use toward their new lives int Los Angeles, but they also knew that it could get them arrested and thrown in jail, and a vampire stood no chance of making it in prison. Who had ever heard of that such a thing: vampires in jail? No, they could not allow that to happen. They could not get arrested or be taken alive.

All they knew was that they must get away, no matter the cost. Whatever came their way, they would have to fight to the death, and they had a feeling that eventually that was what would happen, especially since the vampire hunter had been appearing out of nowhere to accost them.

CHAPTER TWENTY-NINE

1

After leaving Warsaw, Poland to live in the country on a farm, and stay hidden from the authorities. The survivors of the pack settled into the country life and made an effort to live their lives out in a clandestine fashion and remain secretive, while the werewolf hunters sought to bring the pack to an end . . . always looking for them, but not able to locate them in the refuge in the country of Poland.

Crandall and Leona became engaged and were madly in love. They stayed in the country in the commune for several months, until eventually they decided to move back to the city of Warsaw. They wanted to get jobs in the city and go to college at the University of Warsaw where they could pursue careers in business, arts, and entertainment.

While they were their the met other werewolves and vampires and were taken in by the lovely city and the night life. It was a haven for the supernatural creatures and they were young and vibrant trend setters who liked to hang out in the cafés and drink coffee, or beer and vodka at the pubs, and read poetry and sing songs. Life was good and this was the beginning of something great.

Crandall learned to speak Polish quickly and soon was fluent. He became a waiter at a fancy hotel, The Imperial Crown, and he and Leona found a small flat on the edge of the city where they lived together and made passionate love at night.

This was not to be the end of their story, though, because they still had to be aware of the ruthless men who wished to shoot them with silver bullets. Their friends, the vampires, were also on the hit list, and they all were careful to watch behind their backs.

2

Crandall tried to contact Manson and Zoey and let them know that he had arrived at his ultimate destination, but the numbers did not connect. There was no reply from either number, or he was sure that his friends back in the United States of America had suffered some tragedy. He hoped that someday he would find them, maybe on the Internet, or maybe they would call or texts him. Who knew? He would always long to hear from them again.

He went to work the next day and settled into his routine always thinking about his vampire friends in the black Monte Carlo.

He missed them.

He spent his time doting on Leona.

Now, his life was good and only time would tell what would happen next.

CHAPTER THIRTY

1

As if on cue, just as Manson and Zoey had finished loading the illicit cargo and money in the Monte Carlo and climbed inside, behind them a set of bright headlights beamed through the rear windshield, reflecting the rearview mirror blindingly bright.

"Oh, shit," Zoey said. "I knew this was a bad place to stop."

"It's the vampire hunter," Manson said. "He's found us."

"What are we going to do now?"

"We fight him," Manson said. "We have no choice. It's time to bring this to an end. Either he dies, or we die fighting."

"I'm not sure about this," Zoey said.

Suddenly, after robbing and killing Warren, and when they pulled off at a parking lot to reconnoiter and Adrian pulled up in the gray van. Next thing they knew . . . they were in a standoff in Northern California, in the city of Eureka, with the vampire hunter, Adrian Burgendorv in an alleyway in the dark. He had the advantage because he had them pinned into a dead end and there was no exit or advancement in a forward direction.

They would have to fight for their lives.

2

Adrian was prepared and well equipped to deal with the vampires. Adrian jumped out of the van and approached the car with his crossbow raised high. He had wooden stakes attached to his belt and vials of holy water and cloves of garlic in a garland around his neck. He was ready for war, and he intended to end the lives of these to vampires here and now. He knew that they were clever and cunning, and he anticipated their actions. They would either fight or run away, and he would give chase if they chose the latter. He got out of the van and approached the Monte Carlo, the headlights from the van set on high beam and stunningly bright as he crossed in front of the van and stood ready with a crucifix and the crossbow in his hands.

"Come out of the car, you hideous fiends," Adrian called out to them. "I've come to destroy you."

"It's the vampire hunter," Zoey said, recognizing the van instantly.

"What the fuck is he doing here?" Manson said, surprised.

"Get out of the car," Adrian said. "Keep your hands out where I can see them."

Manson and Zoey did not move. They had no intention of going down without a fight. They would do their best to kill the vampire hunter at the first opportunity.

"He can't be serious," Manson said. "What's with this guy? He won't get off our backs. I need to deal with him once and for all." He reached for the door handle and started to open the door in order to get out and battle with Adrian.

"Don't do it," Zoey said, holding Manson's arm. "He's got weapons."

"Yes. But I've got speed and supernatural strength on my side," Manson said. "I can take this fucker out easy."

"I don't know," Zoey said. "I'm not sure I like the looks of this. He might be a problem."

"Only if he calls the cops," Manson said. "And he has not done that yet. So, I'm going to fight him."

"Manson. Please, don't," Zoey said, begging him. "I fear for your life. What will I do without you?"

"Don't worry, dear," Manson said. "I've got this. He is no match for me."

"No. Don't," Zoey said, one last time, her heart sinking in her chest. She had a bad feeling about this.

Manson got out of the car and stood looking at the vampire slayer.

"Finally, we meet face to face," Manson said, hands out at his sides, ready to fight. "You've been a constant pain in my ass, vampire hunter. I intend to be rid of you once and for all now."

"Bring it on, scumbag," Adrian said. "You've had a good run. But it all ends right here and now."

Manson hissed and showed his fangs, his eyes gleaming red like fiery coals, his fingers clutched like rakes, blackened fingernails extended into talons.

Zoey knew that this was going to get bad, she needed to get out and help. She could not just sit by and watch Manson fight the vampire hunter alone. She had more backbone than that and she would have to fight, come whatever may, and stand by her man. She exited out through the passenger side door and joined the standoff that was building in intensity.

"Get back in the car," Manson told her, sneaking a quick glance her way.

"No. I'm fighting with you."

"Excellent," Adrian said, grinning. "Two for the price of one. And now you both will die."

Manson and Zoey became the evil monstrosities of fangs and claws and livid pale flesh with blue veins that was fixed beneath their beautiful facades; beneath their lovely exteriors the vampirism lurked and lived like a hideous beast that was so wretched to look at that it brought fear and loathing to all who looked up on them. Their eyes were glowing like a dreaming demon's with slits for nostrils and rows of razor-sharp teeth behind blackened lips, the facial skin leathery and translucent, showing the mottled flesh beneath.

"Make your move vampire hunter," Manson said. "You are outnumbered."

Adrian had to cover his eyes at the wretched fiends before him. These were no lovely vampires from the movies, on the contrary, they looked worse than Bela Lugosi or Lon Chaney could ever have portrayed in film. Count Orlok from *Nosferatu* was handsome compared to what these to monsters had turned into.

"Yes. But I have this," Adrian said, raising the crucifix and holding it out, the headlights causing the silver figure of Jesus nailed to the cross to glimmer brightly.

Manson and Zoey cringed away from the crucifix, covering their eyes.

Adrian splashed them with holy water and the droplets landed on their skin and sizzled and popped on their flesh.

"No. It burns," Zoey said.

"Stand back," Manson said. "I'll handle this. Prepare to meet your maker, vampire hunter." He rushed at Adrian with claws out at supernatural speed, disappearing and reappearing behind him, stretching out his hands and claws and grabbing the vampire hunter by the back of the head and pulling him backwards, knocking him off balance and sending him tumbling to the ground.

"Not without me," Zoey said, then moved in and they pounced.

Adrian was suddenly squeezed between the vampire as they breathed their foul and fetid breath in his face, trying to bit his neck, but the garlic cloves repelled them and they could not get a good bite, and he splashed the holy water on them in large spurts from the bottle, which hit the intended targets and smoked and hissed, causing them to fall back and allow him to step aside and spin around and fir the crossbow from the hip. The arrow flew straight and hit Manson in the chest, exploding on impact.

"Manson, no," Zoey said, reaching out to him, as she watched in shock and horror.

Manson staggered backward as his shoulder burst into flames. He clutched at the flaming arrow shaft sticking from his chest, where there was a hole with singed flesh and leather ripped and tattered, exposed to the elements.

"Die, hideous beast," Adrian said. "I've toyed with you far too long. This is the end." He loaded another arrow into the crossbow and took aim.

"Zoey," Manson cried. "I love you. You must run. Run quickly and get away from this slayer of vampires. He will be the death of us. Go, now!" He looked at Zoey, his face an expression of dread and loathing, fear and terror, longing and shame. He knew that his time had come, and that death was imminent.

Get in the car and run, Manson thought, sending the message to her.

Zoey: *Where will I go? We are trapped.*

Manson: *You can push his van out of the way with the Monty Carlo. It has plenty of power. Put it in reverse and ram him out of the way.*

Zoey: *But I don't want to leave you. I love you. You can't die on me now.*

Manson: *I love you, believe that. I always will. A tout le monde. Always and forever. Do it now. Before he kills you, too. Go!*

Zoey: *Okay.*

She turned and went quickly to the car, able to move around the vampire hunter while he was focused on Manson, opening the door and getting in behind the steering wheel. She turned the key in the ignition and started the motor.

Adrian, intently focused on Manson, kneeled on one knee and took aim with the crossbow, squinting his eye to gain more precise vision through the sights.

Manson saw what Adrian was doing and lurched forward and ran like a mountain goat directly toward him, his face an expression of intent and rage. They were going to collide, and Manson had every intention of taking the vampire hunter to the grave with him.

Adrian pulled the trigger and the arrow let loose from the crossbow with a twang, spiraling through the air, the explosive tip sharp and deadly, making a straight path toward its intended target.

Manson saw the arrow coming toward him, time slowing down, and he was able to move with supernatural speed and step aside, grabbing the arrow out of the air and snapping the shaft in half.

Suddenly, Zoey put the car in gear and stepped on the brake, revved up the throttle, and made the tires smoke in a massive white cloud, screeching and screaming, heating up with the smell of molten rubber and asphalt permeating acridly into the air.

"Nice shot," Manson said, grinning, licking his teeth. "But you missed." He charged directly at Adrian, claws out, and fangs outstretched, and teeth bared in a wretched sneer.

"I won't miss again," Adrian said. He reached to his side and pulled out a large bladed knife from the sheath, seeing that he was going to have to fight the vampire in hand to hand combat.

The collided in tangle of bodies, rolling around on the ground, Manson getting the upper hand, gripping Adrian's neck tightly, squeezing.

Zoey let her foot off of the break peddle and slammed the accelerator pedal to the floor, the engine revving savagely, roaring like a beast as the car shot backward and smashed into the white Chevy van, colliding in a horrendous crash of smashed and twisted metal. The van rocked and rolled, lurching and shuddering, protesting as it was pushed backward across the asphalt. She applied all the horsepower the Monte Carlo had, and it slowly moved the van back out of the way far enough for her to pull forward and then back again and squeeze through the opening to freedom. She was going to make it, although the moment was bittersweet because she was running and leaving Manson at the hands of Adrian, the vampire hunter, who was now in the process of killing him with his bare hands.

She looked in the mirror and saw Adrian raise the massive knife blade and plunge it deep into Manson's chest, as he fell backward and landed on the ground. He was bleeding from the wound and his mouth. Death was coming quickly. Adrian jumped to his feet and pushed the crucifix to the vampire's forehead, sealing the deal. The crucifix smoked and hissed as it branded the vampire's forehead with a sign of the cross.

Zoey: *No. Manson. Please. I don't want to leave you alone.*

Manson: *Go. Keep going. Don't look back. Just go and keep going. You can make it to Hollywood on your own and make a new life. Don't worry about me.*

Zoey put pushed the throttle down and drove away down the back street with tears in her eyes. She rounded the corner and shot down the connecting street that led toward the exit onto Highway 101 that would lead toward Hollywood.

She had escaped with her life.

Sadness filled her with sorrow as she drove away and left her true love to fend for himself at the hands of the vampire hunter.

3

Adrian had hit his target square in the chest and pierced the heart. The stake protruded from the vampire's chest. He lay on the ground in a pool of blood, heaving and breathing heavy, his fangs exposed, his eyes glowing fiery red. There was a stench of sulfur and death hanging in the air, like a thick fog, palpable, and cloying.

Manson was mortally wounded with a stake to the heart, and he was withering away and dying. He was a portrait of misfortune; his short life had ended too soon. As the life drained away from his body he reverted from the grotesque monstrosity that was a hideous vampire of old, all fangs and wicked eyes, and reverted back to the handsome and charming young man that he was at heart. The curse was lifted in death and he was just a remnant of the mortal man he had once been, now with a stake through his heart, dying in a lot in an alley hundreds of miles away from where it had all started.

"You've finished me," Manson said, clutching the stake in his heart. "Now I must go to oblivion."

"Good riddance," Adrian said. "You are a blight on this world."

"I was human once," Manson said. "I lived, loved, laughed and had dreams."

"Now you must go to Hell and suffer for eternity," Adrian

said. He reached into his pocket and produced the vial of holy water, still half full, and popped the cap and splashed it on Manson, who writhed and spasmed as the water landed on his body, tendrils of smoke rising from the acrid drops that pelted his skin. "I release you to death, vampire. May your soul rest forever in the lake of fire."

"Are you so sure that I will go to Hell?"

"I can only hope."

"Please do not follow my beloved Zoey," Manson said. "Just take my life and leave her be. She is so lovely. She deserves to live a long life. This was not our fault, you know."

"I will do my job," Adrian said, emptying the bottle. "I am cleaning up a mess that started long ago. You are a cursed wretch, and I will not rest until I have completely eradicated your bloodline."

"I am a creature of fate," Manson said, still clutching the stake in his heart. The pain was excruciating, and he was longing for death. "I feel the cold sting of death coursing through my body. Please . . . just finish me now. Make it quick."

"As you wish, fiend," Adrian said. He reached his side and pulled the large bladed knife that was in the sheath. "I will make sure you die and stay dead."

Manson looked at him with loathing and dread, fearing death, knowing his time on Earth was nearing an end. As he breathed out his last breath, Adrian grabbed a handful of the black, hair on Manson's head and raised the blade, arcing it downward and cutting through his neck like a Christmas ham, the meat sliced neatly, back and forth, sawing until the head was released from the torso and came loose with a wet snick of the blade. The expression on Manson's face on the severed head was one of anguish and misery, having died at the hands of the vampire hunter, dead long before his time, too soon, the end a miserable conclusion to a life that had started with so much promise.

Manson's body fell to the ground and flailed around wildly, a headless torso, twitching, kicking, and bucking in the throes of death.

"It is finished," Adrian said, holding the head high like a trophy. He produced a black Hefty trash bag and put the head inside. He would make sure to take it far away and dispose of it properly to assure that the vampire would never be reunited with it and never be allowed to come back from the dead again.

He tossed Ronsonol lighter fluid on the corpse and ignited it with a stick match. The dead vampire began to smoke and smolder and wither away to ashes. Soon he would be nothing but dust and blow away in the wind without a trace of his miserable existence and that was exactly how Adrian wanted it; that is exactly how the world wanted it; that is exactly how it should be in the end. Vampires and mortals were not meant to coexist . . . or were they? One required the other and perhaps it was a harmonious balance.

The end had come for one of the vampires, but Adrian's job had only just begun, because the female vampire had escaped, and there would be more death to be delivered soon. He hurried away from the scene of the battle and exited on to Highway 101 knowing that he would easily catch up with the other vampire.

PART THREE

SOUTHERN COMFORT

"Wretches! ye loved her for her wealth and hated her for her pride,

And when she fell in feeble health, ye blessed her—that she died!

How shall the ritual, then, be read?—the requiem how sung

By you—by yours, the evil eye—by yours, the slanderous tongue

That did to death the innocence that died, and died so young?"

—Edgar Allan Poe,
"Lenore"

CHAPTER THIRTY-ONE

1

Zoey escaped with her life . . . and sped away in the Monte Carlo . . . she had tears in her eyes and knew that her beloved Manson had perished at the hands of Adrian, the vampire hunter. She knew that he would come for her, too, and she could not allow him to take her life as well. Her desire to live was strong . . . Zoey sped away down Highway 101, leaving Eureka, and setting her course and destination toward Malibu. She listened to music that made her sad, as a vampire she was apathetic. Her visage was ghastly and pale, her mood was somber.

She was distraught and did not know what to do without Manson. He had become her entire life over the past few months, and now she was alone. There would have to be a change of plans because she needed to be around her own kind. Now that she was a vampire, she did not know how to react around mortals other than she wanted to rip out their hearts and drink their blood. Being around her own kind made her feel as though she belonged, and Manson had brought her a certain sense of stability, despite that they had been living on the road like nomads, moving from place to place, fugitives from justice, killers on the road.

There was also the situation with the drugs in the back of the car . . . and the money. She would require money to live, but she was not so sure about the drugs. For some odd reason she felt guilty about killing the drug dealer in the hotel room, and the illicit cargo in the back seat of the Monte Carlo caused her considerable stress. She was a heartless creature now, and she could care less about the matters of right and wrong, however, her conscience had vanished long ago along with her mortality and soul; she knew that carrying that much dope could attract undue attention.

She decided to get rid of it, and quickly, because she knew that if the police pulled her over a dog would smell the drugs and she would be in deep trouble. How would she explain having so much money? What if she wound up getting arrested and thrown in jail? It would not turn out well for a vampire, she knew that much for sure, so she made up her mind to get rid of the ill-gotten goods.

2

She found a deserted road that led along a river and she parked quickly, got out and made sure the coast was clear. There was a steep bank at the edge of the gravel parking area that led down into a stream. This was a perfect place to dispose of the illicit cargo. She reached into the car and pulled out the two suitcases full of drugs and money. She tossed the suitcases (Samsonite) over the edge and watched them tumble, end over end, down the rocky hill and into the water below. Somewhere deep inside she felt a sorrow for letting go of the things that would provide and income for her in the future, but she knew that getting rid of it was the best choice.

The current in the river pulled the suitcases downstream, and she knew that they would eventually find their way into the Pacific Ocean, and maybe even drift away to another country. Satisfied that she had gotten rid of the illegal goods, she got back inside the car and drove away. She looked back in the rear-view mirror one last time, feeling regret for having disposed of her only source of income, but it was better this way, she knew that for sure.

3

Now she set her sights on making it to Hollywood, stepping on the gas and steering the monster Monte Carlo down the road with engine revving loudly. She paid attention to the speed limit so as not to attract any undue attention from potential speed traps with police lurking and waiting to pull a speeder over. She was close, now, but she could not decide if it really mattered at this point. With Manson gone, she did not really know what she was going to do after she got there. The plan had started with Manson and Chandler involved and now they were both gone, leaving her alone and confused. She would have to start her life over now, since she could not turn back and go back to Vancouver because that was a life to which she would never be able to return.

She drove carefully through Fort Bragg, and then onward toward San Francisco. She felt like crying, but her emotions were all jumbled and confused and she could not make sense of what she was feeling.

CHAPTER THIRTY-TWO

1

Zoey saw a hitchhiker standing on the side of the road. He was a young man, handsome, well built, but appearing to be down on his luck. He had a green Army duffel bag. She stopped and picked him up. This would be a freebie for her, she thought . . . a quick and easy kill.

They rode along in silence through the darkness, death looming on Zoey's mind. She noticed that the hitchhiker was a cool customer. He sat back, relaxed, not worried about riding with a stranger. He stole glances at her periodically. She knew he was checking her out. It made her feel good to know that she still had it.

"I'm going to stop for the night at a hotel," Zoey said. "You are welcome to stay with me, if you like."

"You trust strangers so easily," he asked.

"I'm not worried about you," she said. "You are too good looking to be a psycho. Besides, I am a powerful woman and I can handle myself. I have a gun, too, if that makes any difference."

"Whoa," he said. "Slow down, little lady. I mean you no harm."

"Good," she said. "Then we won't have any problems. Will we?"

"Nope," he said, hands raised in surrender. "I swear I will be on my best behavior. Scouts honor."

"You were a boy scout?"

"No. But it sounds good."

"Ah. I see."

She stopped at a hotel in Santa Rosa and checked in for the night. She offered the young man an invitation to stay with her.

2

They go to a bar and drink and talk. She learned a lot about him during this time. His name was Virgil Barlow and he was a strapping young lad of Irish and Italian descent. He told her his entire life story, in one long breath, and she listened, trying to pay attention and stay focused.

"Well, let's start of chronologically," he said.

His story started with a broken home with divorced parents early on in childhood . . .

He lived with his grandparents, was a juvenile delinquent, had drug and alcohol addiction and dependencies issues (getting drunk and stoned), reform school (or juvenile detention as they call it nowadays). He liked to drink (Zoey knew she liked him when he said that). He liked music, playing guitar and drums and bass. He had lived in Alaska, Washington, Indiana, Idaho, Oregon, Puget Sound, been to Mt. Rainier, hiked the Cascade Mountains, Olympic Mountains, swam in the Pacific Ocean, hitchhiked through Canada, traveled to Europe (Poland and Denmark), spent time as a homeless man, volunteered at the shelter, hung out with hobos and tramps, dumpster diving, riding freight trains and living free. He was a computer guru (IT technician, programming, and the Internet), had a college degree, a BA Degree, graduated with honors. He liked to work on cars. He had been a painter of portraits and houses. He dabbled in writing stories, had even published a few in magazines. He did not like apartment living, city dwelling, rural living. He despised bullies and stalkers. He was an avid fisherman and loved camping. He liked to watch horror movies and read classic novels. He believed in long-term relationship with a significant other (dysfunction and bliss) but had not found the right girl yet. He was raised as a Catholic and went to church on Sundays when he was a kid, but now he could not stand religion. He had been to too many funerals lately, losing relatives to death, and now he was alone in the world without any family left. He had been to jail many times, and even went to prison, once. He got involved in growing marijuana and magic mushrooms for a while, and he knew a little about horticulture and botany. He was into tools and equipment (big and small) for construction working and fixing things. He had done TV repair (old school). He was against involuntary sex, violence, believed in love, hated anger, fighting. He had broken his in a roughhouse wrestling match while drunk on Vodka. He used to smoke cigarettes. He felt like life was all about waiting until tomorrow. He was working odd labor jobs, washing dishes at restaurants on his way to California. He had been in a few car crashes and busted his skull (contusion) and went to the emergency room. He thought about growing a beard, but was not sure if he liked it, or not. He hated dealing with shysters and thieves (to be or not to be), dealing with assholes (as well as being one). He used to take medication for anxiety and depression, but he was better now. He hated asshole landlords (and some good ones) and would rather live outside in the open country. He was afraid of flying as a passenger in commercial jets and small planes and that is why he chose to hitchhike to California instead. He had been on fishing boats on the ocean in Alaska. He had operated a forklift in a warehouse at a factory in Indiana. He used to drive an old beat up Lincoln Continental. He liked to go mushroom hunting in the forest in the fall. He was into playing a little baseball, football, basketball, and track and field (not seriously and not too enthused). He was also an avid outdoorsman and liked shooting guns, walking and hiking long distances. There was a time when he published books at a vanity press in a basement, but they got sued and went bankrupt. He did not like wearing a suit and tie (briefly). Facebook seemed to suck some of the life out of people, in his opinion. He was suffering from self-doubt, did not know if he had what it takes to become an actor, but desired to achieve something in life, and now he was hitchhiking to California to become an actor in Hollywood.

Zoey listened to the long story, trying to pay attention. She was amazed that this guy had opened like a floodgate and just spilled his guts out, his entire life story, in one big breath. She was bored with the story, but she nodded at the appropriate times. He seemed like a sweet guy and had a sad story, but she did not care too much, one way or the other. She was still missing Manson and still mourning his loss. She was dealing with it. Death did not affect her the way that it did mortals. Her emotions were not tied directly to her heart. She was a cold woman, beautiful, but ruthless and stark.

She wanted to tell the young man to leave while he still could, but she changed her mind. He was prey and she would consume him tonight.

3

Back at the hotel, they had a sexual encounter. It was magnificent.

However, after the sexual encounter, and all that she has learned about the young man and his life and his dreams she felt sorry for him and was unable to kill him.

She let the young man go at after a while, in San Francisco.

They exchange contact information on their cell phones: phone numbers, email, Facebook, etc. . . . and they promise to keep in touch.

He was not aware of it yet, but she had turned him into a vampire.

Someday, maybe they would meet again, but she was in no mood for a long-term relationship and she pushed him away, quickly.

She was not much for long goodbyes, so she drove away and did not look back.

CHAPTER THIRTY-THREE

1

Arriving in Malibu on the Pacific Coast Highway, the final destination, Zoey pulled the Monte Carlo into town in a somber mood. She was happy to have finally made it, but she was without her mate, Manson, and this made her feel a bit subdued and bitter. This was supposed to be their vacation and escape away from the past, where they could start a new life, but now that dream was gone because of the Vampire Killer.

She stopped the car and parked on the side of the highway. It was well after sunset and the night was dark. She could smell the ocean and hear the waves crashing on the beach. A sign said **MALIBU** Surfrider **BEACH PARKING**. This was a famous place she had seen in the movies. It was the home and playground to surfers and movie stars. She walked down the trail past sparsely populated palm trees and over the sandy dunes down toward the water. If she were a mere mortal, she felt she could end it all like a tragedy and fill her pockets with rocks and wade out into the ocean and keep going until she was full submerged and drowned, but she must face life on her own now. There had to be more than this, a meager existence, living in the darkness and riding around in a Monte Carlo.

Whatever the case, she walked to the edge of the water and took off her shoes, letting her toes get sink into the wet sand. The tied came in and out and washed over her feet. It was refreshing and she was feeling a little better now. She knew that things were going to get worse, however, because the doggedly determined Vampire Hunter was still on her tail, tracking her, and intent on killing her. She would have to fight him, and that is what she intended to do; she would sleep the day away in the car, resting up, and then she would meet him face-to-face and stand her ground.

The warmly lit houses and streetlights up and down the beach were beautiful on that evening, and she longed to be a wealthy movie star in a fancy house that overlooked the beach—but, then, did not everybody have that dream? She realized most people wanted to be admired and wealthy, perhaps even famous, but were reduced to being mere mortals with only wistful aspirations to sustain them. She longed to be adored, and now her lover and partner was gone, and this made her feel pain and misery.

With a heavy heart, she turned and walked away from the beach, back to the Monte Carlo. She thought it would be safe to stay there in the parking lot—nobody would notice her parked there during the day and she would go unnoticed, hopefully— for the coming day and sleep, perhaps dream, and rest in her mobile coffin as the living dead must. It was like her Gothic castle on wheels.

She used the keys to open the trunk and climbed inside and pulled the lid down over her. She snuggled into her blankets, smelling Manson on the pillows again, and burrowed deeply into the comfort of her mobile death coach, temporarily at a reprieve from the outside world for the time being. She dozed off and faded away into a deep sleep and dreamed of happier days.

CHAPTER THIRTY-FOUR

1

Malibu at night was a dream. The blue, green, and white sign at the city limits said **MALIBU 27 MILES OF SCENIC BEAUTY** and it was accurate. Zoey drove down the Pacific Coast Highway and stopped at an intersection at a red streetlight. The air was warm and palm trees loomed over sandy scrub and sage brush and random and brilliant lights lit up the horizon in a California paradise. Life was grand from some people in the world and they looked happy to be alive. There were kids out on skateboards and bicycles. It was late at night, but they were enjoying themselves. She saw a couple walking in the crosswalk, holding hands, oblivious that death was watching them from within the Monte Carlo, and she realized that she was now all alone. She was lost without Manson. Her reason for existence had been stripped away from her and now she wanted revenge.

She decided to do something special in memory of Manson. She knew that he had always wanted to see The Hollywood Sign in Los Angeles, and she made up her mind to go there that night and have a few drinks from the finest bottle of scotch whiskey in his memory. She would toast to Manson, the most beautiful and handsome vampire who ever lived, and died, and was taken from the world too soon. He had much to offer the dark side, and it was a shame that he was not around to enjoy this moment as she drove up the Mulholland Highway and parked the car at her destination. The city of Los Angeles lay spread out before her, past the large white letters that spelled out Hollywood with their steel posts and braces holding them in place. This was an iconic scene, and she was loving every minute of it.

Afterward, she was a loose cannon because she knew the end was near, although she had hopes of getting away and running to Europe to live in Hungary. She remembered Stephanie had told her about a place in the country in Hungary where a vampire would live out a life without any worries from the modern world.

First, before she left the United States for good, she decided she would go on a rampage, kill as many narcissistic victims as she could find—which would be a lot in Hollywood.

She went downtown Los Angeles and searched for someone to bleed, on whom she could feed, and rip their still beating heart out of their chest and eat it raw.

CHAPTER THIRTY-FIVE

1

The final conflict in Malibu—Zoey got trapped while she was sleeping through the day in the trunk of the Monte Carlo. Although she had parked in the shade, it is still hot and suffocating, but at least she was out of the sun. The Vampire Hunter used a crowbar to open the trunk and expose her to the daylight.

Zoey was lying in the trunk, wrapped in a thin blanket, her head resting on a silk pillow. She was cuddled up to Manson's pillow, comforted by his scent remnants. She was in a fetal position, slumbering in the sleep of the undead.

"I've got you now," Adrian said. "Awake vampire and face your fate."

Zoey stirred, moaning fearfully in her sleep. She opened her eyes, bright blue irises glittering in the midday sun. She showed her fangs and hissed at Adrian. Wisps of smoke emanated in writhing serpentine streams from her hair. The sun was having a direct effect on her and her skin began to blister and burn.

Adrian raised the crucifix and held it out in Zoey's direction.

She cringed and covered her eyes from the shiny sterling silver cross with a figure of Jesus crucified and hanging limply, nailed at his hands and feet.

"Do what you must, vampire hunter," Zoey said. "I will go to the grave proud and brave. You cannot take that away from me."

"You must die you vile and wretched beast," Adrian said, splashing her with holy water. The drops of water sizzled and spattered like oil and water in a cast iron frying pan.

"No," Zoey cried out. "Don't do it."

She sprang from the trunk, grabbing Adrian and clutching his throat with her claw-like fingers. Her countenance was changing into a hideous monstrosity, a beastly figure of sinister and fiendish proportions. Her face stretched and morphed into a twisted and evil representation of a demonic beast, her eyes slits of flaming and red hatred, her fangs exposed like a jackal, her lips peeled back exposing a mouthful of jagged and sharp teeth. She transformed like a shapeshifter into a devil from the deepest pits of Hell.

"Fare thee well, beast, thing of evil, creature of the night," Adrian said, raising a crucifix and holding it in her face. He held a wooden stake and mallet in his other hand. "You will no longer prey upon the innocent souls. It is your time to die."

Zoey made one final transformation, back into the pretty dark-haired girl that she had been before she was transformed into a vampire. Her eyes were tranquil yet troubled, her countenance that of a little girl with hopes and dreams, a longing to be loved and cared for in life.

"Please," she said. "Please do it quickly. Take me to the eternal damnation that I so deserve. I have been a wretch in this life and no longer deserve to live."

Adrian felt disgust and repulsion. He knew that she was a

cunning beast and she would do anything to trick him into letting her live and go free. Feigning innocence was only one trick in her arsenal of deceit. Although she looked to be sweet and innocent, within she was a wicked and vile creature that had no soul and no conscience or concern for the wellbeing of man.

"I can read your mind," Zoey said, her skin beginning to blister and bubble in the sunlight. "The world changed me. I was forced into this without a choice. I am a symptom of a greater evil that exist and beckons for all mankind. The temptation of sin and evil is strong and alluring. Most mortals will fail and succumb. I cannot be forgiven, but I long to be remembered as a person who loved . . . once. I used to be a good person and loved people. Now I am a wicked soul destined to perish in the fires of Hell."

"You are a liar, you fiendish witch," Adrian said. "I should behead you this instance . . . but I feel sorry for you, all the same."

"Let me go," Zoey pleaded, the blisters on her face were beginning to burst and oozed and wept pus, the liquid dribbling down her chin. "I know I am a wretched creature and have become a servant of the dark side . . . but I can go far away and leave this place for good."

Her gift of persuasion was taking a toll on Adrian.

"I understand what you have been through," he said, bowing his head and shaking it in disbelief. "It is my duty to kill you, but my heart tells me to set you free. I know you were only human once and that you had dreams and desires and did not intend to become the wretched fiend that you are now."

"Then let me go," Zoey said. "I can walk away from this. Leave this all behind and disappear for good. Just one chance is all I'm asking."

"Why should I let you live?"

"Because you are human and you have the capacity to show compassion and empathy . . . unlike me, as I fear my heart had become blackened to the core and I no longer know how to love. Have pity on me, please."

"Well spoken, vampire," Adrian said. "I believe the rays of the sun have already began to take their toll on you. You will burn to death in the sun before you live to see another day. In a act of fair play, I will give you to the count of one-hundred to get out of my sight. If I see you after that I will not change my mind again. Now, go! Before I change my mind. I suspect you won't make it far before the sun cooks you to a blackened crisp. My work will be done for me."

He laughed aloud, realizing that she could not escape, even if she wanted to, and now nature was going to do the killing for him.

Zoey turned and ran away into the bushes, stumbling and staggering as she became disorientated from the sun.

He watched her disappear into the bushes and out of site, and then he looked inside the trunk where the vampires had slept for so many nights and saw an iPhone. It was on vibrate and he could hear a ringtone, Beethoven's fifth symphony, playing from inside the trunk.

"What's his?" he said, aloud. He reached inside the trunk and picked up the phone. He could see the name and number of the caller. It was a call from Virgil Barlow. He was tempted to hit the green button and answer the call, but instead he let it go to voice mail. He tried to open the phone menu and view the contents, but a password screen popped up and denied access. It required a passcode.

"I wonder what it may be?" Adrian said. "Something simple, I'm sure. What about four sixes in a row. That seems appropriate."

He punched the number six in four times with no luck.

"What else could it be?" he wondered aloud. It occurred to him that he knew Zoey's birthday. Maybe it had something to do with that? Could it be that simple?

He punched in her year of birth, 1998, and presto . . . the phone unlocked and he was inside the home screen with familiar icons.

"Let's have a look at the call log, shall we?" Adrian said, to himself.

He thumbed through the menu, found the call log, and observed the most recent call from Virgil Barlow. He saw the voice mail message and clicked on it, putting the phone to his ear, and listening to the message, which came through clearly.

> Virgil Barlow: *"Hello, Zoey. This is Virgil. I bet you've missed me already, huh? No. Just kidding. I know I drove you crazy with my incessant banter. People tell me I talk too much. I know you were so kind to listen to my life story. Anyway, I just wanted to tell you that I've experienced a strange change in my life and physical being.*
>
> *I cannot longer stand the sunlight, preferring to sleep during the day. I have a hunger for rare steaks and cannot stand the smell of garlic. I've always loved garlic and well-done steaks. This is strange.*
>
> *I have been thinking about what you said about vampires and wonder if you were hinting around about something. I had bit marks on my neck after our night together. Did you bite me? Are you truly a vampire? Did you turn me into a vampire?*
>
> *I have to know, because I feel like you did. I understand if you never want to speak to me again, but please at*

least answer this one question. I need to know. I have been feeling like an evil creature lately, and I think it is because of something you did to me. I am heading to Mexico now, crossing over the border and going to a little town called Manzanillo. It's a ways south of Puerta Vallarta and north of Acapulco. I've heard it is a good place to fall off the map. I will try to make a go of it there, making a new life for myself, if possible. Please call me back and answer my question. Just let me know. It's my right to know. That's all for now. Take care and thank you for a wonderful experience. But, I must say, if you've done something to me without my consent, I am ashamed of you. I will forgive you though, because I am magnanimous. I will always be your friend, no matter what. Goodbye, Zoey. I'll be waiting for you call."

Adrian heard the phone beep after the message was finished. He hung up the phone by pressing the red icon button.

"Oh, you poor fool," Adrian said. "I knew she had infected you with her pernicious evil. Now, you too must perish into the eternal flames of perdition. I will seek you, find you, track you down and destroy you. I have you now. You will die, too."

He put the iPhone in his pocket and turned and went back to his van. He took one look back at the black Monte Carlo that had been a transporter of evil and death. It was in the sun like as sinister and malignant Gothic symbol. It saddened Adrian in a certain way, to think about how Zoey had succumbed to vampirism without freewill, because she was just a girl at one time who wanted to live a normal life but had been infected by a spirit of evil and indecency brought on by a modern world that could care less about the individual and was all about glamour, fortune, fame, and style. He thought that as the sun cooked her down to cinders she would die in the sun, and at least she would never know what it was like to grow old; she did not have to suffer and endure that miserable fate.

Adrian started the van, engaged the gear into drive, and stepped on the accelerator. He was leaving the scene of the crime and heading out toward his next target in Hollywood. A vampire hunters work was never done. He turned off the dirt road and onto the highway, speeding up, and racing away into the horizon, the mountains and desert all around him. The sky was clear, and the sun was hot. It was going to be a beautiful day. A good day for killing vampires.

CHAPTER THIRTY-SIX

1

Adrian was drinking a Mai Tai and eating makizushi sushi at The Pagoda Lounge facing the beach off the Malibu coast, preparing for his next hunt—the hitchhiker, Virgil Barlow. He had all the information he required from the iPhone he took out of the Monte Carlo after slaying the vampire, Zoey Lavay. He was writing in his journal, sipping his drink, and reflecting on things past and present. This was a moment to relax, because he knew there were more battles and slayings to come soon. Vampires are abundant on the Earth, even though mere mortals do not know they exist in such prolific numbers, and it was his job to destroy them as quickly and efficiently as possible.

2

Adrian Burgendorv's journal.

January 1, 2020. Malibu—I've finished the hunt for the dynamic duo, the two vampires known as Manson and Zoey. They were a challenging adversary, and the hunt took me all across the West Coast from Vancouver BC, all the way to Malibu, California—and soon I will venture into nearby Mexico to finish off this new vampire, Virgil Barlow—but in the end I feel I have prevailed. I was able to catch the vampire known as Manson and overcome him with my superior abilities to slay vampires, and other supernatural beasts, for which I have been well trained and have extensive experience. I didn't mind taking out Manson so much, for I found him to be a detestable creature with little, or no, redeeming qualities.

Crandall, the werewolf, escaped going east and I may never see him again.

Zoey, on the other hand, filled me with a certain sadness and remorse . . . and I felt compelled to give her another chance. If I meet her again someday, I may not feel so generous. She was a beautiful creature to behold, and it was such a shame that she had been overcome by this hideousness of vampirism. It turned her from a good person into something sinister, evil, repulsive that little resembled her true nature. Although she was a dark beauty, even after the transformation, she changed for the worse. I fear the sun has probably killed her in the desert sand. It is a good thing, in the end, I suppose. There was no remedy, other than death, that could cure her of her condition.

As for my new case, the case of Virgil Barlow, I am anticipating a quick and deft slaying of this newly created vampire. He doesn't even know what he is capable of yet. He is living in Mexico, and I know exactly where he is at, so I will track him down, soon . . . I fear he is beginning to prey on innocent victims already. Soon he will become a full-fledged creature of the night and will stalk his victims in the darkness, a handsome young man who can easily lure male and female victims into his sexually alluring trap and then drink their blood and eat their hearts. These new vampires are savage and gruesome in their hunger for fresh hearts, still beating and bleeding right from the victim's chest. He will undoubtedly create more vampires, as they always do, and they must continue the lineage of their kind. As a result, I must stop them. I must kill them all. That is what I do. I am a vampire hunter. I will stalk the night to rid the world of these foul creatures and keep humanity safe. One thing I have learned from all the years of doing this is that death rides darkly in the night and comes quickly to those who are unaware. We must stay vigilant and strong and fight these evil beasts, no matter what the cost. I will be there, no matter what, to rid the world of this evil curse. That is my pledge, and my word is my bond. I will continue until the last vestiges of life drain from my body, with every dying breath. I will continue to slay these beasts.

Now I will set out on my way to find Virgil

Barlow. I know where he is residing. I have his phone number and address and images, even his Facebook page. I will hunt him down now and put an end to him. That will be the final chapter in Zoey's legacy.

Although I had a moment of weakness, perhaps overpowered by Zoey's powers of suggestion and mind compulsion, I realize that something of that nature will not happen again. I had a moment of weakness, but not ever again. It is still my duty to roam the earth looking for these creatures of the night and I will terminate them completely.

Good night, and God bless.

3

Adrian needed to renew his passport to get into Mexico . . . this could take a while . . . three weeks, if expedited, and six weeks if processed by regular methods. He was looking forward to some sun and fun on the white sandy beaches and beautiful blue water. He would take a vacation and then see if he could find the vampire, Virgil Barlow.

Little did he know that there was a child to be born that would change everything, but that was another story . . . for another time and place. He would just relax and take it easy from here on out. He was getting old, anyway, and he felt like it might be time to retire.

He drove to the beach and parked, cracked a beer, and watched as the crowd passed by in swimming trunks and bikinis, clutching surfboards and cellphones, smiling with perfect white teeth and bronzed skin. This was the life, a life that had passed him by, and now he was old an breaking down, soon to die. He remembered what it was like to be young, but those days were gone now and all that was left was the downhill decline into old age and death.

"At least I can watch the beautiful people having fun in the sun," he said. He sipped his beer, burped, then leaned his seat back. He was exhausted from the past few weeks of travel and vampire hunting. "I think it's time for a nap." He put on his safari hat and tipped the brow forward to cover his eyes.

After a moment he was snoring and deep in a dreamless sleep.

CHAPTER THIRTY-SEVEN

1

Zoey had escaped from the sun that day when Adrian let her go, for her tolerance to the ultraviolet rays was stronger than anticipated, and she did not die instantly from the harmful light. It only gave her an intense sunburn, blistered and singed, on the verge of cooking her to a crisp. If she had stayed out in the sun for too long, she would surely have died, but she was luck and she found her way into a cave in the hillside, and waited for the darkness to arrive. She had been severely burned and there were terrible scars on her face and body and hands, but she was still alive. She had managed to get across the border of Mexico using her mind compulsion to convince the border patrol to let her in to the city of Tijuana. She hid out at night, avoiding the crazies, and making her way to a safe place to hide. She tricked some Sancho, a Mexican pervert in a beat-up Ford Falcon sedan, into giving her a ride. She quickly bit his neck, sucked his blood, picked his pocket, and found he had a few dollars in his wallet, and pushed him out on to the side of the road. She stopped and bought a road map at a gas station and navigated toward Puerto Vallarta. It was a trip of nearly two thousand kilometers, and she was forced to kill more victims for gas money, but eventually she was on the home stretch of Highway 200 going South with only two hundred miles to go. She was getting anxious and excited to see Virgil again.

After a long and hard trip, traveling only at night to avoid the sun, she made it to the city of Mazatlán, where she set up a meeting with Virgil. She contacted him from a pay phone with the words **TELMEX** on the booth.

The phone rang too long, and she did not thing he would answer, then at the last minute, before she hung up, a voice spoke from the other end.

"Hello," Virgil said.

"Is this Virgil?"

"Yes. Who is this?" he asked.

"This is Zoey," she said. "I know I should have called you sooner . . . but I got distracted. I'm sorry. There has been a problem . . . and I need your help."

"You are in Mexico?" he asked, surprised. "What happened? What's wrong? Where are you?"

"I am in Mazatlán. I've been injured in a fight," she said. "I'm coming your way. I have nowhere else to go. Manson is dead. He was killed."

"What? How?"

"I'll tell you all about it when I get there," she said. "I just need someplace to go . . . and figure everything out. I don't know what to do. I was hoping you could help me."

"Of course, I will help you," he said. "I love you. Anything for you. You said you are in Mazatlán? Are you driving?"

"Yes. I have an old car," she said, "but it is almost broken down. I don't know how much farther it will drive before it breaks down. I've been driving it for hours now, nonstop, trying to find you."

"I can meet you in Pureta Vallarta," he said. "Just get in your car and drive there now. I will leave right away to meet you there." He paused for a moment, and then said, "I will be waiting for you in Puerta Vallarta at Palace de Pacifico. It is a nice hotel that overlooks the beach. We can stay there for as long as you need. You can rest after your long journey. I am so happy and excited to hear from you."

"There is one other thing," she said, hesitating.

"What? Tell me anything," he said. "I'm listening."

"I have been disfigured," she said. "I don't look so good. My beauty has been destroyed. . . ."

"What do you mean?"

"I'm scarred from being burned," she said. "I have wounds that are still healing."

"I don't care," he said. "I care about you, not just what you look like. No matter what has happened I will welcome you with open arms."

"Thank you so much," she said. "You don't know what that means to me."

"I understand," he said. "You can explain everything when we meet again, over wine and a view of the beach. How does that sound?"

"Wonderful," she said, a tear forming at the corner of her eye. She was not much for crying, but this was enough to make her break down.

"Now get in your car and drive," he said. "I'm leaving right now. I will see you there."

"Right," she said. "At the Palace de Pacifico. I'm on my way."

"Excellent," he said. "I'll see you soon."

They hung up and each got into their cars and drove to meet each other in Puerta Vallarta.

2

Over the past few days, she had noticed that she was beginning to show her pregnancy. She did not know who the father was, for it could have been Manson, Crandall, or Virgil, as she had sex with each of them in the past few months, but that did not explain the speed at which her stomach was growing—the gestation period was accelerated and much faster than she expected. It had only been a few months, and she had only met Manson since Halloween, prior to that there were men, but they had all used condoms and she was sure they had nothing to do with her current condition, being with child.

She could feel the baby in her womb, it had a presence that was strong already. She could communicate with it, in some strange way, and the will of the little embryo was already vigorous and powerful. She knew that this child was going to be something special. *How would it go?* She wondered. *How would a child born of a vampire live in such a world and what would happen at birth?* She did not like to think about the pain of childbirth or the possibilities, but as she drove down the highway at night it kept coming back to her mind. What was she bringing into the world? Did she really care? Was she beyond the point of no return? Had she become a hideous beast that belonged in the pits of Hell? What had happened to the beautiful young girl that she was only last year? She had changed so much in the past few months that she did not even know who she was any longer. The only thing she did know is that she was a vampire. How was this possible? She had so many questions. Who could answer them?

She drove down the road, the headlights cutting arcs of light out of the darkness, the white and yellow lines on the pavement flowing like long, endless ribbons beneath the car. The sides of the road were sand and sagebrush, rocks, and cactus. There were creatures—lizards, mice, coyotes, and snakes—with glowing eyes that crept and crawled along the ditches and ravines on the side of the deserted road. A scorpion skittered out onto the asphalt and she ran over it, squishing it flat, leaving it behind with twitching pinchers and tail smashed flat on the road. This was Mexico and she was not familiar with this landscape. It was foreign and intimidating and she did not know what to expect.

She wiped her bangs back out of her eyes and focused on the road. She had to make it to her destination. She could not get stopped by the police because that would be the end of the whole mess. What would happen to an American vampire in a Mexican jail, a female now less? It frightened her to think of the possibilities . . . how could a vampire survive in jail and keep the secret? It seemed impossible. Had it ever happened before? She did not think so, but who was to say? A few months ago she would never have believed that vampires existed in the first place, let alone that she would become one, herself, a living beast destined to creep at night and drink blood from unsuspecting victims. It was just not a possibility she had ever considered, but now that it had happened, she could not avoid the actuality.

Up ahead in the distance, she saw a glistening light, there was a small gas station and she saw that it was closed. She looked at the gas gage and saw that it was over half a tank and she thought the old car would make it the rest of the trip on that much petrol. If not, she would have to rely on her cunning and abilities to make it happen, no matter what. Then there was a sign that said, **Puerto Vallarta 150 km**. That was a relief, as she knew that she would be there soon. She could not wait to get to the safety of a familiar friend. It crossed her mind that

Virgil could be angry with her since she had turned him into a vampire, but she hoped he would at least be understanding and forgive her. She intended to ask him for his forgiveness, because she knew that it was a selfish thing to do—and that is why she knew that Stephanie had only done it because she was lonely and wanted companions—and she would fall at his feet and beg him for mercy. She hoped he would be tolerant and kind to her and take her int with open arms.

The human part of her that had feelings and emotions and needed to be loved was still intact and she longed for compassion and companionship. Virgil was her only hope, now, and she was intent on making it the rest of the way to Puerto Vallarta without incident.

3

She pulled into the city of Puerto Vallarta and navigated down the city streets, stopping for directions on how to get to the hotel. She did not speak fluent Spanish, but she was able to articulate enough details and comprehend what the cashier told her in order to drive to the hotel. She pulled into the parking lot, and they finally met each other late in the evening at Palace de Pacifico, and their reunion was bittersweet—they had only spent a short time together when they met a few months earlier and now it was different, and awkward. Virgil was shocked by the scars on her face, but she was still beautiful in his eyes. He hugged her tightly and gave her a passionate kiss.

"Oh, you have been hurt," he said, looking at her face. "Let's go inside. I've already picked out a room." He held up the key with the diamond shaped key tag with the number 6 in a gold serif font. He led the way to the room and put the key in the door, opened it, and motioned for her to go inside.

Inside they hugged each other, a long and emotional embrace.

"You don't know how much this means to me," she said. "I've had a terrible week. Manson was killed . . . and then I got burned. I will tell you everything. Just let me get cleaned up first."

"Absolutely," Virgil said. "Help yourself. I am going to turn the TV on and order some food. Do you want something? I'm sure you are hungry."

"I'm famished," she said. "I've been living off of . . . just what I could get on the way."

He looked at her, knowing what she was thinking, as he could read her thoughts, and she could read his and there were no secrets now. He knew that they were: vampires.

"I know now," he said. "I was only suspicious at first . . . but now I am sure. You have turned me into a vampire. I figured as much."

"I'm sorry I involved you in this—"

"No need for apologies," he said, holding up his hand to halt her speech. "I am fine with it. It's been a blessing and a curse, but I can handle it. I have a much finer appreciation for life now. Go take a shower and get cleaned up and we can discuss the details."

The first thing they had to do was get rid of the stolen clunker Ford Falcon that she had stolen from the Sancho. It was a sure way to get the police alerted to their presence and start snooping around and asking questions.

The next night, after Zoey rested through the day, exhausted from her long trip, the got into a new model Honda Accord and drove the remaining 300 kilometers leaving at sunset in order to make it before sunrise. It was a long and arduous drive with heavy traffic and primitive paved roads, a toll booth along the way, and eventually they made it back to Virgil's little oasis on the beach. He lived in small bungalow constructed out of bamboo, wood, glass, thatched roof of reed grass and palm fronds. It was not much to look at, but it was home, and it kept the light out on bright and sunny days. It overlooked the Pacific Ocean with palm trees, sand dunes, and reed grass. It had electricity, a ceiling fan, air conditioning, kitchen, balcony, and outdoor bathroom. It was rustic but functional, and a vampire could eek out an existence here.

It was a beautiful place, Zoey thought, observing it in the first rays of sunlight.

They knew that they must go inside

4

Virgil treated Zoey with absolute respect and kindness. They would sneak out at night and feed on unsuspecting victims, mostly locals but sometimes they would take a tourist, if the timing was right and they thought they could get away with it, and they ended up leaving the bodies lying the bushes, or alleyways, and trying not to make a scene where they would be noticed killing humans and sucking their blood.

He accepted the fact that she was pregnant, regardless of if it was his child or not; he did not care about that and would accept the child, nonetheless. She was growing exponentially, her stomach as round as beach ball that they were the tourists with every day on the beach. He would put his head up to her stomach and listen to the child's heartbeat.

"Do you have a name picked out?" Virgil asked her.

"Why don't you pick one?" she said back at him.

"How about Alexander?"

"I think that is a wonderful name."

"Then it is settled."

5

It was New Year's Eve and the countdown was winding down with a few minutes to go before it as officially 2020 and the winter solstice was just passed, celebrated by the Druids and pagans for centuries . . . it was a time of renewal for many religions and spiritualists and other assorted walks of life from trailer parks to cathedrals, the Pope in Rome to Wiccans, all were partial to it too, perhaps . . . as they blew party horns and blowouts, threw confetti and popped party poppers, wearing golden hats and drinking Champaign and Vodka.

In Mexico, New Years was called *Fiesta de Fin de Año* and they celebrated with fireworks, food, and alcohol. It was festive and everyone were getting smashed. It would be a night of partying into the morning, lasciviousness, drugs, alcohol, sex, and blood. There would be blood spilled on the first day of the year in Tijuana. Somewhere in the world, vampires would be taken and converted to the undead. The cycle of life and death would continue. There would always be a rebirth, a renewal, the tradition and heritage being passed on through the generations as of old times throughout history. The night breed would continue to live in the darkness and convert mortals. It was a longstanding tradition, and if you are lucky, it may happen to you, too. They could be found in Mexico, too, although the tradition of vampires there was not as significant as the legend of the *Chupacabra*.

6

Zoey went into labor and Virgil did his best to accommodate her, putting down towels, boiling water, producing razor blades and sewing thread and a needle. He was prepared to serve as a midwife.

It would all be unnecessary, however, for the child had made its own decision and began to eat through her womb from the inside out. Her stomach bulged and writhed from the internal activity, and suddenly she cried out in pain. A gout of blood spurted from her lips and down her chin, her cervix dilated blood squirted out from her urethra in a stream.

"Help me," she said. "It's killing me from the inside out."

"What should I do?"

"I don't know."

The beast within her was savage and fast and used its teeth and claws to rip its way out of her stomach. There was sick, wet ripping of flesh as it burst outward and poked its head in a half scream half balling cry of fear and terror, taking its first real breath of air.

Zoey's head fell sideways, and her eyes stared blankly at the wall. She had expired from the birth and lay dead with blood oozing from all her orifices.

The child, opened its eyes and looked around the room, surveying the world for the first time with amber eyes. He was a hybrid vampire-werewolf and Virgil was frightened at first when he saw the little beast, wanting to run away in horror, but after a moment, he realized that it would need someone in this world to take care of it as it matured to an adult.

Virgil saw that Zoey was dead, and he grieved, as much as a vampire can grieve, and then he took the child and wiped off the blood, but the umbilical cord, then swaddled it in towels. Virgil had to admit, the little bugger was kind of cute, in a creepy and monstrously ugly kind of way.

"Well little fella," Virgil said. "Welcome to the world. Your mother has died giving birth to you. You are the last of her lineage and life, I suppose. Your name is Alexander . . . and I will raise you like a son, as if you were my own."

7

Virgil buried Zoey in the sand behind the bungalow, covering her body with lime to cover up the stench of decay, and placing a stone with her name inscribed and year of death. He put flowers down in her remembrance.

Alexander was already growing at an alarming rate, only a few days old but taking on the appearance of a toddler. This was alarming, but Virgil would learn how to adapt. He knew there was much to teach Alexander.

When the moon was full on January 10, 2020, Alexander transformed into the most sinister yet beautiful beast that Virgil had ever seen. He stood back at a safe distance and marveled. This was his son, Zoey's son, her legacy, and he wished that she were here to see it.

"Your mother would be proud," Virgil said, "and I wish she could be her to see—"

Alexander, being part vampire and part werewolf, a hybrid beast, had no recollection or concern for anything in this world and he turned on Virgil, ripping and tearing him to pieces.

"—what is this?" Virgil began to say, attempting to ward off the attack. "No. Stop. You don't know what you are doing—"

Alexander lunged at Virgil's throat, going for the kill.

"I am your father," he said, "and I love you—"

Alexander delivered the final, deadly blow with a flick of his claws and wrist and severed Virgil's head clean from the body, blood spurting out in jets and gouts as the head fell to the ground like a coconut from a palm tree, landing in the sand and looking up at him with terror stricken eyes opened wide and staring into nothingness.

He left the safety of the hut and ran full stride down the beach, a beast in his element, under the full moon, savage and wild, brand new to this world where he would someday rape and pillage the innocent and bring death and mayhem to the inhabitants of the Earth.

The waves crashed and the surf bubbled up on the sand as his clawed feet made tracks in the moist ground beneath him, a trail of tracks behind him, the moon full and bright in the sky. He stopped and howled, beating on his chest, a prime specimen, a new breed of beast to raise Hell and bring terror to all. It was good to be alive and he was happy, the blood of his father still fresh and warm on his lips. He smiled and exposed his fangs, his wolfish eyes glowing green and bright, his nose part wolf, part vampire bat, his features something unseen by mortals. He was a terrifying creature and the stuff of nightmares . . . but when the moon was no longer full, he would return to be the innocent and beautiful creature that resembled the most attractive traits of both of his parents.

He was beautiful when the moon was not full. He was still in a youthful period of development and had all the appearance of a youthful boy. He would find a home. He would find someone to take care of him.

As for now, he would run down the beach and frolic in the moonlight until the tides shifted and the gibbous moon brought him normality and relief from his monstrous curse.

He got down on all fours and galloped in the surf, splashing and prancing, sniffing at the wind and smelling the future. It was going to be a great life . . . he was content to be alive.

EPILOGUE

1

Alexander watched the sun rise over the ocean. He was resting in the shade of a cluster of palm trees. The sunlight was harsh, and it burned his skin, but it did not affect him in the way that it would a pure vampire, because he was a hybrid and he could tolerate the sun in small doses. He preferred the shade, nonetheless, and sat eating a piece of papaya that he had picked off a tree. The fruit was sweet and delicious, and he buried his face in the red and orange pulpy flesh.

An old man, a Mexican fisherman wearing a straw sombrero cowboy hat and white shirt and khaki pants with tire tread flipflops on his feet, was pulling his boat out of the water. It had been a successful day for him, and his boat was full of red snapper and jack fish.

He noticed the boy sitting under the palm trees, alone, eating fruit. He covered his eyes from the son and watched, curious what this little pale skinned, blue eyed boy was doing in such a desolate area. It was rare to see tourists out here at this time of the day and the boy looked lost.

The old man approached the boy and spoke to him in Spanish. The boy did not understand. He tried English, too, but the boy still did not understand, obviously not fluent in either language. Perhaps he was from another country, such as France, but who knew? The old man just wanted to see if he was alright. He had to make hand gestures.

The boy gulped down the last of the fruit and looked at him questioningly with his bright blue eyes.

"You are alone?" the old man asked in Spanish. "Where are your parents? Are you lost?" Then he repeated himself in English, not sure which language to use.

The boy did not answer. He pointed at the boat, then put his fingers to his mouth, making a universal sign that he was hungry. Then, in a small voice, he pointed at himself and said, "Alex." It was the only word he knew. He made the motion of eating food with his finger in his mouth again.

"Is that your name? Alex? My name is Poncho. You are hungry?" the old man asked. "I don't have much to eat, I'm afraid."

The boy named Alex got up and went over to the boat, looked inside and saw the fish.

"Those are not ready to eat," the old man named Poncho said.

Alex did not care. He reached in and grabbed a fish and took a large bite out of the scaly skin, exposing the white and pink flesh beneath, his teeth marks clear around the bitemark.

"Oh, you like it raw?" Poncho said, surprised. "I guess so. Some people like sushi. Not me. Not so much. I like mine fire roasted with a squeeze of lime and some nice steamed rice."

Alex munched happily on the raw red snapper, devouring bones and all.

"You *are* hungry," Poncho said. "We need to find out more about you."

Alex smiled and chewed on the meat.

"Maybe you should come with me," Poncho said. "I'll introduce you to my family . . . they are going to love you." He reached over and mussed the boy's hair; the boy did not flinch; he trusted the old man. Alex broke into a run and sprinted down to the shoreline, getting his bare feet wet in the surf. The old man watched the boy run down the beach at full stride, running and frolicking in the salty waves of the Pacific Ocean.

If they could not find where this boy, Alex, belonged, the Poncho decided he would take care of him. Something about the boy drew him to him; his paternal instinct told him this child was special and needed guidance. Soon there would be lessons to learn . . . and the biggest lesson of life was to stay away from the bad people, avoid the gangs and violence, and stay away from crime (the gangs were bad in the area and they recruited the children young) . . . but for today . . . there was time to play.

"Come on," Poncho said. "I am going to put my boat on the trailer. I have to take some fish to the market. And then we can go to my home and you can meet my family. I will help you."

After the boat was loaded onto the trailer, the old man ushered the boy into the truck and climbed in on the driver's side. He took Alex along for the ride as he went to the market and haggled over a price to sell the fish to the buyer, and eventually they agreed and some men unloaded the fish. Then, Poncho drove home and introduced Alex to his wife, daughters, and children, and grandchildren, and everyone loved him. The allowed him to stay and treated him life family. The time would come eventually to discover what Alex was, and who he would become, but for today he was just a little boy who needed a home and a family and they took good care of him.

2

On the Baja of Mexico, the sun is blazing brightly in the sapphire sky glimmering like diamond as it reflects off the Pacific Ocean. The white sandy beach stretches out for miles, the ocean reaching to the infinite horizon. It is blistering hot. An old pink Cadillac barrels down the beach, whipping up a rooster tail in its wake, the convertible roof down, three men occupying the front seat. They are bleach blonde surfers, hair blowing back in the wind, stubble covered chins, muscles and bronze skin, blue eyes gleaming brightly as they sip their Modelo Especial cervezas. In the back of the car are three surf boards pink, blue, and yellow, high end boards, handmade by a craftsman. These guys are serious surfers. They live for the sport. As the car approaches the engine revs loudly, rumbling, and the pink paintjob on the car is garish and intense. They are coming in fast, fishtailing and kicking up sand . . . the saw the lone, dark, handsome stranger walking along the beach and they pulled over to offer him a ride.

Their names are Stuart, Hugh, and Dupree and they spend their time surfing and sucking up the tasty waves and guzzling down Dos Eques beer by case. They like to sniff cocaine and smoke the Acapulco Gold grown locally, although every now and then they prefer some imported ganja from Jamaica, Afghanistan, or Africa, and they refer to it as "sticky bud" or "skunk bud" and smoke it in a spliff or bong. Life is good for the eternal slackers in the sun, much like the characters from *Point Break* starring Patrick Swayze and Keanu Reeves.

Off into the sunset they rode in the pink Cadillac, Alex in the backseat next to the florescent pink, green, and orange surfboards. He smiled as the wind hit his face. They gave him a beer and he happily accepted, drinking heartily.

3

Alex spent a few days with the beach bums at their *hacienda*, meeting the girls and guys who stayed there like a hippy commune from the 1970s and they all were throwbacks from a distant era with outdated cloths, music, and hair styles. They looked right out of a farmhouse community where Charles Manson might be the guru and leader of the pack.

Alex was slightly amused by the retro styles and slacker jargon and he felt out of place. He was in need of something more. Slouching around, sleeping on hammocks during a *siesta*, and smoking *mucho mota* with nothing to do left him bored and wanting something else. He liked the pretty girls, and he enjoyed surfing on the Pacific Ocean, he even liked the fresh fish cooked over the fire on the beach (it was much better cooked than raw, although he could stomach it either way). It just seemed too laid back with the beach bums and he needed more action. He felt drawn toward the city of Tijuana. It was beckoning to him and he could not resist the thriving metropolis and everything that happened on the streets.

Eventually, he struck out on his own. He hit the streets and lived like an urchin, a vagabond, learning the ways of the nomadic tribes that lived in the tunnels and overpasses along the border of the US and Mexico. He met a dangerous crowd of hoodlums and thugs, the gangs in the turf wars of Mexico, and they took him in, having a heavy influence. He spent many nights running loose in the streets of Tijuana. After weeks of tramping on the streets he decided to go back home to the old Mexican family and see how they were getting along. He wanted to pick up his only worldly possessions: a handmade acoustic guitar and a duffel bag with some odds and ends of clothing.

When he went back to see the old Mexican man and his

family, they were unhappy and told him he must go away. They had discovered his secret, that he was a monster in disguise, and they were forced to turn him away.

He said he understood and left with a saddened heart. They shut the door hard behind him. He never looked back. He would always be grateful for the help they had given him and allowing him to live there while he grew up from a young bow into a young man. He would repay them someday. This was a promise he intended to keep. He would show them that he could be important and have money and be powerful. His mind was made up and his heart was set on becoming someone important. Maybe he could be *El Presidente* someday. Who knew? Maybe.

After a few years of wandering in the streets of Tijuana, involved in crime and drug dealing, he ended up falling in with a rough gang called *"Los Pendejos Cabrones."* He made friends, found connections, and made his way into the Mexican mafia and worked his way up as a thug, an enforcer, and eventually became a head member of the cartel. He was soon promoted to the honorable title of *jefe,* he was now a boss, a leader, a powerful *hombre*, and he ruled with an iron fist and deadly *pistola.*

He was a new breed of cartel leader and he would take over everything, if given the opportunity—and that is exactly what happened: he led a gang of thugs to victory in the street wars in Tijuana—as well as harboring a race of freaks and monsters and misfits living on the fringes of society and outcasts as supernatural entities—into a new age of sex, drugs, guns, violence, and power.

Nobody ever crossed Alex, or at least on intentionally, or they paid a hefty price. He was ruthless and that is what kept him in control. He ruled with fear, but he was loyal to his faithful followers, and they supported him without question.

If anyone made the mistake of getting caught double crossing Alex, he had developed a terrible and frightening solution to deliver justice and retribution. He called it: The Killing Chair.

It was a device he had devised to strap victims down and torture them without relenting until they screamed out for mercy. He filmed it and sent it to anyone else who might have funny ideas about double crossing him for drugs, money, women, territory, or power. It was a successful solution and it worked well, although there were always those foolish enough to tempt fate and when they were caught, they found their way to the chair.

He would be king someday and rule the world from his throne. That was the solemn vow of Alex Vegas (he picked his own last name, modeling it after the character Tony Montana in *Scarface,* except instead of the name of a state, he chose a city: Las Vegas). His story would soon be told to the world and his rise to fame would be chronicled, but for now he sat at his desk looking much like the character from *Scarface* between stacks of cold hard cash and kilos of cocaine and heroin.

He held up his AK-47 rifle and quoted the line from the film: "Say hello to my little friend." He pulled back the lever and loaded a bullet into the chamber. "I got something for you cockroaches."

With mixed blood of a vampire and a werewolf and in position as a cartel drug lord, Alex was now at the helm of a power enterprise and in control of the streets in Mexico, and soon he would be the greatest mafioso leader in the world, bigger than El Chapo or Al Capone.

He lit a cigarette and grinned.

It was great to be alive.

The world was his oyster.

"Hasta lauego, cabrones," he said. "I see you real soon."